THE ADJUSTABLE HALO

THE ADJUSTABLE HALO

BY
KEN ANDERSON

WORD BOOKS, Publisher

WACO, TEXAS • LONDON, ENGLAND

Library of Congress Catalog Card Number: 68-31103

Printed in the United States of America

To the six-footers

In any work of fiction, observation and experience influence what is written. Yet the characters of this story are not purposely delineated as specific people.

THE ADJUSTABLE HALO

Chapter One

My name is Pew.

Jeremiah Pew.

Although I am not an old man, certainly not by St. Petersburg reckoning, my life encompasses that period of mankind's history when, perhaps more so than in any other recorded era, the world has experienced change—change I have observed and often experienced. I deem it pertinent, therefore, to put down in this abreviated form an accounting of some of my most remembered experiences, wishing to be helpful, and not simply to satisfy every generation's inclination to assume the posture of an older brother toward those less familiar with the ways of the world.

Bear with me, please, if you sense no immediate significance in the fact that I scarcely ever remember being called Jeremiah—except, of course, within the family circle. By the time I entered primary school, my friends had all chosen to call me Jerry, making me the first Pew to have his name colloquialized.

The simplification of the surname, though it would have greatly disturbed my forebears, is not meant to evade the fact that I spring from a long and unbroken line of church memberships—dating back, as a matter of record, to one Jeremiah Aldersright Pew, saint, patriot, and my grandfather five times removed according to the chronicles kept by my own father's priestly sire through the agency of his daughter Lydia, my aunt.

Do me the immediate kindness of recognizing from this the beginning of our acquaintance that, although my ancient genitor allowed no deviation whatever from the Biblical cadence of his name, and although everyone now calls me Jerry, you cannot thereby say my forefather was a pious man and, in so saying, indict me with the sin of impiety.

What I mean to say is this. Be we Jeremiah and Jerry, or Jerry and Jeremiah, we could both be pious, or we could both be impious, or, it follows, we could be one of each.

In any case, it will be helpful for you to know that among us Pews the most disquieting of all sins is the sin of impiety. So far be it from me to suggest that Jeremiah Aldersright Pew was not a man of elaborate religious persuasion and performance. Often in my childhood, when other lads pursued the worldly follies of a summer's Sunday afternoon, I sat in Aunt Lydia's parlor and gazed with quite some degree of awe and respect at the array of photographs in her store of heirlooms—the most awesome of all being the ponderous and sonorous visage of my great, great, great, great grandfather.

As I trust I have by now indicated, it is my desire to speak honestly in this putting down of my experiences—more honestly, if you will pardon what may at first sound pretentious, than I can ever recall observing in any of the general run of Pew's now extant. So let me simply say, in regard to those Sunday afternoons, impressed though I may have been with the ancestral splendors contained in Aunt Lydia's front room, I experienced many moments of silent, searing trauma when, on numerous occasions, my eyes beheld the likeness of Jeremiah Aldersright Pew, while my ears heard the far off laughter of companions whose innocuous pranks I had shared on Saturday and would resume on Monday.

Yes, to be sure, I disliked some things about being a Pew.

Many things.

Nonetheless, you will find me most reluctant to admit to any wilful deterioration of ecclesiastical zeal on my own part. My childhood was characterized by what one might simply call a divided loyalty. We Pews enjoyed a goodly measure of esteem, particularly within our church, and this stimulated a sense of personal pride. At the same time, I saw how the zeal with which my relatives expressed their piety evoked disdain, particularly outside our church, and this embarrassed me. Yet the tenets of our family's persuasions became, from earliest childhood, my own concept of the rightly lived life, even in the throes of confusion and rebellion.

Unmistakably, we Pew's are best known for our churchly adroitness, the whole lot of us, and I have often heard my father and those of his lineage point out that the few black sheep of our flock entered the fold by the gate of the altar, not by the gate of the prophets.

For as long as I can remember, and my earliest recollection is of a Sunday afternoon at Aunt Lydia's, my personal frame of reference has been bordered and buttressed and beleaguered by an inherent consciousness of the fact of Providence and the facets of piety.

I should like to emphasize just now, so that you may have further assurance of my desire to be helpful, that I shall not, even by implication, indicate at any time or in any manner the idea of change coming to my life because of the intrusions of those who became Pews by means of the aforementioned altar gate. On the contrary, the infusion of new blood strengthened the Pew stock in many ways, as I shall subsequently enlarge upon.

No, change came because of change, and I trust the events of my life may be of interest to you in the sheer unfolding of those examples I shall give of resistance to change, accomodation to change, and, if I may slightly tip my pen in a continuing desire for the fullest integrity, my own discovery of those potentials in human experience which are impervious to change.

So, with this as sufficient prelude, let me begin my story.

Chapter Two

I suppose people of every generation find reasons to believe they were born at the dawn of history's most significant era. While I offer no such presumption, I could, if time permitted, speak at quite some length of the widening of earth's horizons in my lifetime. For now, however, let it suffice for me to say that, while I do not recall the birth of radio, I vividly remember it's comeuppance.

Radio followed in the aftermath of the first great war, touching the planet men call earth like a magic wand, making our terrestrial habitation suddenly and irrevocably smaller.

As with the first engine, the telephone, the horseless carriage, and the airplane—as with many other modern innovations, dubious and conservative minds greeted the new marvel with reservation.

"It's a fad," said some.

"Good way to get yourself killed by lightning," said others.

"People are making fools of themselves," declared an old crone. "Somebody's moneymaking trick, that's all. Probably a gramaphone of some sort with a record hidden inside where you can't see it."

The Pews, as you have likely surmised, appraised the new marvel with articulate disfavor.

"All this modern science they talk about is the work of Satan," declared Aunt Lydia, "and mankind will rue the day it turned from the plow to look for all these silly gadgets. You mark my words!"

"I predict it'll limit rainfall," said her father, the incumbent grandfather. "Like I heard a preacher say at conference once, they's too much giddiap in the world today an' not near enough whoa."

To me, even though a mere lad, radio appeared as a thing of wonder. It assured me Jules Verne was not a dreamer but a prophet. It ignited my imagination. I sketched radios at school, when lessons bored me. I built mute sets of cardboard boxes, hiding them in the loft of our garage lest my waywardness be discovered.

Ah, yes, waywardness.

For, as I have previously indicated, the Pew tradition was so heavenly oriented it looked askance at anything of earthly origin. Thus the new marvel was promptly added to the list of thou shalt nots and became another of the taboos I was commanded to observe.

I tried.

I limited my initial iniquity to sauntering past houses into which the new marvel had been introduced, studying the aerials, looking upward to the sky to wonder how the human voice could vault across the ether waves from transmitters many miles away.

"Jeremiah," my father asked from time to time, "you haven't gone to anybody's house and listened to the radio?"

"No, sir," I was able to say with fullest honesty.

"Aunt Lydia and your grandfather would be very unhappy," my father then added, "if you disobeyed us."

"Jesus would be unhappy, too," my mother emphasized.

As I said before, my childhood was beset by conflict between my desire to comply and the pull of change. I nurtured inner pride at the thought of our sanctity. I yearned to but once don a set of headphones and experience the new miracle.

One day the inevitable happened.

A friend at school invited me into his house to hear for myself some of the wonders he had been telling me. I might not have yielded, except for the fact his parents were respected church people—a reputation I had never heard disputed, not even among the Pews.

I could not bring myself to flagrant discreditation of my kinsmen, however. As we neared my friend's house, I maneuvered our steps across an open lot, on the pretext of wishing to show him something in the alley leading to the rear door of their domicile, thus avoiding a bold entrance from the more observable street.

I felt a pang of conscience as we came into his house, a desire

11

to turn and flee, to emerge victorious from the tempter's grasp.

"Jerry came to hear our radio," my friend said to his mother.

She looked at me strangely a moment, then smiled and said, "How nice."

She taught a class in our Sunday school.

"C'mon, Jerry," my friend urged. "We can get four stations."

"Last night your father got six," his mother corrected.

We came upon the radio set. It was like beholding Pandora's box, like looking upon a monarch's coffer, like seeing with the mortal eye a caisson of the nether world!

My friend put on the headphones and engaged a switch.

"It takes a minute to warm up," he said.

My eyes widened as I watched him turn the dials.

"Hear anything?" I asked.

He gestured for silence.

"There!" he exclaimed a moment later. "The seed and nursery station. Boy, is it ever clear!"

He removed the headphones and handed them to me. I hesitated taking them, so he put them on my head.

It was wonderful!

Music and voices from the east, the west, from the north and the south, simply by turning three impressive black dials in a ratio compatible to each other. Time passed so quickly I found it necessary to employ a smattering of hyperbole when my father wanted to know why I had not come directly home from school.

By this time you perhaps accuse me of exaggeration. To you, radio is amoral, and the farthest stretch of fiction has no license to portray it otherwise. But, remember, you are the child of change, a younger child than I—all the more reason to hear me completely. For, I re-emphasize, you and I both live in the time of transition. Only as we accept this fact can we most productively recognize those facets of human experience which, being truly absolute, remain forever the same.

It is like a jigsaw puzzle. Fragments, incongruous in themselves, become the mosaic of reality when properly related.

For example, just as many a modern mind would insist time is the mortal enemy of, shall we say, the status quo, so also it became inevitable for my father to know I had been secretly hearing radio broadcasts. He knew I frequented the home of my friend. He knew they possessed the contraption condemned by the Pews.

Normally, he should have gone to the back yard hedge and cut a whipping switch. I had envisioned this eventuality each time I placed a headset over my ears and listened to my friend's radio.

"Now, you stay away from that place, boy," was my father's initial reproof. Later, he modified it to, "There's no sense your being at his house all the time."

But that was all. I was too naive to suspect he had himself stopped in at the confectionary on Main street, where, for the price of a dish of ice cream, one might enjoy a few moments with the proprietor's headset.

I was free to enjoy the new wonder, and there is much I could recount—the afternoon my cousin, hearing radio for the first time, wore headphones for an hour and listened to static, convinced he had some foreign signal; the little crystal set erected in the loft of our family garage and eventually transported to my bedroom.

At this juncture I feel it wise to introduce Uncle Rufus, who had married Aunt Lydia, my father's eldest sister, a quarter of a century prior to my birth. He was founder and owner of Security Mercantile Store, a venture of substantial success in our small community, and was, for the most part, in the good graces of the Pews.

I many times wondered how he so successfully kept favor with the family, for he never became one in mind with the distinctives of our lineage. In retrospection, I see him as the catalyst of change. Others, no doubt, think him an agent of detriment. After you have assessed the facts, you may decide for yourself.

Consider, for example, that day when, without consulting Aunt Lydia, for he knew well what her counsel would be, Uncle Rufus brought to their home a new gramaphone—or phonograph, as they were beginning to be called—and placed it in the parlor.

Aunt Lydia took one dismayed look at the contraption and commanded him to remove it from the house, a circumstance allayed by virtue of the fact providence had endowed Uncle Rufus with both kindly ways and crafty wisdom. Thus one hand gently restrained his spouse, lest she take destructive grasp of the instrument, while with the other hand he placed a record on the machine, turned the spring wind, and lowered the needle arm.

Abide With Me, sung by none other than the renowned and revered Ira D. Sankey, doused the fire in Aunt Lydia's eyes, relaxed her countenance, and set her to spreading word throughout the clan that, subsequent to worship the following Sunday, all would gather at her house for potluck and a wonderful surprise.

Of course, grandfather came.

I observed the deftness with which Uncle Rufus prepared the old fellow for the moment of truth. He not only listened to grandfather's accounting of the good old days but urged the old fellow on with carefully chosen questions.

Then Uncle Rufus brought forth the phonograph, temporarily hidden in the closet.

At first, grandfather resorted to the convenience of his deafness— a chronic limitation. He sometimes heard scarcely at all. It depended upon the weather, upon the phase of the moon, the prevailing disposition of his stomach, or any of several other imminent variables. He could be distressingly hard of hearing or as distressingly perceptive in remarkable synchronization with the convenience of the moment.

(Inasmuch as footnotes would be out of place in a nonscholastic treatise of this sort, allow me a paranthetical moment to add that grandfather always experienced great difficulty making out a sermon, if it happened to touch upon his own shortcomings, and that he could be counted upon for a throaty amen, if the preacher singled out those sins of society against which the Pews staunchly insulated themselves.)

As might be expected, Uncle Rufus had selected *Abide With Me* for the first rendition.

"Turn it up, Rufus," Aunt Lydia urged, "so papa can hear."

"That's as loud as it plays," Uncle Rufus said.

"I heard it play louder," Aunt Lydia countered.

To which Uncle Rufus said, "It depends on the recording, dear. Some have more volume than others."

"Do you hear?" Aunt Lydia called loudly into grandfather's ear.

"How's that?" the old fellow gummeted.

"Do you hear the phonograph? Do you hear the music?" Aunt Lydia pointed to the machine. "It's one of Ira D. Sankey's numbers."

"Sankey?" grandfather exclaimed. "You don't mean D. L. Moody's singer?"

"I sure do," Aunt Lydia told him, beaming.

It was a day for flags and trumpets. The world had come into the Pew circle, to be sure, but it came as a bearer of blessing. Such hubbub of excitement and commendation arose that Uncle Rufus started the record over again.

"Well, I declare!" grandfather effused. "I declare! It's like I heard a preacher say at a conference; that Sankey feller converted nearly as many as Moody did hisself, just by his singin'. I declare!"

"Like Brother Sankey was in the room with us, isn't it, papa?" Aunt Lydia asked.

"How's that?"

"Don't you hear the music?"

"Of course, I do! I'd hear it a sight better if you'd keep still!"

Aunt Lydia blushed. Grandfather cocked his head and swayed to and fro most piously.

Uncle Rufus followed the Sankey selection with a quartet called the Glorious Harmonaires, then a Stephen Foster group, then John Philip Sousa with his internationally famous band.

Grandfather kept time with his foot, like a boy at the circus.

It was indeed a new day in my life. Until that hour, Aunt Lydia's parlor had been a prison to my young spirit. Now, thanks to the benefaction of my beloved Uncle Rufus, it had become the one place I would want to be if I had complete freedom of choice that Sunday afternoon.

After playing the second side of the Sousa record, Uncle Rufus turned to Aunt Lydia, wisely pretending to be seeking her guidance, and said, "Maybe that's enough for now."

A clamor of protest came from the relatives. Aunt Lydia beamed, and looked at her husband as proudly as she might have looked had he been a Pew and she one of the outsiders.

"Play some more," she said. "Play some of the records over again."

Ingeniously, Uncle Rufus selected a disc which consisted of excerpts from William Jennings Bryan's immortal Chautauqua speech entitled, "The Cross of Gold."

"Amen!" gummeted Grandfather, his hearing as clear and keen as a young robin in spring. He had once taken grandmother, a woman no longer with us, to hear Bryan give the speech in Chautauqua Park down at the county seat.

Then, without warning, grandfather put forth his cane, a characteristic gesture whenever he was about to render judgment. He touched the phonograph and asked, "Do you reckon it'll ever take the place of preachin'? I remember a speaker at conference sayin' pulpits would be silenced in the last days. Churches are already closin' down Sunday nights."

This temporary crisis was averted by a particularly eloquent phrase in the speech, which prompted the old gentleman to ask if that part could be played again, in response to which Uncle Rufus lifted the needle and replayed the section.

"Better than if Brother Bryan was here himself!" Aunt Lydia observed. "If you aren't sure of a portion, you can play it again. And, my, isn't that a clear playing machine, Rufus?"

"Can't you keep still, girl?" grandfather protested. "Play it once more, Rufus, so I can get the full wording."

Grandfather asked to hear portions of the speech over and over, with the result that several of the guests drifted away to other sections of the house, Aunt Lydia among them.

I remained.

So did several of the men.

Though I never knew for sure, I suspect Uncle Rufus had earlier whetted their appetites. What I do know is that, after several Bryan encores, grandfather fell blissfully asleep.

Promptly, Uncle Rufus took from the very underneath of the stack of records a hitherto unplayed selection entitled *Milbine and Zack—A Most Hilarious Conversation*.

"I hear your wife has gone to see your mother-in-law," the recording began, it being Milbine who spoke first.

"Yes," spoke Zack secondly, "she went to pick up a few pointers on laying down the law to me."

Following this came such a sudden burst of laughter on the part of Milbine that grandfather awakened with a start.

"How's that?" grandfather asked. "What was Brother Bryan's point there?"

"Say," said Milbine, his laughter having so quickly subsided that I at first thought it to be on account of grandfather, "do you know why birds fly south in the fall and north in the spring?"

"No," said Zack, "unless it's because they don't fly north in the fall and south in the spring."

"Is that Brother Bryan?" grandfather demanded.

"It's Milbine and Zack," said Uncle Rufus, as cool as a glass of Aunt Lydia's lemonade.

"It's who?"

"Milbine and Zack—the vaudeville team from Los Angeles."

"Evangelist?" grandfather asked. "Sounds to me like they's two of 'em."

"Say," said Milbine, "do you know why roosters don't lay eggs?"

"Why?" asked Zack.

"They is two of 'em!" Grandfather turned and bellowed toward

16

the kitchen. "Lydia! What's come over this contraption?"

Aunt Lydia appeared, just as Zack roared with laughter at the statement Milbine had made but which none of us had heard due to the interruption.

"Oh, say," said Zack, "I forgot to tell you. The landlord spoke to me this morning."

"You mean," said Milbine, "he caught you going up the ladder and crawling into the room through the window?"

It took just that long for Aunt Lydia's indignation to detonate. "Rufus!" she screamed, "Remove that record!"

Not waiting for her husband's compliance, she hastened toward the phonograph, and would have taken matters into her own hands, except that Uncle Rufus outdistanced her. He lifted the needle, applying the turntable brake just as Milburn said to Zack, "Say, I hear your wife gave birth to twins."

"What was that point?" grandfather asked.

Uncle Rufus removed the record.

"Did the contraption break down, Rufus?" the old man asked.

"It didn't break down," Aunt Lydia said. "Give the record to me."

"How's that, Lydia?" grandfather asked.

"Give the record to me, Rufus."

Uncle Rufus obeyed.

Aunt Lydia promptly shattered the disc across her knee.

"That will be the end of that!" she stormed. "On Sunday! In our house!"

"I declare," grandfather muttered, having watched his daughter's punitive act. "Some of them things is only good to play once, eh?"

"This kind is!" Aunt Lydia said.

"Must be a might expensive."

Grandfather then settled back for the resumption of his nap.

Aunt Lydia returned to the kitchen, Uncle Rufus having promised not to reactivate the phonograph.

I watched as he gathered together the records he had played, returning them to the storage section at the base of the cabinet. Quite sometime later, years I suppose, I heard it said he placed them together with several other selections, as yet unplayed, among them a record entitled *Milbine and Zack—A Most Hilarious Conversation,* which Uncle Rufus had wisely purchased in duplicate as a protective measure.

Chapter Three

For the first decade of my earthly pilgrimage, I did not realize the downstairs closet in grandfather's house contained a chink in the presumably impregnable Pew armor. Unquestionably, grandfather never intended for me to make the discovery.

But as the old fellow neared the culmination of his days, he grew careless. I wonder if this may not have been the predominant reason Aunt Lydia strived, though vainly, for her father to transpose himself to her house. With all deference to dear Aunt Lydia, she could be expected to have concerns which took precedence over the mere matter of a bloodmate's physical welfare.

During the last years of the old fellow's life, Aunt Lydia assigned to me the responsibility of performing sundry tasks in and about the ancient domicile. Many times, alone in the house but for grandfather, I stood within grasp of the closet knob, wishing I had the courage to open the door and peer inside.

I knew the closet contained grandfather's wedding suit and his wife's wedding dress. I knew it contained such artifacts as the walking stick once used by our clan's progenitor. I knew it contained several sets of stereoptican views brought out for us youngsters on the rarest of occasions. I suspected it contained many other relics and wonders.

But, as you shall discover, I had not the faintest clue its contents included an instrument of evil entrancement such as might have been harbored by Achan or Ananias of old.

The truth became known one warm spring Saturday, when Aunt Lydia summoned me to cut the grass on grandfather's lawn. I loathed the chore, and invariably resorted to an arsenal of excuses. But this particular Saturday found Aunt Lydia in one of her dowager moods. Consequently, she would not be put off.

Had she been allowed sufficient foresight, I am sure she would have blessed me for disobedience. By the same token, I never again felt quite the same repulsion to her totalitarian ways.

Usually, I began cutting along the west side of the house, the front side, but this day I initiated my original effort on the east or back side. Whether this came about providentially or otherwise I shall not attempt to say.

After I had mowed several swathes,, the Morning Flyer signaled its impending arrival. Grandfather's house stood but a block from the railroad tracks, across an open field, and this fact in itself helped lessen the drudgery of Aunt Lydia's demands.

It was a marvelous sight, the great locomotive steaming into town, its plume of black obliterating the sky. In reminiscence, I realize the train, whenever I watched it, awakened in my heart the realization and hope of worlds beyond my own.

On that morning, however, I do not recall being in a philosophical frame of thought. I certainly had no inclination of the impending circumstances. I simply stood, as did many another youngster in the community, and watched the marvel of transportation flaunt its speed and power.

As the Flyer snaked out of sight, I returned my attention to the lawnmower and would have dutifully continued my assignment except for an incredible circumstance. As the rhythmic belching of the locomotive fell to a whisper with the train's arrival at the station, a new sound came to my ears. I at first related it to the hiss of air brakes. Even when I began to hear it clearly, high-pitched and melodic, unmistakable as to identity, I could not believe my hearing.

It sounded like a radio tuned to the seed and nursery station I so often heard at my friend's home, a solo performance by one of the Farmer's Favorite Fiddlers. It came from inside grandfather's house.

It couldn't be!

(I should parenthesize that, like all the new marvels of science, radio underwent incessant refinements, one of the most radical being the development of loud speakers which replaced the initial headsets. Thus not only was an aerial a status symbol in our town, but through an open window one might proudly make known the ownership of an advanced wireless.)

I slowly made my way toward grandfather's veranda.

"Jeremiah!" rang out the voice of Aunt Lydia, guardian angel of Pewdom. She came at me like a blur, grasped my arm with the claws of an eagle, and shoved me toward the sidewalk.

"Grandfather has a radio," I remember saying weakly, as I paused to look back at her.

"He has no such thing!" she exclaimed. "Now you march straight home, and if I ever hear you've let out a peep about this . . . mark my words, boy, I'll. . ."

What she threatened to do, I'll never know, for she sped up the veranda steps like a matronly gazelle and burst inside the house, slamming the door.

I should have gone home in obedience to Aunt Lydia. I certainly owed that much loyalty to our fine Pew traditions.

But curiosity became my undoing.

I ventured onto the veranda, to the large window, and looked in just as Aunt Lydia stalked angrily across the parlor carpet.

In that one initial moment, with my own eyes, I beheld saintly, reserved Grandfather Pew playing a violin. He played with very nearly the comparable prowess of those fiddlers I had heard over the seed and nursery station.

It was incredible!

"Father!" Aunt Lydia cried out.

Had grandfather been afflicted with ears of stone, he would have heard her.

Aunt Lydia grasped the violin and might have smashed it into oblivion, except that she turned and saw me looking on from the window.

"Jeremiah!" she shouted. "Go home like I told you!"

I turned to go, realizing it would mean escape from work. Aunt Lydia, equally perceptive, opened the veranda door before I reached the front walk.

"Finish the mowing, Jeremiah," she said, her voice warm and tender like a cooing dove.

I turned to comply.

"O Jeremiah!" Aunt Lydia sang out.

I glanced back.

"We paid you ten cents a mowing last summer," she said. "I think it should be twenty cents this year."

20

We looked at each other for a moment, as I experienced my first taste of what one might call the political emotion.

Grandfather's fiddling became the prelude to a subsequent unfolding of the new world drama.

For example, Uncle Rufus—having won his point in the parlor—added a new line to his store.

He began selling phonographs.

Aunt Lydia expressed uneasiness, as might be expected, but though she never admitted it, she could no more escape the erosions of change than does the face of granite, furrowed by frost and wind and rain.

Even so, she might have given more definitive protest had it not been for one Sunday afternoon family gathering in her parlor.

As he always did, grandfather asked to hear the "Brother Bryan" records. These Uncle Rufus played, together with Sankey and several new hymn recordings he had stocked in the store.

Then, when Aunt Lydia went to the kitchen to prepare coffee, Uncle Rufus put on a new selection.

"What's that, son?" grandfather asked.

(He had never called another non-Pew by such an endearing name, and had only so designated Uncle Rufus since the advent of the phonograph.)

"It's a violin record I just got in at the store," Uncle Rufus said.

"Fiddlin' music?" asked grandfather, eyes sparkling.

"Fiddlin' music," replied Uncle Rufus, eyes sparkling.

At the first sound, Aunt Lydia came bounding into the room. But she stopped short. There sat grandfather, happily keeping time with his feet. There sat Uncle Rufus in reposed triumph. There I sat, with the smell of new-cut grass in my nostrils.

Aunt Lydia went back to the kitchen.

Within the following month, Uncle Rufus ran a full page advertisement in the community weekly newspaper, announcing another new line at his store. A large supply of the astounding four dial Atwater Kent radios, which featured modern science's crowning achievement, the superheterodyne loud speaker, an exact duplicate of the model Calvin Coolidge had installed in the White House.

Subsequent to the parlor rendition of the new fiddling record, and prior to the arrival of the Atwater Kent line, grandfather had begun daily treks to Security Mercantile Store, where he sat by the hour listening for the most part to fiddling records.

21

"It's a real help to me, dad," Uncle Rufus said, "you playing records all the time draws customers."

But whereas grandfather had touched the phonograph with the hallmark of his blessing, he looked askance at the addition of radios to Uncle Rufus' line of merchandise.

"Son," grandfather said crisply, holding his cane in the monarchial manner, "if you want me in your store, them benighted wireless sets has got to be put out."

"You surprise me, dad," said Uncle Rufus. "What could a man with your kind of discernment have against radio?"

The old fellow touched one of the radios with his cane. As a matter of fact, he nicked the finish just a little, but Uncle Rufus made no protest.

"They's things in this world God has created," grandfather said, "and they's things fostered on us by the devil. Like I remember a speaker sayin' once at conference, the devil wears dress up clothes more'n he does tatters, an' it's up to good church folk to recognize him by his face an' not pay no attention to the style of his britches."

"Did God make your clothes?" Uncle Rufus asked, taking his ammunition from grandfather's arsenal.

"The ingredients, yes, but men had to put those ingredients together."

"Well, dad, it's the same with radio."

"It ain't," said grandfather. "You know the Scriptures, Rufus, how God commanded Adam in the garden to cover his undressedness. The Lord put it in Adam the way to make things, an' that knowledge got histed on down to other generations, just like the original sin itself. That's what you call the grace of God an' the judgment of God seen in side-by-side parallel. Read your Bible, son. See for yourself how this occurs from Genesis to Revelation."

Uncle Rufus contemplated for a moment.

"Now spare yourself from my censure, Rufus boy, an' send them wireless back to wherever you got 'em from!" The old fellow pointed his cane at his son-in-law. "Be a witness to this community, an' bring blessing on yourself an' your store by smashin' 'em publicly."

Grandfather's eyes sparkled, as Joshua's must have sparkled that seventh time around the walls of Jericho.

"That's it, m'boy! That's it! Smash them radios! Glory! Smash em' to smithereens, an' run an ad in the paper to tell folks you're a gonna do it!"

22

"Let's talk a minute about the ingredients that go into a radio."

"How's that, Rufus?"

"You know, dad, there's only one reason why Adam and Eve didn't have radios in the garden of Eden."

"Adam and Eve? One of them vessels of perdition?"

"They could have had one, as I understand it. They just didn't know how to put the ingredients together."

"How's that?" Grandfather cupped his ear, the puzzlement upon his countenance indicating a recurrence of his chronic malady.

"Just as the good Lord made the air we breathe, the sunshine, all for our blessing, so He made a lot of other things. He made the ether waves."

"What was that last point there, Rufus?"

"The ether waves. God made the ether waves so we could . . ."

"Don't believe I'm familiar with what you're speakin' about."

Uncle Rufus looked at his watch. He touched Grandfather's shoulder warmly and stepped to the radio set, which had so recently suffered the patriarch's censure.

It was incredible, Uncle Rufus' genius for timing.

Grandfather held up his hand. "Don't you turn on that thing in my presence, son."

Uncle Rufus turned it on.

"Rufus!" Grandfather gummeted. He touched Uncle Rufus with his cane. Uncle Rufus moved deftly out of range.

"Them things goes or I do!"

Grandfather stood for one historic moment—cane aloft, eyes ablaze, lips firm set. Never had a Pew more majestically displayed the family image.

"I'm leavin' the store, Rufus," he said. "I ain't never comin' back."

The old man turned solemnly, like Lot at the gate of Sodom, and shuffled toward the door.

Uncle Rufus manipulated the dials on the radio, glancing apprehensively toward the departing patriarch. Then, with dramatic fortuity, the radio began to play, softly at first, then in the full glory of the superheterodyne superlative.

Grandfather turned, resolute for a moment, then puzzled.

Uncle Rufus walked away, leaving the old fellow alone.

Grandfather did not leave. He edged slowly back toward the radio, settled comfortably into the chair Uncle Rufus had provided, and for the next half hour listened to the Farmer's Favorite Fiddlers broadcasting from the seed and nursery station some eighty miles away. After that he listened to the news, followed by a mid-morning meditation presented by a clergyman grandfather had once heard with full accord at a camp meeting grounds down along the Middlebrine river.

Toward noon, Aunt Lydia arrived. She had obviously dispatched her father to the store and now came to observe the accomplishments of his mission.

"Papa!" she vociferated.

Grandfather ignored her call.

"He's been having the time of his life," said a woman customer examining a bolt of cloth.

"I 'spect he's fallen asleep," Aunt Lydia said nervously.

"Oh, he's awake enough," the woman said. She winked at one of the clerks, who stood in fullest respect at the sight of her proprietor's spouse.

"He's had another attack of deafness." Aunt Lydia bemoaned. "Seems like he gets strokes of some sort. Only bothers his ear drums."

She went directly to the old fellow.

"Papa," she called gently, touching his shoulder.

Grandfather glanced up irritably.

"Come with me, Come on."

"Quiet, girlie!" grandfather snapped. "I'm checkin' the quality on these instruments before I tell Rufus there which'n I aims to buy."

Chapter Four

Grandfather Pew's purchase of a radio was like the shaving of an Amishman's beard. With this one act, however unintentional, he sounded taps and reveille, lowered the standard and unfurled a flag, tore down the bulwarks and poured a foundation.

I expected fury to errupt, though I realized even Aunt Lydia could no more than tactfully protest an action of the elder clansman.

What happened was a rush of customers to Security Mercantile Store. Every Pew household installed a radio, including eventually Uncle Rufus and Aunt Lydia.

The day we installed the set in our home, I felt like the son of a millionaire. I embraced my father, a singular occurrence in our house, and danced about the parlor in such glee that my mother took hold of me and sat me down.

"Now, Jeremiah," she said, "we're going to be careful what we listen to. It'll be mostly the news and church programs."

"I catch you once listening to foolishness," added my father, "and we'll cut a switch."

"Maybe," said my mother, "it'd be best never to let Jeremiah turn it on except one of us is here to know."

Radio did not instantaneously secularize the family, however. It only became another manifestation of change. Please remember my introductory statement; this is an accounting of resistance to change, accomodation to change, and my own discovery of those absolutes which never change.

Allow me to briefly clarify an aspect of my own thinking as to change.

Prolonged observation of the human episode convinces me that change is the very method of existence, the vehicle of reality, and thus change embodies both good and ill. It searches us out, delineating the primal personality.

Were it not for those who resist it, change might often come without notice. The oddity I have observed is that, at least in the case of the Pew family, resistance would be shown outwardly while, inwardly, my people may have welcomed the innovation. Such a paradox, as you can well imagine, leads to innumerable complications and, in the case of an observant lad such as myself, to confusion and frustration.

For me, the lifting of the ban on radio had a liberating and exhilerating effect. But as I evaluate my past, I also suspect trauma. Though Pew traditions inhibited me, at times deeply irritated me, they gave my life distinction. They also brought stability, for I reasoned that any people who so overtly sought to be pious could anticipate God's choicest favor and, it followed, had less reason to fear His judgments.

So, though I delighted in the turn of events, I also experienced an associated tinge of concern lest our family lose providential favor and, as a consequence, suffer calamities which previously seemed only to befall the wayward and the wicked. Thus I took a renewed interest in Sunday afternoon at Aunt Lydia's and especially in the almost exclusive topic of discussion.

"Did you hear the Uncle Ezra program last night?" Aunt Britta asked one day. "Isn't he just the funniest person, and so sensible in the things he says? It's so cute the way he talks about broadcasting from the powerful little five watter down in Rosedale."

"A body needs to be careful," Aunt Lydia said. "There's good things on the radio, but an awful lot of wickedness, too."

"There's getting to be more and more preaching. It's all in how you turn the dials," Aunt Britta replied.

"Gives folks an excuse to stay home Sundays," said Aunt Lydia.

"I do think radio's cut into church attendance some," Uncle Eliad admitted. "Now when you invite folks to church they can say they hear a sermon right in the living room."

"Well," said one of the other relatives, "isn't it better folks heard preaching at home than not hear it at all?"

"There's the evil of it right there," offered grandfather. "As I understand the prophecies, the devil's program in these last days is to empty out the churches."

"Them anyway that still preaches the true gospel," Aunt Lydia added. "You can see it, too, less an' less of the unconverted coming to church, except Sunday mornings when Pastor don't give an invitation. I listen to radio some. I admit to it. But you mark my words an' see if in ten years time, if the Lord tarries, we'll be wishing there never was such a thing as the wireless."

"The Lord created the ether waves," said Uncle Rufus, "making radio transmission possible."

"But it's the devil who's the prince of the power of the air," countered his wife.

"You think hearin' a sermon by radio's as good as hearin' it in church?" asked Aunt Mabel. She was married to my Uncle Caleb, a hard working man who seldom entered into discussions since he promptly fell asleep the minute he sat down anyplace.

"I'll tell you one thing," Aunt Britta said. "It's a blessing to the shutins. Take Sister Wylie, who's been bedridden for who knows how long. My sakes, but she loves her radio."

"She listens to more than just sermons, I'll guarantee you," said Aunt Lydia. "I've heard it said, though don't repeat it from me, that she listens to a lot of this foolishness they have on, outright worldly programs."

"Well, let her," countered Aunt Britta. "It's precious little cheer enters that poor soul's day."

"It just don't sit right with me somehow," Aunt Lydia said, "We keep bad books out of our homes and then we let the devil wire the world right into our parlors."

"Pshaw, Lydia," Aunt Britta scoffed. "You listen to everything that comes on just like the rest of us."

Aunt Lydia turned up her nose.

"What about you, Rufus?" Uncle Eliad questioned. "Back to that earlier question, is it as good to hear preaching on the radio as to hear it in church?"

"A salesman was in my store last week," Uncle Rufus replied. "Seemed to be a church man. I believe a Methodist. He heard a speaker say that going to church by radio was like courting your girl on the telephone."

Radio was only the beginning.

The Pews accepted automobiles, probably because they facilitated church attendance. The appearance of enclosed sedans, replacing open touring models, met with some resistance, but only slight.

When Uncle Eliad purchased a tractor, he and Uncle Caleb being the only clansmen who tilled the earth, progress met a surprising surge of resistance.

"God made horses and oxen to till the earth," Aunt Lydia declared. "You mark my words, Eliad, you'll rue the day you bought that tractor."

"It saves a man lots of work."

"Don't the Bible say plain as print that man is to earn his bread by the sweat of his brow?"

"Then why don't you go back to a tub and scrub board, Lydia," Aunt Britta argued, " 'stead of that fancy new washin' machine that had a lot of folks at church talkin'?"

Aunt Lydia hadn't expected this kind of confrontation and was plainly unprepared. "How do you know all that smoke and oil won't pollute the ground?" she slowly rebounded. "And them big steel wheels just poke the pollution in. What's going to happen to horses?"

"We still need horses for a lot of jobs," Uncle Eliad defended. "Corn cultivation, hay wagon pullin'. Tractors can't do more than plow, disc, and harrow."

"Suppose they make tractors that'll do them jobs, too?" Aunt Lydia asked.

"That'll be after I'm gone," Uncle Eliad said.

"But you'll have been responsible for starting the trend, Eliad."

"You get rid of your washin' machine, an' I'll trade my tractor for some horses. A feller made me an awful good offer just this week."

Aunt Lydia suddenly found it necessary to retire to the kitchen.

Uncle Eliad did well with his tractor, with the result that Uncle Caleb soon bought a similar model.

"Maybe Eliad can handle a tractor," Aunt Lydia said, "but it'll be the undoing of poor Caleb. When he falls asleep behind his horses, they stop, but a tractor don't have that kind of sense."

"I heard a preacher at the district meetin' last month preach about tractors," grandfather put in. "He says they're a outcroppin' of tanks used durin' the war. Tanks'll be the chariots the Scriptures speak of at the Battle of Armegeddon. He had a verse . . . from Ezekiel, I believe . . . that was pretty plain about it."

I don't know who leaked the story, or if it may simply be apocryphal, but it seems Uncle Caleb did have problems adjusting to machine farming. He supposedly drove up to a line fence one day, while plowing, and from prior habit cried out, "whoa!" instead of applying the clutch. The tractor went through the wire, and, as the story goes, the catastrophe became the reason for his missing midweek service the first time in more than six years.

I do know he experienced operational problems. The tractor he purchased had a penchant for backfiring, or kicking as farmers called it, and one day, attempting to turn the crank by which the engine was started, he suffered a badly fractured arm.

Aunt Lydia could have never more thoroughly enjoyed the vicissitude of a fellow pilgrim, except, of course, if the calamity had befallen Uncle Eliad.

Modern convenience appealed to Uncle Eliad, however, and his next move was to install a home lighting unit. Townsmen could scarcely complain, since they had enjoyed municipal electricity for many years.

Aunt Britta's kitchen became *le place d'avant garde*. She had the best stove, the first ice box, the latest devices.

Then one summer, as his dairy herd began to freshen, Uncle Eliad purchased an electric milking machine.

Aunt Lydia was horrified.

"People are talking, Eliad," she protested, "and you can't blame them."

"It's hard work milkin' that many cows by hand," Eliad defended.

"But what's the world coming to—a time when people won't need hands and feet? And what about your church giving? All that money you spend on the farm!"

"You spend money to make money, Lydia. I figure I can buy ten more milk cows, maybe fifteen."

"I said, Eliad, what about your church giving?"

"What a man gives to the church is a private matter!" Aunt Britta snapped. "It's between my husband and me and God."

"Just as I supposed," said Aunt Lydia victoriously. "You spend money like you owned a bank, and the work of the church suffers!"

"I never said we didn't give," Aunt Britta argued. "I said it's between the Lord and us."

"Except Rufus there," added Uncle Eliad.

Thereupon Uncle Rufus, who served as financial secretary at the church, said that, whereas information on member giving was confidential, it perhaps didn't hurt for the Pews to know that Uncle Eliad was the best giver among them.

Thus was stemmed the tide of Aunt Lydia's protest, and thus flowed on the stream of worldly progress.

Gadgets invaded the home. Electric irons, waffle makers, fans, improved radios—comforts and conveniences of every description. With gentle, unrelenting persuasion, Uncle Rufus provided Aunt Lydia with most of them.

There were exceptions.

Curling irons, with which to alter the divinely intended contour of a woman's head, and cosmetics, with which to disguise the countenance, never merited Aunt Lydia's acceptance, much less her blessing. Even so contemporary a person as Aunt Britta stood firm with her sister-in-law in these matters, as the Pew family struggled to maintain its differentiation from the world.

I could expound at length concerning Pew attitudes to the airplane. Since it emerged during the war, and since its reputation for safety was severely in question, the airplane was looked upon with scorn. Rather than go into detail as to conversations I might recall, let me tell you of the introduction of heavier-than-air transport to our community and how it affected our family.

A young mechanic in our town, who subsequently became an inventor and a factor in my life, built his own airplane.

Dennis Wilding was his name.

His plane, double-winged, roared through the skies above town at unannounced intervals. It was a wonderous sight, and though I neared the age of adolescence, I had not outgrown my yen for such fancies as a toy plane crudely made by my own hand, which I pretended to fly for hours on end.

Government agencies had not yet been formed to restrict aerial conduct, and Dennis Wilding took to stunting and outright foolery across the placid skies.

Aunt Lydia rose up in defiance, commanding her husband to do something. I recall hearing that Uncle Rufus supposedly approached Wilding about the matter, also that shortly thereafter the young pilot soared out of the low-hanging clouds one Saturday morning to all but touch wheels onto Aunt Lydia's rooftop.

"Rufus just stood there and laughed," Aunt Lydia complained. "The town council ought to make a law, that's what should be done, and forbid the plane to fly within the city limits."

30

"In the air," Uncle Rufus said, "there aren't any city limits."

"Suppose he crashes into one of our houses?"

Uncle Rufus did speak to Wilding about the matter. Thereafter, the airplane maintained a higher altitude.

Stunting continued, however, with the pilot adding some awesome and perilous routines to his repertoire. He did tailspins. He cut the motor and glided to his airstrip, calling out to townspeople from the silent sky. He won the heart of a farmer's daughter by dropping love notes. When her father protested, he landed in the farmer's pasture, took the man for a ride, and had no problems thereafter.

He crash-landed one day, demolishing the ship and very nearly himself. After that, he gave up flying and devoted himself to the manufacture of machinist products—a venture destined to add stature to our community and, as I previously indicated, significance to my future.

But whereas the Pews acquiesced to many forms of progress, on one point they all stood staunchly resolute. They deplored the theater and anything related to it, however remotely, holding specific disdain for the silver screen.

We children were not only forbidden to enter the local movie house but must not so much as be seen in its vicinity. Consequently, I developed a thirsting curiosity to look upon anything projected. Slides were used in our school, and I watched every presentation with utmost relish, however erudite the subject.

While in the early years of grade school, I established friendship with the son of the local theater manager. On Saturday afternoons he took me by way of the alley entrance to matinee screenings of silent drama. It was a world unreal, the gnome-like comedians, gunmen falling from dizzying heights and rising to kill again, bejewelled vampires, caricatured policemen vainly striving to keep pace with pandemonium, crisis and rescue in a cascading flow of movement—all like the figment of those dreams one has which are so apart from life as to seem unreal even in the somnolent state.

My father was adamant about the movies, and frequently questioned me.

"Have you ever gone through the door of the theater?" he asked.

"No, sir," I replied, thankful that my entrance was always by the rear, thus justifying my prevarication.

"If you ever do," he said, "I'll whip you so you can't sit for a week."

Tormented of conscience, I would toss in bed at night, promising God to never again enter the theater, but on the following Saturday I invariably returned.

At school, my teachers with increasing frequency projected slides pertinent to subject material in our lessons. Great works of art. Historical sites. Science and industry. My mind was stimulated but it was an activity I never discussed with my parents.

If grandfather Pew had shown himself at my classroom door, when scenes at the Louvre were on the screen, I would have melted in shame. Had Aunt Lydia come, I might have vaulted out the nearest window! It was my responsibility as a Pew to refuse participation in any worldly endeavor, however innocuous aspects of that endeavor may at times have seemed.

With the advent of sound motion pictures, the little theater in our town became the central hub of community activity. Charlie Chaplin and Harold Lloyd had challenged the church's supremacy in community influence, but now came Al Jolson, W.C. Fields, Clark Gable, and a host of others, singing and emoting in sight and sound. Churches suffered humiliating loss in popularity.

Clergymen, who could not fraternize in theistic endeavors, joined forces in attempting to at least prevent Sunday night showings. But, in many churches, Lord's night services had already succumbed, and such clergymen, though they protested loudly, spoke in a minority voice.

The pastor of our church sounded forth in prophetic indignation. Not only did he uncompromisingly denounce the sound motion picture as an implement of iniquity, but he predicted the direst of consequences should any true child of God behold the new device. I did not hear him say it, as my young mind wandered during the preaching, but Aunt Lydia insisted the pastor had gone so far as to warn that blindness might befall a Christian in theater attendance, and most assuredly any such transgressors stood in imminent peril of having their names blotted out of the celestial Book of Life.

So it was with quite some degree of trepidation that I accepted the invitation of the theater manager's son to view a segment of "The Covered Wagon" one Sunday afternoon.

"You've never seen the sound movies," he tempted. "They're just as real as if you were there watching when things happened."

I wanted to leave the moment I entered the building. Never had I so flagrantly desecrated a Sunday afternoon.

32

There was no comparison to the old silent screen pantomimes. Here was life emblazoned before me. It was like a window to the nether world.

"I'd better go," I whispered to my friend. We stood at one side near the front.

"Why?" he asked. "It's a dandy show. I want you to see the Indian fight."

"My dad would lick me like crazy."

"How's he to know?"

My eyes adjusted to the light. I could see the crowd of people in the auditorium. I envied them and feared them. These were the people of hell. I wanted to cry out, to warn them of their folly.

What excuse had I to be in such a place? Suppose someone recognized me and whispered the fact to others in the community? Suppose my father should hear? Even worse, suppose Aunt Lydia were to learn of my debauchery?

"Let's sit down, Jerry," my friend said.

"I'd better not."

"It's coming to that good place, the Indian fight. Wait'll you hear 'em holler, an' the guns an' all."

"Let's go."

"Only a half-hour, like I said. Maybe just twenty minutes."

"Naw."

"Look, he's here . . ." My friend pointed.

"Who?" I asked, and at the same moment saw for myself.

There sat the pastor of our community's most fashionable church! At the movies, on Sunday afternoon!

For one brief moment, his presence assuaged my guilt. But only for a moment. Then I remembered lengthy parlor discussions I had heard. This clergyman was an agent of Satan, the Pews had said, a blasphemer, a Pharisee. It could even be he had *sinned away* the reach of God's grace and was consequently more lost than a drunkard or a harlot or a murderer.

I turned and fled.

Outside, I burst into full speed. Down the alley, across a vacant lot, along a residential street, on and on I ran, my heart pounding savagely, my lungs aflame, my legs aching.

I ran until, exhausted, I came to the church, a gaunt frame structure at the edge of town. I entered. It was utterly empty. I had never seen it empty and silent. It was like a judgment hall.

I walked to the front.

There at the altar rail I prostrated myself and promised God to never again break His law.

I felt peace.

I sensed the breath of forgiveness.

I would sin no more.

Chapter Five

Sincere though my intentions may have been in respect to a boycott of the cinema, circumstances ere long beset my asceticism.

Uncle Eliad belonged to the Farm Bureau, a national fraternity of agriculturalists. Monthly meetings convened in township farm homes, a frequent feature being the presence of the county agent, who gave talks about farming trends and methods. His equipment included a motion picture projector with which he exhibited silent films of general interest, including animated presentations of two new luminaries on the entertainment horizon, namely Mickey and Minnie Mouse.

I regret that you shall not have the opportunity to become better acquainted with Uncle Eliad. He seemed every inch a Pew. Proud. Regal. And, I must admit, pious. Yet he had the innate capacity for accommodation.

I must take time, however, to tell you of a meaningful event pertaining to the first appearance of the county agent's projector within the sanctity of a Pew household.

"We're havin' Farm Bureau next Tuesday night," Aunt Britta said, as she heaped her dish with the potluck bounties on Aunt Lydia's table. "All you folks come."

"How's that?" Aunt Lydia called from the kitchen.

"I say," said Aunt Britta, "we're havin' Farm Bureau Tuesday night."

"I heard you!" Aunt Lydia stalked to the kitchen door. "Is the county agent showing movies?"

"I spect so, Lydia. He always does."

Aunt Lydia went directly to the parlor, where Uncle Eliad reposed with a lap laden with delicacies.

"Eliad!"

"Yes, Sis?"

"You're having Farm Bureau!"

"That's right."

"The county agent will be there?"

"We're expectin' him."

"He'll show movies?"

"Now, Lydia, whatever comes over you whenever . . .?"

"You didn't answer my question, Eliad."

"I didn't?"

"About the movies!"

"He's got an adapter for battery light power. He can even hook up electricity from his car. He usually tries to . . ."

"You're not answering my question!"

"I'm comin' to it."

By now several clansmen had moved in for closer observation of the proceedings.

"Is the county agent showing movies?" Aunt Lydia demanded.

"He wrote us a card, askin' if Britta could have a white sheet ironed, an' . . ."

"Eliad!"

"Of course, he's showin' movies. That's part of the farm program he puts on. You want he should come around teachin' us how to hoe an' how to cut our grain with a scythe?"

Uncle Eliad's neck reddened.

"Did you tell him you'd rather he didn't show movies?"

"No!"

Aunt Lydia clasped her hands and turned to face the others. She addressed them as a prosecuting attorney seeking to convince a panel of jurors. She spoke as a prophetess, standing alone against the relentless onwash of an iniquitous people.

"What's our family coming to?" she moaned.

"They're just harmless pictures," Aunt Britta said. "They're about health or farming, with somethin' extra for the children. Why, you could show them kind of pictures anyplace."

"Harmless?" Aunt Lydia stood erect. "The apple in the Garden of Eden looked harmless."

She turned again to Eliad.

"Maybe you think the county agent's movies do no harm, but I don't," she said. "What bothers me is how we Pews keep giving in and giving in. Nobody stands for anything anymore. Think, Eliad!"

"Think what?" Eliad flared.

"Seems to me," said Aunt Britta, "Lydia's the one that could do with some thinking."

Aunt Lydia turned to grandfather. He sat by the radio listening to an address by a clergyman named Dr. S. Parkes Cadman.

"What do you say, papa?" she asked.

Grandfather lifted his cup. "I could use a little more coffee," he said.

"What about the movies?" Aunt Lydia asked.

"The what?" Grandfather cupped his hand to his ear.

"You heard me!"

"Heard what?"

"The movies, papa."

"I said coffee, girl. I said I could use a mite more coffee."

An undercurrent of suppressed laughter passed quickly through the room.

"Alright, everybody." Aunt Lydia flared. "This is no laughing matter." She turned to her husband, "Rufus!"

"Leave me out of the arguments, dear," Uncle Rufus protested. "I haven't said a word."

"Bring papa some more coffee!"

"That's a woman's work," Aunt Britta muttered. She rose and went for the urn.

"Somebody's bringin' you coffee," Aunt Lydia said to her father. "Now, I want to know what you think about Eliad and Britta having the county agent show movies at their house."

At this moment, however, grandfather leaned toward the radio, as Dr. Cadman reached the eloquent conclusion of his address. Organ music followed.

"What do you think, papa?" Aunt Lydia persisted.

"I don't know what to think."

"Don't know what to think?" Aunt Lydia gasped. "Isn't it plain enough?"

"Seems plain at times, but then I aint so sure. What do you think, Rufus?"

"Oh," answered Uncle Rufus, "I think with the movies it's about like anything else. It can be good or bad."

"Whose talkin' about movies?" grandfather gummeted.

"We are," Aunt Lydia exclaimed.

"Well, I ain't," said grandfather. "What do you think, Rufus?"

"Think about what, dad?"

"About this feller on the radio, this Doctor Cadman. Sometimes I hear him, an' he sounds like he's a real good Bible believer. Other times, I figger he's for sure one of them moderners! It puts me in mind of that feller who spoke Sunday mornin' during the District Conference. How was it he said it? The devil likes to use a cup of truth to mix in a drop of poison error."

Aunt Lydia stalked out to the kitchen.

With but casual urging, I persuaded my father to take our family out to Uncle Eliad's. My father admired his older brother, and often imitated his mode and manner. Uncle Eliad had made life more tolerable for me.

The facts in the case are that the county agent apologized to all children present. The Mickey Mouse cartoon, ordered for the occasion, failed to arrive. So he could only show a short film entitled, "A Busy Day at the Stockyards." It was dull in comparison to the glimpses I had had in the theater, but it was a movie, and so I watched with great interest. It did not seem an evil thing with my own parents present.

Aunt Lydia often said, "Offer the devil a mite and he'll demand a farthing." So it was inevitable that the church itself, the very citadel of righteousness, should come under seige by the magic lamp.

Now it happened, whether fortuitously or diabolically I cannot say, that our pastor resigned to take another charge. During the interim, at such times as the church was not hearing candidates, it befell the lot of Uncle Eliad, he being chairman of the church board, to look after the matter of pulpit supply, and to attend to other circumstances normally looked after by a resident man of the cloth.

One Sunday morning Uncle Eliad asked to meet with members of the board at the conclusion of the worship service, and he read a letter from one of the professors at our denomination's small college requesting permission to present a weeknight illustrated lecture at our church.

"Now I've never met this gentleman," Uncle Eliad said, "but we've all seen his articles in the church paper, an I 'spect read about the trip he made a few months back to the Holy Land. That's where he got these pictures he wants to show."

"Why, yes," Uncle Rufus spoke up. "I've got a salesman from our church down in Farragut City. This fellow calls on me three or four times a year. He was in just last week an' got to telling me about this professor. He was to their church, an' I guess it was just wonderful."

"From the way I understand it," explained Uncle Eliad, "these pictures was mainly took to show to Bible class students at our school. Just on the side, he's showed 'em some at churches near where our school is an' they've went over so well the men down there at Headquarters feel he ought to show 'em to a lot more of our churches."

"Do I understand these are magic lantern pictures and not movies?" Uncle Caleb asked having slumbered through most of the sermon but being now in a state of full wide awakedness.

"That's correct," said Uncle Eliad, "an' he has a machine for showin' 'em. I feel myself they'd be educational an' interesting. The issue we face is whether or not to let him show the pictures in the sanctuary, since we've never did anything like this before."

"Well, my sakes," said Uncle Rufus, "if there's a chance for us to see the Holy Land and see these pictures nice and big so it's almost like being there, I say let's write and tell him we'll be glad for him to come."

"I second the motion!" exclaimed Uncle Caleb.

As is the bent of humanity in general and church folk in particular, the board consisted of several men who sat silently at meetings, especially when controversial issues needed to be expedited, but spoke articulately once they came among family and friends. There was some pro and con discussion on the motion, but it passed without incident. Commotion began to take place after grace had been offered at constituent dinner tables.

Nothing in the church's history; not the charming young widow who came to the community and joined our church on transfer of letter before it was discovered she had been divorced; not the furor which ensued when one of the members committed suicide and several stalwarts insisted the casket be brought in no farther than the foyer on the day of the funeral; not the purchase of a new organ replacing the unit provided from the legacy of a revered pioneer; not the hiring of a janitor to abolish the custom of appointed volunteers; not the remodeling of the parsonage nor the kitchen at the church; nothing, indisputably nothing, had ever so drawn the battle lines of divergent congregational opinion.

"Now they're going to have shows in the church," someone grumbled.

"Before you know," said another, "people will try to bring all kinds of worldliness into the house of God."

"Might as well put in a ticket booth," Aunt Lydia snapped, "just like they have down at the theater!"

"But the man isn't going to show movies," contested Uncle Rufus. "They're slides from the Holy Land. It's no different than pictures in a book, except they're a lot better."

"No," Aunt Lydia agreed, "he's not showing movies. But the day will come when movies will be shown in the church. When that day comes . . . and it's coming, sure as these are the last days . . . whatever spirit is left in our denomination will be forever quenched. May it be after I've gone on to my reward!"

"If someone had taken movies in the Holy Land or maybe on the mission field," Uncle Rufus argued, "what would be the wrong of it?"

"The Lord don't present His message through the prophets of Baalzebub, Rufus." It was grandfather who suddenly spoke up.

"But the motion picture is a new invention, just like radio, dad. It can be good or bad depending on how it's used."

"Ain't the same, Rufus. What's the point in arguin' about it, when it's as plain as the printed Scriptures?"

"It's not plain to me."

"Rufus," Aunt Lydia lamented, "how many times must you be told that the weakness of your Christian life is absolutely no discernment?"

Opposition rose to such intensity, not only in our family but others as well, that several clamored for a congregational meeting.

"How's that going to look?" Uncle Rufus asked. "We've got a good college. We ought to stand behind its program. Now, here's what I suggest. Let's have this illustrated lecture on a trial basis. If it turns out to be the wrong thing, let's learn by our mistake. I'll be the first to admit it. Let's not bury our heads in the sand if the Lord has a blessing for us."

Uncle Rufus prevailed.

Aunt Lydia sulked. Mostly, though, she sulked alone, as once again rationalization imposed the mood of change within the Pew circle.

"As I see it," said grandfather, following a prolonged conference earlier that week with Uncle Rufus at the store, "movies is as wrong as any other kind of worldliness. On account of this, even if it's a good subject, movies can't be shown at church, an' oughtn't to be seen nowhere by nobody that calls himself a Christian. Now pictures that's still on a sheet, like this here professor aims to show, that could be somethin' else."

"Even in church, papa?" Aunt Lydia asked, her voice laden with concern that the patriarch should show compromise.

"Well . . ." Grandfather began. He hesitated, searching for words.

"God made these new things possible," said Uncle Rufus, "so we could better understand."

"You keep out of this, Rufus," Aunt Lydia broke in. She turned again to her father, "Is it right to show such things in the sanctuary?"

"How's that?" Grandfather cupped his hand to his ear.

"You heard me, papa!"

"What she said, dad . . ."

"Rufus!"

"What did you say, Rufus?" grandfather asked.

Uncle Rufus gestured obligingly to his spouse.

"Now just think a minute, papa," Aunt Lydia said. "Here you are in the sanctuary. It's full of people. The usher turns out the lights. No candles or a thing. Why, it would be no different than sitting in a movie show."

"Were you ever in a theater?" Aunt Britta asked, snickering.

"A body turns out the lights when he goes to bed," added Uncle Eliad.

"I'll thank you two not to be smart!" snapped Aunt Lydia. "You think it's right to turn the church into a movie house, papa?"

"How's that?" grandfather asked.

"The slide pictures, papa. Are you going to go see the slide pictures at church?"

Grandfather mumbled under his breath.

"Are you?" his daughter pleaded.

Grandfather continued mumbling.

"Papa!"

Grandfather creaked to an upright position and surveyed the room for a moment.

"Would you?" Aunt Lydia asked, a note of desperation in her voice. "You're the one that should tell us what to do."

Grandfather hobbled away, mumbling, "The Lord gives me one daughter, an' she's got enough obnoxity for a half a dozen women."

The night came for the slide showing, drawing so voluminous a crowd as had not been seen in many years—so many that the ushers brought in extra chairs.

I attended with my parents.

It was a wonderful night. The land where Jesus walked became as real as the landscape around our town, the streets where I ran and played, the clouds in our skies, the sheep along our countrysides.

Of course, a number of the faithful boycotted the meeting. It was, for example, one of the rare times when Uncle Rufus attended church alone. But even among those who stayed away, some could not bring themselves to untempered opposition.

After all these years people still tell of a Scandinavian woman in our church, a goodly soul but dubious about the use of the sanctuary for a picture show.

"I yust ain't sure, Yonnie," she said, when her son begged to attend.

"But it's not movies," the boy argued. "It's just slide pictures, an' they're about places in Palestine."

"Ya, dey say dat," said his mother, "but vunce ya get dere, maybe dey shange to a movie show. I tell you how ve do it, Yonnie. I let you go. If it's yust stand still pi'tures, you stay. But if vun of dem pi'tures start t' vigle, you come right home!"

Chapter Six

You may find it difficult to comprehend Adelia.

She crusaded with Aunt Lydia in the causes of good church-liness, the two seeing eye to eye on most issues although they occasionally scrutinized each other eye to eye in matters of spiritual prominence.

Adelia laid full claim to meekness and humility. If indeed she possessed these traits, they were the non-exhibited variety. In actuality, and often in a most affected voice, she spoke of her crown and its stars—the brightest star of all, the star which impelled her to presume piety more substantial than that of her compatriotess, being the fact Adelia had never married.

She had not even been courted.

Upon the uncomely spinster's frail shoulders rested many heavy burdens. She feared being alone, yet lived by herself with a half-dozen alley cats in a forlorn, psychic-prone house. She heralded her faith, yet feared the judgments of God and spoke frequently of the impending peril of sudden death or a sounding trumpet finding her unprepared. She had migraine headaches and hallucinations by night. She suffered from indigestion, palpitation of the heart, shortness of breath, and chronic billiousness.

But Adelia stood dauntless in the Faith, notwithstanding the goodly number who misunderstood and criticized her in the work she felt providence had ordained for her tongue and hand. She passed out tracts on Main Street, holding a high head when local youngbloods made jests. She visited shutins, loudly quoting verses of Scripture when doorbells and knocking went unheeded.

Adelia enumerated the faults in the preacher's sermons, complained if the choir didn't suit her, grumbled because the church was always too warm or too cold, spoke up profusely at congregational meetings, berated the young people, and beleaguered the church board.

Unquestionably, Adelia was one of the better known members of our church, whose words and ways became the corporate facade in the minds of many noncommunicants.

She also taught a Sunday school class.

My class.

For two tortuous years!

To this day I refrain from singing whenever the hymn "Give of Your Best to the Master" is chosen for congregational participation. Prior to lesson study, every Sunday morning, Adelia led us in song. Always that song. I can see and hear her yet, enraptured, untuneful, sireninig out above the lot of us. I am not sufficiently adept at music to say she never sang a note on proper pitch, but, if she did, I'm sure she never sang it in the proper place.

Loudly though she sang, not one of us dared refrain from joining in the cacaphony. If we did, she would promptly lower her piercing eyes upon us. In due time, I took to moving my lips but emitting no sound.

Prior to my compulsory enrollment in the Buzzing Bible Bees, Adelia's choice of a name for the class, I had successfully withstood her zeal for inducing conversions. Adelia's prize and passion was to see people converted. The milk man drove a mile out of his way so he could service her house early enough to avoid confrontation. The postman tiptoed onto her veranda. Neighbors neglected their lawns and gardens when she appeared.

"Even the devil runs for it when Adelia shows up," folks said.

This is not to say Adelia was doctrinely incompatible to our church. Quite the contrary. Evangelism was the hub and wheel of our ecclesiastical agenda. "Sin, Suffer, and Repent" could have been the title for every Sunday's sermon, morning as well as evening. Our new pastor had a vast collection of fearsome anecdotes about violent deaths, scarlet women, alcohol, wayward children, and broken-hearted mothers, all calculated to impell the listening sinner to flee from his wicked ways.

On Sunday mornings I survived quite happily. Only on the rarest

44

of occasions did the pastor thrust forth the net at noon. On Sunday nights, however, he became a supernal Isaac Walton on the banks of a pond at Saint Bustan's. You could no more expect the benediction to be forgotten, as to presume any Sunday night service would conclude without members of the congregation being instructed to bow for prayer while the pastor admonished sinners and backsliders to identify themselves by raising their hands and coming to the front in a public demonstration of their determination to be converted.

Some were amused at the proceedings, but not I. I sensed a spiritual presence in those meetings.

My thoughts could stray to idle fancying during the sermon, but once the invitation began, I felt as though the fingers of God reached down and removed the church roof so He and His hosts of angels could look down upon me.

"This may be your last opportunity," the pastor would invariably say, as we sat in bowed silence. "Slip up your hand. I'll see your hand and God will see your heart."

The night our community's best known inebriate raised his hand an electrifying awe swept over the audience. He hesitated when the pastor urged him to come forward, probably because so many were looking at him in defiance of the pastor's admonition that every head be bowed and every eye closed.

Adelia had seen his hand go up and, when he tarried, hurried to his side.

"Come forward," she urged. All the church could hear. "Be converted, and you won't ever want to drink again."

He went forward.

It was a spectacle to be remembered. It was historic and majestic, like Saul of Tarsus groping in his blindness toward the heavenly light at Antioch. Our high school basketball team's winning of the district tournament evoked no greater sense of victory.

Adelia accompanied the repentant soul to the altar. Each Sunday night, during the pastor's invitation, she singled out likely prospects. That was why, as I grew older, I made a point to sit well toward the center of the bench.

But though Adelia had spoken to many and had successfully persuaded some to go forward, the sum of her previous triumphs could scarcely equal this.

The glory of that hour lingered for several weeks, as the man made a valiant effort to stay sober and begin living the Christian life. He might have made it had it not been for Adelia. She came daily to his shop, reading Scripture, admonishing him, creating such a spectacle local wags inevitably took to jesting.

One Saturday night, he went back to the bottle, heavy. He never attended church again. When Adelia came to reprimand him, he ordered her out of his sight.

"You never was converted in the first place," she grumbled. "I might have known."

For weeks after that, the spinster's zeal focused upon the Buzzing Bible Bees.

"See what happened to a man who waited too long," she said. "He was so hardened the Word couldn't take root. His carnal appetites deadened his conscience. He yielded to the flesh and sinned against the Holy Ghost."

None of us understood what she was talking about.

Then, singling us out one by one, she would say, "You come forward next time our pastor gives the call. The devil will try to hold you back, but don't you listen."

On several Sunday nights class members whom she had carefully nurtured, mostly girls, raised their hands and went forward.

I wanted to.

Deep in my heart, in agonized sincerity, I wanted to know God in a transforming relationship. I tried to convince myself that going forward would detonate this transformation in my life.

In contrast to the alcoholic, who regressed to the worldly life, others evidenced a saving experience. For each who did, however, there seemed to be a half-dozen others in the church whose lives, though apparently separated from the deadly sins, showed no real evidence of the glow I wanted to experience.

Yet, so long as they had gone forward, so long as they remained faithful in church attendance and adherence to the prescribed mores, all was well.

The death of two men greatly influenced my attitude.

One of them, though he regularly attended our church and was reported to have once requested membership, never got his name on the church roll since he could not point to any specific time of conversion, and, as further evidence of unworthiness, he used tobacco publicly.

(I perhaps should not mention the man in our church, one of the deacons, who privately used snuff. I know, for I once caught him in the act, to my amazement and his mortification.)

Though remiss in the ecclesiastical requirements laid down by our church, the aforementioned non-member possessed exemplary virtues. He supported the church financially. He upheld its cause in the community. But when he suffered a heart attack, succumbing before the pastor could attend to his final welfare, a consequent pall of doom hung over the sanctuary on the day of his funeral, as the preacher spoke of those who come within one step of the Kingdom of God only to plummet into eternal darkness.

A short time later, another man suffered a fatal coronary.

He was known for his shady business dealings. There were stories about his questionable activities in the secluded presence of several women in the community, including the wife of one of our prominent members. Plainly, he had been a detriment to the church's image.

But, though admitting the man was not what he should have been, the pastor sounded a note of victory during funeral proceedings. Why not? This man had been converted in the proper manner. He fulfilled the externals.

I spent many hours deliberating the fate of these two men. I imagined myself to be one of the cherubims at the divine judgment hall, pleading the cause of the good man, demanding justice for the hypocrite.

About this time I also began to discover the differences in churches. Terms such as "fundamentalists" and "modernists" entered my vocabulary.

Only a handful of my friends came from the "fundamentalist" churches. The others, if they attended church at all, were "modernists." They could join church as a matter of routine, not as a result of some deeply emotional involvement. They could imbibe of worldly pleasures. Adelia warned her Sunday scholars of such people. "They are the tares that grow among the wheat," she said. "You shouldn't even play with them."

Frankly, my loyalties tended toward fundamentalism. Partly, I'm sure, because of long association, but also because I sincerely hungered for the reality of God, an experience which seemed of little consequence to the non-committed.

I sufficiently perceived the church's teaching to blame myself for failure in spiritual attainment.

"You can't hide behind hypocrites," was another familiar sermon theme from our pulpit.

Perhaps not.

But a young and lonely soul, striving to find the heavenly way, could surely stumble over them!

For example, I often secured odd jobs on Saturday afternoons.

One of the revered men in our congregation, who had taught the adult Sunday school class for many years, secured my services on three successive Saturdays.

"I don't have my pocketbook," he said, when the final Saturday's work was finished, "but I'll pay you next time I see you."

He never paid me. I know he did not forget, because he quite obviously avoided me for weeks after that until he saw I had given up any hope of remuneration.

On the other hand, one of the alleged modernists hired me to open boxes and arrange stock in the supply room of his store. In addition to an occasional invective, this man smoked a pipe and spoke openly of his drinking partners. He was obviously devoid of transformation aptitudes.

Be that as it may, he paid me a dollar each Saturday, an exceptionally fine wage for a young boy in those times.

Even though at this stage of my life I knew nothing about non-revelationist philosophies and did not question the validity of evangelical dogma, I grew wary of proclaimed believers. I would observe one who seemed exemplary, only to be disillusioned.

I have to this point only mentioned my father.

He was every inch a Pew, staunch, churchly, by ecclesiastical standards a true pilgrim in this wicked world. He had one failing— a violent temper. This he never displayed in church, but he often vented it upon me. He had an enormous voice and sometimes expressed his wrath with such vigor that the house seemed to quake. His favorite hymn was "Love Lifted Me." He might violently berate me for lethargy on Sunday morning—so abusive I could scarcely think of him as a Christian and then gladden the ears of fellow worshipers as he sounded out above the entire congregation with, "I was sinking deep in sin, far from the peaceful shore."

I cannot ever recall my father dealing kindly with me. When I behaved, he ignored me. When I erred, he took my hide.

I might have despaired, had it not been for Uncle Rufus. Though at that stage of my life I had not thought of him as a saintly person, he contributed the one salient consistency to my life, quietly but assuredly bending my loyalties to the conservative minority.

Uncle Rufus did not issue preachments. He never warned me of my sinfulness, or told me I needed salvation. I am not saying he shouldn't have. I am saying that I watched him closely and found in him no guile. Rejoicing with those who took the step of faith in our church, he quietly anguished when some fell by the wayside. In contrast to Adelia, he endeavored to encourage restoration by friendliness and a sincere interest in the person as an individual. In the fullest essence of Christian witness, Uncle Rufus doubtless should have sought to bring about my profession of conversion. He most assuredly could have.

On more than one occasion I sat outside Uncle Rufus' store, or even ventured inside, searching my heart for the courage to ask his assistance. We could have slipped back to his stock room, just the two of us, and knelt among the bins and boxes, as people knelt at church, and there experienced God's presence. But Uncle Rufus never offered me a hint of encouragement in this direction.

Concern for my spiritual welfare mounted, as I observed how procrastination stiffened my resistance to the voice of God, hardening my heart against those compulsions which had at times seemed all but irresistible.

I was two years in Adelia's class. During that time she repeatedly endeavored to persuade me.

"Jeremiah was a great prophet," she told me over and over. "He is called the weeping prophet in Scripture. His heart was tender to the things of God. Won't that seem awful, if you go to hell? Someone by the name of Jeremiah in the pit of fire! Now you get saved! You do it right away!"

On two or three occasions, as a last ditch effort to free myself from her dominance, I promised I would make my profession at the forthcoming evening service. On those Sunday nights I pretended illness so my parents would allow me to stay home. The two or three occasions when I did go, I sat securely within the bench, being particularly careful to select associates who would not themselves endeavor to induce me forward or, if they did, would only whisper a word or two but, when I refused to go forward, would leave it at that.

I particularly remember one Sunday night, after Adelia had been a bit more than customarily persuasive in the Sunday school class. With the very first notes of "Just as I am without one plea," the hymn we usually sang during the invitation, Adelia came toward

49

me. I cringed at first, as though watching the approach of a tornado against which I could find no shelter. Then it occurred to me. I sat well out of her range, with individuals of such corpulence on either side of me that it would be somewhat difficult to make my way to either aisle and equally impractical for Adelia to come to me.

She came to the pew where I sat and, looking directly at me, motioned for me to come. I looked about, pretending to wonder whom she had in mind.

"Jeremiah," she called out.

It was unmistakable whom she had in mind.

When I did not respond, the thing I had long dreaded occurred. She came in after me. My cheeks paled. My eyes turned to glass. My knees weakened.

But then a breath of peace came to my soul. Why struggle any longer? I wanted to be a Christian. I wanted God to touch my life with the miracle of transformation. Why resist her?

Then, with but one fat man and two women separating Adelia from me, I heard suppressed twittering. Looking back, I saw two of my best friends, boys from Adelia's class. Adelia, wedging her way between protruding stomachs and the back of the forward bench, created the most amusing spectacle they had seen in a good while.

That did it.

Just as Adelia reached out to take me by the arm, I bolted in the opposite direction. I stepped on feet, elbowed protruding stomachs. Creating quite a stir, I made it to the opposite aisle.

"That's good, Jeremiah!" she called out. "Go to the front now!"

I very nearly stumbled over the wheel chair of old Mrs. Wylie, the infirm soul beloved in our church.

"God bless you, sonny," she whispered.

I looked at her a moment.

"Let the Lord come into your heart tonight," she encouraged. "It's such a good thing to do."

Glancing back I saw that Adelia had nearly reached me once more.

Every eye was on me, as I high-tailed toward the back and outside.

I raced for home, dashed into the house and up to bed.

Within the half-hour my parents returned.

"Don't be too stern," I heard my mother say, as my father came foot-heavy up the stairs. My heart sank.

He exploded into the room, turned on the light, tore back the quilts with one hand and grasped me with the other. First he shook me. Then he whipped me with the flat of his hand. Then he threw me onto my bed, removed his belt, and mercilessly strapped me.

"Benighted child!" he cried out. "Put your mother and father to shame, will you?" It was many weeks before the last of the welts healed on my skin. I yet bear the emotional horror of the experience.

With only a few weeks remaining until I would be promoted to the next Sunday school age group, and thus fly forever from the hive of the Buzzing Bible Bees, Adelia grew adamant. She prayed for me by name at the beginning of each class. She looked straight at me as we sang, "Give of Your Best to the Master," and invariably turned lesson applications my way.

Yet I successfully resisted.

Then she set her trap.

With the coming of a new spring, I resumed the task of mowing grandfather's lawn. And one Saturday morning, just after the Flyer had thundered by, grandfather called me into the house. (I am sure the passing of the train was to be the signal.) He rarely offered me treats, but this morning he set out a cold bottle of orange soda and a plate of oatmeal cookies, both known favorites of mine. It was like placing fresh cheese in a mouse trap.

When but one cookie remained and the soda was three-fourths consumed, the doorbell rang. Grandfather hurried to answer. I thought little of it.

"Brother Pew!" It was Adelia's voice. "I brought you a bouquet of my first crocuses."

I headed for the back door.

"Jeremiah!" It was Aunt Lydia, engineering the opposite thrust of the pincers. She looked at the table, smiled and said sweetly, "You haven't finished your cookies and your soda pop." I submitted. What else was there to do? I went back to my chair at the table, though I neither ate the remaining cookie nor drank again of the beverage.

Adelia and Aunt Lydia took chairs on either side of me.

"Don't be frightened, Jeremiah," Aunt Lydia said. I admit there was a tenderness in her voice I could not recall from any previous situation. "We are here for your good."

"We have come to talk about your soul's salvation," said Adelia.

Aunt Lydia looked at the spinster sharply. "Let me talk to him. He's my nephew and I understand him."

"Well," replied Adelia, obviously rebuffed, "I'm his Sunday school teacher!"

I had a moment's respite, as the self-appointed evangelism committee became a rules committee. Eventually Aunt Lydia won out. She was a strong woman.

"I'll take the lead, but you put in a word, too," Aunt Lydia said.

For half an hour they pleaded and warned, cajoled and enticed. I saw this as the hour of my long impending destiny. The thought never crossed my mind that I could evade this calculated thrust upon my lost soul.

"Do I get saved right here?" I blurted, surprising them both. The two women looked at each other for a moment.

"I suppose you could," Aunt Lydia said. Her eyes sparkled with anticipation.

"It should be in church," Adelia said. Her eyes flashed with determination.

Once again the course of action was deterred as the two women discussed the matter of transformation logistics.

"Lots of folks get converted outside the church," Aunt Lydia said.

"A few, maybe," Adelia admitted. "But look at Swen Nordquist. A drunkard and a wife beater, a beast to his children, and you know it, Lydia.

"Of course, I know it. But he got converted, right in his bedroom, not two days before he died."

"Yes, Lydia, but even pastor admits it's a good thing he died because he never could have stayed true to the faith."

"Well," said Aunt Lydia, turning to me, "the important matter is Jeremiah. He's young and has his whole life ahead of him."

"Will you come forward next Sunday night?" Adelia asked.

"I might," I said.

"Don't story to me. You've said it before in Sunday school class, and didn't do it."

"I never for sure said," I countered.

"Why wait until Sunday night . . ." Aunt Lydia began.

Adelia promptly countered by saying, "It's best at church. As a public profession. That's the way the Bible says."

"But he can accept the Lord right here in his grandpa's kitchen," "and then go out and give his testimony. That would be according to the Bible, too."

The spinster shrugged her shoulders. "How many ever do it?

Half the people in our church get saved and that's all there is. They never let out a peep." This triggered another exchange of theological views, as I became somewhat like a laundered shirt awaiting the moment of suspension on Monday morning.

To what conclusion my encounter with Adelia and Aunt Lydia would have taken me, I hesitate to say, for just at the point where the irresistible force and the immovable object reached the full point of relentless inflexibility, Grandfather Pew came unwittingly to my assistance.

With his advancing decrepitude, the venerable gentleman developed characteristic weaknesses. For example, his interest span shortened. A subject in which he experienced involvement one moment might completely bore him in the next. He had looked on for perhaps a quarter hour as the two women debated the when and in what manner of my conversion. After that, his eyes began to wander. He yawned several times, and had subsequently creaked off to another part of the house.

I assumed he went for a nap. However, as the inevitable moment approached, whatever its inevitability might have been, the radio began playing in grandfather's parlor. For the first moment or so neither of the women gave any evidence of hearing it.

But I heard it.

I heard the familiar voice of the owner of the seed and nursery station. I heard as the Farmer's Favorite Fiddlers commenced playing their theme, "Turkey in the Straw." I heard grandfather open the closet door, open his violin case, and begin to play.

At that moment, Adelia also heard. So did Aunt Lydia.

"Well, I never!" Adelia gasped.

She sprang to her feet, Aunt Lydia reaching out vainly to prevent her, and marched into the fore section of the house. I glanced at Aunt Lydia. She sat in motionless, unvoiced consternation.

In a moment Adelia returned, more chagrined than when she left us.

"No wonder the poor boy is still unsaved" she muttered, as she headed for the rear exit. Aunt Lydia looked very much as if she had eaten something foreign to the prerogatives of her digestive processes.

Aunt Lydia came slowly to her feet.

"Papa" I heard her whine, as she walked toward the parlor, and as I scampered outside to complete the mowing of the lawn.

Chapter Seven

Although I felt a sense of reprieve, as a result of what happened in grandfather's kitchen, hunger grew in my heart for a glimpse of the assuredness of God. The thought came to me that perchance I could find Him by myself. Perhaps I did not need a preacher or a Sunday school teacher or an Aunt Lydia to show me the way to heaven.

We had an immense family Bible, and one afternoon, alone in the house, I took it from the shelf and placed it on the dining room table.

The Sunday school hour at our church always concluded with students congregating in the sanctuary, where each scholar was given an opportunity to stand to his feet and quote a Bible verse from memory. Some of the children learned a new verse each week. Others learned a new verse occasionally, but for the most part they reverted to something short and simple, such as *God is love* or *Draw nigh unto God, and He will draw nigh unto you.* Adelia stressed Bible memorization among the Buzzing Bible Bees and often had us stand to recite verses in unison. I forgot many of them. Others became permanent segments of my memory.

As I sat with the Bible that day, one verse in particular came to my mind. *Thy Word is a lamp unto my feet, and a light unto my path.*

I opened the Bible, and a prayer rose from my heart. I wanted God to help me understand. I wanted to find Him, to know Him, to let Him be to me what He had been to Daniel and David, to Stephen and Peter and Paul.

I grew expectant.

I began to read.

What with all the religiosity of our church, it is strange no one ever introduced me to the Bible itself. All I heard and observed surrounded the book with a kind of mysticism.

Catechism classes were not emphasized in our church. Our denomination looked askance at any reliance upon sacraments for salvation, believing a man's redemption to be possible only through the evangelistic procedure. We did have what was called a Bible study class, and which the pastor often announced as "the so-called catechism class," and I never missed a session. We learned by rote, questions and answers, but though the pastor taught the course with priestly fervor, it seemed to be something apart from the Bible itself.

On this particular day, however, it had come upon me that, if I read the Bible with a searching attitude, it's meaning would surely come to me. I read with careful determination, searching out every word, and yet my mind wandered. When this happened, I read the same verses over and over. Engrossed in my search, I was unaware of my mother's reappearance in the house.

"Where is your Sunday school book?" she asked, resting her hand upon my shoulder.

I looked up.

"You can't study your Sunday school lesson without a book, can you?" she asked.

"I'm not studying my Sunday school lesson," I said.

I will never forget the look of surprise that came to her face as she asked, "Then why are you reading the Bible?"

I didn't know what to say. I felt as though I had done something wrong. Then my mother said, "That's nice, Jeremiah. You should read the Bible every day."

My eyes must have expressed something of my yearning spirit, because she asked, "Did you want to ask about something?" This brief involvement of her spirit to mine was unprecedented and, I'm sorry to say, never repeated.

"Do you understand the Bible?" I asked.

"Of course," she said.

"You can read anyplace and understand?"

"Of course not."

The contradiction of her two replies confused me.

"The Bible is God's own word," she said. "You can't expect it to be easy to understand."

Except for teaching me a table grace and a bedtime prayer, making sure I was washed and dressed on Sundays, and frowning if I fidgeted during daily Bible reading and prayers, I could not recall my mother ever having previously spoken a word of spiritual encouragement. This then was like a new day.

"Do you understand the Bible?" I asked again.

"I?" she asked.

"When you read it?" I replied.

"I told you it isn't an easy book to understand. That's why we have a minister and Sunday school teachers."

Grasping at straws now I asked, "How do Sunday school teachers learn about the Bible?"

"They must study hard," she replied. "Each teacher gets a special manual which explains the lesson. The people who write the manuals have had many years of special education, learning about the Bible."

"Why isn't it written the same way we talk?" I asked.

"Jeremiah!" her eyes flashed. "The Bible is written the way God intended it to be written. That's something we never question."

"Oh," I said.

That concluded our discussion. My mother returned to her work. I closed the Book, put it back on the shelf, and went outside.

Our house lay but a short walk from the western edge of town, where a bordering road separated residences from a spectacular outreach of rolling farmland. Here I often came at sunset to behold in boyish awe the flaming demise of the day. Sunset, more than any other temporal phenomena, stimulated my thoughts about God.

Sometimes I imagined I saw His presence in the contours of a smouldering cloud. I smiled, as one does to a friend nearby, hoping God would notice from whatever distance He might be. Another time I hummed the melody of a hymn. It was "Give of your Best to the Master," and it startled me, for I had no recollection of ever associating myself with the tune except in the company of the Buzzing Bible Bees.

But whatever or wherever, God always seemed far away, unmindful, unapproachable. Lest you accuse me of being a child plunged into some kind of traumatic mysticism quite apart from normal childhood, let me first take your side of the argument and agree that, most certainly, I experienced religious frustration. But

56

I also encountered numerous other children my age who wondered about God.

On occasion, when the pastor delivered a sermon on impending judgment, we discussed the possibilities of this judgment befalling us. The pastor delivered many sermons on prophecy. He expounded Daniel's vision of seventy weeks and the image in Nebuchadnezzar's dream. He preached about the vials and the seals and trumpets, celestial creatures with flaming eyes, the four and twenty elders. All of these had to do with the imminent return of Jesus Christ, an event which might occur before the passing of another week and which filled me with such fear that I would awaken in the night, fearful lest the event had occurred, then be comforted by the snoring of my father in the adjoining room.

In fairness, I must tell you many of our pastor's predictions have been borne out by history. He predicted the return of the Jews to Palestine, the restoration of Jerusalem to Israel. He predicted the revival of the old Roman Empire in a modern United Europe. At a time when both nations seemed eternally docile, he predicted the angry emergence of Russia and China. He predicted the ecumenical movement and particularly the fraternization of Protestants with Roman Catholics.

He also made mistakes.

You may be sufficiently familiar with the Bible to recall that it speaks of an antichrist appearing at the consummation of the age in which we now live.

Our pastor believed Benito Mussolini to be this man!

I remember the night our sanctuary reverberated with the declaration, "The coming of the Lord draweth nigh, Beloved! Watch Mussolini. He is fulfilling in detail the Bible's prophecy of the Man of Sin. Let me warn you, my unsaved friend. In the light of events happening now in our world, I expect the return of Jesus Christ in not more than two years! Those not ready will be left behind, lost, to go through the Great Tribulation!"

As I mentioned before, response to evangelistic invitations had begun to wane. But that Sunday night three adults and fully half a dozen children raised their hands and went to the front. If the congregation had sung one more stanza of "Just as I am," I probably would have joined them.

Again and again during the ensuing weeks, my friends and I discussed the sermon. We all agreed it would be a fearful thing for Christ to return, suddenly snatching up into the clouds those who

57

were ready to meet Him, leaving the unconverted to the merciless Antichrist.

We formed a secret trust. On the coming Sunday, if our pastor again preached about the second advent, all of us would go to the front.

On the following Sunday night, the pastor changed to another of his favorite evangelistic themes, namely, "The Unpardonable Sin." But this did not quiet my determination, for he made the need for conversion more compelling than ever. He never gave a full definition of the unpardonable sin, though he succeeded admirably in sounding forth the warning that it was possible to so tantalize the Spirit of God as to remove oneself from the very possibility of being converted.

That night several more raised their hands in response to pastor's invitation.

"I will see your hand," he called forth, "and God will see your heart! The Holy Spirit will know you are not resisting the voice of the Lord."

I raised my hand—quickly up, quickly down, both hopeful and fearful of the pastor's seeing it.

Anticipation welled in my heart.

Though many hands had been raised, only a few went to the front. Consequently, soliciters like Aunt Lydia and Adelia took to the aisles.

I sat directly on the aisle.

Somehow, Aunt Lydia overlooked me. But Adelia came. She stood, arms folded, looking down at me with a most sombre countenance. Her eyes were cruel, her lips firm set.

She said not a word. She made no gesture.

She left me to go to another prospect!

Chapter Eight

My eyes first looked upon a deck of playing cards one summer afternoon at Uncle Eliad's place.

It was during the threshing season, out along the grove sheltering his farmstead. In those days, farmers organized what was called a run—eight or ten men banding together to share the cost of a threshing machine and then going from farm to farm in a kind of commune until the completion of each summers' small grain harvesting. Every farmer provided a hay rack, manned by himself or his son, or, in the case of those more enterprising, by a hired hand. These racks were horse drawn into the fields, piled high with grain bundles, and hauled back to the machine for threshing.

Strong men loaded their racks quickly in proud exhibition of their prowess. Others, or so it was told me, had a knack for building a hollow load—making it appear they had a full rack, when in reality they did not. In either case, men would hurry their loading in the hope of reaching the machine sufficiently ahead of time to allow for repose in the shade.

Sometimes the threshing machine jammed, or encountered minor breakdowns, and this would give the haulers added respite, in which case one of the men invariably brought out a deck of cards. Such an occasion transpired that afternoon at Uncle Eliad's.

I remember watching in mute awe as several men engaged in a game of rummy. It was like looking into the kingdom of the damned, seeing the implements of Satan in flaunted view.

"Cards are the wickedest thing there is," Adelia often said. "Bad as liquor and tobacco, and can be worse, because they lead you to these things. Gamblers and harlots and people who go to pool halls and all sorts of sinners play cards."

As a matter of record, one of the known sharks in our town was a handyman, often hired by the town council to do concrete repair. When frost upearthed a stretch of sidewalk past Adelia's place, this man was dispatched to repair it. Adelia not only stood on her veranda and proclaimed the gospel as he worked, but she proudly wore a path on her lawn grass afterward rather than set foot on the benighted masonry.

One Sunday night, our pastor preached a sermon entitled "Playing Cards and the Road to Hell."

"Each of the cards has an evil meaning," he said. "It all stems back to the Middle Ages and the revolt against the church of Rome. The King represents God. The Queen represents the Virgin Mary. The Joker was designed as the blasphemy of blasphemies, for it represents Jesus."

His documentation was thunderingly convincing.

To think I now watched the game being played on Pew soil!

Aunt Lydia frequently urged Uncle Eliad to put his foot down during threshing season and at corn shelling bees and forbid the use of tobacco among unregenerates working on his premises. I cannot conjecture what she might have done had she known that Uncle Eliad looked down upon the nefarious pastime from his lofty vantage atop the straw stack and offered no protest.

Now I cannot say with certainty that Uncle Eliad saw the men at play. He did look in their direction. He looked searchingly. But a playing card is a small object, and there was a constant swirl of blown chaff around my uncle as he stacked the straw. It may be he simply did not see well enough to ascertain the gravity of the situation.

I certainly hoped so.

Actually, however, we Pews were not without sin in the case.
We played rook.

Aunt Lydia protested the fact most vociferously, and it goes without saying she never permitted the appearance of a deck in her parlor. But Uncle Eliad and Aunt Britta championed the game, and family forays to their farmstead inevitably terminated only after a few hands.

Rook was never played in grandfather's presence. Give the old fellow a full meal, however, and he was soon asleep. When he awakened, the cards would be deftly put aside, a skill at which our family became quite proficient and which, as I shall soon point out, sheltered the clan from certain censure.

"Shame on you!" Aunt Lydia would protest, whenever a game began. "What kind of Christianity is this, playing cards?"

"It ain't cards," Uncle Eliad would say. "It's rook."

Aunt Lydia was not one to reason out a case. Cards were condemned because of their history and their use in gambling. Rook was a game of numbers.

"No different than dominoes," I heard Aunt Britta explain. She seldom wasted any time currying Aunt Lydia's favor, and well knew Uncle Rufus' spouse accused her of introducing the game, even though evidence pointed rather conclusively to Uncle Eliad having picked up the vice at a Farm Bureau convention.

It particularly unnerved Aunt Lydia when her kinsmen played on Sunday afternoons. Though she never outwardly said so, this may well have been the reason why she invariably discouraged Sabbatical occasions at her brother's farm. But occasions did occur in spite of her obstructions.

"You'll live to rue the day you ever began playing this terrible game," she prophesied one Sunday afternoon. "You mark my words!"

Within the year of that pronouncement, Aunt Britta invited us all to her house for the purpose of celebrating her husband's fiftieth birthday. Grandfather ate heartily and by two o'clock had slipped into the master bedroom for some afternoon slumber.

"Let's play rook," Uncle Eliad said.

"It's Sunday, Eliad!" Aunt Lydia snapped.

"You'd rather we sat around and gossiped?" asked her brother.

Aunt Lydia sulked into the parlor.

Eight players drew sides (Uncle Eliad had two decks.) and began playing around the spacious dining room table. Uncle Eliad was a titan at the game. He could bid with near flawless accuracy. When he played, he remembered every trick that appeared on the table and quickly surmised who held what in his hand. It was no mean accomplishment to upend Uncle Eliad.

On this particular afternoon, two strokes of ill fortune befell the reigning champion. He drew discouragingly dull hands, and he played opposite Uncle Rufus, who was in many respects the equal of Uncle Eliad. It was said he kept a deck at the store and played with town cronies on quiet business days, though I never knew this to be assuredly verified.

In any case, hand after hand went awry for Uncle Eliad. Even when he bid cautiously, he sometimes went set. There would be a poor pickup, or his partner would be weak in trump, or some other whim of the game would go against him. He was a good sport about it but became obviously distraught.

Then his fortunes began to change. He won the bid with a poor hand, but was nobly assisted by his partner. Next he drew two excellent hands and played them with finesse. His spirits soared.

"You just don't like it unless you can win, do you?" Aunt Britta chided. Only on the rarest of circumstances did she speak out against her husband. But then, of course, in this particular instance she happened to be a partner on the opposite team.

It was at a moment when Uncle Eliad was in his highest spirits, appearing certain to turn into victory a game which had seemed hopelessly lost, that a motor entered the farmyard.

"Red is trump," announced Uncle Eliad, paying no attention to the exterior arrival.

"I think somebody just drove up," Aunt Britta said. She was not in a position for a good view of the window.

Uncle Eliad led with the red ten. Knowing his tactics, it was plain enough that he held a formidable hand.

"Play," he said to Uncle Rufus, who sat to his left.

Uncle Rufus studied his hand, then laid down a red seven. It was Aunt Britta's turn, but she did not play.

For a knock was heard at the door.

"Hey!" someone called out. It could not have been more alarming had the house been afire. "That's the preacher's car out there!"

It subsequently turned out that grandfather had mentioned to the minister about the forthcoming gathering and suggested he drive out. This is of minor importance. What matters is that a scurry ensued such as my eyes had not previously beheld.

"I'll go to the door," Aunt Britta said. "Eliad, you cough real loud, if you hear the preacher's voice and the cards still aren't all put away."

"So," Aunt Lydia sputtered, "you get caught in your sins!"

"Not so loud!" Uncle Eliad whispered.

The door opened. We heard Aunt Britta greet the minister and his wife with appropriate civility. Everyone sat quietly in the dining room. Uncle Eliad did not cough.

"Hypocrites!" Aunt Lydia snapped.

"Careful, dear," cautioned her husband. "The minister'll think you mean him."

The newcomers entered, and took chairs near the table. A stiff exchange of dialogue began, slowly giving way to more amiable speech.

"It's such a lovely day," said the minister's wife. "We didn't know if we should come or not, but it was so nice for driving."

"We're glad you came," sang out Aunt Lydia.

I believe I was the first to see the minister's wife look curiously at the floor near where Uncle Eliad sat. Then Aunt Britta took notice. She nudged her husband commandingly.

"We've had awfully good weather this season," said Uncle Rufus. Whether it was his intent or not, I cannot say, but he diverted the lady visitor's attention.

"What's wrong?" Uncle Eliad whispered to his wife.

"The floor," she replied.

Uncle Eliad looked at the floor. There, looking as big as a barn door, lay the red ten.

"Dear," said the minister's wife to her husband, "sit over here by me so you can see folks better."

My spine chilled.

But enterprising Uncle Eliad thrust forth his foot, completely covering the glaring evidence of prior debauchery.

Aunt Lydia detected what was up and decided to make the most of the situation.

"Shall we go into the parlor?" she asked, looking squarely at her brother.

Aunt Britta hurried to her feet. "A splendid suggestion," she said. "It's more comfortable there. Pastor, you and your wife go first."

"This is fine," said the minister's wife.

"We'll only stay a short time," said the minister. "I want to go over my sermon again before the evening service."

"What's that topic again you announced for tonight?" It was grandfather who had been awakened by the commotion and was delighted to see the clergyman.

Uncle Eliad bent forward to retrieve the red ten. But the minister's wife put her gaze upon him, so he brushed some lint from his knee and returned to an upright position. He winced. It seems his legs cramped easily.

"Let's go to the parlor," Aunt Britta again suggested.

Uncle Eliad massaged the under muscle of his protruded leg.

"Yes," he said, "let's go to the parlor."

"What'd you say you was preachin' on tonight?" grandfather asked the minister.

"I'm speaking about 'The Little Foxes who Spoil the Grapes.' "

"It's from the Song of Solomon," explained his wife. "It's about the little sins we often overlook."

Aunt Lydia moaned softly.

As the time passed, Uncle Eliad's discomfort worsened. He tried to advance his chair, but it was on a throw rug Aunt Britta had made and this prevented it's ease of movement.

"I just remembered, Eliad," Aunt Lydia said. "You've never shown Pastor those wonderful pictures you took of the Christmas decorations." Her eyes drifted to his foot.

"With that flash powder?" asked the minister. "I'd like to see them."

"Go get the pictures, Eliad," Aunt Lydia commanded.

"I'll get them," Aunt Britta said. She hurried away, muttering, "He's like any man, I guess. Can't find anything, if it's in the house."

It turned out that Aunt Britta couldn't find the pictures either, and she and Uncle Eliad carried on a loud conversation across the house, as he tried to explain where he had put them.

"Land sakes, Eliad!" exclaimed Aunt Lydia. Mischief and reproof sparkled in her eyes. "Go help her."

"She'll find 'em," Uncle Eliad said. He rubbed the muscle of his leg.

Aunt Britta didn't find them, and it was only with the utmost dexterity that Uncle Eliad retained his foot upon the red ten and parried his sister's every suggestion that he go to his wife's aid.

"We'll see them some other time," the preacher's wife said.

"I'll bring them to you," Uncle Eliad promised.

Uncle Eliad slid to the edge of his chair. He maneuvered from side to side, seeking comfort. But he never once lifted his foot, though he was able to move it and its quarry to a more equitable position.

The minister and his wife stayed for almost an hour. Gradually, Uncle Eliad became more reposed. Aunt Lydia gave up her quest to bring about exposure. But then came the moment of truth. As was his custom, the clergyman asked for the Bible.

"Would you get it for me, Eliad?" he asked. "I believe it's right behind you there on the buffet.

As though he had forgotten the red ten, Uncle Eliad turned to comply. But Aunt Britta swept past him, touching his knee.

The minister read a long portion. I watched Uncle Eliad. He seemed at peace, like one who has submitted to the inevitable.

"Let us kneel," said the minister, when he had finished reading.

I watched tensely as Uncle Eliad lifted his foot and turned to kneel. Aunt Lydia watched. Aunt Britta watched. The minister's wife watched. So did Uncle Rufus and the others, who were aware of the inclement circumstance.

As though in rehearsed chorus, we all sighed. Uncle Eliad had managed to maneuver the red ten back toward the rug and then slide it underneath.

Chapter Nine

Faithfulness in marriage was a staunch Pew tradition.

Indeed, no one associated with the church took the vow of marriage with so much as a fleeting suspicion the marriage might end in divorce court. This is not to say marital bliss circumscribed each union. There were happy marriages. There were content marriages. There were endured marriages. There were miserable marriages.

To me it was a kind of game, watching young couples in courtship—the gallantry of the males, the starlight sparkle in the eyes of the maidens. Then, following marriage and the honeymoon, I took note of how quickly the knight's armor tarnished, how quickly the sweetheart became merely the spouse.

Whereas the Pews never issued a manifesto on marriage, I observed attitudes and picked up occasional comments, sometimes not meant for young ears, which gave me a generalization of the nuptial state in our clan dwellings.

With the exception of Uncle Eliad and Aunt Britta, I never thought of any of my aunts and uncles as being in love with each other. My own parents, though my mother never affronted her husband's temperment, seemed, in the externals of their relationship, more like brother and sister than husband and wife.

Neither my father nor my mother so much as implied the mechanics of life origins in my presence. A pregnant woman was said to be in the family way, but that was the extent of dialogue relative to procreation.

On the street, however, I secured a vivid education in the subject of sex. Woman was for man's pleasure, I learned, and the curtailment of virginity an enobling male conquest.

Newlyweds came under special discussion, and I once heard a young husband speak with stunning frankness about his new nocturnal habits. The next time I saw his wife, a great pity welled in my heart, and I found it difficult to comprehend that she appeared jovial in the presence of an acquaintance she had encountered on the street.

Pregnancy was a kind of shame. When it occurred, women all but vanished from public view.

I found it difficult to comprehend my parents ever participating in the connubial relationship, so unchaste had the act become in my scheme of values and, for that matter, so unlikely did this kind of intimacy appear possible on the part of my stoic progenitors.

I recall one Sunday afternoon, just prior to the marriage of one of my oldest cousins, when parlor talk grew rather frank about the possibilities of it being a good marriage.

"She's an affectionate girl," Aunt Britta said, "and they do seem to be head over heels in love with each other."

"That won't last long," Aunt Lydia observed.

"Oh," Aunt Britta agreed, "they'll settle down some, I suppose, but I think their love for each other is real."

"Well," Aunt Lydia rebuffed, as though she were the young virgin in question, "you don't have to be hugging and kissing all the time to be in love."

At this juncture, older family members got to reminiscing. They recounted tales of courtship and romance in the horse and buggy days. Said Uncle Eliad, "I remember the time I was taking Britta home from young peoples' meeting. Ordinarily, we didn't pay no attention. The horse would just naturally turn in at her place. But that night he walked right on by and took us three miles down the road before I realized what was up."

Aunt Britta broke into hearty laughter. "Eliad often said he was sure the horse glanced back a couple of times and saw it was no use to hurry me home."

"Foolish talk!" Aunt Lydia protested.

"Now, Lydia, we all know how you always held yourself back so people wouldn't know you were really in love with Rufus. But remember that time you thought you were alone in the house? You didn't know I'd been sleeping in the parlor. Rufus came to call . . ."

"Eliad!" Lydia snapped.

"You did a little dance on the rug and . . ."

"Eliad!"

"You twittered like a bird."

"Eliad, you be quiet."

As though he had not heard his sister's remonstrance, Uncle Eliad added, "But when Rufus appeared at the door, you were as serious as a burro mare. He asked for a kiss, and you told him to sit down while you poured him a glass of lemonade. That's when you discovered me on the parlor couch."

"At least our courtship was proper!"

"We all know that, Lydia," Aunt Britta said.

"Your trouble was that you took so much bones making sure everyone knew how proper things were that people almost got suspicious," Uncle Eliad said. He was fearless of his sister but had such a kindly way about him she was always caught off guard. "Now take your honeymoon."

"We never had a honeymoon," Aunt Lydia defended.

"Well, whatever you called it." said Eliad.

"We went to the national conference."

"And you stayed in a hotel."

"We stayed in a hotel."

"Every night you made Rufus there stand out in the hall while you got ready for . . ."

"Eliad. Now that's enough." Aunt Lydia exclaimed.

I glanced at Uncle Rufus, expecting him to be pale with anger. On the contrary, he was red with merriment and hard pressed to deny an outburst of laughter.

"One night," Uncle Eliad continued, "you kept him out there so long somebody complained there was a prowler in the hall. When the hotel sent a man up to check, Rufus was in an awful plight. Isn't that right, Rufus?"

Laughing merrily, Uncle Rufus said, "I let on at first like I couldn't find my key."

"That's the first time I ever heard that," Aunt Lydia interposed.

"I didn't want to say I had been put out in the hall by my own wife," Uncle Rufus continued. "So I just did the best I could to talk him into going back down. He asked me what room we were in and . . ."

"Rufus!" Aunt Lydia snapped.

"Go ahead, Rufus," Uncle Eliad urged.

"Well, I told him it was the room I was standing outside of, so he knocked on the door. Lydia made such a fuss because she wasn't dressed yet, so he figured out right away what my situation was."

"Now that's enough!" Aunt Lydia insisted.

As I said, my awakening to the intricacies of life origins came primarily from boys in our community. They were shockingly vulgar to my sensitive spirit, tales of community conquests for the most part. I pretended to share the philosophy that woman was made for man's convenience, but only so as to avoid ostracization.

Victorian though our family attitudes were, these attitudes became enough a part of me to insulate my mind against an acceptance of street philosophy. We had a few books in our house. I read avidly, often a book a day during holiday periods, and treks to the library occurred at frequent intervals. So I naturally pursued each of the few volumes contained in what was called our book case.

There was one volume my mother had been given as a maiden. It was titled *Searchlights on Dark Corners*. By my twelfth birthday, I had secretly read it twice from cover to cover—several chapters, eight and ten times. It was utterly platonic. Love was a poem, and marital intimacy too sacred for print. Deftly, it alluded to the whispered trail from maidenhood to motherhood. Noble was the young man who had none but pure thoughts for the damsel of his heart. Marriage was a garden and offspring the fragrant blooms of a morning in spring.

The book profoundly influenced me.

So, as the dawn of adolescence awakened creative urges within my body, a girl became a thing of beauty, delicate like a flower, radiant like a shaft of sunglow.

One summer, Dennis Wilding hired a man to head his sales force, since Dennis had developed a couple of new products for which there was sure to be considerable demand. The new family purchased a large brick house near the edge of town. Adjacent to the house was a small barn once used as a livery stable, which the new family converted into a garage, a storage and play area.

The Halford Vamps became the talk of our town. They were fashionable and worldly. They converged upon the whirl of society with a Parisian flair, and in a fortnight they headed the list of people to be invited for special functions. They not only boycotted every church in town, but Mr. Vamp invariably mowed his lawn on Sabbath mornings, while his attractive wife sunbathed or tended her flower garden.

Mrs. Vamp organized a bridge club. Her husband began talk of putting in a golf course.

"They'll bring a curse to this community," Aunt Lydia declared. "You mark my words."

They had several children, among them a daughter my age, a proud and pretty girl who, by her twelfth birthday, flaunted a figure of Hellenistic grace. She became the talk of boys my age, the envy of the girls.

Her name was Hillary.

Apart from sharing a bag of popcorn on Saturday night, or sitting together at school functions, childhood romances in our town were limited mostly to being able to say, "He is my boy friend," or, conversely, "She is my girl friend."

Hillary changed this.

She championed the cause of adolescent suffrage. High school seniors dated her, a girl not yet in her teens. Other girls patterned her exploits.

Hillary ignored me. We Pews are not a comely lot, apart from our reputation for solemnity. I could hardly expect the girl to show the least interest in me.

Then one Saturday, just before school resumed, Mr. Vamp, having heard of my good hand at odd jobs, summoned me to their dwelling.

"I've been going to get that barn cleaned out, sonny," he said. "But it just doesn't look like I'll get to it. Here's a dollar. My wife and I'll be out of town a few hours, and I probably won't be here before you finish. Everybody tells me you're a good worker and an honest boy."

He took me to the barn and showed me what he wanted accomplished.

"It won't take very long," I said. I felt guilty accepting the dollar without indicating the simplicity of the assignment.

"You do a good job," he said, "and I'll be happy. My wife's been after me for weeks, and I can't put her off any longer."

I plunged happily into the work. Never would I have earned a dollar more easily. In two hours' time, I had the bulk of the job finished. Only a few moments of tidying remained.

"It looks a lot better than it did," someone said.

I turned. There stood Hillary, in this private circumstance more attractive than I had ever known a girl to be.

"H'hello," I said.

70

"Hello," she returned. She looked at me as though we were old friends.

"I thought you went away," I managed.

"Just my mom and dad. They left us kids at home. I decided to come out and see what you were doing."

"I'm working," I said awkwardly. "I'm cleaning up here where your dad said I should."

She laughed, obviously at me. My cheeks reddened.

"Your name is Jerry Pew, isn't it?"

I nodded.

"My mother and father talk about your people a lot. You're awfully religious, aren't you?"

I wanted to be defensive, but the girl had me cowering instead.

"I'm all finished." I said. "I guess I'll go now."

"Why?"

"Because I'm all finished."

"You don't have to go just because you're finished."

I started toward the door. She stepped into my way. I could have easily brushed her aside, but she was like fine glass. I didn't dare to touch her.

"Do you think I'm too old to play with dolls?" she asked.

"I don't know anything about playing with dolls," I said.

She laughed. "You say funny things. I like that. You know something? I'm more interested in you than any of the other boys my age."

I felt my ears grow hot.

"I've had dates with boys in high school. My mom doesn't like that. She thinks I should be more interested in boys my own age."

She came to within the touch of me. I backed away, nearly stumbling over a small box. She continued coming until I had backed against a stanchion and could retreat no further.

She laughed and turned aside a moment, giving opportunity for me to slip away. I saw a few more items I could attend to, such as the box over which I had so nearly tumbled.

"You go to that real religious church, don't you?"

"I guess so," I admitted.

"We don't go to church any place in this town. We might start going sometime, but it sure won't be to your church."

The words cut. I accepted them in silence, quickening the pace of my activity so I could be finished and on my way.

"Do you like your church?" she countered.

71

"Nope," I said.

I stood erect, jolted by my admission. I had never before spoken to the discredit of our church. I had never in any way denied the faith.

She looked at me questioningly. She stepped into the area where I was working and walked a semicircle about me as though I were a contemplated purchase of merchandise.

"I'll bet you're as religious as anybody there," she said. She snickered. "Have you been saved?"

"No," I said.

"Cross your heart?" she asked.

I didn't answer. Adelia said crossing your heart was a sin.

"Are the people at your church like the Holy Rollers?"

I shook my head.

"People in your church can't go to shows or dances or anything, can they?"

"I guess not," I said.

"Can you dance?"

"Nope."

"Shall I teach you?"

"Now?" I asked. "Here?"

"I could teach you real easy."

She offered herself to my embrace, but the pages of *Searchlights on Dark Corners* flashed across my mind. Not until the betrothal should a man take a woman into his arms. I shied away. She looked at me. I thought I saw sympathy in her expression.

"Do you ever go to the movies?" she asked.

"Sometimes," I replied.

"I'll bet." She came closer once more. "My mother and father think it's awfully funny the way your preacher tries to get everybody to come to the front of the church to get saved. Are you sure you've never done it?"

"I've never done it," I said.

"You're lying."

"I'm not."

I continued to work. She watched every move. I felt her eyes upon me like the crack of a whip. I wished she would leave.

She didn't leave.

When I finished, she said, "You're a good worker."

I looked at her now, surprised to hear flattery from her lips. She smiled, tossed her shoulders, winked at me.

"Y'know something?" she asked.

"What?" My heart was pounding.

I began putting the tools away.

"When I first saw you and a girl told me you were from the funny church, I thought you were kind of homely. You aren't, though. You're just awkward. If you had a neat mom and dad like mine, you'd be all different."

"I would?"

"Sure. Wouldn't you like to be different?"

"Maybe."

She circled me again. She was scrutinizing me, but also flaunting her charms. Passion and fear welled up in my chest. I wanted to grasp her. I wanted to run.

"Are you grown up?" she asked. A wildness came to her eyes, replacing the proud candor of earlier moments.

"I'm twelve," I said.

Again she laughed, abruptly sobering.

"Well," she said haughtily, "I play with dolls. I don't care who knows it. I play house, too. That's why my father had you clean the barn. I'm going to make a playhouse right there where you finished cleaning. I'll only be in the eighth grade this fall. Maybe then I'll quit playing with dolls. Maybe I'll make a playhouse and play in it once and then never play in it again."

"That's up to you," I said.

"Here's an idea. Why don't you help me make it?"

"I ought to go."

"Please."

Her charm overpowered me. I set to work at her command.

"This will be the kitchen," she said, "and this will be the dining room and living room, and here can be the door where we come in."

I moved boxes and barrels, which she had been keeping in anticipation of this day, improvising furniture, making room divisions. In half an hour, we had finished. She surveyed the accomplishment happily.

"You're nice," she said. She touched my arm. It was like an electric charge surging through my body. "I planned to take a week doing this."

"It was easy," I said.

Her eyes sparkled, as she took my arm firmly. "We could play a little while," she said. "We could pretend this is our house. I'm the wife, and you're the husband."

"Don't you have a boy friend?" I asked.

She laughed and said, "Some of those high school guys I go riding with sure would be surprised, if they knew I played with dolls." She grew suddenly serious, "I'd rather have a boy friend who wasn't too big to play fun things."

In all my life, I had never been so enraptured.

We played for a long while. I pretended to go to work, while she in turn pretended to shop and mind the house, and then I would come back. When she put her arms around me, I was evasive but increasingly less each time the event occurred.

She brought food from the house. A smaller brother and sister came out to the barn to pretend they were our children, but they quickly wearied of fantasy and went outside to play.

"I like it better this way," she said, "only you and me."

"I suppose maybe I should go home," I said.

"No!" she protested. She put her arms around me again, clinging. I stood meekly, hands at my side.

"You should put your arms around me like I put mine around you."

I tried but couldn't bring myself to do it.

She laughed. "You sure are bashful," she said. "Haven't you ever made love to a girl?"

"Huh, uh."

"And you're twelve years old?" she exclaimed. "Is it a sin in your church to make love to somebody?"

"I guess not."

"Then make love to me," she purred.

It was enticing, like the offer of candy. I wanted to put my arms around her, to smother her with kisses as I had seen love made in the movies, but there was no strength in my arms to do it.

"Some of the high school guys sure do make love to a girl," she said. "I got scared one night. We were parked by the football field, and I got out of the car and ran home. Did that guy get mad."

She set me squirming once more, as she studied me pensively, taking her tactic from any of several screen sirens.

"I'd lots rather have a boy friend my own age," she said. "Wouldn't you rather have a girl friend your age?"

"I guess I would," I replied.

"Would you like me for a girl friend?"

"Maybe."

"I'll bet your folks wouldn't like that." She was haughty again.

"Well, let me tell you something, Christian boy. My dad's going to be the richest man in this whole county. He's going to be richer than anything. If you married me, you'd be pretty awful lucky."

I was like wax, melting before the flame of her wiles.

"Would you like to be the one that marries me?"

"Y-yeah," I managed.

I took a step toward her, expecting her to open her arms to me. Instead, she put her hands on her hips and said, "Let's play house some more," and as quickly as that she reverted to childhood.

On and on we played, far into the afternoon.

I made a sofa of boards. When it was finished, she sat down and pulled me beside her, moving close against me.

It was exhilarating.

"Put your arm around me," she whispered.

I did, but sat like a Grant Wood figure.

"Now kiss me," she said.

"I'd better not."

"Why?"

"Somebody might see us."

"There's nobody here."

"You can't always be sure," I said.

She jumped to her feet and skipped nymph-like across the play area, laughing. She turned and looked at me. "You're the funniest boy I ever saw. I've kissed boys lots of times, and you won't even do it. Why are you so bashful?"

"It's just the way I am," I said.

"You put your arm around me on the couch. Didn't you like that?"

"Sure."

She slipped down beside me once more and put her arms around me. I put mine around her.

"Wouldn't you like to kiss me, too?"

"I guess I would."

"Then why don't you?"

"Maybe a little later."

She pushed away from me and skipped across the play area.

"You're a Holy Roller!" she sang out cruelly. "You lie and won't admit it. That's a sin, to lie. My dad says church people are no better than anybody else. Sometimes they're worse."

We heard the sound of her parent's automobile approaching the barn. "They're back!" Fear rose in her eyes. "You'd better go."

75

To this I heartily agreed, and made my way toward the door at the rear of the barn. She followed. The doorway was in a completely obscured area. As we reached it, she grasped my arm and turned me toward her.

"Put your arms around me again," she said.

I did.

"Kiss me."

She turned her face up toward mine, closed her eyes. I hesitated a moment, thinking she would become impatient and draw away. She didn't. She simply waited.

I kissed her.

It was a new taste to my lips. It swept through me like a fire in the wind. I leaned forward to kiss her again, but she pushed herself free. The doelike softness of her eyes turned hard and fierce. A sneer came to her lips.

"That's the end of that!" she said. "Now, you go and don't you ever dare tell anybody about this. If you do, I'll call you a Holy Roller in front of everybody!"

Stunned, I stumbled out the door and headed toward my home.

That evening, as he always did following mealtime, my father read a chapter from the Bible. Usually my mind drifted. But now I heard every word. My father's voice was like the voice of a prophet, the words he read sounding judgment upon my soul.

I tossed in bed for hours that night. Surely I had broken God's law. How could I expect anything but condemnation to fall upon me?

Yet, might there not be one breath of hope? Sunday night, when the sermon concluded and the minister once again gave the call for salvation, if I delayed no longer. . . .

I do not recall the subject of the pastor's sermon, except that it was delivered in a most impetuous manner, a clarion cry across the stormy waters of life, a summons to be done with iniquity, to make the crooked places straight, to be at peace with God Almighty.

"I'm going to ask that every head be bowed and every eye closed," the pastor concluded. "If you're here tonight, and you want to be saved, put up your hand. I'll see your hand and God will see your heart."

Up went my hand. I did not wait for him to say more.

No more hands were raised.

Alone, at the first strains of "Just as I Am," I walked to the

76

front. A wave of approval came from the crowd, like a quiet but audible breeze. It encouraged me.

Infirm Mrs. Wylie touched me and said, "God bless you, Jeremiah."

I knelt at the altar.

"Are there not others who will join this brave lad tonight?" the minister asked.

Though I was unaware of it at the time, Adelia had gone to the two other boys who, from among the Buzzing Bible Bees alumni, remained spiritual holdouts.

Apparently because of the example I had set, she experienced little difficulty persuading them to join me at the altar. I must assume their sincerity, for it took courage to walk to the front of the church, the object of everyone's attention.

As they knelt beside me, we exchanged glances. Both seemed every bit as serious about the matter as I was, and I had never before been more serious about anything.

Unfortunately, however, Adelia insisted upon sole responsibility for leading us to the moment of decision, all three of us having been members of her Sunday school class.

I do not wish here to make light of Adelia's sincerity—I make every claim to the validity of my own. I believed this to be the great moment of my spiritual destiny, and I sincerely sorrowed for my sins and wanted the righteousness of God to envelope my life.

But something went wrong.

Adelia, enthralled, chattered at us with a cascade of words, at times becoming so incoherent I could not understand what she was telling us to do. We listened, all three of us, attentive, trying to get the sum of what she said.

On and on Adelia rambled, until the boy next to me began to smirk. Partly from tension, I giggled. So did the boy next to me.

Adelia grasped each of us by the collar.

That did it. We began to laugh so uncontrollably it became pointless to pursue the initial intent of our coming.

My father whipped me without mercy that night. I had desecrated the altar of God. I had brought shame to the church. I had dishonored our family.

"God may never speak to your heart again!" he shouted.

I believed the words to be true.

Chapter Ten

Alongside the water tower, directly adjacent to the town park, lay the circus grounds, fully two acres of undeveloped land deeded to the community. Small circuses, itinerent vaudeville and stage troops, carnivals, and, in the earlier years of my childhood, the last of the Chautauqua circuits pitched their tents on the plot.

To the Pew family, consequently, anything that took place under a canvas was sin.

Early one morning, a Friday in mid August, townsmen observed a small group of negroes erecting a tent. Children came running from half-eaten breakfasts. Men paused on their way to work. Women drew back their curtains and observed from a distance. A man of colored skin was a rarity in our town, apart from the erection of a tent on the circus grounds.

"Good morning," said Uncle Rufus, he being the only onlooker to offer a greeting.

"Lovely morning," said the negro who appeared to be in charge of the function.

"Sure is," said Uncle Rufus.

The leader went on with his duties.

"Seems nice enough," Uncle Rufus quietly commented to a man nearby.

"Whatever he's up to," said the man.

"I don't 'spect it's any mischief."

"I wouldn't say that. I've heard you never can trust a nigger."

"Colored people are just as good as anybody else," Uncle Rufus said rather sternly.

In a small town like ours, of course, people did tend to hold any stranger suspect. For myself, I was impressed from the outset by the glow and dignity of the newcomer. Tall and portly, with the bearing of a senator or a good auctioneer—the two highest secular distinctions in our area—he greatly impaired my concept of the negro as a simple creature who sang songs and made funny faces while eating large slices of watermelon.

"Is it a minstrel show?" a lad of high school age called out.

"We feature good music," said the negro.

So that was it! A minstrel show!

But no advance posters had been put up around town. And had they secured permission for the use of the grounds?

Someone hurried off toward the marshal's house.

"Let's three or four of us lend a hand with the tent," Uncle Rufus suggested, as the leader of the group and two other men finished spreading out a sizeable canvas.

"I'd say keep hands off, Rufus," said one man.

"What on earth for?" Uncle Rufus asked. "Come on!" he called. "Who'll lend a hand?"

A half-dozen men responded.

So, with my uncle as foreman, a crew of men rolled up their sleeves and went to work.

"God bless you, gentlemen!" said the leader.

I heard one of our townsmen swear. "Ain't it always that way?" he muttered. "Show me a nigger that's a card shark or runs a red light house, an' he'll still be religious!"

"You oughtn't to say such a thing," Uncle Rufus reprimanded. "And especially not so loud."

"It don't matter how you talk to a nigger."

"It sure as goodness does!"

I was proud of Uncle Rufus!

Presently the marshal arrived.

So did Aunt Lydia.

"Rufus!" Aunt Lydia henpecked. "Do you want me to go down and open the store?"

Aunt Lydia then became aware of my presence.

"Jeremiah!" she sang out. "Come to me this immediate instant!"

I obeyed.

"My sakes," she muttered, grasping my arm savagely, "you won-

79

der if anybody cares anymore what it means to be a Christian."
She held me firmly and called out to her second intended prey.
"Rufus, did you hear me?"

Uncle Rufus heard. He glanced at his wife, as he affirmed his
grip on one of the tent ropes.

"He'll get his pockets picked," she grumbled, "an' then maybe
he'll wish he'd listened."

Aunt Lydia drew considerable attention, a circumstance she
never seemed to find disturbing, and I began to squirm in an effort
to escape her grasp. I would have a good deal to live down among
my associates.

But then the marshal upstaged my aunt. He was a big, profane
man with a glib tongue and an ulcerated ego.

"Say," he bellowed, "what's going on here?"

At that moment, two of the colored men's sons, one of them a
boy my age, came carrying a large painted sign, somewhat worn
from use, which read:

REVIVAL MEETINGS
Every Night
Evangelist John Wesley Sommerford
Faith in a Dying Savior and a Risen Lord!

"Well, I do declare!" exclaimed Aunt Lydia, releasing her tenacious grip upon my arm. She stared at the sign in transfixed amazement.

"Good day, sir," said the leader, extending his hand to the marshal. "My name is Sommerford. May I ask yours?"

"It don't matter," the lawman said. "You see my badge. I'm the
marshal. Who gave you permission to set up your show in our
town?"

"It's not a show, officer," said the evangelist.

Uncle Rufus saw the sign. He nudged the marshal. The marshal
glanced at Uncle Rufus. Uncle Rufus pointed. The marshal turned
and looked at the sign. His mouth opened slowly in obvious surprise.

"I assumed our preaching mission would be welcomed here, as
it has been welcomed elsewhere. Therefore, I did not come to you
with a prior request."

"You're a preacher?" the marshal said.

"An evangelist," Mr. Sommerford smiled warmly. "Is there any
problem?"

"Well . . ."

Uncle Rufus spoke up. "The circus grounds is for any worthy group to use. Isn't that right, Marshal?"

"What if we had a circus coming in this afternoon?" asked the marshal. He fingered his badge. "Suppose we had some organization scheduled to use these grounds?"

"But there were no placards anywhere announcing an event," said the evangelist. "So we surmised it would be quite in order for us to erect our gospel tent."

"Say," said the law officer, pushing back his cap and scratching just above his forehead, "you talk fancier than a white man."

"I've come to proclaim the message of One who has power to save men's souls and heal their bodies."

"How's that?" the marshal asked awkwardly.

"May I ask of your relationship to our lovely Lord?"

"Don't evade the issue!"

"There is no greater issue."

I looked up at Uncle Rufus. His eyes gleamed.

"We've got churches here already, y'know," said the marshal.

"We offer the hand of fellowship to all churches," said the evangelist, "if they truly love our Lord and sincerely proclaim His message."

"Did the preachers know you was comin'?"

Uncle Rufus now interposed himself. "Welcome to our little town," he said. He shook hands with the man. "I got so busy helping with the tent, I forgot to introduce myself."

"I saw it was you who took the initiative," said Mr. Sommerford. "I'm greatly obliged to you."

"It's a sad part of the world," said Uncle Rufus, "where people won't lend a helping hand."

"I trust you are one of my Lord's own," said the evangelist.

"That I surely am," said Uncle Rufus warmly.

"Now back to this matter of the permit," said the marshal, attempting to interrupt.

"We'd better get back to putting this tent up," said Uncle Rufus.

"As I was sayin' . . ." the marshal began.

"Uh, Marshal," Uncle Rufus interrupted, "would you have a minute to bring some of those fence stakes over there by Mr. Sommerford's truck?"

The marshal looked at Uncle Rufus a moment, like a lad who has just been had the best of in marbles, then returned to his car and drove away.

81

The Reverend John Wesley Sommerford became town talk by high noon.

I lingered on the circus grounds, lending a hand as the platform and benches were erected in the canvas chapel. The evangelist's son likewise assisted, and we slowly struck up a friendship.

"My name is Luther," the boy said.

"Mine is Jerry," I reciprocated.

"Are you a Christian?" Luther asked.

"Are you?" I quickly retaliated.

"I surely am."

"It was my uncle who suggested for men to pitch in and help put up the tent."

"I thought maybe he was your father."

"Nope."

"Is your father a Christian?"

I nodded.

"Your mother?"

"Yep."

"Ask them to help spread word for people to come tonight."

People came, filling two-thirds of the tent.

"This is a glorious beginning," said the evangelist. "God bless you all. I pray that you may have come, and will continue coming night after night, not to hear the words of a man but to hear and to heed the voice of God."

"Amen!" Grandfather called out.

"Thank you, my dear brother," the evangelist said.

Grandfather sat two rows from the front, his hearing so keen he caught every word. Uncle Rufus and Aunt Lydia occupied seats on either side of him. I was directly in back of them.

"Say," I heard grandfather whisper to Aunt Lydia, as the sermon began, "he's quite a preacher."

Aunt Lydia nodded, beaming.

"Good as anything you'll hear at conference," he added a few moments later.

"He's real good," Aunt Lydia agreed.

I concurred.

In fact, I gazed with a considerable degree of envy at my new friend, Luther. The social implications of pigmentation had not yet prejudiced my attitudes. I could have as proudly been the son of John Wesley Sommerford as to be sprung from the loins of my own father.

82

I had never heard such eloquence. I had never seen anyone who seemed so captivated by the Son of God. I am told he preached for over an hour. It seemed less than twenty minutes.

"Ah, my dear friends," emoted the evangelist, as he concluded, "when God flung the stars into the farthest blue of space, He had but to speak. When He formed the mountains, He used His fingers, gently, like an artist working with clay. But when He wrought salvation, He rolled up His sleeves, and He sweat drops of blood."

"Amen!" Grandfather called out. "Glory!"

It was his profoundest outcry and a ripple of amusement coursed through the congregation.

My ears reddened.

"Now our Lord wants to do a great work in this community," the evangelist continued. "He wants to wash hearts stained with sin and make them white. He wants to bring new happiness into your home. He wants to lift you from discouragement. He wants to touch your body and make it whole. He wants to walk the streets of this lovely community in power and great glory, and He will, my friend, He most surely will, if you will dare to believe Him."

"Say," gummeted grandfather, as he greeted the evangelist at the close of the service, "like I said to Lydia, my daughter here, that's near as good as some of the best preachin' I've heard at conference."

"Thank you, sir," said Mr. Sommerford. "But please give glory to God. I am only His servant."

He and grandfather shook hands. You would have thought grandfather was shaking the hand of President Coolidge or the Republican congressman from our district. (Our Governor was a Democrat.) He squared his shoulders, bounced on his heels, and looked anxiously about to ascertain who of prominence in the community might be observing.

"I sure never thought I'd get to hear a nigger preach before I died," grandfather exclaimed gleefully.

Mr. Sommerford stepped quickly back, as though someone had struck him. The word, "nigger," had seemed normal to my vocabulary, but never again after that moment.

"I say," grandfather repeated, "I sure never thought I'd get to hear . . ."

"Colored man! Colored man!" Mr. Sommerford corrected.

His eyes showed hurt and indignation. His lips trembled. The pleasantness of countenance, with which he had greeted grandfather, now grew ill-disposed.

"Let us address all of God's children with dignity," the evangelist said, when he regained sufficient composure to speak. *"God hath made of one blood all nations of men,* the Word tells us."

"How's that?" Grandfather cupped a hand to his ear. "Say, you look a mite peek'd. I s'pose preachin' sermons, like anything else, is harder on a nigger than a white man."

Aunt Lydia nudged her sire. "Use the word darky, papa!"

"How's that, Lydia?"

Mr. Sommerford was a man of divine gifts, there was no questioning it, but, being human, he also possessed mortal attributes. Plainly, he lost any sense of rapport with grandfather who, though feigning innocence, put up a resolute guard against the evangelist.

"You'd best not get uppity," grandfather warned. "I heard our district superintendent say a proud preacher is . . ."

"I apologize, if I seemed vain," Mr. Sommerford interjected. He offered his hand.

But grandfather was spoiling for trouble. He did not offer his hand.

"Come, papa," Aunt Lydia urged. "Let's go."

Grandfather stood firm.

"What is the problem, my poor brother?" the evangelist asked. "Are you not one of the Lord's own?"

"Now listen here, mister!" Aunt Lydia broke in. "I'll thank you to apologize for that statement!"

"Apologize?" Mr. Sommerford seemed genuinely surprised.

"It may interest you to know my father has been a stalwart in our church for over sixty years! He has never backslidden, not even once!"

"How's that, Lydia?" Grandfather asked.

"You can hear!" Aunt Lydia momentarily addressed her indignation to her father. "Now stop that foolish deafness and help me. This man's trying to put our family in a bad light."

"He is?" Grandfather huffed.

At this juncture, Mr. Sommerford excused himself to speak with others. Aunt Lydia took grandfather's arm and moved him out into the night.

The damage had been done, the lines of battle drawn.

In humiliation the following morning, I heard grandfather in Uncle Rufus' store loudly expostulating about "that coon preacher," as a sizeable group of people listened, several of them being among the town's benighted.

"I think you're wrong, dad," Uncle Rufus opposed. "I believe Mr. Sommerford is a . . ."

"Rufus!" Grandfather broke in. "Sheep is sheep, and goats is goats!"

He brought his cane down upon the counter so resoundingly it broke into two pieces, thus adding fuel to the patriarch's fury, since the cane was of illustrious lineage.

"Yep," said grandfather to Mr. Sommerford that following evening, "I've got your kind figured."

"What do you mean, sir?" the evangelist asked.

Word of grandfather's antipathy having spread through the community, a number of people lingered about the tent.

"You aim to keep buildin' up people's excitement night after night," grandfather said, "so by Sunday afternoon you draw a bigger crowd than any circus that ever desecrated this plot of ground. I figger you'll lift an offering of upwards to a hundred dollars."

"That's more than a month's pay for an honest working man in this town!" Aunt Lydia put in.

"Our needs may be supplied," Mr. Sommerford said quietly, "so we will not need to ask for any offerings. We haven't thus far, you know."

"Hmph!"

Grandfather turned and, brandishing his newly purchased cane to clear the way, hobbled out of the tent and into the night.

"Papa's right," Aunt Lydia said. "There's something strange about that preacher. For one thing, I don't believe it's right for a darky to be giving the Word of God to white people. Why do you suppose the Lord has us send missionaries out to Africa?"

"I do like his spirit," said Aunt Britta.

"Anybody can put on," Aunt Lydia argued.

"Do you reckon he'll get anybody healed?" Uncle Eliad asked.

"He's no healer," Aunt Lydia scoffed.

"It might be he could heal people," Aunt Britta countered.

"Then why don't he do it?" Aunt Lydia asked. "No, he'd rather just talk about it, so's to build up attendance."

"I'd like to see him heal Mrs. Wylie," Uncle Caleb said.

"That dear soul," observed his wife. "How she suffers and never once complains."

"Even if healing was for this dispensation, which I doubt," said Aunt Lydia, "Mrs. Wylie's too far gone. But back to this point of money. I'd sure like to know . . ."

"Aunt Lydia," I broke in. I had never before interrupted such proceedings but at this moment could not restrain myself.

"What is it?" she snapped.

My tongue froze momentarily.

"I think Jerry's taken by the evangelist," Uncle Rufus said.

"I was playing with Luther Sommerford today. That's Mr. Sommerford's boy. He told me . . ."

"Jeremiah!" Aunt Lydia's tongue terminated my words like the slice of a knife. "I give you firm orders to stay away from that boy. What's coming to our family anyway?" She grasped me by the shoulder. "You're a wayward soul, boy! A wayward soul. You like the colored preacher, do you? You would have blessed the Pharisees and cursed the disciples! You poor dear."

I almost spit.

Let her doubt, I reasoned. I would believe the more, with neither qualm nor question, and my confidence would become the encouragement God needed to show His greatness.

My confidence waned, as the nights passed, not my confidence in God or the evangelist but in the likelihood of a miraculous visitation upon our town in the face of our family's defiance. I tell you with pain that Uncle Rufus and myself were the only voices uttered on the evangelist's behalf. Even Uncle Eliad and Aunt Britta seemed little more than amused by Mr. Sommerford's presence in the community.

"Don't it say in the Bible somewhere that the devil can heal people?" Aunt Britta asked.

Her words gave me renewed concern.

"Have you seen real miracles?" I asked Luther Sommerford. We spent a part of every day together.

"Many times," he said.

"Like what kind?"

"Healings mostly."

"People bad sick?"

"And crippled, too. Sometimes we've needed food or money, and my father has prayed and God sent just what we needed. We were in the south one summer. Only colored people came. They were all poor. The offerings were so small my father stopped taking them. But we needed two hundred dollars to finish paying for the tent, or have the company we bought it from take it back. When the meetings were over . . . the last Sunday night . . . we all stayed in the tent to pray. We had to have the money the next morning."

"What happened?"

"About midnight a white man came into the tent. He said God woke him right up in his sleep and told him to give my father two hundred dollars. He hadn't even been to any of our meetings."

"He gave your father the money?"

"Four fifty dollar bills."

"Wow!"

"Didn't I tell you a church in Chicago, a colored church, took an offering and sent to us? So we maybe won't need to take any offerings here."

"I never heard of meetings without collections," I said.

"My father never asks for offerings, if we have enough money for expenses. Even then he doesn't do it, if he's prayed and feels God doesn't want him to."

John Wesley Sommerford was most certainly the greatest man I had ever seen. On Friday night, prior to the benediction, Mr. Sommerford said quietly, "We have proclaimed the message. We have shown you the food God has for your hungry hearts. Now the time has come either to reward your faith or to rebuke your unbelief. Sunday afternoon we will see what God can do among us."

A chill of anticipation fingered my spine.

"Bring those who are sick among us," the evangelist continued. "Whether the sickness be great or small, God is able to heal."

Grandfather and Aunt Lydia sat adamant and silent.

"That son of the Hamites is up to something," grandfather said to standers-by at the conclusion of the meeting.

"He'll hurt God's cause in this community," chimed in Aunt Lydia. "You mark my words."

The following night the evangelist spoke on the topic, "God is a God of Miracles."

Now I had heard about miracles since I was knee high to a hymn book. During my two years in the Buzzing Bible Bees, Adelia frequently alluded to such events as the marriage feast at Cana, the pool of Bethesda, the raising of Jairus' daughter. I believed those miracles transpired exactly as recorded in Scripture.

But they were history.

Now a man had come to our town proclaiming that God was as much a God of miracles today as He had been when the Israelites crossed the Red Sea. He could give sight to the blind. He could open the ears of the deaf. He could make crooked limbs straight. He could cure all manner of diseases.

I believed it and could not reconcile the piety of the Pews with their questioning of God's power.

"Now, I'm not limiting what God can do," Aunt Lydia said during a family discussion prior to the meeting the following Sunday afternoon. "But this is a benighted age. There's ten times more wicked being born into the world than there are people added to the church. God's power is put forth these days to convert the sinner, not to make people feel better. What do you say, papa?"

"How's that?"

"What do you think of the colored man?" Uncle Rufus put in.

"I think he bears watching," said grandfather.

Uncle Eliad spoke up. "There is one point," he said. "From reports I've heard, not about this man but others, these evangelists that come around and make a big to-do about healing are sometimes pretty clever when it comes to money. Yet this Sommerford feller don't seem after the money side at all!"

"He bears watching," grandfather repeated.

"You've heard some of the reports, haven't you, Eliad?"

"Like what, Lydia?"

Even though in her own house, Aunt Lydia looked about as though for possible eavesdroppers. "Rufus said there was a couple people in the store who thought they had had their pockets picked by . . ."

"Lydia!" Uncle Rufus scolded.

"I didn't say they said for certain," his wife whimpered.

It was unprecedented for Uncle Rufus to assume this degree of domestic dominance.

"There's one thing that makes me suspicious," Aunt Lydia said. "If this Sommerford is so right, why don't preachers in town back him? That young Pentecostal from Arathon came the first few nights, but even he quit."

"Some of the preachers have been there," Aunt Britta said. "I've seen them."

"I heard someone say," said Uncle Caleb, "that the Methodist and Presbyterian preachers drove up one night after the preachin' started an' looked an' listened from the car for half an hour."

"It just could be." Uncle Rufus said facetiously, "Evangelist Sommerford speaks so good it makes a white preacher jealous."

"Foolish talk." Aunt Lydia scoffed.

"Well," said Aunt Britta, "this afternoon's the acid test. We'll see if anybody get's healed. I'm getting awfully curious."

Just prior to the meeting, I spoke again with Luther.

"You've really seen miracles performed in other places?" I asked.

"Lots of times," Luther assured me.

"But what kind?"

"Just like in the Bible."

"Anybody raised from the dead?"

"Not that."

"Blind people?"

"Well, nobody that was all blind. There have been people who could hardly see. Lame people who walked good again. People with cancer cured so their own doctors wouldn't have believed it, if they hadn't seen it!"

"And God has sent you money?" I asked hesitantly.

"Just yesterday morning again."

"How?"

"My father said I mustn't talk about it. He felt he shouldn't ask for any offerings in this place because . . . I'd better not say."

"You pray and got the money you asked for?" I primed.

Luther nodded.

"They're beginning to sing in the tent," he said.

"Boy," I mused, "if I could just see one miracle."

"It isn't right just to want to see miracles," Luther scolded. "A miracle isn't something God does like . . . like somebody does a magic trick or something. Miracles are to show God's power, to give people faith, to help them really believe."

This was exactly why I wanted to see a miracle.

I knew God had made the rising and the setting sun. He made the trees. He fashioned the gold of autumn and the cold of winter and the green of spring. I knew He was great and powerful, but He was also far away. If I could see one miracle, if it could happen in Mr. Sommerford's tent that afternoon, then I would know God was near, near enough to touch me, to hear the searching cries of my heart, to give me faith.

"Are there always miracles at places where you go?" I asked.

Luther shook his head.

"Why not?"

"Sometimes there aren't enough people who will believe God can do it."

"Not enough?"

"God doesn't just go around doing miracles. People must ask Him for them. People must believe He can do it. They must be sure it will happen. If too many people don't believe, then many times God can't do it, or anyway He won't."

"Does it take many people to believe He can?" I asked anxiously.

"Sometimes there only needs to be one person."

"And how many people, who don't believe, can stop it from happening?"

"It depends."

"How many would you say, just to guess?"

The low growl of thunder sounded from the western edge of town. Luther turned. His eyes grew troubled.

"It could rain," I said.

My friend nodded.

"What if your father prayed and asked God not to let it rain?"

"He already did."

"He prayed?"

"Yes."

"Then . . .?"

"Let's go into the tent. Otherwise my father will scold me."

Night after night, I had listened to John Wesley Sommerford proclaim the God who could do miracles. Night after night, my confidence had grown. If all others disbelieved, I would remain true.

I would believe!

I would be the one whose faith would unleash the power of God!

Though he called himself an evangelist, Mr. Sommerford did not conduct evangelism in the manner to which I had grown accustomed at our church. His mission seemed to be that of testing the faith of our community. With each night's sermon, he had told of new and wonderful experiences in which he witnessed the power of God. He assured his listeners this same power could be shown to our community, if we sufficiently believed.

Now the hour of manifestation had come.

Although there was the threat of rain, a throng of people crowded the tent to capacity, with a hundred or more seated on the grass outside. I would have had no place to sit, except for joining Luther beside his mother, unmindful of Aunt Lydia's indignation.

The evangelist spoke more eloquently than at any of the previous meetings, declaring the power of God, heralding the role of faith in the detonation of that power.

Grandfather, who had taken a seat at the very front, like a fight fan at ringside, looked on with a haughty air.

"Get to what you said you was goin' to do!" he called out.

The evangelist looked at him squarely, without so much as a moment's pause in his flow of oratory. So eloquent became that oratory even grandfather fell under it's spell. And, as always, good preaching made him sleepy.

He dozed.

Aunt Lydia awakened him.

He dozed again.

"Let us never forget," declared Mr. Sommerford, "the exceeding greatness of God's power is not in the farthest flung star of outer space, not in the resplendent forces of nature, not in breath of life itself, but in the redeeming mercy of Calvary and the transforming power of the empty tomb!"

"Amen!" gummeted grandfather, forgetting himself for a moment.

Aunt Lydia nudged him sharply. A twitter passed through the audience.

"But God does show His power in the physical realm," Mr. Sommerford continued. "He does this to strengthen our faith in His spiritual power."

"Stay awake, papa," Aunt Lydia urged. "I think he's coming to it."

"God is able to come into this tent right now," the evangelist proclaimed, "and show His miracle working power."

Grandfather, wide awake, called out, "Do it, then!"

The speaker paused. He looked down at grandfather. I thought I saw anger flash in his eyes. Quietly, he said, "God cannot show His power to those who question it, my dear brother."

"How's that?" Grandfather cupped his hand to his ear.

The evangelist stepped to the side of the pulpit, like a good comrade who has paused to speak with a friend. Quietly, convincingly, he urged those in attendance to join him in the confidence of God's miracle working power.

I listened so intently, leaning forward, a mere touch could have tumbled me from my seat.

Mr. Sommerford asked any who were ill and felt the need of prayer for healing to come to the front of the tent. He asked them to come quietly, to come with the conviction that God, not man, could heal them.

Several came. Tension gripped the audience.

I glanced back to the crowd. Near the rear of the tent sat Mrs. Wylie in her wheel chair. She was weeping.

God, I breathed silently, *if Mrs. Wylie gets up from her chair and walks, I'll become a Christian!*

One by one the evangelist laid hands upon those who responded, asking God to touch their bodies.

I bowed my head, but my eyes would not remain closed. I peered up toward the platform, anticipating a visible manifestation.

I saw nothing.

Two or three of those for whom the evangelist prayed claimed some improvement in their physical condition. Members of the evangelist's party stood about the seekers in concert prayer. There was weeping in the audience. But no overt manifestation.

Grandfather stood and called out, "Bring some of the real sick ones." He turned to the audience. "Caleb, wheel up Mrs. Wylie."

I looked at Mrs. Wylie. She held her hands toward the pulpit, like a child pleading for bread.

"Come, my dear sister," Mr. Sommerford invited. The confidence in his voice fueled my faith.

"Yeah, bring 'er." Grandfather sparkled with enthusiasm. "Bring 'er, Caleb. Eliad, you help him."

"Sit down, papa," Aunt Lydia admonished.

Obediently, Uncle Caleb and Uncle Eliad went to Mrs. Wylie's chair.

"Shall I come?" Mrs. Wylie called out to the front.

"What is the Lord saying to your heart, my dear sister?" replied Mr. Sommerford. "Have you the faith He will heal you?"

"I only want the Lord's will," said Mrs. Wylie.

"Bring 'er, boys." Grandfather urged. "Bring 'er."

"Quiet, my friend," Mr. Sommerford rebuked grandfather. "Let us be loud in God's assembly only from the glee of the Holy Spirit in our hearts."

"No excuses there!" Grandfather defied, sitting down. "Either you can heal her or you can't."

"I can heal no one," said the evangelist. "Only God has that power."

"He's makin' excuses." Grandfather accused.

Uncle Rufus laid a hand on grandfather's shoulder. Grandfather turned to him defensively. Uncle Rufus smiled and stroked the old man gently.

Uncle Caleb and Uncle Eliad began to wheel Mrs. Wylie toward the front. The audience was electrified. My heart pounded like a sledge.

92

"There you go!" Grandfather called out, hopping to his feet and waving his cane toward the pulpit. "See what you can do with that one!"

"In the name of my Savior, I rebuke you!" the evangelist cried. "Sit down!"

"Go on." Grandfather was like a gleeful little boy. "You straighten her up an' nobody'll question all this blow you've been givin'."

"Sit down!" Mr. Sommerford repeated.

Uncle Rufus tugged at grandfather's coat, but he would not sit.

The crowd grew restless, mob-like, mumbling among themselves. Some agreed with grandfather. Some wanted him thrown out of the tent.

The evangelist held up his hands for quiet.

The crowd complied.

Uncle Caleb, Uncle Eliad, and Mrs. Wylie reached the front. Mrs. Wylie's head was bowed.

"Let's see y' heal her." Grandfather again challenged. The evangelist ignored him.

Instead, with penetrating sadness in his voice, he apologized to the audience for the turn of events.

"Believe me, my dear friends," he said, "God is a God of miracles. I have seen Him do mighty things. But it would be folly to continue this meeting. This old man has scoffed Almighty God. May the Lord have mercy upon him and bring him to repentance in these last days of his life for he has denied this community its right to see the power of God made manifest."

So electrifying had been the circumstances of the meeting, few people realized storm clouds had darkened the skies.

"Now listen here!" Grandfather cried out. "You lay hands on that woman!"

An immense, precisely timed clap of thunder shook the very earth.

"The thunder is the voice of God!" the evangelist called out to grandfather. "It is the evidence of His displeasure upon your un- belief."

A furious burst of wind swept into the tent, billowing the top like a sail. Rain began to fall in torrents. People ran for their cars.

Without formality, the meeting ended.

It rained throughout the remainder of the afternoon, rained on into the night, but at dawn the next morning, when early risers looked out upon the circus grounds, tent, vehicles, and people were gone.

93

Chapter Eleven

To grandfather and Aunt Lydia, John Wesley Sommerford had been an imposter whose ersatz spirituality withered in the face of their iridescent righteousness. To the community, he was another of the unique happenings—like a circus, like vaudeville, Chatauqua—which briefly intercept the monotony of life and then move on.

But to me he had been a prophet. His sure step and firm hand had led me to within a glimpse of that precipice from which vantage point one looks across the chasm of unbelief into the boundless yes of God's existence.

To within a step he took me.

Had Mrs. Wylie forsaken her wheelchair, could she have leaped to her feet as the evangelist declared one might, leaped and run and cried out praise to the God of heaven, then Jerry Pew would have believed as Elijah believed, as David and John the Baptist, as those other heroes of the ancient parchments whose exploits I had never been able to acclimate to Christianity as the Pews lived it.

I blamed my grandfather and Aunt Lydia, priest and priestess of Baalzebub. Their unbelief held back the flow of celestial power. They flaunted the Holy Spirit, denied restoration to Mrs. Wylie, withheld faith from my heart.

I was gripped by a sense of enormous loss, like the absence of a nearest friend, like the snuffing out of one last candle in a strange and forboding darkness.

My friends summoned me to play, and I joined them. I was not an adept athlete but, in a game of softball, vented my frustration by timbering the ball farther than the most stalwart participant. Shortly thereafter, my normal skills, impaired by preoccupation, caused me to perform so ineptly that my teammates asked me to surrender my position to another boy who arrived during the third inning.

I walked a lot. To this day, when I wish to do some thinking I often walk. I came one afternoon to the western edge of town, vaulted a fence and strode across some summer plowing, sweet-smelling in the sun.

I envisioned myself as John Wesley Sommerford proclaiming the power of God to a willing audience. I imagined great miracles, and I was not proud, for it was God who gave the power. I was only proud that I was John Wesley Sommerford, not Jerry Pew. My skin was dark and it was beautiful, my hands were like fine ebony, and my speech was soft and glowing.

"God is doing great things in this town, because you people believe!" I cried out, my voice arousing a pheasant into frightened flight. I laughed, pretending the noisy bird to be someone like Aunt Lydia, who fled from my presence because my skin was black, because my words unclothed her hypocrisy.

"Let the hypocrites go!" I proclaimed. "Then they will not stand in the way. Now we can see miracles."

I picked up a clod of dirt to throw. Something about the earth caught the mood of my thoughts.

Here I was, alone, heart-yearning to witness the arm of God, to see and to believe. Grandfather did not know I was in the fields, alone, seeking. Aunt Lydia did not know. Might it then be that I, all by myself, possessed the right to challenge God to prove Himself with the performance of a miracle? There would be only my faith and His omnipotence involved. There would be no one to disbelieve.

The thought both stimulated and frightened me.

I looked heavenward.

If my motives were wrong, displeasing to God, surely clouds would roll across the heavens. Lightning would spew forth the fire of His anger. Thunder would utter His condemnation.

But the skies were blue, clear and bright and warm.

It was like coming into a supposedly empty room, seeing no one, yet sensing the gaze of someone watching, concentrating upon my every act and motion. Here in the fields it seemed that someone watched from above me, smiling, reaching down as though to touch me, as a tall man extends a downward hand to touch a son with whom he is pleased.

I felt surrounded by gentleness and strength. I heard no audible voice, but there were whispers in my soul—impelling, reassuring, possessive.

I would do it.

I would ask God to show me a miracle.

Musing, I crumpled the earth in my hand. It fell upon a stick. Should I pick up the stick, as Moses lifted the rod of Aaron, and command it to become a serpent? I stooped to take the stick but refrained.

Perhaps I could ask God for the faith of Joshua and command the sun to remain fixed in the sky. The thought excited me. I would run through the streets of town, as people stood in terror beholding the sky, and I would cry out, "Now you must believe! Now you see that God is a maker of miracles!"

I would fly through the streets. Yes, one miracle would spawn another. I would fly over the houses, over Adelia's house, over Aunt Lydia's. Then they would know I was not a hopeless sinner. They would know I had looked into the face of God. They would know He had smiled His blessing upon me.

But then I remembered Luther Sommerford's words of caution. I remembered sermons in the tent. The evangelist had not promised strange miracles. He said God purposes to bless our lives. He dispells sorrow with gladness. He supplants sickness with health.

I walked on for a good distance, beyond the plowing to a quiet meadow, beyond the meadow to a creek, and sat upon the creek bank contemplating the water. Anticipation filled my heart. Some great thing would soon happen. I did not know what it might be. It did not matter. The knowingness was enough.

I began to sing:

> Give of your best to the Master.
> Give of the strength of your Youth.
> Clad in salvation's full armor,
> Join in the battle for truth!

Odd I should sing that song. I did not sing it as I had done with the Buzzing Bible Bees, restrained and insincere. I sang out boldly, as one of the Crusaders might have done, as John Wesley Sommerford would do.

I took to my feet once more and went closer to the water. There was a path trodden by cattle. I walked briskly, began to run, following the path. My feet had never known such lightness. I ran and ran, up the side of the bank, down again to the water, on and on like a bouyant spirit caught effortlessly in the breeze. Could this be the first touch of a miracle, this nimbleness of foot, this freedom of spirit?

At last I tired. I came upon a spring and, as I had done before in childhood frolic along this watercourse, stopped to drink. The water had a newness to it, sweet, strength giving. In quenching my thirst it awakened hunger for food.

A cluster of ground cherries grew nearby. I picked several. They were full ripe. I ate them heartily. But like fine hors d'oeurves, they only whetted my appetite.

Again, subconsciously, I took a handful of earth. It was moist from nearness to the spring. I squeezed it into a firm oblong, bearing the mold of my fingers.

The earth—my winged feet—the feathery lightness of my spirit.

Then the drink at the spring, satisfying and yet whetting hunger, not hunger for food alone but a hunger that was like my lightened feet and heightened spirits.

Was it all part of a heavenly purpose, all a prelude to the miracle God had chosen to display before me?

Would the miracle be a providential provision of food?

Manna perhaps!

I waited expectantly,

> . . . clad in salvation's full armor,
> Join in the battle for truth!

Nothing happened, no manifestation from above nor on the earth before me. There was nothing except an odd-shaped stone, which I had not previously noticed. It had the appearance of a loaf of bread.

Could this be it, my miracle? Did not Jesus have the power to change stones into bread? Did He not perform miracles, so His followers might have food, and so they could see the sureness of God? Did not I strive to be one of His followers?

I walked to the stone. I stood above it, looking down. I lowered myself to one knee. I reached out to touch the stone but withheld my hand.

Could I? Would God?

If only I had someone to help me. But there was never anyone. I only knew people who talked about God, told you how to invoke His wrath, but one could not show Him to you.

The hunger grew in my stomach and in my heart. Slowly, as one venturing into an unknown, I placed my hands upon the stone.

"Please, God," I whispered, "I haven't asked for many things. I believe the evangelist could have shown Your power. Please, God. Make this stone . . . please . . ."

I closed my eyes. The feel of the stone was like the feel of earth, clutched tightly. It seemed to soften beneath my touch.

Bread! I wanted bread!

Bread such as my lips had never before known, bread such as the five thousand were once fed, bread broken upon golden tables, shared among Cherubims, eaten by the angels.

"Please, God," I continued, desperate now in my pleading, "make this stone become a loaf of bread. Please, God!" I cried loudly. I began to weep. "Please, God! Please! Please!"

I clutched the stone. It no longer felt soft and living. It was hard and cold, cruel and dead.

I fell across the stone, sobbing, unable to understand. I tried to pray but no words formed on my lips. It began to come plain to me. God had refused to show Himself.

Why?

A terrifying thought struck me, its thrust lifting me upright.

Satan had tempted Jesus to turn stone into bread. But Jesus didn't do it. Frightened, I searched my thoughts, trying to remember any time in the Savior's life when He performed the miracle I had sought to bring about, fashioning a stone into bread.

There had been no such time!

I could come to but one conclusion. The devil had tricked me into blasphemy.

I rose slowly to my feet. Smitten. It was as though I had prostrated myself before a judge, seeking pardon, and now, having been denied that pardon, stood to receive my sentence.

I hurried homeward. Whereas my feet had been light, now they were leaden, and my lilting spirit a vanishing memory.

"Jeremiah!"

A voice repeatedly called my name, as I neared our house. It was a harsh voice, piercing, demanding. It took a moment before I recognized it as the voice of my mother.

I ran to her.

"Jeremiah," she exclaimed. "Where have you been?"

"Only out in the fields," I said.

"Come quickly into the house." She grasped me by the arm and thrust me through the door. "Wash yourself, hurry, while I lay out a clean shirt and trousers."

She began to weep.

"What's wrong?" I managed to ask.

"It's grandfather," she sobbed. "Aunt Lydia found him, lying on the floor. Now you hurry, Jeremiah. We've got to get over there right away."

It was God's judgment, fallen upon grandfather because of my sinfulness. It would surely fall upon me.

Chapter Twelve

Grandfather Pew lingered for several weeks, being of hearty stock, but at the end of summer, like a stalk of grain spent and withered, he died.

I silently bore the conviction of guilt.

By now, having followed me this far in the accounting of my story, you perhaps think I suffered from perpetual neurosis.

This is not so. There were many carefree moments. I laughed and played as boys do, and shared the pranks of others. There is much I could tell you of this, if the purpose of my story were autobiographical.

But that is not my purpose.

My objective is to show you the imprisoning grip of legality, the sham of spiritual contrivance, the inability of mere mores to withstand the erosion of time.

To be sure, I had a sensitive spirit. I have often wondered what my lot in life might have been if I had been the son of a poet, or if perchance Uncle Rufus had been my father and Aunt Britta my mother, or if I had been conceived and born in a more secularized wedlock.

By the time I entered high school, I had taken upon myself much of the manner of my fellows. In fullest honesty, I should say I hid my real spirit, as so many mortals do, as we Pews were particularly adept at doing, in exchange for the fabrication of an outward appearance which more suitably accomodated my surroundings.

My fellows did not see me as a gay blade. I retained a measure of aloofness to dissolute practices. Though not an egg-head, I enjoyed school and did well in academics, cementing many a friendship by casual tutoring. I dismayed Aunt Lydia and unnerved my parents by joining high school thespians and earning the supporting role in the junior class play, a circumstance so cataclysmic as to discourage any subsequent effort to appear in the senior class presentation, though our drama teacher all but promised me the lead part.

I dated occasionally, mostly girls from our church, taking them to congregational events; it was more serving as an escort than dating, as the event was coming to be known.

Through the years, I nurtured a flame for Hillary Vamp. She was the most personable and beautiful girl in town, at times the epitome of worldliness, as often a proper debutante.

Hillary was in the junior class play. I played the role of a shy student, and in one scene was supposed to put an arm about her waist. She unnerved me so that I couldn't bring myself to do it, and the drama teacher—supposing my problem to be puritanical —revised the scene.

"Don't be such a dummy," Hillary muttered backstage. The words cut me, and yet there may have been a tinge of pathos in her voice. I wasn't sure.

With the passing of grandfather, the Pew clan ceased to be a patriarchy. None of the sons had been groomed to bear the standard. Instead, the mantle fell onto the drooping shoulders of Aunt Lydia who, among all his children, had been the apple of grandfather's spiritual eye.

I do not mean to say the Pew stance disintegrated with the passing of the patriarchs. One would more accurately say there was a resurgence. Aunt Lydia saw to that. She counseled my father, cajoled Uncle Eliad, pampered Uncle Caleb, and stimulated the loyalties of those, like my mother, who yielded themselves pliably to the mold.

As for myself, a new persuasion bid for my spiritual interest. It seemed plausible, uncluttered, and it catered to the smoldering hostility I felt toward my clan.

I speak of Mr. Mack, the young history teacher who came to our high school during my junior year. He was a man among men, so eloquent I often thought he might have been a preacher, so personable he could have sold me the colors of the rainbow, so dedicated he forsook the better life he might have had to be a teacher.

Mr. Mack was a skeptic.

He didn't believe God created the world in six days. He didn't believe the Israelites crossed the Red Sea on dry land. He didn't believe there was once a giant named Goliath. To Mr. Mack, the book of Jonah was as much a work of fiction as Gulliver's adventures in Lilliput and Brobdingnag. He even questioned the validity of the New Testament, though he expressed profound admiration for the Man of Nazareth. as he called Him, and at times he spoke eloquently of the failure of Christo-centric western civilization to conduct itself within the potential of its ethic.

"Do you believe in evolution?" a girl asked in class one day.

"Do you not believe in it?" Mr. Mack countered.

"I'm not sure."

"Excellent," Mr. Mack exclaimed. "To not be sure is to have the mind of a true student."

His words awakened memories of my prior search for a God of miracles.

"What about miracles?" I asked.

"What about them?" he replied.

It was Hillary Vamp who spoke up at this juncture. "Belief in miracles is just a lot of fanaticism, isn't it?"

"Is it?" Mr. Mack asked.

"Well, don't you think so?" Hillary asked. Her question had apparently been in reaction to my statement, but Mr. Mack's response drew her off guard.

"I think about a lot of things," the teacher said. "So should you. Think about everything you can."

"What about miracles then?"

"What about radio? What about combustion engines? What about heavier than air flight? What if man one day builds a rocket that takes him to the moon?"

It was as unsure of herself as I had ever seen Hillary!

Secretly at first, I resisted Mr. Mack's juxtaposition to the Pew tradition. Deep had been my hunger for the God of the Bible, utterly sincere my quest to experience His presence. But Mr. Mack was also sincere. As the months passed, it troubled me to find him more consistently sincere than my observation of congregational stalwarts. He did not flagrantly attack the Bible and the faith of the fathers. It was the questions he asked. It was the force of his logic. It was the genuiness of his humanity.

102

Though Mr. Mack questioned historical events in the Bible, he openly advocated the Book's teaching.

"The Bible is the focal point of history," he said. "The problem is that men have fought over its doctrines and fine points, when they should have united behind its message of love for all the world."

I never forgot those words.

I developed an affinity to Mr. Mack, as much as students fraternize with their teachers, and became one of his stellar students. In fact, I was salutatorian of my graduating class, a circumstance largely attributable to the inspiration of this man upon my life—and, might I add, a circumstance which seemed to arouse as much pride in Aunt Lydia as if I had been the finest trophy of the sanctuary altar.

Many times I wanted to talk with Mr. Mack about my frustrations. I believe he sensed them. He could hardly have lived in a community so small as ours without an awareness of Pewdom. But I did not have the courage. For, though he profoundly undermined the ecclesiastical foundations of my childhood, I could not bring myself to completely embrace his philosophy. I could not verify his denunciation of the Bible, as every jot and tittle the Word of God, by posing questions indicative of my own departure from the faith once delivered.

My becoming class salutatorian involves Hillary. As I became more and more one of my generation, she lessened her antagonism toward me. Once, during our senior year, I very nearly asked her for a date, but at the last moment lost courage.

Though boys migrated to Hillary's side at school functions, vied to sit beside her in the classroom, promoted her for class offices—for Homecoming Queen and Belle of the Prom—she dated only on the rarest of occasions.

Legend surrounded her.

Halford Vamp, her father, was said to have schemed his way into control of Dennis Wilding's industrial firm, and in so doing he brought the establishment to such a financial stature as to make the Vamps the first millionaires in our entire geographical area. This circumstance in itself surrounded Hillary with an aura she in no way endeavored to dispel.

It was further said that Hillary had boy friends in Chicago, that far off metropolis to which the family made frequent sojurns. Young tongues were sure she conducted clandestine affairs with city swains, affairs which made amusing to her the oogling of local youth and the envious glances and whispers of girls at school.

She occasionally dated boys in our area who were much older than she. One in particular was known for his nocturnal conquests. He made veiled claims of alleged exploits. Some of the community youth believed him, others questioned, most disbelieved.

In the matter of school honors, Hillary and I came to somewhat pronounced odds. She was a good student by virtue of innate cleverness. I did well in school because Mr. Mack had set my mind ablaze.

The winning of valedictory or salutatory honors interested me only in a normal sense, my greater concern being to one day have a finely schooled mind like that of Mr. Mack. To Hillary, however, academic esteem was another status to be sought. She fully expected to be named class valedictorian, would have settled for salutatorian, but when honors were announced, it was disclosed that, by a mere fraction of a grade point, I had earned salutatorian honors and Hillary stood only third in the class.

"I should have known you were buttering Mr. Mack for this!" she snapped at me. "Well, I suppose you need some kind of relief from the monotony of what your life must be."

Ironically, Halford Vamp had that year announced the giving of full scholarships to the state university for the two academic winners. Town gossip insisted he did this as company publicity, thus hoping to arrange for Hillary's education at lessened personal expense for himself, at the same time improving his reputation in the community.

"You're going to cost my company a good deal of money," he told me. "I expect you to make the most of it. Maybe you better think about showing your gratitude by coming back here to work for me after you graduate."

Aunt Lydia did her utmost to bring about my matriculation at the college sponsored by our small denomination—her utmost being the offer of a year's tuition. I decided against it, partly out of rebellion, partly because of Mr. Vamp's benefaction, but mostly because I had heard the school was more a Bible training center than a liberal arts institution.

"You mark my words," declared Aunt Lydia one Sunday afternoon early that September. "Jeremiah will turn against us. The precious seed we have sown in his heart these years will be trampled underfoot. All those big universities do is prepare the way for the athiestic overthrow of our country."

Uncle Rufus saw my resentment. "Now don't rush to conclusions, dear," he said.

"You know I'm right, Rufus," Aunt Lydia snapped. "It's bad enough for young people who have made a profession and go to the university. Look what happens to so many of them. Jeremiah here is unsaved."

"But he has a clear-thinking mind."

"That's exactly the point," countered Aunt Lydia. "He'll learn all those evolution things, all these arguments against the Bible, and because it's done in the name of education . . ."

"Ah, for cat's sake," I exclaimed, springing to my feet, almost overturning my chair. "I get sick of you always making me out to be some kind of a devil."

"Jeremiah!" my mother gasped.

It was the first time I had countered Aunt Lydia in this manner. It felt good. I was a man now, could say what I pleased, and I meant to do it.

"What good is your Christianity," I continued, "if it has to be protected all the time? If it can't stand against reason, if you have to defend it by calling black white and white black, then what's the sense of it?"

"Already," Aunt Lydia gasped. "You see?" She pointed at me like the aim of a gun. "This is just the start. God have mercy on us. You mark my words."

I went outside, slipped into our family car which by that time had a radio, and further desecrated Pew sanctity by tuning in a Sunday afternoon baseball game. In a few moments, Uncle Rufus came out. Our eyes met. He smiled. Without speaking, without either of us saying anything, he opened the car door and slipped in beside me.

"Who's ahead?" he asked.

"Yankees. Want me to turn it off?"

"Seems like they never lose a game," he said, ignoring my question. "I thought when Babe Ruth was gone, and now Lou Gehrig, that the Yankees would start to go downhill."

We sat for five minutes. The Yankees were playing the Philadelphia Athletics and were in the process of a runaway. Losing interest in the game, I turned to Uncle Rufus and said, "I suppose you came out here to talk to me."

"Not necessarily."

For the first time in my life, I looked at him skeptically. He smiled. (Parelli of Philadelphia lined a two run homer into left field, saving the A's from a greater disgrace.) Uncle Rufus turned up the volume button. I turned it down again.

"What did you want to tell me?" I asked.

He chuckled. "You are a wise lad, Jeremiah."

I waited. He rolled up the window halfway, ran his finger idly along the rim of the glass, and rolled the window down again.

"It isn't all bad, the things your people stand for," he said at last. "Now take the business I'm in. Putting things up in fancy packages is all the go now. A lot of new brands are coming out. Some of it is pretty inferior. But it sells, because it's packaged to appeal to people. Some of the older brands, products that have been tested through the years, aren't doing as well because the manufacturer keeps using the same old-fashioned package. It's the same product, just the same, a lot better than some of the new stuff."

Though I thought lightly of Uncle Rufus' words that day, I gave them subsequent appraisal during initial weeks on campus. For one thing, I experienced chronic homesickness. I was surrounded by throngs of students my age, none of whom knew me, few of whom seemed to want to. It unnerved me—homesickness—I who had so long desired the freedom my new setting proffered. But it was more than being torn from the natal roots. It was the newness of everything, the fact that, from the first day of school, I discovered the university classroom to be in multiples more demanding of my intellect than Mr. Mack's classes had been.

My beginnings were in what is known geographically as the corn belt, where one would suppose a state university to be somewhat out of pace with, for example, the Ivy league. Not so. Our campus had its share of matriculates who equated a Bachelor of Arts degree with economic success, but it was likewise peopled with students who reached out to the horizon while grinding their heels into the status quo.

Whereas I had been in rebellion against the legalistic mores of my lineage, I now grew hostile toward the liberality of this new world. My profoundest difficulty lay in trying to condition my thinking to the panoramic broadmindedness of university students, particularly sophomores. I wanted freedom. I loathed, or thought I did, everything Aunt Lydia expounded. But I was not about to blaspheme God, acclaim man and the earth episode as the ultimate reality, and champion the repeal of the Ten Commandments.

Particularly the seventh commandment!

The young males of my community had not been what you would call exemplary in matters of virtue. Whenever they congregated, talk invariably centered around one of three subjects—athletics, automobiles or amative conquests. Nevertheless, chastity was a trait most admired in a girl, and a young woman devoid of the vestal graces was rarely considered a proper choice for marriage.

Modern collegians, on the contrary, looked upon promiscuity as the new freedom, the master stroke of suffrage, in which woman gained companion status with man as his equal in the quest for pleasure.

"Ah," said a dormmate one day, gazing out across the sprawling complex from the window, "the world's biggest bedroom!"

"The loss of two fears has brought modern man to a new plateau of experience and search," said a sociology professor. "Man has lost his fear of God and his fear of pregnancy."

I had heard Aunt Lydia speak about modern teachers as men of the cloven hoof, destroyers of the faith, degenerates, profligate, spiritual assassins. Until the appearance of Mr. Mack in our community, I believed her. Because of Mr. Mack, I anticipated new frontiers of mental stimulation.

Admittedly, I had not anticipated smoke-filled classrooms, much less lectures in which profanity and bawdy frankness became commonplace. I have since discovered that, at least on our campus, it befell those who taught freshmen the task of shocking and disrupting prior thought patterns, to strip us of our fledgling concepts, reduce us to mental and emotional nudity, and thus compel us to fashion new garments of thought and behavior.

Perhaps I am guilty of hyperbole. For certain, many came to the campus and accepted routinely the new world of ideas. As certainly, I do not wish to reduce faculty members to conform to Aunt Lydia's descriptive techniques. But seldom did they mention the Bible or truth received by revelation. To them, all the world was observable phenomena. Man had the intellect and was fashioning the tools with which to catalog and control that phenomena.

My initial cowering resulted not only from Aunt Lydia's influence but from my own belief in a personal God, as compared to the *elan vital* of the man to whom science is virtually a religion. It is possible that I saw the disciples of materialism as a threat, because they were such real people by comparison to the veneered personalities surrounding my childhood. Thus their credo was a more blatant threat to my ultimate hope of one day discovering God.

There was a winningness about these men. They did not moor their minds in narrow, bigoted coves of thought. They launched out upon the high seas in search of truth, adventures—brave men who refused to accept the existence of a horizon, men to whom discovery was never a point of arrival, but always a launching site for new exploration.

"Liberalism," said one professor, "is by definition simply a better word than freedom. The true liberal refuses to settle for the status quo. To him, there are no absolutes, no need for first causes, no God or gods worthy of obeisance, if such divinities bind the spirit and circumscribe the mind."

Huxley, Darwin, Nietzsche and Freud were the new heroes, supplanting St. Paul and Moses, and perhaps even Jesus Christ.

Every fact of existence, including men's minds and wills and the flow of human history, depended upon and were reducible to physical processes. Logical positivism was the only real intellectual honesty. Man could be sure of nothing beyond the phenomena of personal experience.

Most startling of all to my compartmentalized mind was the de-mythologization of our national heroes. The Pilgrims were social misfits from England; George Washington had strong personal motivations. Did Abraham Lincoln use the slavery issue for purely political purposes? Was not Woodrow Wilson a pious ego maniac? How patriotic were those early pioneers who raped America's forests, bled the land for all its fertile worth, and trampled over each other in the rush for gold? Wouldn't the average citizen look askance at the stars and stripes if in some other clime he could find an economic strata more conducive to the good American life?

Silently, but at times resolutely, I withstood the flagrant iconoclasm—on occasion almost suspecting myself to be a Christian by Adelia's and Aunt Lydia's definition, so strongly did I question onslaughts against Pew ideologies. With each passing week, however, I felt myself giving ground for I seemed to stand completely alone. I could not detect the existence of the slightest minority who in any sense shared my apprehensions.

It seemed plain enough. My church and my people had lost their way in the search for truth. They had fixed their eyes on but one star, unmindful of the galaxies in the endless vault of attainable knowledge.

By mid-December, when I returned for the holidays, I had wandered afar from my childhood convictions, most assuredly now one of the lost ones, an unregenerate soul, numbered among the transgressors.

On Christmas Eve, we gathered at Aunt Lydia's.

"Well," said Uncle Rufus, "how is life at the university?"

I smiled wanly but gave no audible reply.

"A lot different from life in the old home town, I suppose."

"It sure is," I said.

"I always regretted that I didn't get an education."

"It really does something to you. Even the little taste I've had so far."

He eyed me closely.

"You begin seeing things in a different way," I said.

He led me on rather craftily, as I think back to it now, and soon I was sharing classroom concepts. It was obvious that some of the ideas startled him. It amused me.

"Well," he commented, when I paused a moment, "it seems those professors have done a pretty good job of weaning you."

I bristled. "They are broadminded men" I retorted. "The most exciting thing about the university is being among people who aren't prejudiced!"

"From what you've said," Uncle Rufus countered, "they sound real prejudiced to me."

"Prejudiced?" I half-shouted the word. It was the farthest thing from my mind—prejudice on the university campus?

"Don't you think so?"

"Prejudiced?" I spoke the word more softly now.

"Can't you be prejudiced about other things besides what folks believe around here?" He chuckled. "Seems to me, it isn't just people who believe the Bible who are prejudiced. People can be just as prejudiced against the Bible, as they can be prejudiced for it."

Uncle Rufus' logic caught me unprepared. I looked at him in mute admiration. At that moment, I esteemed his intellect as much as that of any of my professors.

"Now it seems to me that if people were really broadminded, the way you say, they'll look at both sides."

"I never thought of that," I admitted quietly.

"Another thing I'd keep in mind, Jerry," Uncle Rufus began, then suddenly broke off speaking.

"What?" I primed.

"Well, I'm talking too much, maybe. Like I said, I never had much for an education."

We looked at each other a moment. He must have sensed the eagerness with which I awaited his comment. In any case, he said, "What seems to me, listening to you tell how some of these professors put up questions about the Bible that you can't answer, well, what I'd say, Jerry, is a man should keep in mind that, just because we maybe don't know the answer right at the moment, it doesn't mean there isn't an answer."

"I knew it!"

Like the unanticipated crack of thunder, Aunt Lydia's voice overpowered our conversation. Unknown to either of us, she had been standing by, listening.

"Everybody," she called out, "come here! Come!"

Pews hurried to the scene, as though fearful of finding one of their number physically stricken.

"Our precious Jeremiah goes away to the university," she wailed, "and it's only been just these few weeks, and now he comes back to deny everything that was taught to him. I told you."

I stood to my feet, ruffled. "What are you talking about?"

She looked at me for a moment, then stalked to my father. "I told you to mark my words. You could have kept him from going to the university. I offered to help with tuition at our own school. But, oh no, you wouldn't listen to me!"

"Look here!" I called out.

Uncle Rufus stepped to my side. He motioned with his hand for me to calm myself.

Aunt Lydia began to cry.

"Well, there's one blessing," she sobbed. "Papa is gone, so he doesn't have to face this day when the first bearer of our family name turns against the Lord!"

"Don't talk that way, Lydia," Uncle Rufus said. He went to his wife's side, "Jerry is just going through a stage. He's trying to find himself. That's all. Be a little patient with him, and. . ."

"Oh, what do you know about patience?" she cried out. "I'm the one who has to be patient. Now listen, everybody, you know this is partly our fault. We've let the things of the world come in upon us." She gestured toward me. "Now we see what it's cost us. Let's get on our knees before the Lord. Let's do it right now—this blessed Christmas Eve. Let's get right with the Lord ourselves and let's pray for Jeremiah, pray that he will see his sin and turn to the Lord before it is forever too late."

She moved quickly about the room and, as though hearing an

invisible scythe, reduced everyone to a kneeling position, everyone except Rufus and myself.

When she came to us, Uncle Rufus whispered, "Be careful, Lydia."

"Kneel, Rufus!" she demanded. "You, too" she said to me.

Placing a hand firmly upon our shoulders, she pushed the two of us to the floor. I wanted to resist but, quickly assessing the situation, decided it might be the easier route to accommodate her eccentricity.

It had been a long, long time since I had knelt.

In that moment, very briefly, I felt a surge of that childhood emotion when I had sought for faith. Might faith come now even under these strange circumstances?

I doubted, but the old hunger was in my heart.

Aunt Lydia began to pray.

She gave God a resume of my life's history. She confessed my sins for me. Her voice was a kaleidascope of moods—like the wail of a lost puppy, like the roll of thunder, plaintive and vindictive, a cry of helplessness and a pronouncement of judgment.

I listened for awhile, listened until my mind began to wander, as it had wandered in church when I was a boy, as it wandered when I sat under Adelia among the Buzzing Bible Bees, as I knelt obediently beside my parents at midweek services.

Quietly, I took to my feet, slipped unobserved into the hallway, donned my topcoat, and went outside and home.

Chapter Thirteen

As resolutely as I once walked to the church altar, determined to forsake the world and give full allegiance to heaven, I now renounced Aunt Lydia's theomania in exchange for a pragmatic approach to the *who* and *why* of myself and the world and the universe surrounding me.

I looked at the university campus through a new set of lenses. Whereas it had once been a hostile place, undermining my view of things, it now became the center of my world, a laboratory and an observatory, probing the past, dissecting the present, and looking candidly and fearlessly into the future. Though located in an area often designated as one phase of the Bible belt, as I previously indicated, our state university was *avant garde* in many ways.

Existentialism, for example, did not become an intellectual fad until the years following World War II. Camus had only written the first of his novels, Jean Paul Sartre, the "pope of existentialism," was as yet unbathed by the fires of the great war out of which he and Camus were destined to share new perspectives of savage man's civilized state. On our campus, however, Sóren Kierkegaard was the revered master. Lost at first in the intricacies of his definition of *existenz,* I came slowly but with growing excitement into a working comprehension of his philosophy.

It will no doubt seem strange to you that the spawning ground for my new search was not so much the classroom, nor the university library—both of which became increasingly meaningful to me—but rather an off-campus coffee house known simply as *Friends of Faustus,* where the repeal of the eighteenth amendment made possible, if not always legal, the purchase of spirited coffee as a stimulus for thought and discussion.

I assume no need to enlarge upon *Friends of Faustus* as being by no means committed to the ecclesiastical viewpoint.

While I was in high school, America plunged into the chaotic depression years. Panic struck many in our community. In the darkest months, suicide reached epidemic proportions.

Pewdom survived without incident. Though spirit-oriented, our people knew the value of a dollar. While other farmers burned grain as fuel, Uncle Eliad took to truck farming, specializing in sweet corn and melons. The enterprise did so well that he sublet Uncle Caleb's land and took his brother into partnership. But most Americans suffered deep economic losses, giving rise to radical change in the relationship of government to private enterprise.

Franklin Delano Roosevelt emerged onto the American scene, introducing the doctrine of NRA and the New Deal as a progressive panacea for economic depression and social inequity.

"How can you spend yourself to prosperity?" asked a more conservative coffee sipper one evening. "I've heard the forecast that our national debt may be raised to fifty, maybe even a hundred billion dollars."

"What does it matter? Did you ever figure out the interest on a billion dollars at five percent? If the national debt went to, say, eighty billion or so, our government would go bankrupt."

"No, it wouldn't!"

"Yes, it would. Why wouldn't it?"

"Simple economics. Suppose, for example, you own a piece of land worth ten thousand dollars. You borrow five thousand dollars to improve that land, with the result that land becomes worth twenty thousand dollars. You still are just paying interest on the five thousand but, already, it's doubled itself. So now you borrow ten thousand dollars more and your land increases in value to forty-five thousand dollars."

"And a better trick yet," another sipper added, "is that you don't borrow this money from a bank, but from funds you've set aside from the land's earnings."

"That's right. The land increases in value because of its productivity, and the productivity becomes your borrowing source."

"Does that mean," I asked, "according to your theory, the government could increase the national debt to an unlimited figure?"

"So long as it's held in ratio to the increase of our gross national income."

I was skeptical, not fully comprehending, but it was a new day for the world, revolutionary, exciting, and I reveled in the dawn of it.

Realism was the mode for literature. Men like John Steinbeck, Somerset Maugham, and Ernest Hemingway had stripped the novel of its platonic garments, chiding man to once again walk the earth in search of fig leaves with which to cloth his nakedness.

I began to understand why my teachers looked askance at the nation's heroes. They had not brought forth upon this world a "land of the free and the home of the brave," but rather a machine in which common man was the working parts—the privileged few were the only real benefactors. This was changing.

"You know, it's a funny thing," said one of the better known erudites one afternoon at *Friends of Faustus.* "Here's this Hitler fellow. He's got some great ideas. But I don't figure him. He has the same objective as Marx and Lenin. Yet he gets all ruffled if Joe Stalin so much as glances toward the west."

"Their objectives aren't the same at all," responded one of the others.

"Well, of course, they are. Both plead the cause of the common man. Both advocate the overthrow of the privileged minority. Read *Mein Kampf* and *Das Kapital.*"

"*Mein Kampf* mainly states Hitler's foreign policy. But that's not the issue I'm driving at. Karl Marx advocated international communism, a system in which existing governments would be overthrown by the revolt of the working class of each country. Hitler, on the other hand, believes in a Germanic master race destined to rule the world."

"So what?" someone spoke up. "We believe in a master American race."

"We do? You're talking about the Sioux and the Iroquois."

More often, discussion centered around those subjects which pertained to the gratification of man's more basic existential drives— a kind of sophisticated lewdness.

"Religion is the real essence of what we're after," I heard someone say.

"Religion?"

"Now, hold your fire until you hear me out. Watch this guy Kierkegaard. He gets to me. According to him, you don't discover God by abstract demonstration. You don't even find Him in nature. Religion is purely an inward experience. It's sensory. All these people going around in sackcloth and ashes, so to speak, denying themselves the available pleasures in order that they might somehow please God, have missed it. Whatever it is, if it lifts me, projects me out of my humanity into a spiritual experience, that's religion. A glass of beer, a girl out along a grass road—hallelujah!"

"Man," another of the group observed, "you sure must miss some of the paragraphs when you read Kierkegaard."

"Why?"

"What about the suffering bit? In order to become a Christian, as I understand Kierkegaard, a man has to pass through despair."

"You can't buy all of Kierkegaard any more than you can't buy all of Plato or Nietzsche," a girl spoke up.

"Or Freud" someone jested.

The laughter intensified, as a voice from the back exclaimed, "Man, I buy all of Freud."

"Pleasant dreams!" the girl called out.

As the merriment subsided, one of the former spokesmen said, "Back to Kierkegaard, what about his views on immortality!"

"Doesn't most everybody believe in some kind of immortality?" someone asked.

"Immortality?" There was this one chap, a senior, known for his leftest opinions and his licentious pursuits. It was he who spoke now. "The only immortality anyone can lay proof to," he drawled, "is a man's ability to induce gestation."

"I'm a Descartes man myself," the senior continued. "That boy scratches me right where I itch. *Dubito ergo sum!* That's my philosophy, gives a man lots of latitude."

Thus did the heroes of the Bible lose relevance in my thinking, being supplanted by such names as Machiavelli, Thomas Paine, Charles Darwin, Sigmund Freud, and Albert Einstein.

I found meaning in the brush strokes of Van Eyck—shared the restlessness of Pintoretto—was challenged by Botticelli, the sensitive and poetic painter who had risen to greatness from the home of a common tanner. I could identify with the passionate rebelliousness of Van Gogh, the escapism of Gauguin, the penetrating seriousness of Cezanne.

All of these many influences made me increasingly an orphan spirit, severed from home ties, dislodged from prior foundations, at times a ship with neither sail nor anchor. I was a wayward sheep, the first of the blood line to defame the faith. Yet one landmark remained, to which I again and again turned for positional reference —my Uncle Rufus.

I loathed homeward jaunts and might have avoided them entirely had it not been for this man. I would put him out of my mind completely days at a time, and then he would drop me a postcard or some circumstance, often trivial, would remind me of him, so that invariably the days preceeding a school holiday turned my thoughts homeward.

Uncle Rufus took to reading, I discovered, so as to more adequately share conversation with me when I came home. It was remarkable, his capacity for productive contemplation. At times I envied him.

With Aunt Lydia, it was another matter. She either lacked the capacity for mature thought, or had so circumscribed her mind as to shunt its earlier capabilities. I delighted in confusing her with questions and logic.

To my amazement and discomfort, Uncle Rufus began to take sides with her. This had not happened before. I tried to dismiss the fact casually, but it kept coming back, the remote possibility that, even in Aunt Lydia's frame of reference, there might be a reality I was missing.

If only I could have overlooked Uncle Rufus, I could have given myself completely to the embrace of New World philosophy. But he was a catalyst, always there, quietly tantalizing me with the hint of reality.

We often hunted and fished together when I came home, seldom talking about anything other than the exploit of the day. Occasionally, he drove to the campus to attend athletic events. I introduced him proudly to my friends. He was colorful, the kind of character one might expect to find in a novel, and it pleased me the frequency with which my friends mentioned him.

"How's good ol' Uncle Rufus?" they would ask, when I returned from a few days at home.

That was my sustaining problem. Whenever I saw him, under whatever circumstances, Uncle Rufus had that quiet confidence, the profound simplicity, of being at peace with himself.

Chapter Fourteen

I joined a fraternity, with full intentions of becoming "one of the boys," and did participate in many of those diversions by which collegians are frequently defined. I had my first taste of the inebrious spirits, so besotted myself one weekend I turned my room into shambles, my exploits becoming one of the establishment's chief non-academic topics of conversation for the next several days, and causing me such personal chagrin that I renounced alcohol and thenceforth limited imbibing to occasional sips of wine. I intended to fully identify, and I endeavored to convince myself this was my intent. However, I could not so easily unleash myself for the moorings of my childhood. Even casual devilment smote my conscience. I was at all times on guard.

But I tried.

One of the frat men came upon a magazine advertisement extolling the virile charms of Arabian water pipes—a contraption dating back to the pre-Aladdin era, in which tobacco is drawn through a chamber of water before reaching the smoker's mouth—and a subscription was taken to raise the cost of the object.

I was elected project chairman of the Hubble Bubble Committee (that being the pipe's English-Arabic name), which simply meant it fell my lot to collect the necessary funds and dispatch the order. I chaffed at myself for experiencing qualms of conscience over the venture. As a boy, I had on occasion joined other lads sequestered in fields of tall corn adjacent to our town where, finding ears

117

with dried silk, we made improvised cigarettes. I had on fewer occasions used tobacco itself—but only rarely, since for a Pew to be suspected of tobacco on his breath was as evil and unanticipated a circumstance as for a Pew to set foot upon a dance floor, enter a movie house, or do manual work on Sunday.

"When's the pipe coming?" the boys would ask, teasing me. "You sure you didn't pocket the money?"

"I've got the money order receipt," I would defend.

At last, the parcel arrived.

Frenzied excitement heralded the event. We drew the shades— for mood not secrecy—pushed back the furniture, and sat in a circle on the main room floor. Like sheiks met for council on a desert oasis, we passed the instrument about, taking turns drawing smoke from it and blowing the acrid fumes across the room.

A somewhat accomplished amateur photographer in our group took a number of exposures. One of me happened to be the most descriptive of the lot and was thus subsequently chosen for appearance in *The Magus,* our campus year book.

I took great care to make sure Aunt Lydia never saw the volume.

Progressively, I became less sensitive to the trampling assunder of old mores. For, in spite of conscience qualms, I experienced liberation. I was no longer on observation by the folks at home. I could do as I pleased.

There was a goodly measure of satisfaction in this.

I bought a fur coat, the symbol of the college male in those days. I wore horn-rimmed glasses and became a party goer. Sinclair Lewis emerged as my literary idol. I embraced political liberalism. I helped burn the dean in effigy. I knew all the Pat and Mike jokes. I never missed a Mae West movie. I slept until noon on Sundays.

By the usual definition, I was collegiate.

Yet I failed to earn the fullest acceptance of my fellows. For, in the foremost of all campus diversions, namely the dissolute life, they came to suspect me of prudery.

Weekends were given to licentious endeavors, and the ability to recount flamboyant adventures insured stature in the eyes of one's comrades. Sex had become a status symbol.

A chap, who roomed immediately across the hall from me, earned the distinction of being named the establishment's official sexologist. He not only possessed an encyclopedic knowledge of Pompeiian procedures but kept an elaborate catalogue of sorority row conquerables, complete with case study details and telephone numbers.

He also listed the unconquered, and kept a detailed record of efforts extended toward, as he put it, "correcting the situation." Sunday afternoons were largely spent in discussing the prevalent status of such maidens, and those frat men, who succeeded in adding names to the victor's roster, received a hero's acclaim.

I tried to appear interested. I hated myself for being puritanical, while at the same time I resisted the casual efforts of fellow fraternities to amend my circumstance.

Then one Sunday afternoon, when I once again had nothing to report, the aforementioned champion of the cause summoned the house to action.

"Look," he said, "we try to look after the girls on campus, and here we have one among us who isn't part of the battle."

He turned to look squarely at me. So did all the other men.

I squirmed.

"Jerry, friend," he continued, "we're your brothers. We can't let you suffer."

"Don't you guys worry about me," I said awkwardly.

It was an odd moment. Though the circumstances of misconduct were utterly reversed, I felt as though I were in Aunt Lydia's parlor again.

"Men," the spokesman continued, "as Crown Prince of Hormonia, I decree the forthcoming weekends—however many it takes —to be devoted in a joint effort to convert our wayward brother."

Dates were arranged for me each subsequent weekend. In every instance, the girl had been appraised of my dilemma and agreed to be cooperative.

Yet I did not defile myself. It was as though I were guarded by an unseen presence, who deftly maneuvered circumstances, so manifestly on occasion it was frightening, so consistently it was reassuring.

Each Sunday, fellow initiates congregated in my room, insisting upon an hour by hour accounting of my Saturday night foibles.

"What's the matter with you?" my foremost benefactor asked.

"Nothing," I countered.

"We don't allow wierdos in this place y'know."

"I'm no wierdo."

"What are you then, a Sunday school boy?" Disdain deepened upon his countenance. "That must be it. One of Billy Sunday's boys."

He leaped to his feet, turned an agile handspring, and hopped onto a nearby chair.

Flailing his arms, he cried out, "Down with drink and the devil! Down with. . ."

"The Eighteenth Amendment!" one of the others called out.

"Down with Billy Sunday!" called out one of the others.

Whereupon several of the men took the self-appointed evangelist in hand, with such resulting commotion my situation was tabled.

The following Tuesday one of the less vociferous came to me.

"You better get with it, Jerry," he cautioned. "If you don't want to play our brand of ball, you should get yourself another team."

He spoke kindly. I could tell he had been in conversation with pressure factions, who had discussed the possibility of my expulsion from the house.

"I think I know your problem," he said, "and I think I can help you. Isn't the problem a lack of suitable surroundings?"

I didn't understand.

"I'll fix you up," he said. "There's a little hotel out in the country where my girl friend and I go. The manager's a great guy, caters to college students on weekends. I'll ask my girl to find somebody. You know, somebody who'll make it easy for you."

He was intense, like a crusader, an evangel, and I feared. I could maneuver myself on a date, but going with a girl to a hotel was another matter.

"You want to go, don't you?" he asked, eyeing me with skepticism.

"Well. . ."

"Do you or don't you?"

I gave reluctant approval.

As the weekend approached, I grew increasingly apprehensive. At night, long after the others had fallen asleep, I relived my childhood. I thought of John Wesley Sommerford and his pronouncements of divine judgment. I thought of Uncle Rufus. I thought of the Buzzing Bees. I thought of my sunset contemplations.

By Saturday afternoon, I took violently ill with an aching head and an upset stomach.

"I'm sure sorry," I apologized to my fraternity brother.

"Tried aspirins?" he asked.

"I've taken six." (I lied. The headache was a mercy to me.) "Aspirins don't even faze it."

"Can you get over to the infirmary? You still have a couple hours."

"I'll just sleep it off."

"We'd better call a doctor."

"Naw, I'll be okay."

He looked at me skeptically and left the room.

Two weeks later the offer was repeated. Again I accepted, for during those interim days I had repeatedly castigated myself for failing to seize such an alluring opportunity.

Saturday came. My head began to ache. I took an aspirin. My stomach felt upset. I walked to the campus drug store and purchased a small dose of bismuth.

When my accomplice entered the room, as departure time neared, I was dressed and waiting.

"You're going through with it," he said.

We looked at each other silently for a moment. I suspected what he was thinking.

"When you begged off last time, I thought you were pulling my leg."

"I was pretty miserable," I said. "I was sure sorry to fowl things up for you the way I did."

He grinned. "It worked out fine. You never have any trouble finding substitutes."

We left.

The girl was pretty. She appeared rather young, more like a high school junior than a college freshman. She eyed me curiously at first, but seemed to like what she saw, for she smiled and took my arm.

"Into the back seat, you two," my accomplice said.

Laughing, the girl pushed me ahead into the car. I would have preferred being more chivalrous. She lunged in after me, moved close to me and took my hand.

In a moment, the car sped away.

"Weekends sure are a relief," she said. "I liked high school better'n college. Do you?"

I shrugged my shoulders. A reply to this kind of observation seemed utterly pointless.

"Have you ever been to this place we're going?" she asked.

"No," I said.

"It's nice to get away from the campus, don't you think?"

"It's a change."

"Have you ever seen me around before?"

"No."

"You're a freshman, like me, aren't you?"

"Right."

121

"Do you have a car?"

"No."

From the front seat came, "How you two doing back there?"

"Okay," I said.

"Except he hardly talks," the girl whimpered.

I tried to make conversation but with difficulty. It was hardly in place to discuss erudite matters, even had she seemed the scholastic type, and I was much too inhibited to introduce conversation more appropriate to the intent of the situation.

I felt pity for the girl. She seemed out of context, not only because of her juvenile appearance but because of a pathetic shallowness. She had obviously been sent to college.

Mostly, I pitied her because of her willingness to give herself, being reasonably endowed with the necessary facilities for promiscuous encounters and dependent upon these qualities for popularity.

She snuggled closer, lowering her shoulder in an effort to encourage me to put my arm around her.

I didn't.

I felt like a kidnapper, like an assassin.

I began to whistle softly, abruptly stopped, startled. The tune had come from my subconscious reservoir. The words now leaped into flame in my mind.

> *Give of your best to the Master.*
> *Give of the strength of your youth.*

"Hey," my girl chided, "aren't you human?"

I turned to her.

"Do you always just sit there like that, when you're on a date?"

"Well. . ." I could think of nothing to say.

She inched slightly away. I put my arm onto the back of the seat. She moved closer again. I lowered my arm to her shoulders. She turned to me, her lips coming close to mine, and I drew her to me, kissing her fiercely.

"I thought maybe you didn't like me," she whispered. It was like the fright of a little child.

"I think you're terrific," I whispered in reply.

"Do you really?"

"Sure."

It had been a sudden impulse, this decision to unleash the animal in my breast, and I felt a new sense of freedom. Why not? What sense did it make, groveling in the remnant memories of an antiquated morality?

122

For the next half-hour, I played to the full the role of a good brother, as our fraternity described one.

"You're a keen kisser," the girl whispered. "You're the nicest guy I ever dated."

I made no comment.

"Am I the best girl you ever dated?" she asked a moment later.

"Sure," I replied.

"Honest?"

"Hey!" I called out to the front. "How much farther is it to that hotel?"

"About ten miles," the driver responded. "I can't drive very fast with just one arm."

"We're going to stop to eat first, aren't we?" my girl asked. "I'm hungry!"

"Hungry?" The driver chuckled. "You can always eat."

"I'm so hungry my stomach aches." She turned to me. "Aren't you hungry?"

"Anything you say."

We drove to a small truck stop. It was well we did, for the little diner was brightly lighted, and I could once again look clearly at the girl.

She had become quite infatuated with me. She moved her chair tightly against mine, making it difficult to eat. She cooed at me, giggled at my remarks, whether or not they were meant to invoke levity. She rolled her eyes and puckered her lips and winked.

She was pitiful.

I came to my senses again, disdaining my prior display of beastliness, and would have forsaken the food and left had I had the courage.

I didn't have the courage.

Consequently, by the time we reached the hotel, where a number of other college couples were noisily congregated in the lobby, I totally despised myself.

"Here's what we do," my fraternity brother explained. "You and I register for a room together. The girls do the same thing. That way everything stays hoyle for the innkeeper. The police closed a place about five miles from here because kids came in on the Mr. and Mrs. routine."

I felt a momentary reprieve.

"Don't just stand around. Go ahead and register. You pay for our room. I gave my date the dough for theirs."

I registered.

"Just one night?" the clerk asked.

"Y-yes," I spoke with effort. My mouth felt dry and dirty.

"That'll be four bucks."

I paid.

A pudgy bellhop picked up our small hand luggage and showed us to our room. He opened one of the windows, checked the bathroom, waited for his gratuity.

I had never taken a night in a hotel before. I didn't know how much to tip. My companion took two small coins from his pocket and pressed them into the bellhop's hand.

"You'll notice that door over there, gentlemen," the bellhop said. "Actually, this room, and the one next to it are adjoining, in case we have parents with children or salesmen traveling together. The door locks from both sides."

He winked and left.

My companion promptly unlocked the door from our side. "The gals will be up in a minute," he said. "They'll unlock their side."

"You're sure they'll be in that room?" I asked awkwardly.

"Idiot. That's the way they run this joint."

I was nervous. I paced the floor. The room was cool, but I began to perspire.

The bellhop brought the girls. A moment later, the lock clicked on the inner door.

"Open it," my companion said casually.

I just stood there.

He went to the door and opened it.

"How about a little privacy?" his girl called out.

Entering their room, he retorted, "Go hang it on your nose!"

They both laughed.

My girl came. She stood in the doorway a moment.

"I guess this is our room," she said. She closed the door. "Should I lock it?" she asked.

I didn't answer. I couldn't.

She came slowly toward me.

"Uh," I blurted, "I'm sorry."

"Sorry about what?" she sang merrily.

She came fully to me and placed her arms around me. I lifted my arms to embrace her, a surge of desire momentarily quieting my apprehensions.

I was utterly mortal in that moment. I wanted the girl, cheap

124

though she might be. But there came upon me a larger compulsion, fearful like those Sunday nights of my childhood, when the pastor of our church flung forth the net of divine invitation.

I freed myself from her grasp, took hold of my hand luggage, and moved briskly to the door. She came after me, clutching my arm.

"Where are you going?" she asked.

I turned to her.

"Don't go!" she begged.

She was frightened, as though fearful of being alone in that room.

"I've got to," I said. "I'm sorry to stand you up this way. But I've got to go."

She struggled to forbid my exit. We caused considerable commotion, so much our next room companions appeared in the adjoining doorway.

"Be quiet, you fools!" my fraternity brother called out.

My girl turned to him. It gave me a moment's advantage, sufficient to be gone.

I must have made a strange spectacle, as I scampered down the stairs, dashed through the lobby, and broke into the flight of a thief outdoors.

I hurried to the hamlet's edge, out onto the main highway leading back to the city, and was shortly picked up by a passing truck, relieved lest my fraternity brother came angrily in search of me.

Early the next morning, I gathered my belongings and moved out of the fraternity house into a private residence offering a vacated student room for rent.

For several weeks after that, when men from the fraternity house saw me around campus, they called me "the eunuch." I took pains to avoid encounters, and by midsemester the whole affair had blown over.

But I did not forget. The episode plunged me into a prolonged period of deep introversion, during which time I almost totally ignored the opposite sex. Introversion gave rise to introspection, as I tried to analyze myself. Was I simply ridden with complexes, my mind scarred by the traumatic influence of people like Aunt Lydia and Adelia? Had my childhood search for inner righteousness been motivated only by a fear of divine judgment? Or was there a higher good, and, if so, did an inner compulsion lead me toward it, a compulsion yet resident within my being?

I gave myself to academic diligence, both as an escape mechanism and as a further search for ultimate truth.

Then one day I met Vaneta.

It was a casual meeting, such as can occur on campus without formal introduction, and at first I thought little of it. I did not so much as ask her name, nor share mine. We had probably seen each other often, without noticing, because our meetings grew more frequent. We both ate at the same cafeteria. We would meet in the library. Two of our classes convened in the same building at the same hours. Before long, we began walking together to and from the cafeteria and the classrooms. Then one morning, we formally introduced ourselves, Vaneta Logan and Jerry Pew.

"I'm a home ec major," she said. "I guess we girls get the reputation for being a little stuffy, but it's not really all that bad."

"I'm in business administration," I replied.

She was like a choice flower in comparison to the girl who had so nearly blighted my life. Perhaps this was why I felt such an immediate attraction to her, the reason I overlooked her shyness, the Victorian mannerisms I came later to see as prone to make her aloof. She was color and fragrance and warmth to my frustration and loneliness.

I liked her.

One afternoon, I suggested we simply take a walk. She expressed reluctance but agreed to go. As we strolled, I took her hand. She drew it away and became quiet, responding only briefly when I spoke to her.

"You're a pleasant contrast to most girls I've met on campus," I said.

"Thank you."

We walked on silently. She guided our course back toward the campus.

"Got another class this afternoon?" I asked.

"No."

"You live in a sorority?"

"No."

"One of the dorms?"

"Yes."

"Shall I walk with you to the dorm?"

"No, thank you."

During the ensuing two or three weeks, whenever we met, she was polite but invariably had an excuse for not accompanying me. I tried to be casual, partly because I felt affronted, also because it seemed so intriguing to find this kind of specimen on campus.

126

She gradually restored me to her good graces and we were frequently together again. When I suggested dates, however, she always had an excuse.

I endeavored to remain casual. Indeed, I gave frequent thought to abandoning all interest in the girl. More than on one occasion, alone in my room, I wondered if there might be any similarity to the maidenhoods of Aunt Lydia and Adelia and the present mannerisms of Vaneta—a most frightening contemplation.

Then, late in May, home economics majors sponsored a banquet. Vaneta invited me to be her guest.

It was our first date. I was delighted.

Somewhat to my surprise, I found home economics majors a personable lot, so much so I might have begun looking for an alternative to Vaneta, except that she was like a dormant bud come into sudden blossom that evening. She introduced me proudly to her friends. She made me the center of her attention with those poised courtesies befitting a girl of good breeding. And, although only a freshman, she was chosen to give a report on the progress of initiates in the department, an assignment she dispatched with the ease and lucidity of a senior.

"You gave an exceptionally good report," I complimented, as we walked to her dorm later in the evening. "It was an honor to be your escort."

She made no audible comment but took my hand. It felt soft and warm and clean. I held it firmly.

"When we first met," she said a moment later, "I wondered about you. There seem to be so few decent fellows anymore."

"You could say the same for girls."

"You prefer decent girls?"

"Sure do."

We walked quietly another moment.

"Do you know many other girls on campus?" she asked.

"A few."

"You've dated some of them?"

"Some of them."

"Nice girls?"

"I doubt it."

Again we walked in silence.

Then she asked, "Do you date often?"

"It's been weeks since I had a date," I said. "I guess I about gave up looking for somebody like you, Vaneta."

She squeezed my hand affectionately.

When we reached her dormitory, I took both of her arms and turned her toward me. The moon shone full and her eyes caught the silver of its glow.

"May I kiss you goodnight?" I whispered.

"Not yet, Jerry," she replied. "You're awfully nice, and I like you, but please not yet."

"May we have more dates?"

"Anytime you say."

Thanking me for the evening, she went quickly into the building.

I walked slowly back to my room. There was a song in my heart. There was gratitude.

I stopped outside my house and looked full into the brightness of the moon. I remembered the Buzzing Bible Bees. One of Adelia's favorite topics had been the angels. She often quoted a verse from the Bible, the words of which I could not at that moment recollect, in which God promises to surround His children with angelic custodians.

Had this been my good fortune? Had God kept me clean for Vaneta? Might it be that my past confusion and frustration were providentially ordained circumstances for the purpose of molding me and leading me to the discovery of truth and goodness?

God seemed nearer to me that night than He had ever been before!

Chapter Fifteen

Immediately prior to the outset of my sophomore year the mustached Austrian, once the casual topic of academic discourse at *Friends of Faustas,* gained history's hall of villany. Maddened by the pursuit of his own destiny, he made *Deutschland Uber Alles* a political theme instead of a national goal, dared Europe and the world to play his game of chess, thumbed his nose at the Union Jack, set upon a crusade to exterminate the Jewish race, and subsequently poured his *panzer* divisions across Europe like molten hate from a burst ladle.

In the Pacific, Japanese war lords looked beyond their islands for economic and population respite.

Campus doers urged the boycott of products bearing *made in Japan* labels. Students of German extraction spoke of Hitler as a good man gone mad, sure to be overthrown by his people.

"It's all a lot of preplanned international politics," I heard one upperclassman say. "FDR is steering us right down the road to war."

"You're nuts!" he was told.

"Wait and see. Hoover was a good man, maybe the last of the good presidents. He saw the depression as inevitable in the economic cycle. But FDR is an egomaniac. He's got to succeed. I think he'll manipulate us into war to stimulate the economy."

"Man, you're so prejudiced you think the angels are all Republicans and the devils are all Democrats."

Multitudes of young males left school to enlist in the armed forces.

I felt some of the pressure myself, even, though not a pacifist, I both feared death and revolted at the thought of taking another's life.

But my strongest compulsion was to complete my education, a pursuit involving the pleasant alchemy of familiarization with the ways of commerce and a stimulation of one's intellectual appetite for the humanities. I also wanted to become better acquainted with Vaneta.

She was like a fine painting, admired the more with each beholding, yet rarely touched. There was a vivacious wholesomeness about her, a genuineness which somehow compensated for her aloofness.

Since adolescence, my dreams had been of a girl who would overtly express affection in good taste but also in good abundance. Vaneta did not fulfill this dream. When she eventually permitted our first kiss, it was as though the endearment were exchanged between brother and sister.

Yet it never occured to me to sever our relationship so I might seek another. I was the one campus male with whom Vaneta could entrust her virtue, a fact sufficient in itself to stimulate my fullest loyalty.

Between Christmas and the New Year I visited her home and had a most pleasant encounter with her parents, finding them much to my liking and, to my delight, being substantially acceptable to them. They were stalwart church folk, though gold of a different ecclesiastical vein from the Pews. They were Presbyterians, one of the denominations highly suspect in the eyes of my clansmen.

The Logan's operated a large farm. Until that time I had thought of Uncle Eliad as the finest of farmers. Vaneta's father not only tilled twice the amount of land but employed principles of agronomy foreign to either of my landed uncles. He had about him the air of a farmer but would most adequately classify as a country gentleman.

It was Vaneta's mother, and her married sister, Winona, who gave me insight as to the girl I considered marrying. The mother, a charming woman, had regality about her, a manner of good breeding such as one might expect to find in the gubernatorial mansion. Winona exuded refinement, but perhaps without the poise of her mother. Both were paragons of propriety, at times warm and outgoing, but always with that edge of gentility by which the Victorian Age is most commonly characterized.

I admired these women.

I feared them.

It occurred to me that, in the two husbands, I might find some of the answers I sought as to what I could expect of Vaneta were she to one day share my wedlock.

The father and mother were quite obviously well-married. After so many years, a nuptial relationship betrays itself, be it poorly oriented or blissful. There was a glow between these two people. I wondered, though, if it might not be as much respect as affection. The father's first love was farming, the mother's her house. Both dispatched their domestic responsibilities with finesse. I wondered if, in lieu of the flame of passion, these two, from the outset of their marriage, had found expression in their related duties more than in the physical aspects of their union.

I suspicioned so.

Winona, some eight years Vaneta's senior, seemed to offer more clues. She was an individual, sure enough, but so in awe of her stately mother as to be somewhat bound by the proverbial apron strings. At times Winona betrayed her facade and gave vent to a smallness I have always despised in women, that of a tongue glib to recount the shortcomings of others. It would only be a small remark, a matter overheard in the community, or brought to mind by a figment of the conversation. Invariably, the mother, with the merest turn of her head, silenced such talk. To her credit, I recall at least one occasion where Winona herself bit off the conversation, like a child, seeking to break a habit, that restrains itself at the onset of a wrongdoing.

Winona's husband, Pierce Roberts, was as flamboyant an individual as I had come upon in a good while. He sprang from one of the community's best families, farm folk who envisioned great furrows for their son but, ere he finished high school, realized he had a thumb green for commercial tender, not for the tending of crops.

He had dimensional talents. He played a half-dozen musical instruments with varying degrees of excellence. His Carusonic voice kept him in high demand for weddings, funerals, civic events, and one or two solos at the band concert each summer's Friday night. (He could sing Carrie Bond's *A Perfect Day* as though it were being sung for the first time.) In high school he lettered in three sports, captained the forensic team, and was elected Attorney General of Boys' State.

Thus he could have been any of a number of things. He could have been a lawyer, a real estate promoter, a teacher, a banker, a bandmaster, an actor, a merchantman. He might even have been a preacher.

He chose to be a salesman.

You can never quite document such things but, from the outset, I suspected his choice of vocation to be somehow inspired by his marriage. Let me again hasten to say that, by the usual standards, he and Winona had a good marriage. The Roberts and the Logans once thought in terms of Winona marrying Pierce's younger brother, a chap born one year prior to the young maiden. But, when he was a junior in high school, the boy lost his life in a farm accident. So, despite the fact Pierce graduated from high school the year Winona finished eighth grade, the two were brought together—by their choice, by parental encouragement.

"She's a good kid," Pierce told me. He winked. "Too bad these Logans only had two daughters. You're lucky the second one hasn't been picked already."

Then, as though having dispensed with that subject, he spoke of the world with which he encompassed himself Monday through Friday of every week.

"I've been wanting to visit your town," he said. "I sell for Harvest Craft. You'd know a man by the name of Vamp. I forget his first name."

"Halford Vamp."

"That's it. He's after Harvest Craft like a leech. Wants to sell to our company the worst way. No wonder, with HC the biggest farm implement firm in the business. Vamp sat across from me at a dinner in Chicago a couple months ago. He's a little on the obnoxious order. How's he looked on in the community?"

"He's providing my school tuition through a scholarship," I said. It surprised me to find myself conveying the information in such a defensive tone of voice.

"I hear he's really pulled the wool over the eyes of the guy he works for," Pierce said. "This inventor there in your town."

"Could be," I said.

"Looks like the war's going to change business procedures for a lot of us. These Russians invading little Finland has me stumped. All it's done is to show the Germans how weak the Russians are. You watch. Hitler'll clobber Russia before this is all over.

"I just read in the paper where a Finn ski-mounted division almost wiped out a whole Russian column. One of the captured Soviet soldiers was being registered in a prisoner-of-war camp and got

132

his first look at a fountain pen. He was flabbergasted and asked to show it to his buddies. None of them had ever seen such a thing before. Imagine it. A fountain pen. I guess we just don't realize how advanced we are in this world. I'll tell you one thing. If we get mixed up in this war, it'll be over in a hurry."

Vaneta seemed genuinely pleased with the rapport I established among her kinfolk and expressed enthusiasm when I suggested she visit my home at semester break.

"I'd better caution you," I said. "My people are pretty straight-laced."

"I'm sure I'll find them very nice," she said. "I don't ever want to be a prude, Jerry, but I am a little old fashioned in my own thinking."

"I like you that way," I said.

Back again on campus, I further conditioned Vaneta about pre-dominant Pew peculiarities.

"I'm anxious to meet them," was her reaction.

And so the day came.

Vaneta did so well with my parents I grew somewhat anticipant of her first encounter with Aunt Lydia.

Ambivalent by nature, Uncle Rufus' spouse greeted Vaneta with an initial coolness. It was good. It brought from the girl's person-ality an effusiveness I had not previously witnessed. Slowly, assured-ly, she won Aunt Lydia's favor, evidencing such a genuineness of spirit as to completely disarm the woman.

"Are you a Christian?" Aunt Lydia asked.

"Well, of course," Vaneta replied warmly.

Thereupon my Aunt surveyed my chosen one with penetrating scrutiny.

"You know what born again means?" She asked.

I cringed.

"It's a term Jesus used in the Bible," Vanetta replied.

"You know that Jeremiah there has never been converted, don't you?"

"Jeremiah?"

"I guess I never told you, Vaneta," I broke in. "Jerry is a simpli-fication of my given name."

Vaneta came to me. She put her arm around my waist. She said to Aunt Lydia, "Jerry is the finest young man I've ever met."

Aunt Lydia promptly changed the subject.

Later, I overheard her say to Uncle Eliad, "She even looks like a

133

Christian, don't you think? I guess it must be true, like I've heard it said, there aren't many, but there are a few Presbyterian churches that are still fundamentalistic."

Thus did Vaneta Logan come into full acceptance of the Pew family.

The following October, I proposed marriage. It was evening. We had gone for a walk in a large park near the university.

"But we're only juniors," Vaneta said.

"I'm not asking you to marry me now," I told her. "I just want to be sure nobody else gets you."

She moved into my arms, turned her lips to mine, kissed me fully for the first time, and for one rapturous moment I wondered why I had harbored any apprehensions. Then, deftly, she went out of my grasp again. She took my hand, and, skipping, pulled me with her.

"Let's walk," she said.

We moved silently through the quiet darkness, hand in hand, two people given to each other, trusting each other, sharing the ecstasy of a dream coming to fulfillment.

It was a profound experience. This girl belonged to me. I belonged to her. Yet, I had never once claimed possession of her body. Surely, I comforted myself, this was a kind of righteousness. Perhaps it really was true after all, that God, who seemed so completely inaccessible, had never been far away.

The war continued in Europe. France fell. The battle for Britain raged. Insanely, Hitler spread his military might into Africa and eastward into Russia. Victory for the Axis was to be decisive for the future of Europe.

Conscription of young American males approached the stature of full mobilization.

Then came December of my senior year.

December 7, 1941.

"Shall I enlist?" I asked Vaneta. "If I do, I can maybe get into some kind of office work. If I wait for the draft, I'll graduate, but I'll also probably end up in the infantry."

I waited for the draft.

July 15, 1941, I left for basic training at Fort Leonard Wood. By early winter I was at Fort Ord in advanced weaponry, and then I was transferred briefly to Fort Campbell.

It is mostly irrelevant to my story, those long, treacherous years

134

in the army. Though I hated the thought of war, and had a profound disrespect for many aspects of international politics, I was a loyal citizen and extended every effort to be a good soldier.

As an infantryman, I recognized the possibility of being called upon to make the supreme sacrifice. This figured prominently in the metamorphosis of my self-discovery and in the dimension of Vaneta's love. That love became increasingly obvious through the exchange of letters between the high school, where she had taken a position, and my various military addresses.

I spent the following Easter at Vaneta's home, after stopping briefly with my own parents enroute to be with her.

On Easter night, she and I walked arm-in-arm along a cluster of trees adjacent to their farmyard. An awesome display of the *aurora borealis* was in progress.

"When I was a kid," I said, "I thought the northern lights were reflections of the sun off the icebergs instead of electrified particles shot out from sunspots."

"They make me think about God," Vaneta said simply, "especially coming this way at Easter time."

"I guess I could say the same."

A sensational spray of light mushroomed across the full of the north.

"Makes you think this could be the night Christ returns," I said.

Vaneta stepped away from me. It was momentarily startling, as though I had unintentionally offended her.

"What do you mean?" she asked.

"Doesn't your church have teachings about the return of Christ?"

"He comes for us when we die."

"I guess, but there's also the time when He will come in the clouds and all the Christian people will suddenly vanish from the earth. They'll go up to be with Him."

"I never heard such a thing," she said.

I got the impression she thought I might be joking with her. I dismissed the subject. She asked no questions. We walked side by side for a few moments. She again put her arm about my waist, and I put mine about her's.

"Jerry."

"Yes?"

"As you look to the future, mixed up like it is for us now, do you have a feeling God is anywhere in it?"

"I feel God led you and me together."

"So do I." She walked quietly for several moments before adding, "But I wish I could feel closer to God. Is He close to you, Jerry?"

"I guess not."

We paused. The lights in the north vaulted high into the sky. Vaneta nestled into my arms.

"I'd like to know more about God," I said, "but my tribe, especially Aunt Lydia, has me pretty mixed up on religion."

"I'm mixed up, too."

"But we're clear on one thing," I said. "We love each other."

"I love you, Jerry. I love you."

We kissed savagely.

Our love deepened during those brief days. Though buttressed by propriety, it became increasingly intimate. Vaneta was a complex person, but she was completely genuine. I felt at times a strong desire to discuss Christianity with her. It was a subject she never broached except for our brief Easter night comments.

Whereas the Pew's made much of spiritual amenities, religious practice was limited among the Logans. They did say a memorized table grace, but there were no family prayers, no reading of the Bible, nothing of piety save a tranquil approach to life and faithful attendance at church on Sunday mornings.

Vaneta and I did not see each other again for the duration of the war—the war in Europe I should say. I was sent to England for further training, serving also for a short term as an instructor.

Loneliness and uncertainty beset me. Letters from Vaneta sustained me. It was that time in history when England began to put from its image the remaining vestiges of the Victorian era and to enter the spiritual vacuum by which it would be characterized long into the post-war years. Consequently, the moral breath of the nation became stifled, and homesick American soldiers were provided with frequent opportunities for clandestine diversions.

I remained dauntless in my loyalty to the girl who had given me her heart.

It was in London where I met Lucky—a brash, hulk of a man with a twist to his philosophy of life quite different from anything I had previously encountered.

"Yeah," he said, when we first met, "call me Lucky. I'm here, ain't I, not down in North Africa playin' shoot-you-last with Rommel's boys?"

He invited me to spend a Saturday night with him at Piccadilly.

136

"These English gals are great news," he said. "You don't even have to be lucky. All you gotta do is be the same place they are."

"I've got a girl back home," I said. "I write to her Saturday nights."

"I suppose you think she sits around doing the same."

"She's a great girl. She's waiting for me."

Lucky looked at me in sheer unbelief.

"You'll get your 'Dear John' letter one of these days," he said. "Be smart, an' keep a jump ahead of her."

In the next months I met many GI's whose girl friends had forsaken them for deferred males at home. Yet my confidence in Vaneta never wavered.

In January of 1943, Roosevelt and Churchill conferred with Giraud and DeGaulle at Casablanca and, at FDR's insistence, drafted a plan to settle for nothing less than Hitler's unconditional surrender. We knew that could mean the necessity of retaking Europe, inch by inch.

The following month Rommel made a frantic effort to break out of the Allied claw in North Africa. He failed. Before the middle of May, a quarter of a million Germans and Italians surrendered.

"That'll give the paper hanger somethin' to think about!" Lucky effused. "Maybe we won't have to invade Europe after all."

Early the following month, however, we were both assigned to the Seventh Army, commanded by Lieutenant General Patton—affectionately known as "Old Blood and Guts" to his fighting men.

On July tenth, the British Eighth Army, under Montgomery, and the U.S. Seventh invaded Sicily. I lost contact with Lucky, being assigned to logistics after the beach-head had been secured. The invasion came off rather badly. We lost a lot of men, and I wondered about Lucky.

In September, we invaded Italy—the Allies first thrust back onto the continental mainland. Again I was fortunate. I was assigned duty in Salerno, while the main force moved inland.

London was Edenic compared to Salerno. There's nothing quite like war to turn a man's thoughts heavenward and at the same time disrobe him of his basic decency. Wine and women were for the asking, as men tried desperately to take full sips of the cup they called life lest death greet them on the morrow. I couldn't give Vaneta details, because of tight censorship, but she caught the implications of my letters, for she repeatedly wrote, "I love you, Jerry. I trust you. I'm waiting for you to return."

June 6, 1944, the Normandy invasion occurred. While in England, I had presumed I would be part of such an invasion. Instead, the 7th Army regrouped, now under General Patch, and on August fifteenth, following D-day, I stormed ashore in southern France.

Ten days later, Paris was liberated. But in those ten days, I was to see the raw and blooded hand of war.

We moved quickly, one hundred and forty miles in eight days, but at times we met stiff Nazi resistance, when men fell all around me. I stepped over their bodies. I heard them cry in pain behind me. It was incredible that I should be unscathed.

One day, as we mopped up scattered resistance in a French village, I stood outside a small restaurant. Something struck my back.

"God!" I cried aloud. It was not profanity. I thought I had been hit by some kind of armament.

"It's me, you ol' devil, you!" a voice rang out.

I turned.

"Lucky!" I exclaimed.

We embraced, pounding each other on the back, as, with eloquent blasphemy, Lucky expressed his joy at our reunion.

"I thought the Krauts must've got you for sure," he said.

It showed in his eyes how much I had come to mean to him. I was surprised and honored.

"I've had some pretty nervous moments wondering about you," I said.

"You have for sure?" he asked.

"For sure."

"Well, ain't that somethin'—anybody givin' a honk what's come of me? Where all you been?"

I told him.

"I wished you luck many's the time," he said, excited at the fruition of his benevolent hexing. "Man, I've had mine. Remember that fat kid in Quartermaster?"

"Johnson?"

"Yeah, well, he got clobbered down there on that Sicily deal, so I put in for his job an' I got it." Lucky grinned and held up crossed fingers. "My captain raised hob so I got put back again, but it was after the worst of it. Remember Sykes an' Juniper an' guys like Bemis an' Spellman? They got wiped out, just about the whole bunch of 'em, while I was ducked out on the Quartermaster deal. Remember that scared kid, that real little guy? Forget his name. Got his leg shot off. But not me, not ol' Lucky!"

138

"How about that?"

"Your woman still writes to you?" he asked.

"Letters get better every time," I said.

"She must be one of the rare ones. I should meet her. Maybe I could sneak her away from you."

"Not a chance."

"Wanna lay money to that?" he challenged.

"You'd lose."

"Hey, you got her picture? You never showed me."

I took out my wallet, handed it to Lucky, who studied Vaneta's photograph closely. The leer that had been in his eyes dwindled away.

"Man," he said, thrusting the wallet back to me, "you c'n have 'er."

I bristled for a moment, but Lucky was several sizes bigger than me, so I held my peace.

"How far down the road are you with that babe?" he asked.

"I plan to marry her."

"How's she sample?"

"What do you mean?"

"What do I mean?" Lucky laughed and whacked me across the shoulder so hard I nearly fell forward. "Buddy, tell me true. Did you chicken from them gals at Piccadilly because you was true to this blossom in your billfold or because you ain't got no fizz in your tank?"

"Come off it!" I bristled.

Lucky studied me closely. "You for real on this?" he asked. "Look, all I wanna do is be your friend. If you got cool britches, that's your business, an' so we let it go at that. But I figure you're as human as I am, buddy, an' so I gotta talk to you like a friend. I know women. I know their types. I can tell you in half a minute if a girl's easy or difficult or impossible. This chick you say you're holdin' the flame for, this babe . . ."

He shook his head.

"What's wrong?"

"She's bad business, Jerry. Believe me, pal."

"She's a wonderful person!"

"Yeah, like to knit an' crochet, an' patch your pants, an' maybe cookin', but she's bad news otherwise." He thought a moment, then shrugged. "I guess maybe you ain't so dumb as I first figgered. Sure, marry the girl. You got yourself a good cook an' housekeeper.

But when you want some livin', friend, be sure you got a list of phone numbers you c'n depend on."

It was incredible, the crass humanity of this basically wonderful person.

"Hey," he continued, "I didn't tell you the rest of what happened to me. After I got shoved back into the outfit, like I told you, I was sent out on patrol at Anzio. We run into a pocket of Nazis, an' they opened up on us. Couple of the guys got their numbers pulled. I was hit in the shoulder. Real nasty hole." He grinned. "It was my luck, huh?"

"Where'd they hospitalize you?"

"Salerno."

"You character! I was stationed there for months. I'd have come to see you."

We walked down a gutted street.

"Listen to them skies," said Lucky. There was no artillery fire, not so much as the drone of one plane. "Ain't it pretty?"

We entered a small inn, badly damaged by shell fire. The manager was there, a spunky little old man methodically clearing away the debris.

"Parlez-vous, mon ami?" Lucky bellowed. "Speak any English?"

"Only leetle bit," the man said, without bothering to look up.

"Then how about somethin' to drink an' a little food?"

The man stood. His eyes blazed. His lips trembled. He raised his arm angrily, stooped and picked up a slab of plaster fallen from the ceiling.

"Food!" he growled. He walked to our table, tossed the plaster on to it, muttered something in his own language, and disappeared.

"What's his problem?" Lucky picked up the plaster, broke off an edge, held it to his nose as one would do to food of uncertain substance. "He's a little down on his luck. He forgets the Luftwaffe cropped his roof instead of his head."

"He's old enough to have gone through all of this twenty years ago," I said. "These French've really been hit."

"Any minute you're alive around here," muttered a soldier who joined us, "you're up on your luck."

"Exactly!" Lucky exclaimed. He tossed the plaster over his shoulder. "That's me! Always up on my luck."

"Always?" the soldier asked.

"Since the day I was born. The doc thought I was dead. Shoved me off to a table on the side. My mother had a bad time of it so he

140

give his attention to her. Then one of the nurses thought she saw me move a little. The doctor checked. Sure enough. I had some heartbeat left. They went to work on me, an' before ma and me left the hospital, I could kick an' bawl as loud as the best of 'em.

"I fell out of a upstair's window when I was five. Should've busted my neck. But there was one bush—just this one on that whole side of the house—an' I fell head first into it. Only got a few scratches.

"Almost drowned another time. But I didn't. I was up on my luck. Had an uncle who drove a truck. Train hit 'im an' killed 'im that quick. I was supposed to have ridden with 'im that day but didn't.

"Then I had pneumonia right before all them fancy drugs they're comin' up with now. Doctor give me up three times. But my dice was rollin' seven come eleven, an' I made it."

"Do you wear a fetish or something?" I asked.

"A what?" He was a man of simple vocabulary.

"A good luck charm?"

"Nope. Don't believe in such things. You gotta think lucky. People who carry rabbits' feet and saints medals and things like that do it because they're scared. You can't be lucky when you're scared. Naw, you gotta think lucky."

He leveled his finger at me. "Now mind you, most people do play their luck when things are pretty normal for them. A guy back home drives his car. He knows people are gettin' killed on the roads every day. Maybe he takes a few chances. There's no cherry top in the rear view mirror, so he gooses it. What's to worry? He's pretty sure it ain't his day to get it.

"Same thing over here. We got a lot of boys countin' daisy roots. I ain't sayin' this is true with all of 'em. I've got enough to just look out for myself. But they were scared sick, a lot of them guys. They was expectin' to get shot up, an' so they did.

"You know somethin'?" he continued. "I d'know if you're the religious kind or not. It don't matter. But from what I've seen, the more religious somebody is, the more scared he is of bein' down on his luck. That's what makes people religious. They get scared. They want the Man up there to work all the angles in their favor.

"I'm no God-hater. I figure He's the One who fixes the odds. You can't blame Him for dealin' a bad hand for the guy that gets scared of his shadow the first time trouble turns up. That ain't me. Believe in your luck, an' it won't let y'down."

The very next morning, as we moved on, the ominous roll of artillery fire rose like thunder out of the distance.

"How about that?" Lucky wrinkled his forehead. "The Krauts must be kickin' up a little resistance."

"You know they won't back up all the way to Berlin," I said.

Whatever credence I may have placed in Lucky's claim to benign fortunes succumbed to circumstances the next afternoon. For, though resistance was crumbling all across southern France, we ran head on into a determined segment of the remnant German army.

"They're encircling us!" came the cry.

The sound of fire power heightened. The tempo of activity stepped up. Like trapped animals, we struck with our full force against the encircling walls. It was an inferno, the relentless din, the screams of men struck down, men dead and dying everywhere I looked.

A soldier came to me, an unlighted cigarette in his mouth, and asked for a match. I began to tell him I had none but never completed the statement. A shell burst nearby and a fragment shattered his skull. One moment he was alive, talking to me, the next moment a man with half a head falling like a thick rope to the ground.

That's the worst of war's hell. You are always dying. You breathe deep. You grit your teeth. You run your fingers across your head, across your heart. You could live another sixty years back home, but you're potentially dead here. All that has to happen is for somebody to aim at you instead of at the next guy and the "black angel pulls your time card," as the guys sometimes put it. It happens fast. It happens mercilessly. It happens all the time. At any moment, it could happen to you. There is never a moment when you can be absolutely sure.

Even Lucky found it so.

We were assigned to take a hill. We thought we could take it by surprise. We miscalculated. The enemy let us get almost to the top and then opened fire. We were shot down like rabbits in an open meadow. I was hit in the shoulder. Lucky got it in the chest. He fell into my path.

I crawled into a small ravine. Using my good arm, I pulled Lucky with me.

"Medics," he moaned. "Call 'em. Call the medics."

He cursed violently.

"We're trapped," I told him. "Nobody can get near this hill until we get some artillery or air back-up."

"I'll die, if I don't get a medic." He put his hand to his chest.

He took it away. It was red wet.

We lay there for awhile.

"Take a look," he whispered, weaker than before. "I'll make it if they can stop this bleeding. Get me back to a doctor."

I looked.

"There's nobody," I said.

"Then I'll die," he repeated. He was no longer the confident, relaxed Lucky. He was scared.

I opened his shirt. It was a nasty wound, inches off from his heart and bleeding badly. I ripped my own shirt, laid a wad across his wound in an effort to stop the blood. The wound quickly drenched the cloth. The flow of blood continued.

"I'm down on my luck, man," he whispered.

I didn't say anything. I didn't know what to say.

"Y'know how to pray, Jerry?"

"Not much." I said. "Sorry."

"Know anything about the Bible?"

"A little."

"Say some of it for me."

I raked my brain. It was numb. I could only think of one verse.

"Draw nigh unto God," I said, "and He will draw nigh unto you."

"That's from the Bible?"

"Word for word."

"Say it again."

"Draw nigh unto God, and He will draw nigh unto you."

"What does it mean?"

"I'm not sure."

Lucky looked up at me, eyes glistening with fear. I breathed a prayer. My mind went back to childhood Sunday nights at church.

"Gotta get some religion, Jerry." Lucky's voice seemed to weaken with each word. "Help me."

"The Bible tells us we're all sinners," I began.

Lucky looked up at me anxiously.

"It tells us God sent Jesus. He died on the cross. He died for our sins. Then He was resurrected. Our sins caused His death but couldn't hold Him in the grave. As I understand it, that's why He can forgive us."

"How do I get my sins forgiven?" Lucky gasped.

I thought hard, trying to remember.

"How?" he repeated weakly.

"I . . . I'm not sure."

His eyes opened. He looked at me. It was as though I had been the one who inflicted his mortal wound. Impulsively, I fumbled for my canteen and offered him a drink.

With his remnant strength he blew away the water as it came upon his lips.

"God," I prayed, "this guy's going to hell, if I don't help him."

Suddenly, I thought of John 3:16.

"For God so loved the world," I began.

Lucky closed his eyes.

"Hey, man!" I called out.

"Read the rest of it," he mumbled.

"For God so loved the world, that He gave His only begotten son." I knew the verse as well as I knew the name of my home town, but the words came hard to my memory, like a blur, like something far away. "He gave His only begotten son," I continued, "that whosoever believeth in Him, should not perish but have everlasting life."

"How?" Lucky asked. His eyes remained closed. His strength was all but gone from him.

The din of battle increased, shells bursting so near us I could not speak, could not think.

Then, wth the coming of a lull, an idea came to me.

"Raise your hand, Lucky," I whispered.

He opened his eyes, closed them again.

"Just put up your hand," I whispered. "I'll see your hand, and God will see your heart."

He didn't move. His eyes remained closed.

"Put up your hand, Lucky," I repeated.

Slowly the dying soldier raised his hand. His eyes opened. They searched the sky for one moment, then became like orbs, remaining open, as his arm fell limp upon his chest.

Chapter Sixteen

No man, who participated in the great carnival of death, can ever be the same again.

I, who loved and respected life, had killed and watched men die, subsisting by those Machiavellian values which deem the individual meaningless. Virtue lay with the man smart enough to out-think his opponent, the man with the quickest draw, the surest aim— the man deft at parrying another's thrust so he can bury his own bayonet deep into the bowels of his adversary. If war has any glory, it is in that most sodden of all hypocrisies whereby men unleash their Adamic motivations and win the hero's laurel for desecrating the noblest intentions of the Creator.

You join the battle. You spare yourself by slaughtering others. You hate. You curse, You see other men as pigs. You forget they have mothers, wives, children. What does it matter if some of them be artists, musicians, craftsmen, teachers? They are devils now, and it is virtue to destroy them.

And when the battle's ended, when the smoke clears and your flag unfurls above the conquered land, it is shame to have not killed, it is glory to have shattered skulls and disemboweled, to have left a baby fatherless, to have broken a mother's heart.

Glory! Glory! Glory!

I do not say the soldier is a lesser human. Some of the best fighting men I met hated war. They didn't want to kill. But most everyone, as did I, fell into the awesome mentality of the soldier at the height of battle. It takes its pound of flesh, war does.

I'm sure there have been just causes worthy of men's lives. Doubtless there will be again. But if more politicians had sons the age of soldiers, and if it could be ordained that, in any war, each politician's son would be the first to die, arbitration would take the place of armaments and spare the shedding of blood on many a battlefield.

When the war is ended, when the victory cheers have died away, the bands stop playing and you want to forget. You don't talk about the battles. You never share the gore of it. You bury it inside you. There it stays, festering, to haunt your dreams at night, to imminently remind you that you know how to hate and kill and ignore the sacredness of life. You can never again identify fully with the beauty of sound and sight and feeling. You will always be somewhat blind and deaf, a man living and a man dead.

Perhaps then, in the fullest sense, the texture of my marriage to Vaneta falls as much to my responsibility as to hers.

As the end of the war in Europe grew near, I wrote frequently about setting a wedding date. Occasionally, she reacted. Often, she made no mention. Never did she express the kind of enthusiasm I wanted to hear. She wrote good letters. She obviously held me in deep affection. Yet, even when she used the pen, her aloofness was made manifest.

It irritated me.

I remained in France until VJ day, but shortly thereafter I boarded a ship for New York and the mustering out process.

It took the sight of Vaneta to convince me the war had actually ended, and that it was no dream, my coming home. She came alone to meet me, and those first hours together, just the two of us, were profoundly endearing. "I love you, Jerry," she whispered, uttering the words as her lips searched mine. "I've missed you so much."

"Got a date for the wedding?" I asked.

She snuggled her forehead beneath my chin. "Let's not talk about that now," she said. "Let's just be together."

We drove to her home.

"Good to see you, Jerry!" her father greeted. Uncle Rufus himself had never welcomed me more warmly.

Her mother kissed me, and tears came to her eyes, as she said, "We've prayed for your safety."

"My parents have been so concerned about you," Vaneta told

146

me, as we walked along the grove bordering the farmstead. "They both admire you very much."

"I appreciate that," I said.

We strolled quietly for a few moments.

Then I asked, "When can we plan the wedding?"

"We will need to make plans," she said.

"Soon."

"I've signed a contract for teaching and . . ."

"Teaching?" I broke in. "Forget about teaching."

"But I've signed a contract."

"Break it."

"Well . . ."

My temper flared. I stepped away from her. "You haven't changed your mind about me, have you?"

She didn't answer. I turned her briskly toward me.

"Jerry!" she complained.

"Have you changed your mind?"

She remained quiet.

"Tell me!"

"Didn't you read my letters? Didn't they tell you how I feel about you—only you?"

I apologized, but the damage was done. We were soon amiable to each other, but not as we had been in the first rapture of reunion. Neither of us spoke further about a wedding. It was painful. I had moments when I would have terminated our relationship. But Vaneta was schizo-romantic and the moment my own confidence waned was invariably the moment she would be the warmest to me.

On Sunday, Vaneta's mother convened Logan relatives for a sumptuous dinner. It was the first time I had met all of them. I was obviously on display, but didn't mind. They were impressive, charming people.

"What'll you be doing?" Pierce Roberts asked.

"I've hardly given it a thought," I replied. "A guy gets so all that really interests him is to get home. I suppose I should be worrying about a job. With the war over and so many coming back, I suppose work may be a little scarce."

"That I doubt," Pierce said, "at least for a long time. Consumer commodities'll be in scarce supply for a long time. At Harvest Craft we look for the biggest boom in the history of farm machinery. Which leads me to something that may interest you. I talked with one of the men from Dennis Wilding Manufacturing in your town.

147

I guess this Vamp character has about frozen Dennis right out of the plant. There's no love in your town for Vamp, as I hear it. Anyway, rumor has it Vamp wants to hire you."

"He does?"

"Figures you owe it to him on account of the scholarship deal."

"Then I won't work for him."

"I wouldn't say that, Jerry. You strike me as the makings of a real good businessman. I think Vamp needs somebody like you— needs you and knows it. Somebody the town'll have a lot of respect for, and still be somebody that can throw his own weight in the business."

"So what should I do?"

"Play it cagey, that's my advice. Vamp'll likely give you a big song and dance about what a break it is for you to work for him. He won't mention the scholarship, probably, unless you hedge. Well, don't hedge. Just think a move ahead of him. Act real interested. Show appreciation. But make sure you get a good description of the job and the potential. Get it in writing."

I appreciated the advice. At that moment I thought of Pierce Roberts as the light I'd look to again and again, as I sought to carve my niche on a few rungs of the business success ladder.

I returned to a hero's welcome. The band played. The Superintendent of Schools and the Mayor gave short speeches. And it was Halford Vamp who gave each of the returnees—there were several of us—a certificate of honor from the city but which he had had printed.

"Good to have you back, Jerry!" he exuded. "Sure hope this town can hold you. We need young blood like yours."

"I've prayed for you every day," Aunt Lydia said.

She had grown older. So had Uncle Rufus.

"I appreciate your prayers," I told her.

"But you're still not converted?"

I smiled but didn't answer.

The second morning after my return home I received a telephone call from Halford Vamp.

"We need a young executive with a good business head," Mr. Vamp said. "You'd work right under me, Jerry, and move into our organization on one of the top rungs of the ladder. How about being my guest for dinner tonight? Come over to our house where we can talk about it."

Hillary met me at the door. My heart missed a beat.

"Jerry," she exclaimed. "I haven't seen you in years. Come in. I'm dying to talk to you." I stumbled inside, unable to keep my eyes off the woman. She was vivacious and alluring, with the same iniquituous glint in her eye. I felt a compelling urge to draw her into my arms.

She took my coat. It was like watching a performance, the subtle rhythm of her movements. She hung the coat and came to me.

"I don't suppose you've thought about me since we graduated from high school," she said.

"You and your husband are back for a visit?" I asked awkwardly.

"No husband," she said, tossing her shoulders.

I stared at her, not knowing what I should say. I knew she had married her first year out of high school.

"He was overseas?" I asked, supposing him to be one of those who didn't make it.

She shook her head. "His father had an in of some kind. Kept getting him deferred."

"Oh."

"We were divorced two years ago."

She brushed some lint from my lapel. The touch of her hand quickened my pulse.

"I'm the kind that's slow to learn." She sighed. "I married a playboy. I should have used my head and chosen someone solid and dependable."

A touch of pathos came to her face. Her eyes searched mine.

Neither of us spoke.

After a moment, she touched my arm and said, "I believe dinner is ready. Let's go to the table."

Her father dominated the mealtime conversation. He was a profane man, even in the presence of his wife and daughter, and he gave me a nutshell autobiography. Chief among his accomplishments had been the securing of majority stock in the Wilding corporation and building it to thrice its size during the war.

"Now I'm looking for someone I can develop into the organization," he said. He glanced at Hillary, then back to me. "Dennis just isn't the businessman type. He knows that. Frankly, I think he'd like to get out of the company entirely. I've got a lot of spark left, but even I won't last forever. I need to be thinking about new blood, young blood. My own boy is still just a kid."

There was no evidence of Pierce's warning that Mr. Vamp would be trying to take advantage of me. I was puzzled about this.

"You're probably thinking about getting away from the old home town," Hillary said.

Her father gave me no opportunity to reply.

"Why should he leave here?" There's going to be a lot of lay-offs around the country, with war plants closing down. But we're going to grow here. We've already switched mostly to civilian contracts. I'm working on Harvest Craft. If we ever land those boys . . ."

"An acquaintance of mine sells for HC," I said.

"That so?"

"His name's Pierce Roberts. He works out of . . ."

"Sure, I know Roberts. Don't know that he can do us too much good, but then I'm sure he can't do us any harm. How do you happen to know him?"

"He, uh . . ." I glanced at Hillary. My cheeks reddened.

"It doesn't matter. Look, Jerry, I'm offering you a job that a man might take twenty years working up to no matter how many college degrees he had. Are you interested?"

"Yes, of course," I said, glancing at Hillary.

"You can get married, settled down, and have yourself a good thing in this community."

Hillary studied me closely, intent to know my reaction to her father's words. It came to me, unbelievingly but without question, that they had multiple designs upon my future. It was a good discovery, for in that moment, in precisely how it came about I cannot say, I knew I loved Vaneta. But I also remembered Pierce Robert's advice.

"What say?" Mr. Vamp primed.

"I'm grateful for your offer," I said, "and I'll sure think about it."

"Think about it?" He nearly lunged from his chair. "You understand the kind of offer I'm making, don't you?"

"I appreciate it," I said. It was difficult to appear poised.

"Daddy, don't shout," Hillary interceded. "Jerry just got out of a nasty war. He needs time to adjust his thinking."

Mr. Vamp grumbled something, then resumed eating. Hillary and I made small talk for awhile, about school, about all she had done in the past years, with the exception of her marriage. This she never mentioned.

"You had a girl friend on campus, didn't you?" Hillary asked.

I nodded.

Her countenance fell. She looked at her father and mother. Mr. Vamp cleared his throat and fixed his gaze upon me.

150

"You have a wedding date planned?" he asked awkwardly.

"There's no wedding date," I blurted.

A look of relief came to Hillary's face and to the faces of her parents, and I felt a pang of guilt. I felt I should tell them how it was with Vaneta and me, since this seemed of such obvious importance. But I was a soldier now. It had been kill or be killed, not live and let live. Perhaps the battle for all of life would be this way. That certainly seemed the case in dealing with Halford Vamp.

"Shall I drop by your office in a day or so?" I asked him, as the meal concluded.

"Why, uh, yes, Jerry. That'd be fine."

"Maybe you could draw up a letter for me—a presentation of just what you have in mind."

"Sure, sure," he said. He winked at his daughter. "Y'know, Hillary, this fellow strikes me as a crackerjack of a business man."

Hillary smiled and there was wonderment in her eyes, as they attempted to search deeply into my own.

By week's end I had in my possession a written job offer, signed by Halford Vamp, and added to in several areas by his own hand where I requested additional considerations.

"Jeremiah," Aunt Lydia reacted, when she learned of my new position, "you have no business being associated with that ungodly Halford Vamp."

"But it's only a job in Wilding's company," Uncle Rufus said.

"Does Mr. Vamp hire any of the people from our church?"

"A few."

"For what kind of jobs?" Aunt Lydia continued, promptly replying to her own inquiry. "They work in the factory part. Halford Vamp will see to it poor little Jeremiah never does get converted. He won't have a born again Christian in a prominent position. You mark my words."

The following weekend I went back to see Vaneta.

"I'm sorry I was a little rough," I said "about the wedding date."

"It was my fault, too," she told me. "And I've been thinking about the wedding. I need a little time to get ready. How about early February? That will give my school time to find a replacement for the second semester."

She melted into my arms.

That night I told her about Hillary.

"I don't care about her," I said, "But I'm sure she and her dad have plans in mind. Shall I refuse the job?"

151

"Take the job," she said, "if it's the kind of work you want. I trust you completely."

On Monday, I began work as administrative assistant to Halford Vamp.

I proceeded cautiously. For the first two weeks, I concentrated on learning the business, stationing myself in various areas about the plant. Halford Vamp was a genius in many ways, but he lacked perspective in basic organizational procedures, and I was able to suggest changes which both pleased him and benefited the organization.

For two months, I did not mention my marital plans to anyone, not even to my parents or Aunt Lydia. I wanted nothing to disrupt my efforts to establish myself in Mr. Vamp's firm, so much so that I foolishly offered little resistance to those manipulations of his which brought me into encounters with his daughter.

The most ingenious of these devices occurred one morning when Mr. Vamp called me into his office.

"You're doing a whale of a job, Jerry," he said.

I thanked him.

"You've exceeded my expectations. Far exceeded them, frankly. You may have noticed there's an empty office next to mine here where we've kept some of our accounting equipment. I had all that taken out yesterday and a new desk and chair moved in. Other embellishments can be added later. The office is yours, Jerry."

"Mine?" I'm sure my ego flaunted into full view. "Well, thank you, sir."

"You not only have an office," he said, taking my arm, "but your own private secretary. Come on. Let's have a look."

As we stepped out into the corridor leaving his office, I could see into the door of mine. There was an impressive new desk. There was a high back chair.

He entered ahead of me.

It was not until I stepped inside that I saw my new private secretary.

Hillary Vamp!

I told Vaneta the following weekend.

"If she's a good secretary, what's the difference?" was her reaction.

I did not detect the slightest variance in the confidence she had expressed in me. Instead, she wanted only to talk about wedding plans.

152

"I'm anxious to get information into the newspaper," I said. "I may not be the apple of every girl's eye around our town, but I'm still anxious to let it be officially known I'm unavailable."

Whereas Vaneta looked with candor at Hillary's proximity to my commercial responsibilities, Aunt Lydia reacted as might be anticipated.

"You've encouraged this, Jeremiah" she accused. "Shame on you. The Lord gives you a beautiful girl like Vaneta and you begin showing attention to a divorced woman."

"I dictate letters to her," I defended. "I treat her the same as any other woman who might be my secretary."

"A likely story!"

"It's true."

"Does Vaneta know about this?"

"Why don't you write and ask her?"

Aunt Lydia wrote. She would have done so without my suggestion. Vaneta's reply must have convinced her, for she did not again breach the subject. Then, too, Vaneta and I decided upon a nuptial date and I promptly supplied the information to our local newspaper. It appeared on Thursday.

When I came to work Friday morning, Hillary was in her father's office. I went to mine, expecting her to come in with the morning's work, as was the custom, but she didn't come in until ten o'clock.

"My father wants to see you," she said curtly.

My heart sank.

"Close the door," Mr. Vamp snapped, as I entered. He did not look up from some letters he was signing.

I did as he told me.

He left me standing there, as he finished the letters. I expected the worst.

"Well, Jerry," he said at last, looking up, "you surprised us by this announcement in the paper."

"Surprised you?" I asked innocently. "Why?"

"I didn't know you had a girl picked out."

"I've had her picked out since I was in college," I said, bravely adding, "I didn't think it had anything to do with my job."

He was taken off guard by this.

"You were right, of course." He turned his chair to the side and sat for a moment looking out the window. Without turning back, he continued, "Perhaps you don't realize that my daughter has admired you for many years."

I made no comment. He stood, came around to the front of his desk, and sat on the edge looking up at me. "To be real honest with you, Jerry, it's a good thing I didn't know about this girl friend business. I probably wouldn't have hired you. But you're proving to be a valuable man—a good deal more valuable than I thought."

"I'm glad to hear that," I said.

He studied his hands for a moment.

"We, uh," he searched for words, still studying his hands, "my daughter . . . Hillary . . . well, the announcement of your coming marriage is quite a shock to her. She . . . just this morning . . . she asked to be relieved of any responsibility here at the organization."

Vaneta and I were married the tenth of February.

"God has given you a wonderful bride, Jeremiah," Aunt Lydia said with uncharacteristic tenderness. She wept profusely at the wedding. "Make it a Christian home. Let the Lord come in right from the start."

I wanted to take her advice. Though the years of carnage had to a degree seared my emotions, I looked upon marriage as totally sacred and wanted my relationship with Vaneta to find its highest meaning.

We had a good honeymoon. It did not fulfill the visions of my earlier years. But there was warmth between us, an affinity of abiding proportions.

"I want to be a good wife for you," Vaneta said winsomely. "It will take time for us to adjust to each other, but I'll do my very best. I promise."

Perhaps we could have achieved an early profoundness in our relationship. We were amiable. We enjoyed being together. But marriage is an art, perhaps the finest of the arts, and fulfillment can only be achieved under proper conditions.

It disturbed me that I should experience qualms concerning our union, that I should wonder if I had settled for less than my connubial lot might have been. It was not that I held a candle in my heart for Hillary. I would surely have been much less happy had I married her. As I said before, the war took its toll on my emotions. Having seen life in its most sordid hues, I suppose, I should not have anticipated extremes of beauty and endearment. I certainly should have known Vaneta's innate serenity would make for what one might kindly call domestic tranquility.

That described it—domestic tranquility.

When I was of romantic inclinations, she complied. But she

154

seemed as contented, indeed more so, if I simply came home from work, partook of the fine cuisine she always prepared, and then settled myself comfortably in the living room to relax or read.

I could not avoid thinking back to childhood, when I amused myself observing how quickly chivalry and gallantry gave way to marital norms among couples in our church.

"She's a good girl," Pierce Roberts observed one weekend, when we motored downstate for a family affair. "A lot like my wife in many ways, I suppose, but maybe a little different in others." Though he had not posed it as a question, there was obvious inquiry in the conclusion of his remark.

When I offered no comment, he said, "They're real great people, these Logans. The girls have been raised a little straight-laced, but over the long pull, that's a lot better than having a wife you can't trust. Me, I'm gone so much, but Winona's as dependable as the courthouse clock."

Accustomed to a more active life, Vaneta grew restless, and the following autumn she took a position instructing home economics in our local high school. On the other hand, the demands of my employment required the most stringent regimentation of my time and energy. Mr. Vamp, rebuffed to his effort to arrange a substantial suitor for his impulsive daughter, demanded quantity and quality in my every performance. I rarely disappointed him. On more than one occasion I surprised even myself at the facility with which I carried out his orders. But keeping a firm grip on the demands of my job took more and more of my time, even to the extent of preoccupation during the few hours of the week when Vaneta and I were together.

She never mentioned it. She never complained. We both seemed to accept the fact that most marriages were this way. Why should ours be different?

To my unvoiced dismay, Vaneta became the apple of Aunt Lydia's eye. Where I had failed to meet my aunt's qualifications for excellence, my wife excelled. I had enough respect for Vaneta not to believe she permitted overt instruction in the theocratic manner, nevertheless, I began to detect noticeable Aunt Lydiaisms in my wife's household attitudes.

I could have overlooked the situation. The circumstances of my employment offered numerous opportunities for authoritarian involvement. But I was determined not to settle for a role similar to what had been imposed upon my Uncle Rufus. So we had a few quarrels. I prefer not to enlarge upon them. They were small, my reaction to a trivial purchase, my refusal to go along with some suggestion for household improvement. There were evidences that she tried to comply with my right of domestic leadership.

She became active in church affairs, and in this I could offer no protest. I attended Sunday mornings, but neither had nor sought so much as a whisper of influence in religious matters. I suppose I was more proud than disturbed that she became one of the most prominent young mesdames in the congregation, called upon to plan menus, special decorations, and to supervise outstanding church events.

As the months passed and I became more and more involved with my work, I grew less and less concerned about her handling of our household details. She made decisions relating to maintenance. She looked after all provisionary shopping. When I fell behind on payment of obligations, because of my stringent work schedule, she took over the checkbook. She was a multi-dimensional woman. She had a mind of her own and could have handily managed a life of her own.

One afternoon, returning from the plant, I discovered workmen in the process of replacing the roofing on our house. I was tired, edgy.

"Vaneta!" I stormed, as I entered our dwelling. "Do you want me to call those men down from the roof or are you going to do it?"

At first, she appeared startled, hurt.

"What's going on up there?" I demanded.

"They're fixing the roof," she said, her eyes flashing.

"It's something we discussed?"

"It needs fixing!"

"I said, is it something we discussed?"

She glared at me. Her lips quivered. She was as angry as I have ever known her to be. I stalked toward the door.

"What're you going to do?" she demanded.

"Order those men off the roof."

She hurried ahead of me and challenged my further progress.

"Step aside," I said, trying to be more reposed.

"You want to make fools of both of us?"

"You've already made a fool out of me," I said, "so it might as well be both of us."

I tried to push her aside. She struggled to forbid me.

"Perhaps you forget," she snapped, "that my earnings also go into our checking account. Is there any reason why I can't fix the roof out of my income?"

I didn't call the men off the roof. It needed repair, and I should have attended to it. In the several weeks following, I became so engrossed in my responsibilities that I was relieved to see Vaneta reassume the making of decisions I had denied to her in our quarrel.

I began to make frequent out-of-town trips on behalf of our company. In the summer when Vaneta was not involved at school, she sometimes accompanied me. For the most part, however, she preferred to remain at home.

Sometimes I traveled with Mr. Vamp, as, for example, the autumn when we went to a toolmaker's convention in Chicago.

"I want you to go a couple of days early," Mr. Vamp said. "Make a few client calls for me. Then we'll meet you in Chicago."

"Some of the other men are going?" I asked.

"No," he said, as though not understanding the reason for my question.

When I checked into the hotel in Chicago, I understood the plurality of his previous statement. His wife and Hillary were with him.

Deftly—though I confess I did not make myself as unavailable as I should have—Hillary arranged for us to be together, usually just the two of us.

"Vaneta seems like quite an exceptional person," she said one evening, as we had dinner in the hotel dining room. "I don't see her often. I suppose we aren't in the same circles."

"Her school responsibilities keep her busy," I said.

"School and church," Hillary corrected. When I nodded, she continued, "She doesn't seem the type for your church."

"You don't think so?"

"Do you?"

"I guess not."

"What are your attitudes toward the church?"

"I attend."

"I guess the place has simmered down some. A few years ago it almost had the reputation of being Holy Roller."

I shrugged my shoulders.

She lit a cigarette. It was the first time I had seen her smoke. I didn't like it. In my eyes, smoking was unbecoming to a woman.

"You won't mind my being terribly frank, will you?" she asked.

"Go ahead." My curiosity rose.

"Around town, people notice that you and Vaneta probably wouldn't win honors as the happiest couple in the community."

157

I lowered my eyes.

"Isn't it true?"

I looked up to her again but didn't speak.

"Hate me if you must, Jerry, but I'm crazy about you. I know I have the reputation for being the kind of person who apparently doesn't appeal to you. But I could change. Is there any chance of your getting your freedom from Vaneta and at least considering me?"

I was speechless.

"I'm being terribly forward," she said at last, "but I can't help myself. I made a terrible fool of myself with my first marriage. It looks like you've made your mistakes, too, though maybe a lot less seriously than I did. I want a good life, Jerry. So do you. So please don't hate me for what I've said. I can't help myself. Believe me, Jerry, I know what it could be like for you and me. I really do."

I lost my head. While my Puritanical background once again forbade indulgence in the ultimate option of such clandestine affairs, those next three days and nights in Chicago, spent mostly with Hillary, caused me to look with new perspective at my marriage.

We saw little of the convention. I accompanied her shopping. We went sightseeing, to the theater.

"Your dad'll fire me," I said late one evening, as we walked toward the hotel."

"He does, and he'll have me to deal with," Hillary assured me. "Don't you worry. He loves you like his own son."

As we entered the lobby, she startled me by suggesting I come to her room.

"I'm sorry," I said. The words came as though by impulse. "I can't."

"Marriage must be like a prison sentence to you," she sighed.

"It isn't something I can take lightly," I admitted.

"Nor do I!" She put her hand on my arm. "I want you, Jerry! I won't give up 'til I get you."

She turned and walked briskly to the elevator.

I went outside. I walked the streets for an hour or more—both disgusted at myself for not yielding to her persuasiveness and at the same time grateful that I had not in totality betrayed my vows to Vaneta.

Returning to the hotel I went to the newsstand for an early morning paper. Sleep was my farthest inclination. I had just made the purchase when a hand rested upon my shoulders. It was Pierce Rob-

158

erts. I was so taken off guard by the sight of him, I could not collect my thoughts for a moment.

"Haven't seen you around," I said at last. "I should have known you'd be at this kind of convention."

"I haven't noticed you in any of the sessions," he said. "I did see your boss at the dinner this noon." There was a searchingness in his eyes. I turned from them.

"You, uh, you seen me around before now?" I asked.

"How's Vaneta?" he said.

"Vaneta?"

"Your wife."

He looked up at me from having casually observed the headlines on a stack of morning papers. My cheeks reddened.

"She's fine," I managed to say.

He yawned.

"Maybe we can have breakfast together," I suggested.

"I've got a customer for breakfast."

"Some other time."

"I leave on a noon train."

I cleared my throat nervously.

"Give Vaneta my love," he said and turned abruptly to head toward the elevator.

I left a note in Mr. Vamp's box and caught an early train the next morning. My mind was in turmoil throughout the homeward journey. Was this to be the sum of my life? Would I always live in a beclouded world? Conventioneers disgusted me with their shallowness. But might it not be the thorough worldling found more of reality in his libertine philosophy than I could ever hope for in my straddling of the path of anticipated vice and aspired virtue?

I was at ill sorts with myself when I arrived home late that evening. My wife came to the door at the first sound of my arrival.

"I have wonderful news!" she told me.

She moved warmly into my arms. "What's the news?" I asked.

"I won't be teaching next semester."

"Why?"

"Silly," she said, nestling her head on my shoulders. "We're going to have our first baby."

She looked up at me again. I felt dirty and cheap. I saw my wife as a creature both pure and wonderful.

"I love you, Vaneta," I whispered.

"I love you, Jerry."

Chapter Seventeen

I suffered silent castigation of conscience those next weeks, somewhat assuaged by reminding myself I was only guilty in God's sight of vicarious consortment with Hillary.

Vaneta became my most prized possession. True, ours might not be a marriage with deep emotional embellishments. It may have lacked in that rare welding of two personalities which seems to characterize some unions. Perhaps so. But our love was creative. The body of this dear one I had taken to wife now nurtured a child I had sired.

I brought Vaneta gifts. We went for rides along the river road, more commonly known as lover's lane, parking beneath the vast overhang of an ancient cottonwood, and made plans for the new life we would soon bring forth.

"Let's keep our marriage this way," I said one evening, as we sat along the water. "A marriage doesn't need to go to weeds."

"Do you think ours has?" she moved away from me slightly.

"I didn't say it has," I replied. "I only said it doesn't need to."

"But it isn't always the way you would like?" she probed.

"Not always," I admitted. "I'm sure that's as much my fault as yours."

"What bothers you?" she asked, settling close to me again.

"Sometimes we don't seem very close to each other."

"Isn't that normal?"

"Is it?"

"We can't expect to be emotional toward each other all the time."

"But we could have warmth all the time."

She moved completely away from me.

"Can't we?" I asked.

"Don't we?" she countered. For the first time, I saw a question in her eyes. "I assume you are implying that I am only partially satisfactory to you as a wife."

"I didn't say that."

"I didn't say you did," she snapped. "I used the word imply."

"Please, Vaneta. . ."

I reached to draw her to me. She restrained my hand.

"Do you have other interests?"

I looked away.

"Jerry! Tell me!"

"I have never touched any woman but you. I never will."

We sat, silently watching the water.

"We're being silly," she said, after a moment.

"I'm sorry," I said.

I could see she believed my denial of unfaithfulness. I was greatly relieved.

"If we had an incompatible marriage, Jerry, you'd have some grounds for complaint."

"I don't mean to complain."

"You should hear some of the married teachers at school. The trend these days seems to be to talk openly about one's personal life. It's something I never do, and I hope I can expect the same of you. But I do hear these girls talk. They think of their husbands as . . . as something to be tolerated."

"I appreciate you, Vaneta."

"And you've been awfully nice lately. I'll try to be worthy of it, Jerry."

In all our marriage, we had never spoken more openly to each other. It was good. We became more communicative, more considerate of one another. Vaneta had the poise and qualities of enduring greatness. We could build a good marriage.

Let me now take some moments to assess the situation at our church, as a prologue to a series of significant occurrences.

During the last of the war years, Adelia became critically demented, necessitating her committal to an institution where she expired. Aunt Lydia remained vociferously extant, the unofficial chairman of every committee, but she rarely made any attempt whatever to negotiate the salvation of my soul, having, I suppose, relegated me to the ranks of the hopelessly lost, and having largely transferred her kindred affections from me to Vaneta.

I regularly attended church, out of habit for the most part but also in deference to my relatives. Vaneta taught a Sunday school class. She sang in the choir. She was the youngest woman ever to be elected chairman of the Dorcas Society, a woman's organization devoted to monthly meetings which consisted of thirty minutes of sewing for the poor and a considerably longer period of sipping coffee and circulating the latest gossip.

The anticipation of a vital faith ebbed in my heart.

I do not wish to be critical of clergymen. Specialists in prophylaxys and therapy are as necessary for the spirit as for the body. In the case of our church, however, we were asked to endure the declining efforts of a man who, at least in my opinion, had never been one of God's stronger exponents.

He had served our church since prior to Uncle Eliad's episode with the rook card.

In our small denomination, only a handful of congregations could be classified as top rungs on the conventicle ladder—being limited to those pastorates in the city and those which, though rural, enjoyed substantial membership, ours falling into the second category.

It seems our pastor never received a call from a city church, nor from a sufficiently prominent rural constituency, and so he remained with us.

By virtue of that hypocrisy which at times characterizes churchmen, he was never openly told to leave. But the mood of the congregation was unmistakable. Even Aunt Lydia privately admitted she was praying for the Lord to lead him elsewhere—either in a vertical or perpendicular direction.

He grew irritable. He castigated his hearers in every sermon. God's hand had moved mightily in the earlier days of his ministry, he declared, but now was stayed. Blame lay solely in the worldliness of the membership.

His memory began to fail. He often repeated the same illustration in a sermon. One Sunday morning he actually preached the identical discourse he had offered the week before.

Yet, so long as he received no call elsewhere, the membership could do nothing about securing a new minister. Discontent spread through the congregation. Attendance dwindled. I never attended

Sunday evenings but was told he had barely a dozen hearers one summer's Sunday night, mostly members of the Pew family.

"I wouldn't criticize our minister for the world," Aunt Lydia said one Sunday afternoon. "He has served our church well for many years. But it beats all he don't have sense enough to quit."

"Where would he go?" Aunt Britta asked.

"That's his responsibility," said Aunt Lydia.

"Preachers are just like the rest of us," added Aunt Britta. "They like to know where the next meal's coming from."

"The problem we face," said Uncle Eliad, "is that our churches don't have a retirement program like the bigger denominations do."

"It's just the modernistic denominations that do that," Aunt Lydia said. "If a preacher don't see he has God to supply his needs, then how's he to give us faith?" As an afterthought, she added, "He could at least get a job selling Bibles."

"What do you think, Rufus?" Uncle Eliad asked.

"We've got a good-sized church. . ." Uncle Rufus began.

"When they come," Aunt Lydia interupted.

As though he had not heard his wife, Uncle Rufus continued, ". . . blessed with more than enough means to retire our pastor."

"Say now," said Uncle Eliad, "there's an idea."

"What sense would that make?" asked Aunt Lydia.

"Remember that missionary speaker we had?" Aunt Britta put in. "He said in the Philippines somewhere all they need is ten families— all of them tithing—and they could have a pastor of their own. We must have fifty or sixty families."

"You mean we'd have to pay his living expenses the rest of his life?" Aunt Lydia asked. "I sure wouldn't be in favor of that, an' I don't s'pect a lot of the others would either."

"What would you be in favor of?" Uncle Rufus asked.

"Hasn't he saved any money?"

"You know yourself how prices have gone up since the end of rationing, and his salary certainly hasn't gone up accordingly."

Uncle Rufus could pose such questions because, as it turned out, this man of integrity had a plan. He told me about it the following week or I perhaps never would have known. To this day I question how many members of the church are aware of my uncle's spiritual philanthropy.

Our denomination sponsors a small home for the aged, by coincidence less than one hundred miles from our town. Uncle Rufus motored to the institution one day and suggested to the manager, himself a retired clergyman, that it might be wise to establish a chaplaincy. The manager, who had been responsible for both temporal and spiritual matters in the small institution, reacted most approvingly to the idea.

"The only problem," he said, "is our limited budget."

"Would you be willing to give the post to someone in exchange for room and board?" Uncle Rufus asked.

"To the right man, yes," the manager replied.

On the first Sunday of the following month our pastor read his letter of resignation, in that instant repossessing the lost love in the hearts of his hearers. Aunt Lydia wept when she met him at the door. So did others.

When the time came for him to leave, the Dorcas society sponsored a farewell supper, at which time such flowery eulogies were spoken as to render the occasion very nearly ridiculous in my eyes. The pastor was delighted to go, the congregation eager for his departure, but all expressed utmost regret over his leaving.

Once again, it was Uncle Rufus who salvaged the occasion.

"Life is like climbing a mountain," he said, highlighting his remarks. "It takes all of our energy to reach the top. Once we reach the top, we must start down the other side. We never pause in our travel. We keep moving all the time. It behooves each of us to ask the Lord to help us so that our descent into the valley on the other side of the mountain is as much a blessing to others as God intended climbing the mountain to be."

"Well," put in Aunt Lydia glowingly, "even if it was my own dear husband who said those beautiful words, I certainly want to go on record as thanking our pastor because this has been so true in his life. The only thing I would say is that his ministry is still so appreciated here it doesn't seem he's started into the valley yet. He's still climbing!"

She said more. But I didn't listen.

As was intended, our pastor's resignation necessitated the calling of another shepherd. To chronicle the events pertaining to that situation would require a volume of its own. Suffice it to say that at no time does a congregation so effectively project its fullest spectrum as when the time comes to call a new minister.

Once again Uncle Rufus proved to be the man of the hour. He had his sights on a young man in his early thirties by the name of Mallory, one in a crop of rising young pulpiteers whose accomplishments appeared frequently in the denominational weekly.

"We've got one of the oldest churches in the congregation," Aunt Lydia opposed. "So we should have an older man. Don't that make sense?"

"I agree with Rufus," Aunt Britta said. "We should call a man who'll give some fresh, young blood to the congregation."

"I could expect that!" Aunt Lydia flared. "You always want the opposite of what I suggest. If I recommended a young man, you'd be for somebody old."

"That's not true," said Aunt Britta. She was not beyond contesting Aunt Lydia tooth for tooth, but her spirit was benign at this moment. "Some older men can keep fresh and appealing to a church. Others—well, like the man we just got rid of—they get all crotchety an' maybe do as much harm as they do good. But a younger man . . ."

"They can be a peck of problems," Aunt Lydia intercepted. "They come in and want to change everything. They want the church decorated. They want the Sunday school reorganized. They put down the older, wiser leaders and cater to the young and inexperienced. We'll rue the day we call an upstart to our pulpit. You mark my words. 'Twouldn't surprise me none if he'd want us to tear down and rebuild a whole new church. Wouldn't that be a sweet howdy-do?"

"This is a good man Rufus has in mind," Uncle Eliad said. "I think he's just what our church needs."

"Is he fundamentalistic?" asked Aunt Lydia.

"He's a graduate of our own school," said her spouse.

"That makes it sure?" Aunt Lydia questioned. "In this day and age? I guess nixie."

During the foray that ensued Uncle Caleb dozed lightly. He would awaken when a stringent point was stressed, then his head would drop once more.

"As I see it," said Aunt Britta, "we need somebody to appeal to the young people."

"Not just the young people" put in Uncle Rufus, glancing toward me, "but the young couples, too."

"I'm against it," declared Aunt Lydia, "and so are some of the other older people who care what happens to our precious church."

"What do you think, Caleb?" Uncle Eliad asked.

His voice was resounding, which was one of the reasons he was repeatedly elected chairman of the church board. Uncle Caleb bolted upright as though an alarm clock had rung and it was harvest season.

"What's that?" Uncle Caleb muttered.

"Who do you think we should call for our preacher?" Uncle Eliad asked.

Caleb was taken off-guard. He looked meekly around the room. He looked at Aunt Lydia, at Uncle Rufus, at Eliad and the others. He even looked at me, though participating in the ruckus was not my intention.

"Do you think we should call an older man or a younger man?" asked Aunt Britta. She said "older man" softly and "younger man" with volume and articulation.

"Well," drawled Uncle Caleb, "I guess I go along with Lydia."

Aunt Lydia's eyes sparkled.

"Yep," Uncle Caleb continued, "I go along with you, sis. I think it's time, like you say, we call a younger feller."

Aunt Lydia sagged in her chair, as such an outburst of laughter reverberated throughout the house I was sure for a moment that great-great-great-great grandfather raised an eyebrow on the wall portrait that helped perpetuate his memory.

Aunt Lydia lost this particular battle, but she was not about to forfeit the war. She took to the telephone, to calling on people, speaking up in Sunday school and church. It even became obvious, so I am told, that she championed the cause in her prayer at each mid-week meeting.

Uncle Rufus never flinched, not only winning his case, but, with his inimitable genius, retaining the tacit goodwill of his wife.

Pastor Mallory began his ministry among us on the first Sunday in July.

"He's such a nice chap," said Aunt Britta, as the clan discussed his inaugural sermon at the inner sanctum of Pewdom.

"Myself," said Uncle Eliad, "I might like a man whose delivery is a little more like what you might expect from a preacher but . . ."

"Now you're showing some discernment!" Aunt Lydia broke in. "We've called him. He's here and now we have to live with what we've got. I realize that. But I don't see how any preacher can claim to have the unction of the Holy Spirit on his ministry when all he does is just stand up there and talk to you like it was the two of you out in the street or something."

"Like I started to say," Uncle Eliad intercepted quickly, as Aunt Lydia drew breath, "I had a reaction similar to yours, Lydia, but several times I looked around the congregation and the young people never took their eyes off of him. I saw that. Never once."

"What does that prove?" Aunt Lydia scoffed. "Of course the young people liked him. The worldlier a young person might be, the more so. They'd like any preacher who just talks easy to them, 'stead of sounding forth the pronouncements of God."

"What do you think, Rufus?" Uncle Eliad asked.

"I have no comment just now," Uncle Rufus said quietly.

"Of course, you don't." Aunt Lydia vociferated. "For once you see how right I was. I told you we shouldn't have called him. You mark my words. We'll rue the day we ever let ourselves drift into such folly. Now maybe as a teacher he's fine. But that man's no preacher, and you all know it.

"Now, I don't want to sound unchristian about all this—not one iota—so I do say I appreciate the concern my husband showed about getting a pastor." She turned to Uncle Eliad. "It's you, brother of mine, that'll be judged for this. Oh, where has gone those glorious days when the men of our family took the lead in the church and saw to it the right was always done? Well, I don't mind telling you I'm spending more and more time in my little prayer chapel."

(She had a small upstairs room set aside for prayer and meditation—a noble facility except that she publicized it so widely.)

She wrung her hands and moved toward the kitchen. In times of spiritual duress, Aunt Lydia went for the coffee pot as some men do their pipes.

"What do you think, Jeremiah?" Uncle Eliad asked.

"I don't particularly care to be part of the discussion," I said.

"How do you expect Jeremiah to have any spiritual discernment in a matter like this?" Aunt Lydia paused in the kitchen doorway. As she addressed the question to her brother, she cast judicial glances toward me.

"I'd just like your reaction," Uncle Eliad said, speaking to me as though he had not heard his sister's words.

"To be real honest," I said, "the things he spoke about made a lot of sense."

"Now you see," Uncle Eliad exclaimed, pointing a weather-worn finger at his sister.

"Do I see what?" his sister retorted.

They went at it hot and heavy. I touched Vaneta's arm.

"I think we should go," I whispered. "You know what the doctor said about your getting some rest every afternoon."

We slipped away unnoticed, except for Uncle Rufus who saw us to the door.

"To bad about all the ruckus," he said, "You kids encourage Pastor Mallory all you can. Our church needs a man like him."

Vaneta and I strolled quietly for a few moments.

Vaneta broke the silence.

"Jerry," she said.

I put my arm on her shoulder.

"Sometimes I get terribly confused as to what a Christian really is."

We walked quietly again.

"Don't you?" she asked.

"It's the story of my life," I said.

"You're such a dear person," she said. "So believable. And yet . . ."

At Vaneta's insistence, we attended the evening church service for the first time in many months. I was surprised at the size of the crowd, fully three-fourths as many as had attended morning worship.

"Things are looking up," I said to Uncle Rufus, as we stood in the foyer.

"We've got a good minister, Jerry," Uncle Rufus said. "He's real good."

I could not give you an accurate gist of what Pastor Mallory spoke about that night. I confess my mind wandered. It was not that I was disinterested in his sermon—his talk, as Aunt Lydia would put it—but I took to reminiscing. The sanctuary of our church had profound significance for me. Here I had witnessed weddings and funerals, baptisms and professed conversions. Yet, though my heart had been many times stirred to pause and contemplate the gates of righteousness, it was here I had been repeatedly confounded in the quest for spiritual meaning.

There was credibility in this Mallory fellow. It became momentarily his undoing in my eyes. I had for so long associated ecclesiastics with other-worldness. I could not be sure of a man who spoke of heaven in an idiom so terrestrial as the pulpit manner of this man.

At the conclusion of his discourse, Pastor Mallory stepped to the side of the pulpit. Nonchalantly resting one arm atop the sacred desk, he looked out at the audience and said, "If God has spoken to your heart tonight, let me be of help. Nothing in all the world is more important, nor more attainable, than the salvation and blessing God offers your life.

"My wife and I thank God for the privilege of serving you," he continued. "Humanly speaking, we realize it was you who called us. In the fullest sense, however, we believe it is God who has sent us. My wife joins me in the sincere desire to be helpful to you, every one of you, whatever your spiritual need may be."

After the benediction, as is typical in sanctuaries, congenial hubbub filled the air. Parishioners talked about the weather, their and varied and sundry subjects.

I chatted for a moment with Uncle Eliad, not noticing that Vaneta had slipped on ahead of me. She returned in a moment and stood shyly to one side, until Uncle Eliad and I had parted and I was alone.

"Do you mind going on home without me?" she asked.

I was taken back.

"I was just talking with Pastor Mallory's wife," she explained. "I need to see them for a few moments. She said she and her husband will drive me back to the house."

Vaneta turned and left. I went outside, got into our car alone, and drove home.

Chapter Eighteen

In the parsonage living room, counseled by Pastor and Mrs. Mallory, Vaneta professed conversion.

"I've been religious all my life, as long as I can remember," she told me, "but Christ was never personal to me, not in the way Pastor Mallory explains it. Maybe I was a child of God before. I'm not sure. But I am sure now."

"I'm happy for you," I said.

"Are you really, Jerry?"

"Of course."

"Yet you yourself . . ."

Our conversation led into the first dimensional sharing of our respective backgrounds. We had spoken superficially of our childhoods, the highlights, the adventures, but not until now did we exchange keys to the innermost parts of our minds, to the traumatic and definitive molds into which our personalities had been formed.

"In my home," she told me, "Christianity was the way of goodness. We honored God. I wouldn't say we discredited the gospel, but the real essence of Christianity lay not in recognizing or confessing one's sin but in the continued effort to be a good person, keeping the Ten Commandments, living by the principles of the Sermon on the Mount.

"There's a richness to that kind of life, Jerry. But there's emptiness, too. Everything I did seemed to bring me just one step short of God. But I honestly believe I've found Him, simply by fulfilling the conditions that are really so very clear in the Bible if one will only take the time to recognize them."

"For as long as I can remember," I said, "I was surrounded by people who made a big production out of the theology of salvation. Yet for them, life is some kind of an endurance test. The more you avoided frivolity, the surer you were of the joys of heaven."

We talked for hours, unfolding our pasts.

"You know more about the Christian faith than I do," she said. It was a startling thing to hear. "It's true, Jerry."

I yawned, playfully pinched her cheek, and suggested we retire.

But we did not sleep. We continued talking for another hour or more.

At last Vaneta said, "How can you know so much about the Christian faith and yet not be a Christian?"

"That's a good question."

"I want you to be like me, Jerry."

I made no immediate comment. Her head was on my arm. I turned her face toward me and kissed the bridge of her nose. We were quiet a long time.

At last, I said, "Maybe I am a believer."

"Do you think so?" There was a surge of eagerness in her voice.

"Aunt Lydia wouldn't think so."

"But do you think so?"

"I'm not sure."

"Why don't you make sure, like I did tonight?"

"How was that?"

"About all Mrs. Mallory did . . . Mrs. Mallory and the pastor . . . they turned to several verses in the Bible, one after another, and let me read for myself about, well, the fact all have sinned, all people, and that Christ died for our sins, and that our only hope, our only possibility of righteousness, is in Him. What is so meaningful, Jerry, what the Mallorys made clear to me, is that faith, really knowing God, is simply taking at face value what the Bible says. God has done, in Christ, everything He can for us. The doing of salvation is all finished. All we do, what salvation consists of, is to acknowledge what God has done and thank Him because He did it for us—for me, for you."

I pondered her words for a moment.

Then I said, "Know something, sweetheart? I've been exposed to the salvation machinery, our church an' all, since I can remember, and this is the first time I ever heard it put simply."

I felt a soft quiver in her body.

"It's the truth," I said.

We were quiet for some time. This was the way Vaneta was. Effusive one moment, withdrawn the next. I knew I had said nothing that could possibly offend her, so I waited.

"Jerry," she half-whispered, "couldn't you trust in the Lord right now, the way I did?"

I recognized the seriousness of her suggestion, but all the same it amused me. I chuckled and said, "Wouldn't Adelia turn over in her grave if she knew I got Christianity lying in bed beside my wife?"

"Jerry!" Vaneta scolded.

"Sorry, sweetheart," I apologized. "You'll have to forgive me. My resentment for the soul hunters is pretty deep. My suspicions, too."

"Don't you want to be a Christian?"

"More than I want to breathe."

"Then . . ."

"Let me watch you for a few weeks. I'll be a willing student, I promise. Maybe you can help me get some of the scales off my eyes."

I kissed her and turned to sleep.

Change did come to Vaneta's life, an inner radiance, a new openness, but there were also elements disturbing to me—one in particular. Aunt Lydia heard the news and promptly engulfed Vaneta in a surge of attention. Apparently she saw an opportunity to salvage what the Pew family had lost by my spiritual defection. I cringed at the prospect of my wife becoming a second Aunt Lydia.

By this I do not mean to say Vaneta lacked perspective and could thus be readily swayed into Aunt Lydia's legalistic view of things. In fact, I think she reacted tongue-in-cheek to much of Aunt Lydia's assertiveness. However, Vaneta was by nature a serious-minded person and could be expected to respond with gravity to the unfolding of those conservative tenets on which our denomination had been founded, those tenets which presumably accompanied the spiritual decision she had made. I spoke with her about it.

"Look," I said, "you're drawing into a shell. I thought faith was supposed to give freedom, a bouyance to life."

"It does, Jerry," she replied. "Mrs. Mallory stopped by just this morning and that was the main thing we talked about."

"Mrs. Mallory was here this morning," I scowled, "and I'll bet my Christmas bonus Aunt Lydia was here this afternoon."

172

Vaneta turned away. It irritated me.

"Old Mother Superior was here this afternoon, wasn't she?" I scoffed.

"Jerry, shame on you!"

"Wasn't she?" I insisted.

"She has a perfect right to come to our house any time she wants to."

"Sure she does. And I'm supposed to sit by and cheer her on while she tries to fossilize you the way she must've started being by the time she was your age!"

"I don't think you're very fair with your aunt sometimes!"

"Okay! Okay! Now you're laying down your cards. The old gal's giving you treatments on how to wither up an' be holy, so lesson one is it's a sin to criticize Saint Lydia, right?"

"Jerry!" Vaneta screamed at me.

I was blistering, and kept up my barrage of defamation until Vaneta burst into tears and went to our room and slammed the door.

Fortunately, we didn't have a lot of scenes like this. What happened was that I convinced Vaneta to go easy on any favorable comments concerning my aunt. Also, the two women worked out a trysting procedure whereby Aunt Lydia came and left during my working hours. The sad part of it all was that, instead of being helpful as I had rather sincerely hoped might be the case, Vaneta's spiritual metamorphosis tended to draw us farther apart.

I did note an attitude on the part of Pastor Mallory that disturbed me, while at the same time nurturing my slow acceptance of him as a truly credible Christian. He remained aloof. I think he wanted to reach me through my wife. I am certain he recognized my unvoiced spiritual hungers but suspected the fragility of my confused spirit. Vaneta wanted to become the avenue over which divine discovery would at last penetrate my life. I think perhaps she might have been, even though she became largely incommunicative in spiritual matters. She gave herself to many hours of Bible reading—evenings mostly when we might have talked together—and I presumed her seriousness to be as much from the natural timidity of anticipating the birth of her first child as from religious inclination. In any case, as the time neared for the appearance of our firstborn, Vaneta and I became more distant than at any time in our marriage.

Two and three times a month my boss asked me over to his house for evening discussions. Hillary was always there. I hated myelf for enjoying those hours with her, comparing her feminine litheness with the temporary obliqueness which characterized my wife's physical appearance.

"How is Vaneta?" Hillary would ask. I could tell, from the way she said it, she hated my wife's name. "You will soon have your first baby. That will be nice."

One evening it was just Hillary, her father and I—Mrs. Vamp having retired early—when my boss received a telephone call that kept him in a far part of the house for half an hour.

Hillary took a chair near mine, positioning herself in a manner which, though not improper, made obvious her efforts to facilitate my awareness of her.

"I guess you reap what you sow in this life," she said. "I treated you like a dog in high school. You know why?"

"Why?"

"You remember that day when we had just moved to town and my dad hired you to do some work in the barn?"

I well remembered.

"I was terribly curious about you. I really wanted you for a boy friend. You know, in a puppy love sort of way. But you were so introverted.

"When we were seniors in high school, I began to see you in a new light. I never let you know. You had the scourge of your church, your family associations."

She inched her chair closer.

"All the time, what I really wanted was stability. Someone like you, Jerry. Oh, don't hate me. Please don't even be offended at me. I wouldn't try to take you away from something you really want. If Vaneta meets your needs, then the best of everything to you."

Tears came to her eyes. I had never before seen this shade of her emotions.

"But if you ever should realize that . . . that Vaneta really isn't for you . . . that you aren't happy together . . . don't throw your life away, Jerry. You're too nice a guy."

For the next several weeks, I couldn't get Hillary out of my mind. I became preoccupied with thoughts of her at work. I delayed returning home at night, finding excuses to stay at the office in the hope she would come in and find me there. I would drive past the Vamp residence on the frail chance of intercepting her along the street. It was in my mind to run off with her, leave Vaneta and the Pews and my background forever.

Then, coming home to my wife, I silently castigated myself for so much as the thought of betraying this one who bore in her body the living extension of myself.

Yet the time came when I very nearly gave vent to my moral wanderlust. It was scantly three weeks prior to the birth of our child. I had had a rugged day at the office. Mr. Vamp, just returned from two weeks on the road, didn't approve of some decisions I had made and treated me badly. He had a tongue like the bite of a whip, like snake's fangs, and continually resorted to it to accomplish his ends. So I was both tired and irritable when I returned home to find Vaneta weeping, Aunt Lydia by her side.

"Something wrong?" I asked.

"I'm surprised you even ask the question," Aunt Lydia snapped.

She pointed to Vaneta, sobbing quietly. I went to comfort Vaneta. Aunt Lydia stepped in the way.

"Don't you touch her!"

"What on earth's gotten into you people?" I snapped.

"It's the devil that's gotten into you," Aunt Lydia replied. "Been in you an' never driven out."

I grasped Aunt Lydia's arm firmly. "Now look here!" I cried out. "Will you stop all this childishness and let me know what's wrong?"

"Will you tell us the truth about you and that divorced libertine named Hillary Vamp?" Aunt Lydia snapped back.

My knees went limp. I felt the color drain from my cheeks. It was as though someone had struck me full force in the stomach.

"I'd like an explanation," I said weakly.

"So would we," said Aunt Lydia. She pointed to Vaneta. "That's your wife, Jeremiah, soon to bear your child, and you bring shame upon her."

"I . . ."

Pouncing cat-like, Aunt Lydia slapped me hard across the face. I felt the color return to my cheeks. Hate rose like kindled fire in my heart. I wanted to strike her back.

"Aunt Lydia," I pointed to the door. "Leave my house!"

"I will not!"

She could not have stood more firmly had she been nailed to the floor.

"I have every right to ask you to leave, and you have no right to stay, if I tell you to go."

"Jeremiah!"

"Go!"

"Then that confirms it. You have no explanation. You're guilty."

"I'm not guilty of anything." I pushed Aunt Lydia toward the door. "Now you go."

"Come with me, Vaneta," she called. "You can stay at my house."

"I'll stay here," Vaneta said quietly.

As I put Aunt Lydia out the door, she called back, "You'll be sorry, Jeremiah. You mark my words."

Vaneta stood blowing her nose, as I returned to the living room. "What's this all about?" I asked.

She took a letter from her pocket and handed it to me.

"It's from Winona," she said.

"Something wrong with your folks, or . . .?" Then it hit me. Winona's husband, Pierce Roberts, that night in the Chicago hotel lobby.

I gave the letter unread back to Vaneta.

"Pierce saw me with Hillary Vamp in Chicago?" I asked numbly.

Vaneta burst into a fit of uncontrollable sobbing and fled from my presence. I heard her go to our bedroom and close the door.

I paced the floor. Where could Pierce possibly have seen me, under what circumstances, that would give him any reason to level accusations? And why had he waited this long? I sensed the pointlessness of my own questions. He had seen me with Hillary. There had been no question of her designs when we were together. He may have come upon us at a moment when, from her manner, he was left without supposition as to what our relationship had come to.

Why had I consented to spend any time with her? Sure, I told myself then it was necessary to facilitate my good graces with Halford Vamp. But I also enjoyed her attentions, and every moment we were together. I was the fool of fools!

Was this the inevitable roundelay of life? Crisis upon crisis, perpetual unfulfillment, the desire for good but the continual confrontation with evil? *It's not fair God*, I breathed. *I've tried. I'm human, but I've tried. Don't play with me like a cat, God. Destroy me, but don't torture me!*

Vaneta's Bible lay on the couch, beside it the letter from her sister Winona. I took the letter and tore it into minute pieces. In sheer disdain, I crumpled it and took it to the half-bath off from our kitchen, flushing it out into the sewer.

Returning to the living room, I picked up the Bible and would have rent it likewise but for the sense of awe it held over my life.

I did clutch it angrily, as one would strangle the neck of an adversary. I twisted it in my hands and when I heard the binding tear, I threw it back upon the couch.

I went outside and got into the car. I sat there a long time, not thinking, for my mind was awhirl. At last, I started the engine and drove away.

I drove past Aunt Lydia's house. There was that little room upstairs she proudly referred to as her prayer room. The light was on in the room. Doubtless she was on her knees, praying for me, likely imploring judgment upon my life. I laughed at the thought of her praying. After the laughter, I bit my teeth hard, grinding them.

I drove past grandfather's house. Uncle Caleb had moved to town and lived in it now. The strains of "Turkey in the Straw" touched my thoughts. I laughed again. I laughed loud and long. I pounded the wheel with my fist, pounded and pounded. When I had my fill of pounding, I wasn't laughing any more.

I drove out of town. It was late. The moon was bright. There were no cars on the road. I accelerated, faster and faster. I laughed again. It seemed idiotic, laughing this way, and I took measures to suppress the outburst, an effort substantially aided by a glance at the speedometer. I was cometing through the darkness at eighty-five miles per hour. Suddenly, a stray calf loomed out of the night. I veered, barely missing the animal, momentarily losing control of the car in a stretch of loose gravel.

I slowed to snail's pace. For a long time—an hour, perhaps two— I drove slowly. I paid little attention to where I was and in the course of time found myself along the river road. A couple was parked. They drove away quickly. Inevitably, the suddenness of their escape from my headlights turned my thoughts again to Chicago and Hillary and the letter from the Pierce Robert's household.

I stopped the car and again hit the steering wheel with my tightly doubled fist. In torment I walked along the river—the pressure so intense I felt as though the top of my head would burst.

"God!" I cried out. "I never touched that woman. I've never defiled myself with any woman. Don't other men have temptations? Is Pastor Mallory only aware of the body of his own wife?" I began to weep, to weep and then to sob, sobbing in great gasps of breath. I was not ashamed. I felt like a man crying.

Long after midnight, I returned home. I entered our bedroom in complete silence.

"Where have you been?" Vaneta asked. She sounded frightened.

"I drove and walked," I told her. "I'm sorry to awaken you."

"I haven't slept," she said. "Turn on the light."

"I don't need any light."

"Turn it on," she said softly. "Please, Jerry."

When I refrained, she reached across the bed to a table lamp and snapped the switch. The light blinded both our eyes momentarily, so I did not at first see the hurt upon her countenance.

"Have you been seeing Hillary Vamp often?" she asked.

"I never see her."

"Is that where you have been now?"

"I have done as I said, driving and walking."

"With her?"

"Vaneta will you . . ."

"Tell me."

"I have been alone."

I could see her plainly now in the dim illumination. I saw more of hurt than anger in her eyes. She struggled to refrain from weeping.

"I love you," I said simply.

"Don't make the hurt worse."

"It's true. Please believe me."

I wanted to take her into my arms. I wanted to throw open the door to my past, to be transparent about my infatuation for Hillary, but also to make known the truth of my loyalty.

"We shouldn't have come to a small town," she said. "Then it wouldn't matter so much."

"Vaneta," I pleaded, "there's nothing to matter. I've never betrayed you."

"Please."

I sat down on the edge of the bed. She touched my arm. I reached to take her hand but she withdrew it.

"You wish you had never married me?" she asked.

"That's a crazy question," I said. "Crazy."

"What shall we do, Jerry?"

"Do?"

"If it weren't for the baby . . ." Her poise faltered. She could not speak further. I reached to take her into my arms. She restrained me but permitted me to hold her hands.

"I never touched Hillary in Chicago," I said. "When we were children, twelve years old I guess, I kissed her once. But I've never touched her. I've never touched any woman but you. Not anyone.

178

In France . . . England . . . in Italy . . . women threw themselves at us . . . beautiful girls . . . young . . . but I never touched one. Not one, Vaneta."

She came once more into control of her emotions.

"What about Chicago?" she asked.

I told her about Chicago. I told her of Hillary's apparent interest in me during our senior year in high school. When her marriage failed, she conspired with her father to bring about an arrangement for me. I did escort her in Chicago. But I was clean. I had been true to my marriage vows.

"I wish I could believe you," Vaneta said. The words cut like a knife.

"What about the letter from your sister?" I asked. I was becoming desperate. "Your brother-in-law is being fair with me? He doesn't say he saw me in any situation . . .?"

"Didn't you read the letter?"

"I tore it to bits."

"You didn't read it?"

I shook my head.

"Shall we talk to Hillary?" I asked.

"I couldn't stand it," she said. "If you want her . . ."

"Vaneta, will you be sensible? I want you. Are you telling me to leave?"

"No."

"We can stay together?"

"Yes."

There was a long silence. Then I said, "I'll go to the guest room. I won't bother you any more than necessary."

As I suspicioned, Aunt Lydia spread the story. It was done properly, I'm sure. "You know I wouldn't speak a word of this," would be her way of doing it, "but I just wanted you to know so you can pray about it."

Vaneta and I lived like strangers in our own house. I tried to be considerate, fearful of prenatal injury to our unborn. Wherever I went I felt eyes staring at me. In my office, I could hear whispers behind my back. It was a kind of hell.

Then came that awesome morning, several hours before dawn, when Vaneta came to the guestroom where I had taken up sleeping.

"I'm sorry to bother you," I heard her say, as I awakened from her touch. "Do you hear me, Jerry?"

"I hear you," I said, sitting up.

"It's the time."

I dressed, helped her to the car, and we drove to the hospital.

"I thought I could wait until morning," she said. "I didn't want to bother you."

I took her hand, grateful that she didn't withdraw it.

"How are you doing?" I asked.

"I'll be all right," she said.

I caressed her fingers, then pressed her palm firmly against mine.

"I love you," I said, not taking my eyes off the road.

She squeezed my hand.

At sunup, as I sat waiting in the obstetrics lounge, our doctor came to me. "Congratulations," he said, extending his hand. "It's a boy. He looks like a dandy."

Chapter Nineteen

We named our son Gerald Rufus. I wanted him to be Jerry but not Jeremiah.

Vaneta insisted I choose the name. She was lovely in the hospital. The sharing of a new life began to bring us together again. She never alluded to our recent abrasive circumstances. She seemed willing to forget the past in the hope of building an endearing future. It was second best, settling for anything but her full trust in me, but I was not without gratitude.

Aunt Lydia came the first evening. I was about to leave, to ignore my aunt, but Pastor Mallory and his wife also came.

"We heard the wonderful news and just couldn't stay away," Mrs. Mallory greeted.

"Congratulations," added her husband, grasping my hand warmly.

"Well," huffed Aunt Lydia. "This is hardly the time for light talk."

"It's a happy time, isn't it?" asked the pastor's wife, managing a smile.

"At least we don't have to question who the father is," Aunt Lydia snapped.

"Aunt Lydia!" Vaneta protested.

I glared at the old dowager. I wanted to order her out of the room but held my tongue. She obliged by leaving. "Gerald Rufus Pew," she muttered. "That's a slap in the face, if I ever heard one!"

Pastor Mallory and his wife moved closer to the bed for a more intimate look at little Jerry nestled in his mother's arms.

"He's so handsome," Mrs. Mallory complimented.

"Why not," said the pastor pleasantly, "when you consider who his parents are?"

Vaneta laughed. It was like a little girl laughing at the sight of flowers or a new toy. It was warm and real. It had been a long time since I'd heard gaity in her voice.

"We know you two want to be alone," the pastor said.

"Not the two," said his wife merrily, "but the three."

The pastor put his arm around his wife's shoulder and drew her to him momentarily. It was beautiful to see.

"I wonder if we might offer a brief prayer on behalf of your new son," he said.

"Please do," Vaneta said. She turned quickly to me and asked, "Is it all right, Jerry?"

"Of course," I said.

I will never forget that prayer.

It was as though I had slipped back to early childhood, back to the setting of the sun, to strolls across the meadows when I felt the nearness of God.

Pastor Mallory prayed for little Jerry's physical well-being, for his body to grow strong, for his mind to be alert, for good eyesight, for the love of life. He prayed for Vaneta and me, asking God to give us wisdom that we might never lose the excitement of being parents.

"Let them be artists, Lord," he prayed, "fashioning the raw material of this young life into a splendid, living example of grace and goodness."

I could scarcely keep tears from my eyes.

Before they left, Pastor Mallory touched my arm and said, "We've missed you at worship. Don't wait too long to begin setting a good example for that boy. These youngsters become observant sooner than we think."

"Good-bye," Mrs. Mallory said. She stooped and kissed Vaneta. "God bless you."

It was the first time I had seen the minister and his wife in such informal circumstances. I had previously thought of them as professionally competent. I had now seen them as genuinely human, people who served God but in a context impressively dissimilar from the Pew frame of reference.

182

I came back to Vaneta. Her cheek rested against our son's forehead. She looked up to me and reached for my hand. She placed it on young Jerry's head, resting her hand upon mine.

Neither of us spoke. There was no need.

It was a mystic moment. This woman of my choice, the fruition of our union, myself. Silently, I breathed a prayer acknowledging a fourth presence.

"Jerry," Vaneta whispered.

I withdrew my hand and moved to a better view of her eyes.

"I'll try to be the kind of wife you want me to be. I'm independent. I've always been that way. But I love you. I forgive you for anything that may have happened."

My heart leaped in gratitude.

She drew my lips to hers, and we kissed tenderly.

"Do you believe me?" I asked. "I've told you the truth, sweetheart. Honestly, I have."

"Let's not talk about it now," she said.

I searched her eyes, eager for any clue that she might give credence to my claims of innocence. I found none. But I could see her reaction to the disappointment I could not help showing. Tears came to her eyes, tears of tenderness, moist with the flow of her heart.

She took my hand and held it against her bosom.

"It's been a long time since I felt the beat of your heart," I said. Neither of us could say more. I turned away to regain composure. She began nursing our newborn.

Our son became the hub of life to Vaneta and me. We shared the many chores his coming imposed upon our household. I did everything within my means to provide her with convenience, snatched at any excuse to come home each day for lunch, to avoid so much as a moment's delay at the work day's conclusion.

"What did he do?" I would ask, as I came into the house, and she would enumerate every detail.

We sang to young Jerry. We laughed hilariously, when for the first time he showed us his smile, watched breathless the evening he followed with his eyes the back and forth movement of my hand. At times, we rollicked as little children. At times, we were like ponderous philosophers.

"He's wonderful," I said one day, holding young Jerry in one arm and clasping my beloved with the other. "I'm more and more convinced that I could never have been the father of a boy this fine had you not been his mother."

She rested her head on my shoulder, looking down at our son. "It's certainly the truth, isn't it, Jerry? A baby is a gift from God." A gift from God!

The sound of those words fell upon my ears like the first melodic chord of an orchestra, like music audible only to those who love, those who drink deeply from the fountains of life's goodness. I became engrossed in the thought of it.

Until the doorbell rang.

It was Aunt Lydia, distraught about something.

"Anything wrong?" I asked.

"I've been miserable all day," she said. "I hardly slept all night. I've spent hours in my little prayer sanctuary—hours and hours and hours."

"Why?" Vaneta asked.

"This dear boy," Aunt Lydia said. She came and put her arm around me with the first expression of endearment between us in a good while. "Jeremiah, God has given you and your wife a wonderful baby."

"We were just talking about that," Vaneta said.

Aunt Lydia walked over to young Jerry's crib. "I wish you could have chosen a different name," she said. "It's a rebuke to our whole family."

"I wanted him to be called Jerry," I said. "Jeremiah is old-fashioned now."

Vaneta stepped to Aunt Lydia's side and put her hand on the old woman's shoulder in an act of arbitration.

"Dear little baby," Aunt Lydia cooed, petting young Jerry's cheek. "Aunt Lydia prays for you day and night. She spends many hours in her prayer sanctuary, praying just for you. Just for you, sweeticums."

"We appreciate your prayers," Vaneta said.

Abruptly, Aunt Lydia stood erect and stepped away from the crib, addressing my wife and me.

"I musn't dilly dally," she said. "The Lord spoke to me early this morning, when I was on my knees in my little chapel, and I must be about the doing of His commands."

I glanced at Vaneta, finding some courage in the realization that she seemed as puzzled as I was.

"Sit down, you two," Aunt Lydia commanded. "Sit on those two chairs so I can look at you."

We complied.

"Jeremiah," she began, "we have a great family heritage. I suppose it's part of the signs of the times, the ending of the age, that this heritage seems to be dying. Well, as long as I have breath, as long as I have a mind to think, it's my duty to uphold that heritage among those of our family God intended to benefit from it.

"Forty years ago, when I was the age of you two, it was unthinkable that there would be a backslider in the Pew family. It was just unthinkable. Why? Because we were a people united in obedience to the Lord.

"In many ways, I sympathize with you, Jeremiah. You are accountable to God for your lost soul, but, in a way, our family is also responsible. Worldliness began to creep in when you were a boy. It's worldliness that hardens the heart. There was once a spirit of revival in our church, but worldliness quenched that. Like I say, it's the signs of the times.

"So I sympathize with you, Jeremiah. Maybe Aunt Lydia has been a little firm with you at times, and you haven't liked it, but it's always been meant for your good."

She began to whimper.

"I know I'm not appreciated by many people in this community. I'm not appreciated in our church. It's because I won't compromise. People know it. They don't like it. But they respect me for it just the same."

"What are you getting at?" I broke in. "If you've come to preach a sermon, we hear those in church."

'Don't be cross, Jerry," Vaneta urged.

"When was the last time you attended church?" Aunt Lydia asked judiciously.

"Jerry has promised that we will be attending regularly," Vaneta said.

"Hmph" Aunt Lydia scoffed. "Even church isn't the way it was in those grand old days. Oh, I know everybody's all taken up with the Mallorys. He preaches a fundamentalistic message, so people like me, people with a little discernment, aren't supposed to complain."

"I think he's wonderful," Vaneta exclaimed.

"Of course, you do, dearie. I understand that. You are like your son—just one of God's little newborns."

"But whatever could you criticize about Pastor Mallory?" Vaneta asked.

"Like I said, he preaches a fundamentalistic message. But you know yourself he has absolutely no fire in the pulpit. He just stands there and talks. It's no wonder a lot of the old folks fall asleep. I even doze myself sometimes."

"But I find his messages very communicative," Vaneta said. "Truth isn't made any more important by shouting it."

"It's unction I'm talking about, dearie. You don't understand. I realize that. I suppose it doesn't bother you either, the worldly ways of our pastor and and his wife."

"The worldly ways?"

"Let me talk, Vaneta. The young people love him. Of course they do. He jokes all the time when he's with them. We're all embarrassed by the way he goes to ball games, both he and his wife. Do you know what I heard just this week? I found out he plays golf every Monday morning."

"But what's wrong with that?"

"What's wrong with that? In the first place, it's the pleasure of sinners. In the second place, it's a waste of time. In the third place, it's unbecoming to a minister. And as if that isn't enough reason, I suppose you don't know they sell liquor out there at the country club."

"But Aunt Lydia . . ."

"Look," I broke in, "I don't suppose Aunt Lydia came here to tell us about her theological frustrations. Get to the point."

Aunt Lydia cleared her throat.

"I appreciate you, Vaneta," she began. "I think you've shown wonderful growth in the Lord. You have no idea what a relief it was when I heard that you was converted. I had the idea you might be a Christian when we first met. That would have been wrong, you know, you a believer marrying Jeremiah, a non-believer. But I didn't protest. I suppose it was wrong not to. But I prayed about it. I did a lot of praying. I was so anxious for Jeremiah to have every good influence possible.

"Now you are a believer, Vaneta, and that's wonderful. You have this sweet little baby. But mark my words, dear ones, trouble is just ahead if your husband keeps resisting the grace of God."

"Like I said, Aunt Lydia," I interrupted acidly, "we'll be going to church to listen to sermons."

"Don't be cross," Vaneta interceded. "Please, Jerry."

"I'll come right out with it, Jeremiah," Aunt Lydia said. "Do you never intend to be saved?"

It was a blunt approach and threw me off-guard.

She pointed to the crib. "Do you mean to say, Jeremiah Pew, darling, that it is your intention to go through life as an unbelieving father, as a poor example to that precious baby?"

"I intend to be a good example to my son," I said.

"As an unbeliever?"

"Are you sure I'm an unbeliever?" I asked. The words came so unexpectedly they startled me.

"Jerry!" Vaneta exclaimed. Her eyes brightened momentarily.

"Are you sitting there trying to make us think you have accepted the Lord?" Aunt Lydia scoffed, "You that never attends church. You that runs around with a divorced woman while your own wife . . ."

"Aunt Lydia!" Vaneta protested. "Please!"

I sprang to my feet.

"I'm not finished yet," the old woman snapped. "Sit down."

I didn't sit down.

"Sit down, Jeremiah!"

"Please, Jerry," Vaneta pleaded.

"This is my house," I said. I struggled to remain calm. "I'm going to talk now, and when I've finished, that'll be the end of it."

"Please, Jerry." Vaneta came to me.

I pushed her gently aside.

Aunt Lydia just sat there, glaring at me. It wasn't often anyone frustrated her delusions of supremacy.

"Ever since I was a little boy, Aunt Lydia," I began, "I've wanted to know God. It was the deepest hunger of my life."

"Well, then . . ."

"Be quiet," I demanded curtly. "Remember, this is my house."

Aunt Lydia settled back in her chair, folding her arms.

"I'm sick till my belly aches," I continued, "sick of the kind of Christianity that makes some kind of an ogre out of God and a female neurotic out of Jesus."

"Jeremiah!" Aunt Lydia gasped. "That's blasphemy."

I waved my hand so violently for her to keep quiet, waved it so near her protruding nose, she sulked back, frightened.

"I've wanted to know God. Nobody knows how much. I wanted to find some meaning in life. I used to walk the fields, Aunt Lydia, hours and hours I walked the fields. You want to know why? I was trying to find God.

"Sure, I know the proper way was to build up an emotional typhoon and come bawling to the front of the church on a Sunday night. Well, I wanted to do that, too. I tried. You have no idea how sincere I was.

"But all I ever heard was thou shalt and thou shalt not. I saw very little Christian love in people's hearts. Remember the Buzzing Bible Bees? What a farce! Adelia wanted to get us all down to the front so she could put some more stars in her crown. She didn't have any real love for the kids in her class. You know she didn't. Getting us converted was just her way of being important.

"Remember when the negro evangelist came to town? That was one of the greatest men I ever met. He had a message for this community."

"He was one of those money raising holy rollers," Aunt Lydia blurted, "and my dear father put him in his place."

"Your dear father frustrated the power of God," I countered. "And speaking of Grandpa . . . rest his soul . . . what about the consistency of his life? What about his love for barn dance music? What about his lack of tolerance toward others?"

Tears came to Aunt Lydia's eyes. She looked helplessly toward Vaneta. There was anguish in the old woman's face, whether from remorse or mortification, I could not ascertain, but I pitied her, and would have tempered my vilification but for the sheer surge of desire to speak my feelings.

"What about yourself, Aunt Lydia? You've always looked at yourself as a fine example of a Christian. But my problem is I spent too many Sunday afternoons in your parlor. Pious talk and gossip. I was weaned on it and raised on it. It sickened me.

"Even as a little kid I had respect for other people. It hurt me when you used to talk the way you did about people around town. Sure, you found things to criticize, but there were things to criticize about you, too.

"And there I was, a little kid who really wanted something. I used to lie awake nights wishing I could be a Christian. I wanted to be. But if I became a Christian, I wanted to be a real one. I wanted God to control my tongue. I wanted Him to control my attitudes toward other people.

"You probably think I'm some kind of devil or something. I'm a human being, Aunt Lydia. I want all that there is to life. I went through a war. I don't talk about it, and I never will. I lived in the face of death for weeks and months. I was willing to die, hundreds of my buddies did die, so men could enjoy freedom in this world.

"This is going to be hard for you to believe. But there were times during the war . . . one time especially . . . when I believe God used me. That's right. I believe God used me, maybe to help a dying man find faith. I'm not sure.

"I've never mentioned it and won't give any details now because, as a kid, I saw so much of people trying to be indispensable to God that, frankly, it made me sick.

"No, Aunt Lydia, by your definition, I'm not a Christian. One of the main reasons is that I never saw Christ in you or in a lot of other people in our church. That's not a good excuse, I know, but it is a reason. Maybe I never will be a Christian. I don't know. But if I ever do become one, it won't be from the help of someone who disillusioned me all my life. It will be with the help of some Christian I can believe in, someone who gives real evidence of the liberty and radiance conversion is supposed to give.

"I'm not questioning your salvation. But I am saying you're just wasting your breath, if you think I'm going to salvage your fractured ego by pretending to be one of your converts, so you can cry out to the world that the great cause of the Pew clan has at last been reconstituted.

"Sure, I know, you figure you have a sword over my head. This Hillary Vamp deal."

"Now, you've . . ."

"Quiet, Aunt Lydia!"

She kept quiet.

"Okay, let me tell you something. I happen to love my wife. I think maybe she's beginning to realize how much I love her. I know that if I were to confess adultery with Hillary, Vaneta would forgive me. I know that not confessing such a sin would hurt her deeply, and I would not intentionally do anything to hurt my wife.

"Okay, listen, both of you. I did not, I have not, and I will not touch Hillary or any other woman. My vows are to Vaneta, and I intend never to break them. That's the truth, and if it takes till I die, I'll stick by that story because it happens to be true."

Aunt Lydia stood. Without speaking, she walked to the door. Vaneta accompanied her.

"I'll pray for you, dear girl," she said and departed.

Vaneta came to me. We embraced, but neither of us made further comment.

My affrontation of Aunt Lydia was the shot destined to be heard throughout the congregation. She did indeed salvage her ego by moaning out her new burden to fellow congregationists. I had sinned away my day of grace. I was possessed of a demon. I had blasphemed God in her presence. I had spit upon the cross. I was of all mankind most wretched.

Beginning the following Sunday, Vaneta and I regularly attended Sunday services. I suppose I went partly in defiance of Aunt Lydia, for the elucidation of my inner feelings toward the woman had a profound effect upon me personally, but I was also concerned to be my best for Vaneta and our son.

"You know, Jerry," Uncle Rufus said one day when I stopped by his store. "I wish you could take a more active part at church. We need some young blood. There are too many of us old ducks muddying the water. With a man like Pastor Mallory here, it's time younger men take over."

"I hardly qualify for any position," I said. "I'm not even a member."

"Oh," Uncle Rufus said, "we have folks active in the church who aren't members. We have several Sunday school teachers. Some of the people in the choir."

"I don't know enough about the Bible to teach a Sunday school class," I said, chuckling, "and every song in the hymn book is pitched too low or too high for my limited range. Besides, if anybody ever put my name up for a position, some of the most pious ones would start dragging skeletons out of my closet."

"Don't be bitter, Jerry," Uncle Rufus said kindly. "I don't know if it means anything to you or not, but there are lots of folks who don't believe the gossip that was spread about you and Hillary."

I was startled at his words. He had never before mentioned the situation. I knew he had not spoken lightly.

"You're serious?" I managed to say.

Uncle Rufus nodded.

"Tell me one person who doesn't believe it," I said eagerly.

"I don't believe it," he said.

"You don't?"

"I suppose I should have talked to you," he said. "It's just that I don't like to meddle in things."

"Why don't you believe the stories?"

"I know the Vamps too well. Halford Vamp wouldn't stop at anything to accomplish his purposes. He's taken control there at the plant and made poor Walt Wilding old long before his years. I'm afraid his daughter is cut out of the same bolt of cloth. Oh, I venture to say she may have given you moments of temptation, Jerry, because you're human, just like the rest of us, but I've got enough confidence in you to believe that if you say you never touched the girl you never touched her."

"Thanks, Uncle Rufus." I took his hand and squeezed it warmly. "It's true. I never touched the girl."

Uncle Rufus smiled.

"I'm on the church board, as you know," he said.

"I can't remember a time when you weren't."

"Oh, I've been off a few years, but I've been on a lot, too." He puttered a moment with some stock.

"One of the problems we've been having," he continued, "is setting up ushers. It just seems nobody wants to buckle down to the responsibility. We'll get some ushers set up and maybe they'll show up on Sunday and maybe they won't. Or we've had men come on the Sunday they were supposed to usher and forget all about it. So I suggested to the board the other night that we set up an usher's committee. Well, they appointed me to be chairman. I got the committee together, and we put down the names of some of the young fellows in our church, some of them that aren't used much, especially putting down the names of those that are dependable."

Uncle Rufus stood erect and looked directly at me. "You know, Jerry, your's was the first name suggested."

"I appreciate that!" I exclaimed. "I appreciate it a lot." Then I asked, "But would I qualify?"

"Sure, you would. Oh, we've got a few who tend to be a little persnickety. My own missus is a little that way, as you know. She means well though. So do most of the folks at church. People can look real perfect until you get to know them. Then you begin to see all the little faults and shortcomings."

The following Sunday morning, just after she had placed young Jerry in the nursery, Vaneta pinned a carnation to my lapel. "You look so nice," she said.

Frankly, I was as nervous as a child at his first Christmas program.

Aunt Lydia always came early and sat near the front, and thus did not become aware of my new appointment until the offertory prayer had been given and I turned, collection plate in hand, and started up the aisle.

When I attempted to give the plate to her, she just sat there, holding her offering in her hand. I finally gave the plate to the next person, by-passing Aunt Lydia and her unbestowed offering.

Needless to say, she sounded forth vigorous protest ere the day was out.

"The very idea" she spewed. "An unbeliever having to do with official church functions."

"Now, Lydia," Uncle Rufus said, calming her, "ushering is a matter of convenience, not just a spiritual service."

"It's just another of the giving-ins that's happening in our church."

"No it's not. Jerry wants to help. This is a little thing he can do. It means a lot to him, and it means a lot to the folks in church, too."

"Hmph!"

She withdrew her protest. But she sat sulking whenever I passed near her in the sanctuary on behalf of my assignment.

It was a little service, but for me it was the first time the people of God had recognized me as anything but one of the damned.

It was good.

Every Sunday, something stirred in my heart, when I would hear Pastor Mallory say, "And now, the ushers will please come forward to receive the tithes and offerings."

Chapter Twenty

It had puzzled me many times what there is about faith that so seldom takes the measure of a man, why woman symbolizes righteousness, why supreme efficacy lies with mother's prayers, the sainted way learned only at her knee.

I thought I had reasoned out the gist of it.

In the supernatural genders, I supposed, angels were feminine and devils masculine. Somehow, though David felled Goliath and Daniel encountered lions, they were genteel, men of quiet water courses and fragrant bowers who played harps and sang psalms. They did exploits, to be sure, because God was with them. This I understood. But it was the profane and the damned—the Philistines and the Amorites who had the wind in their faces and thunder in their words and fire in their loins.

I respected preachers. It was part of my heritage to do so. Yet I saw them as the epitome of what faith was to mean to a man. Preachers had unsoiled hands. They were men without passions, delighting in piety. They avoided such banal acreages as ball diamonds and circus grounds and the midway at the county fair. There was often a feminine manner about them. They were nice men and took life seriously. When they came to your house, you put on your best manners and spoke of the sick and the dead, the inevitability of meeting God. And before leaving, the preacher would pray. You became uneasy. Everyone sighed when he was gone and became themselves again.

The preacher was man at his best for God.

It was not until Pastor Mallory came that this image in my mind began to tarnish and to fade. I grew vitally interested in the church, felt myself a part of it, not simply because my long trauma had been remarkably assuaged by the responsibility of serving as an usher, but because of the awakening of a new anticipation in my heart.

"You're doing real well," Uncle Rufus complimented. "We haven't had such good ushering in years."

One never fully evades the mannerisms of childhood, perhaps should not try, and I confess I beamed as a boy at the hearing of my uncle's commendation. Even Aunt Lydia came to accept my role, conducting herself with civility if not congeniality. And Pastor Mallory took note of my attitude and deftly won my confidence.

One Sunday evening, as we shook hands at the door, he said, "Say, how about a few holes of golf some morning this week?"

"Sounds great," I replied.

"Take a look at your schedule tomorrow. If you find you can open up some time, give me a ring."

We arranged to meet on the golf course Tuesday morning at seven o'clock. For several holes, we just played golf. I'm fairly adept with the woods and irons, but when we reached the sixth tee he was two up on me.

"You've got a good game," I said.

"I like golf," he replied. "That's half of success in any venture. I relax when I play golf, relax and do a lot of thinking."

He stroked, hooking the ball slightly down the green. "See, I tried to talk to you and right away I'm off my game."

I laughed, as I pushed my tee into the turf and positioned the ball.

"I should add," he continued, "that I enjoy golf most when it's combined with conversation. It always ups my score but makes for a more enjoyable morning."

I took a couple of practice swings, then stepped back. We were alone on the course. I tapped my shoe with the club, stepped up to the ball, limbered my arms again, and swung.

"Beautiful" he praised.

The ball sailed squarely down the fairway, coming to rest a comfortable nine iron shot from the green. I turned to him and said, "I like a little conversation during the game, too. As a matter of fact, I've been wanting to talk to you about some things for a long time."

"Okay," he said, "I'll meet you on the green. You look like about one under par." As he walked away, he called over his shoulder, "Be patient. I'll get there."

I experienced a strange emotion in that moment. The nearest description I can give is the way I felt the summer Uncle Caleb became president of the County Farm Bureau Federation and introduced me to the governor of our state at the annual picnic.

As we lined up our putts a few minutes later, I said, "Aren't you held in suspect a little bit by your fellow clergymen?"

I surprised him.

I putted, missing the cup by a foot or so. It didn't matter—I'm an avid golfer, but it didn't matter.

"Go head," he said.

I put the ball into the cup, took it out, and stepped back to wait his putt. Instead, I saw him coming toward me, his ball back on the fringe of the green. He was so serious, I at first thought him to be ill-disposed with what I had said.

But he smiled and asked, "Why should I be held suspect?"

"Because you don't fit the pattern."

He got my message.

"Well," he said warmly, "one of my extra-biblical doctrines is that God was not the originator of ruts. God never duplicates His craftsmanship. Every human being He fashions is an original. Men try to fit into preconceived patterns, but that's not God's intention. *Be not conformed,* He says. *Be transformed.*"

"That's what I was trying to get across," I said. "Clergymen, as I've observed them, conform to a . . ." I held my tongue in cheek. He smiled, went back to his ball, and hit the cup with flawless accuracy, thus equalling my score for the hole.

"See what I mean?" I exclaimed. "In my experience, a preacher playing your brand of golf makes as much sense as a bartender teaching a Sunday school class."

"Well," he chuckled, "I know at least one ex-bartender who teaches a class every Sunday. But by that kind of reasoning, I suppose I should be a former clergyman."

We walked to the next tee.

"Don't misunderstand me," I said. "I'm not saying you disqualify as a preacher. What I do say is that, incorrectly I'm sure, I never associated virility with men of the cloth."

He looked at me soberly, then stooped to fix his tee.

"Get what I'm trying to say?"

"I surely do, Jerry."

We continued the game. As play proceeded, my greens-mate

developed an uncanny arm and eye, not so much accuracy at the tee and the cup but the ability to stroke his ball in proximity to mine so that, for fairway after fairway, we walked together. We talked about clergymen for awhile.

"In a sense," he said, "we're men of the arts. Then, too, I'm not sure anyone can give a pat description of virility. But I know what you mean, Jerry. It irritates me, many times, the feminine overtones of so many descriptions of Jesus."

"That's another thing that's bothered me."

"It relates to the image of the clergyman, to the format many of them seem to feel they must fit into."

We separated momentarily in the course of our play.

Together once more, we continued the discourse.

"It's understandable why spiritual contexts tend to have feminine overtones," Pastor Mallory said. We paused in the shade of a big oak, waiting for an energetic threesome to play by. "Nature has its storms, its tragedies, but we think of it primarily in terms of beauty. If we agree that God created our world, then we naturally relate the comeliness of nature with the personality of God. We speak of Mother Earth."

"Or Mother Nature," I added.

"And I like that. It fits. Women are, in a sense, the best of God's creation. Their bodies function much more spectacularly than ours. It's a tremendous thing, the mechanics of gestation and birth. We call woman the weaker sex. In a way, they are. But they outlive us."

We stood a moment, watching one of the passing golfers execute an especially difficult shot. "Not bad," Pastor Mallory commented.

"But back to what we were talking about, Jerry, have you ever wondered why God didn't make both sexes more identical? Well, He didn't, and every well-married man is surely grateful for it. It doesn't work out that way, unfortunately, but, obviously, God intended woman to be charming. They're most believable when they are. So, you add it all together, the capacity of woman to create, the innate qualities of a charming woman, and one just naturally ascribes spiritual qualities to them."

"But nobody wants a female God!" I declared.

"Precisely. And it's pretty clear in the Bible that God intended spiritual vigor to be more masculine than feminine.

"It is?"

"God created man in His image, then from man formed a woman to help him. Help him, Jerry—not rule him."

196

I sighed. "My problem is, I've met so few women in my life, women of any age, who had the charm, you know, the personality a man really admires in the opposite sex. I've seen a few. There were a couple of women in our church—I had one for a Sunday school teacher when I was just a little kid—and they were really something. I wished either one had been my mother. But . . ."

"Women, just like men, miss God's intentions for them," Pastor Mallory said. "And I don't mean to write off the woman who takes spiritual initiative. God's work would be in sorry straits if women didn't take the initiative in many cases. But it's men who really miss the mark, Jerry, and I think the basic problem is that the devil, the master craftsman at perverting thought patterns, has so sentimentalized vital Christianity that the average man, who's looking for excuses anyway to minimize his need for God, hasn't a clue as to what real faith really is."

I was captivated by his words.

"We sing about 'gentle Jesus, meek and mild.' I remember a chorus at a youth camp one summer. The words went something like 'He saves me so neatly, so sweetly and completely.' Nauseating! Oh, I'm not saying Jesus was dispossessed of such attributes as meekness and mildness. I'm not saying He didn't express gentleness. But He did it from a position of strength. A strong man can be tender—a strong man can show kindness.

"Ah, Jerry, my heart aches. The average painting of Jesus makes Him look like . . ." He didn't finish the sentence. "Jesus, was a virile man, the noblest specimen of masculinity ever to appear upon this earth. I believe that. He spoke, and the winds and the waves obeyed His voice. He drove a hundred men—maybe a thousand, I don't know—drove them single-handed out of the temple. Demons trembled and fled at the sound of His voice. After He had gone without food for forty days, the devil himself tried to outwit Him and was ignominiously put down. And in the Garden of Gethsemane, when He prayed that the cup might be removed, it was not the cup of suffering, not the cup of responsibility—not at all, Jerry— I believe that, being human as well as divine, He prayed that His human breath might be sustained long enough so He could get to the cross and finish the job. He wanted to bear the full brunt of suffering, the full of it, man, so our atonement would be completely assured!" There was turbulence in Pastor Mallory's countenance, thunder in his words and lightning in his eyes. There were tears, too. This was a virile man.

"I'll tell you something," he continued, having calmed himself.

"If you want to think about Jesus, to comprehend Him as fully as the human mind can do, I tell you what—fill your mind with masculine thoughts. Think of the greatest physical exploits men have accomplished—athletes, soldiers, orators, engineers, kings and diplomats. Men, Jerry. Think just about men. Put women out of your thoughts, completely out. When you have built your thought patterns to an imagery that is exclusively masculine, you have just taken the first step in being able to think about Jesus. He's more than all that. Much more. But unless you think of Him as the virile Christ—loving and tender but tenacious and authoratarian—you're really not thinking of Him at all. He's the Creator, Jerry. The Bible tells us *all things were made by Him*. God the Father is the source of all things. God the Son is the Creator, the Architect of Genesis who became the Carpenter of Galilee to redeem our lost souls."

My God, my soul cried out, why didn't somebody talk like this to me twenty years ago?

The threesome was gone, and we continued our game. Pastor Mallory resorted to the tactic I had previously observed in him, and profoundly admired, that of not coming at you like a man of conquest, obvious in his determination to add you to his list of fallen rebels. As we played, we resorted to casual conversation. I asked him about his background, where he had gone to college, how he met his wife, what he thought of our town, all the time wishing to return to the previous subject.

"Isn't it about time we change the subject and talk about you?" he suggested, as we both came in a miserable three over par on the eighth hole.

"You're quite an iconoclast," I began.

"Easy now," he chided, "I said let's talk about you."

"I'm getting to that," I told him.

"Okay," he said, "shoot."

"I'll just do that." It was my turn to be jovial, as I stepped to the tee and sent my ball nicely down the number nine fairway.

He swung with equal dexterity, landing a good thirty yards beyond my effort.

"Well," I continued, as we walked leisurely, "for one thing you've worked havoc with the traditional image of a fundamentalist preacher in this town."

"So?"

"That in itself takes the starch out of a lot of notions I've built up over the years."

"Such as?"

"The list is pretty long."

"I've got all morning."

So I began to talk. It was easy, words flowing from my lips as though I had planned everything I would say. By the time we reached the tenth green, I had highlighted the frustrations of my childhood, the deep disallusionments of hypocrisy, the almost total lack of adult spiritual guidance, the legalism, the fear, the unpalatable indoctrination.

"I probably sound like the world's foremost malcontent," I said.

"Or like someone giving a resume of my own background," he said.

His words struck me silent with astonishment.

"It's true," he said, coming within inches of dropping a fine putt.

"I'm afraid this is the history of a lot of people who came up through the ranks of American evangelism, as you and I have."

"You don't sound bitter," I said. "That's my problem."

"I was," he told me. He smiled. In the penetrating warmth of that smile I felt a compelling rapport. "I was very bitter, Jerry, until I discovered the reality of Jesus Christ."

We played quietly for awhile. I suspect he wanted to give me time to evaluate the turn of conversation. When the silence grew prolonged, he said, "Actually, a woman served as the spiritual catalyst in my life. My father pretty much fit the pattern of the inept evangelical, but I had an angelic mother. She was a great woman. She took the spiritual leadership in our home. My father expected her to. I'm sorry you couldn't have known someone like her, Jerry. I'm very sorry. Our world would have few problems if every boy in it had a father like, well, like your Uncle Rufus, and a mother like mine."

"I envy you," I said.

"My mother is the reason why I'm a believer. If she'd been like my father . . ."

". . . you'd probably be like me," I concluded, when he hesitated a moment.

He looked at me, making no comment.

"My observation," I said, "has been that when people experience conversion, or whatever you choose to call it, they tend to go into some kind of bondage. They become inhibited."

"Has this been true of your wife?" he asked bluntly.

"I'm not sure. She has always been a very noble person. But I'll

199

tell you one thing. Her conversion hasn't improved our marriage."

"That's not the issue."

"Shouldn't it be?"

For the moment, I thought I had him off-guard.

"No," he said, "the complexion of your marriage is your responsibility. That's as God intended it to be."

"How do you mean?"

"I'd be glad to talk to you about it sometime. Just now, though, it would be a little like putting the cart before the horse."

Again we played quietly for several minutes. Then he said, "Even though my background was frustrating, I'm prone to be sympathetic toward it. I really am, Jerry, and in saying that I'm not trying to shout down your obvious hostility toward some of the elements of your past. I can be sympathetic because God has permitted me to see my past in perspective."

"The reason you aren't bitter," I asked, "is because of a . . . a transformation in your attitudes?"

"Partly. The acceptance of Christ as personal Savior involves transformation. Strategically, though—and I know I lay myself vulnerable in saying this—conversion has mainly to do with putting right the past, the old Adamic dereliction, and, of course, conversion lays the foundation for one's spiritual future. But robust spiritual development results from spiritual laws which operate from an entirely different plateau, you might say."

"You're putting me farther into the dark."

"I'm sorry. I'm not trying to make it sound complicated. Virile Christianity is a profound experience, but it need not be complicated.

"Let me approach it this way, Jerry. The only way to God is through Jesus Christ. That's as plain in Scripture as the simplest geometric axiom. But far too many evangelicals . . . fundamentalists, as we are often called . . . stop at the birth plateau and entirely miss the intended growth plateau of spiritual development."

I began to understand.

"As I said, Jerry, I'm sympathetic. I'm not meaning to be critical when I say that evangelicals have failed, often miserably, in proclaiming the new birth but omitting the new life, seeing conversion only as escape from hell and admittance to heaven, missing the here and now dynamic of the Bible's message."

"I read you now," I said, "loud and clear."

"What I'm saying is simply this, Jerry. I don't question the per-

200

sonal salvation of members of your family who, you say, have inhibited you. Frankly, there's every reason to believe that, if the status quo is maintained, they'll end up in heaven and you'll end up in hell."

"That's not fair!" I flared.

"Truth is never unfair," he said. "When it seems to be unfair, it's only because someone has distorted it or withheld it from us, preventing us from reacting to it in our own best interests."

He selected a club from his bag, studied it pensively.

"Of course," he continued, "we sometimes call truth unfair, when we are unwilling to face its issues."

"*Touche,*" I said.

"Now, I'm not defending the fact that our ecclesiastical forebears settled for an inhibited, legalistic Christian life. There are historical reasons for this, though not necessarily justifications. What they were actually doing, Jerry, was accepting the grace of God for personal salvation but then depending upon their own personal initiative for righteousness. There isn't anything in all the world more frustrating.

"They were sincere, Jerry. Give them credit for it. They meant this quest for righteousness to be for God's glory. They really did. They gave us a background we can build upon. They taught us through their mistakes. The "thou shalts" and "thou shalt nots" many times simply consisted of their efforts to do nothing which would offend the unconverted."

"Your analysis begins to make some sense," I said.

"I only give it as my own analysis. Not for a moment would I try to impose it on you. My sole concern for you at the moment is that you might come to a personal knowledge of God's Son."

"I'm listening," I said.

He had me in the palm of his hand. His voice was saying what my childhood ears had listened for in the wind, his poise and confidence bringing into comprehension the mystic entity I at times thought I saw in the sun's afterglow. He reawakened old hungers and at last offered sustinence. I felt at times a breath of rebellion, a remnant reaction from the past. I gave it no heed, as I opened my mind to this man.

"No one can possibly be a total person," he said, "if he denies Christ the place He wants to fill in his life. There's an emptiness, a falling short, a feeling of just spinning your wheels, until the miracle of regeneration occurs.

"Jesus said, "You must be born again." That sounds pretty naive to a lot of people. Actually, it's just about the most profound statement of all times. It takes a combination of certain forces to bring about physical birth. Every child born into the world . . . except the Son of God Himself . . . came into existence as a direct result of those forces. No one could be more naive than to suggest physical birth might occur otherwise.

"But physical birth is not enough for a man to become the complete personality God intended. This takes spiritual birth and the ensuing spiritual life. Here again there's just one way it takes place. No sense trying to fabricate some other way. It's pointless."

"How does spiritual birth take place?" I blurted.

"Through an act of faith," he replied.

Our eyes met. Inevitably, my mind swept back past the years to Adelia and Aunt Lydia and their efforts to bring about my conversion. Could it be possible they, revolting as they had been to me as people, had sought to bring about the same experience this man obviously wished to occur on my behalf?

We played on.

The eleventh hole, the twelfth, the thirteenth.

As we stepped up to the fourteenth tee, I said, "It seems incredible that so many people in the world could be wrong about God."

"Yes, it does," he admitted, "especially when God has so clearly made His plan known."

"Clearly?"

"Clearly."

"Okay," I said. I tried to be nonchalant. "I'm fair game."

"I happen to believe in a personal devil," Pastor Mallory continued. "If knowing that two plus two equal four were strategic for a man's personal salvation, I'm sure he'd find some way to make the world believe two plus two equal five."

"Come again?"

"To the average person, Jerry, the Christian life is so ponderous and complicated as to be virtually unattainable. It's the devil's lie."

"You're not saying people like Adelia and my Aunt Lydia are tools of the devil."

"Not tools necessarily."

"Then what?"

"It's a little off the subject. If you ever take to reading the Bible, spend a few sessions with the sixth chapter of Ephesians. Then maybe you'll understand my theory that Satan works harder inside the church than he does outside."

"Deacons are devils and sinners are saints?" I asked.

He didn't answer. I saw the silence as his rebuke.

"Okay," I primed, "let's get back onto the subject. How has God made salvation simple, as you say?"

"In the Bible, Jerry."

"Don't people read the Bible?"

"Do they?" he asked. "Do you?"

"Well . . ."

"Oh," he said, as he sent a high looping drive down the fairway, "I don't deny that people read the Bible. But one's attitude is important. Too often," he continued, "men read the Bible in search of vindication for their own ideas."

"I'm not sure I understand," I said as we walked.

"It's the difference between Christianity and religions," he explained.

"Christianity is one of many religions isn't it?" No one ever more adeptly laid himself vulnerable.

"Religion is man-made, Jerry. Sincere though it may be, it stems from a man's ego, from his conscience, from that insatiable something within us that demands righteousness. Because we are human, we like that righteousness to be something we can point to and claim as our own doing. Christianity . . . really valid Christianity . . . is the discovery of life. It goes back to what I said. No one is a complete person without Jesus Christ. That's the difference."

"I'm confused." I said.

We reached the fourteenth green.

"You're sure it isn't rebellion?"

"I don't mean to be rebellious. I guess my problem is that I have absolutely no faith."

As though the words were on the tip of his tongue, Pastor Mallory said, "Take a good look at me, Jerry. I have no faith either."

I stepped back, startled.

"It's true," he insisted. "I have no faith."

For the first time, I began to grow skeptical. I felt he was putting me on, making light of my limited theological knowledge.

"What do you mean?" I finally managed to ask. "Great day . . . if a preacher doesn't have faith . . ."

"In a sense," he admitted, "it's a play on words. Basically, though, it's true. That's the very essence of successful Christianity, the absence of a self-generated faith.

"Now, obviously, faith motivates my life. I've got a lot to learn on this score, but its my ambition to have every moment of my life —everything I do, Jerry—motivated by the principle of faith. When I said I had no faith, I meant that I possess no faith generated from within myself. The faith that regenerates and builds us into valid spiritual beings is not a faith we generate ourselves, but a faith implanted from outside. Religion is generated inside men. Christian faith comes from an outside supply, from God Himself."

I listened like a child.

He took out a small New Testament. For once, the sight of the Scriptures did not offend me. Conversely, I hungered to know more.

"I was an unbeliever when I went to the university," he continued. "Proudly, though not very honestly, I called myself an agnostic. There was a Christian in our dorm, one whale of a guy, and he had discovered the liberating life in Christ. He was as genuine as a slab of solid gold.

"We did a lot of talking. Sure, I threw out a few questions he couldn't answer. When he couldn't answer something, he admitted it. He never tried to fake his way.

"He took a long time bringing me to the point where I was ready to let God give me faith. It started one evening, one Saturday evening, when most of the crowd was out painting the town red. He opened his New Testament, just as I've opened mine here, and showed me this verse. He asked me to read it, just as I'm asking you."

I glanced at the top of the page. It was the book of Romans. He pointed to one verse. I read, "So then, faith comes by hearing, and hearing by the Word of God."

"Mind reading it aloud?"

Aloud, I read, "So then, faith comes by hearing, and hearing by the Word of God."

"The faith God's telling us about there is the genuine article, Jerry."

A chill of excitement touched my frame.

"Is it faith generated from inside a person?" he asked.

I shook my head. I felt a little bit like a boy at Sunday school being interrogated about the lesson. I didn't mind. "It comes from the Bible," I said. The glow of anticipation rose in my heart.

204

"My friend made me a dare," Pastor Mallory continued. "He dared me to read the Gospel of John three times. The first time I read it, I could think whatever I cared to think. The second time, I was to begin paying closer attention to its claims of Christ, to what Christ can do in a recipient life. The third time, I was to be in a spirit of honest openness, inviting God—even if I honestly questioned His existence—to reveal Himself through the words I read."

"What happened?" I asked eagerly.

"Why don't you try the experiment for yourself," he said. "Maybe you'll have the same result I had—what began as an experiment turned out to be a transforming demonstration."

Chapter Twenty-one

It is an awesome experience to have long searched for God, to retrospect across years strewn with the debris of unfulfillment, and then to stand at last in imminent anticipation of the veil rent, the clouds rolled back, the darkness dispelled, the reality of God made sure.

I had at times envied those people who seem to pass through life devoid of spiritual compulsion, people to whom God matters little —neither His judgments nor His blessings. And at times I wondered if fellow savants at *Friends of Faustus* were correct in asserting that God was a mere figment of the imagination inscribed within the mortal frame of reference by religious forebears who had in turn been indoctrinated by their own peers. True, I had suspected genuineness in people like Uncle Rufus and John Wesley Sommerford. But man is by nature quantitatively persuaded. I was no exception. Once gone from my home community, I beheld what seemed to be a world of unbelieving men. How could I nurture credence for the faith of people like Aunt Lydia and Adelia when I sat at the feet of learned men who looked at microbes and galaxies and declared them devoid of mystical forces?

If the relativists are correct, and the universe is indeed contained within itself, if person and personality may be reduced to atoms in motion, if experience is existential and not universal, then where does an infinite God reside and how does He demonstrate extratemporal phenomena?

On the greens, I had been as a boy again, the boy of the open fields and the circus grounds and the Sunday night sanctuary. But in the aftermath of my golfing date with Pastor Mallory, conflicts ensued within my mind. Though I am aware childhood follows man to the grave and that some humans become at best grown children, I had become more man than boy. There were the afternoons and nights at *Friends of Faustus* to be reckoned with. There were the blood-soaked years in Europe. There was the memory of so many who had for so long distorted my image of the pious man.

And there was Vaneta.

What had I seen of transformation in her life? How did she differ from myself in divine relationships? Did I indeed want transformation? Did I believe it possible for anyone?

I could reject Pastor Mallory's reasoning entirely. Perhaps I should. Like my kinsmen, I had once been persuaded that the God who blessed Abraham and Joshua was the God who now condemns Einstein and Bertrand Russell. I could be done with religious sentimentality. I could inter the God of the patriarchs and hail the gods of the test tube, the assembly line and the launching platform. Did I not need to at last recognize this maturity of thought and be done forever with my past? Such a mentality might at last heal the trauma and release my mind for productive concepts.

Then I remembered what Pastor Mallory had said. I was to read the Gospel of John three times. I could think what I wished during the initial reading. I was to pay closer attention on the second.

And on the third reading . . .

I had not opened the Bible in years.

I did not return to work that day, following my golf date with Pastor Mallory, and I did not call Mr. Vamp to explain why. I pocketed a small copy of the New Testament, not showing it to my wife or informing her of my intentions, except to say that I might be late returning home.

"Are you going to the office?" she asked. I was still dressed in my golfing togs.

"No," I said.

I kissed her and left. My first impulse was to get into the car and drive out along the river road and into the country where I could be alone. However, my search for God reverted my thoughts to childhood, and I struck out by foot to the western edge of town, across the fields to the meandering stream where I had spent so many hours in youthful contemplation.

Having made sure I was unobserved, I took the New Testament from my pocket, turned to the Gospel of John and began to read. I tried to concentrate, but my mind wandered. I would read for several moments without paying attention to my reading, unmindful of what my eyes had seen, as memories of the past blurred the pages, memories of Sunday night sermons in our church.

Our pastor had several favorite phrases which appeared repeatedly in his sermons. "I love this blessed Book. It is more to me than life itself. If the Bible is strange to you, sinner friend, it's because you are a stranger to God . . . The Bible says it, beloved, and I believe the Bible from Genesis 1:1 to Revelation 22:21 . . . A changeless Book in a changing world . . . It's sin to question this blessed Book . . . Believe this message and be saved. Reject it and be damned."

I could hear Grandfather Pew's resounding amens and remembered the aversion that grew in my heart against the Bible, feeling an essence of that aversion now. It was like anger, like a malady, like a shelter from Aunt Lydia. I would have given up except for the third stage of Pastor Mallory's proposal.

I was to read with a prayer. If there was a personal God, if He revealed Himself through the Scriptures, then He was to reveal Himself to me.

God, I prayed silently. If . . . I caught myself—startled.

Prayer had come to my thoughts without my volition. A simple thing perhaps, but it quieted my doubts and stimulated my hopes.

I once more opened the New Testament:

> In the beginning was the Word, and the Word was with God, and the Word was God. The same was in the beginning with God. All things were made by him; and without him was not anything made that was made. In him was life; and the life was the light of men. And the light shineth in darkness; and the darkness comprehended it not.

It was like a prelude, like the rolling of drums before the curtain rising. I put aside Pastor Mallory's counsel to first read the book in an academic frame of mind. I would plunge into stage three and read with the anticipation of either an encounter with God or a cessation of searching to know Him in the context of revelation.

I read eagerly. The baptism. The calling of disciples. The marriage at Cana. Nicodemus. The woman of Samaria at Jacob's well. The feeding of the five thousand.

208

People, living and needing, touched by the Son of God.

I saw Jesus teaching on the mountain. I saw Him spit upon the ground and make clay to anoint the eyes of the blind man. I heard Him command Lazarus to arise from the stink of death, saw Him wash His disciples feet, break bread with them, pray for them.

Confidence rose and waned in my heart, rose and waned.

This was history, the acts of Jesus vividly chronicled, but nineteen centuries had passed. How could I relate the sayings and the events of antiquity to the needs of my heart in the Twentieth Century?

Yet I read on:

> Let not your heart be troubled: ye believe in God, believe also in me.

I prayed again and again, inviting God to show Himself greater than my unbelief.

> I am the vine, ye are the branches; He that abideth in me, and I in him, the same bringeth forth much fruit: for without me ye can do nothing. If a man abide not in me, he is cast forth as a branch and is withered; and men gather them, and cast them into the fire, and they are burned.

Did these utterances relate to me? Was I not like Judas who denied Christ? And should the miracle of transformation touch my heart, might not I, like Peter, deny my Lord?

I stopped reading and walked along the creek, sensing discovery, wanting to believe, wondering, wavering. I thought again of Pastor Mallory's counsel. In my first reading of the Gospel, I could think whatever I pleased. But I should read it again, asking God to reveal Himself, to implant faith within my heart.

"Lord," I prayed audibly, "if it really is possible to discover You, make it happen to me now."

I reopened the book: "Faith comes by hearing," I remembered Pastor Mallory quoting, "and hearing by the word of God."

"I've got to find faith." I whispered.

Faith.

It comes by hearing.

By hearing the Word of God.

> Then saith he to Thomas, Reach hither thy finger, and behold my hands; and reach hither thy hand, and thrust it into my side;

209

and be not faithless, but believing. And Thomas answered and said unto him, My Lord and my God. Jesus saith unto him, Thomas, because thou hast seen me, thou hast believed: blessed are they that have not seen, and yet have believed. And many other signs truly did Jesus in the presence of his disciples, which are not written in this book: But these are written, that ye might believe that Jesus is the Christ, the Son of God; and that believing ye might have life through his name.

"Be not faithless but believing." I scanned back across the reading. "Blessed are they that have not seen, and yet have believed . . . and that believing you might have life through his name.

Believing!

As the blind believed, the faint of heart, those burdened by their sins and seeking peace. These things were written that I might believe—believe in the power of Christ, in His personal concern for me, knowing that, though I did not, as Thomas, feel the nail prints, the wound of the spear, these wounds were for me. There was mercy for my sins. There was pardon. There was peace. There was a door ajar, a wisp of light.

Faith comes . . . by the word of God.

Faith, the elusive, mystical quality, that living thing which is beyond life and above death, yet meant to be as much of life as breath is, as much and more. And it was not a thing in skirts, not a taskmaster, but a virility, a strength, an everlasting answer.

Faith!

I wanted it!

I wanted faith!

"Savior," I prayed, "I believe. I believe You were and are and will always be. I believe You met the needs of men in your day upon earth. I believe men are the same today, and You are the same . . . the same Lord . . . just as I've read here. I believe . . . help me, God! . . . I believe You can meet my need."

I can't explain it. It would be pointless to try.

The discovery of God must be experienced, every contact ordained by the Almighty for each individual need.

Holding the book firmly in my hand, as a rescued man continues to clutch the rope that has drawn him to safety, I lifted my eyes skyward and whispered, "Thank You, God! I believe what I have read. I take it for myself. Thank You, God. Thank You!"

Faith materialized in my heart—not faith I had generated, not religious opinion, not a creed, but the living aura of God.

I was being transformed!

210

Give of your best to the Master.
Give of the strength of your youth.
Clad in salvation's full armour,
Join in the battle for truth.

The song burst from my lips!

I walked up from the creek bank and out into the field.

I had paid no attention to the time of day, but now saw the sun low in the sky.

I watched the sun set.

I watched and worshiped.

I did not worship the glowing orb, nor any divine countenance imagined in its flaming splendor, but stood in awe of its Creator, the reality of whose existence was no longer like the setting sun, always beyond grasp, fading from view, but instead like the sunrise, fuller and brighter with each moment of beholding, surrounding me with warmth and light.

Chapter Twenty-two

I am aware that the phenomenon of religious conversion is held highly suspect by our pragmatic world.

Small wonder.

I was to learn that the devil is a staunch ecclesiastic. He delights in overt displays of mortal righteousness. He lauds those doctrinal distinctives which fragment Christian fellowship. His disciples number those human beings who sing "I'm the Child of the King" on Sunday morning, "nor silver nor gold hath obtained my redemption" on Sunday night, and whistle "I Got Plenty of Nothing" the remaining six days of the week.

None-the-less, the discovery of faith swept me into the effulgence of spiritual exaltation, and I wept as I took Vaneta into my arms that evening, telling her what had happened. The following morning, I stopped at Security Mercantile Store to share the news with Uncle Rufus. Thereupon I hurried to work, walking resolutely into Walter Vamp's office to give my witness. I also called Pastor Mallory and thanked him for the guidance he had given.

Vaneta seemed a little frightened. Rufus gripped my hand and smiled silently. Mr. Vamp swore and said, "I suppose that's good, Jerry."

It was Pastor Mallory who established an immediate affinity with my spiritual experience.

"A man doesn't become a total human being," he said, "until he lets Christ add the spiritual dimension you have just found."

"It's actually so simple," I said. "Why do people make it seem so complicated?"

I shall always remember his reply. "Simplicity is the most profound aspect of existence," he said. "Simplicity demands humility. It offers no opportunity to be proud of great personal achievement. Man accepts simplicity in the physical world. Two parts of hydrogen and one part of oxygen transform two gases into a life-sustaining liquid. Addition, subtraction, multiplication—these can be extended into complex forms. The basic elements, however, are utterly simple. Take the most advanced mathematical problem, reduce it to steps and what do you have? One, two, three, four, five—knowledge most children obtain before they start school.

"But though conversion involves a simple formula—your need, God's provision for that need, your acceptance of that provision—the living out of the divinely implanted faith is the only procedure God has designed for mortals to experience fulfillment. When a man avoids this procedure, or when he complicates it, he lessens or denies the flow of God's grace into his life.

"You see, Jerry, God designed you with two purposes in mind. First, so you might be the recipient of His merciful grace. Second, so you could humbly glorify Him before men through the transforming evidence of that grace in your life.

"And this is at all times a personal experience. Christians have their greatest problem in the search for conformity, trying to fit themselves into a predescribed mold. There is uniformity in Christion experience. Without it, there would be little basis for fellowship among believers. But uniformity, Jerry, stems from the fact that it is the same God revealing Himself to each believer through His Son, and not because fallible human beings, who call themselves Christians, prescribe set forms of conduct and procedure by which one supposedly stands in favor before God.

"We must realize," he concluded, "that the one great truth of redemption is freedom. Freedom in Christ. Freedom to become the human being God envisioned when He designed us . . . every one of us, Jerry . . . as individuals. After God made each of us, you know, He threw away the mold. There aren't two identical snowflakes. There aren't two identical people. I'm a new student in these matters, but I am becoming more and more convinced there should not be two identical Christians."

I could not be expected to sense all the nuances of what Pastor Mallory told me. Indeed, as I was to subsequently learn, he had only begun to search out from the Scriptures the truths indicated that day.

What he said meant essentially three things to me. First, and most important, his words guided my thinking in those early stages of spiritual adventure. Second, his words spared me the error, into which I most surely would have fallen, of endeavoring to make my Christian life a carbon copy of his own. Third, his words prepared me for inclement circumstances I would soon face.

In regard to the third aspect, I should have suspected something afoot. In the excitement of my new discovery, however, blinded by the sheen of spiritual newness, I overlooked many things. Around town, I gave undaunted witness to what had happened in my life. As a boy, I remembered others doing this and thereby invoking ridicule upon themselves. Through Pastor Mallory's counsel, I sought to be forthright and tactful in my witness. Consequently, though I'm sure there were those who made light of my testimony, I found myself being more accepted by the men of our community than had previously been the case.

Pastor Mallory did not say so, being too kind and astute, but in his continuing counsel I sensed that, in the past, townsmen had simply taken me for granted as another member of my family who, in perhaps a different way, demonstrated the hypocrisy they ascribed to all religious fundamentalists. Like a new brother, for indeed he was, he encouraged me to relate myself vitally with community endeavors. I volunteered my help for special projects. I attended town meetings where items of civic importance were discussed. When several of the younger business men began talking about the need for a junior chamber of commerce, I joined their circle, shared my ideas, offered to help.

Because of my initiative, it came to be said that the junior chamber, or Jaycees as it was called, came into being considerably sooner than had been anticipated. Also, because of the initiative I had shown, members of the new group elected me their first president.

That was the fell swoop. For my picture appeared in the paper, showing me receiving congratulations from Mr. Vamp, who now served as mayor of our town.

Aunt Lydia awaited me in our living room when I arrived home from work that afternoon. It had been months since she and I had been together in our own home, for whatever purpose. She held the weekly paper in her hands. I could hear Vaneta off in another part of the house looking after our son.

"Jeremiah!" she bellowed, shaking the paper at me like a court summons. "There will be a family meeting at my house Sunday afternoon. I have told Vaneta to see to it you are there."

She tossed the paper onto a nearby chair and stomped out of the house. Glancing toward the chair, I saw my photograph prominent on the front page of the paper and surmised an inkling of Aunt Lydia's motivation. I waited for Vaneta to come, certain of her having been duly informed by my aunt.

"Vaneta!" I called, when several moments passed without her presence.

She did not come.

"Vaneta!" I called again, much louder than before.

I was sure she heard me. Yet she did not come. So I went to her.

She was in our room, seated on the edge of the bed, half-heartedly playing with our son.

"Didn't you hear me call?" I said.

She looked up but did not speak.

I began to think back. From the outset of my professed conversion experience, Vaneta had reacted strangely. Of late, she had grown distant in many of her attitudes toward me. But, so swept up in my new enthrallment, I had overlooked it.

"What's the matter?" I asked. For the first time since my conversion, anger rose in my thoughts. "What's eating on Aunt Lydia anyway? And what part do you have with whatever it is?"

Tears came to her eyes. As quickly as it had risen, my anger subsided. I stepped over to her, put my hand on her shoulder.

"What's wrong?" I asked.

She took little Jerry into her arms, stood and moved quickly toward the door.

"Vaneta!" I called out.

She hesitated at the doorway, turned and looked back at me.

"What do you care what Aunt Lydia thinks?" she snapped. "And what do you care about me or about our son?"

I followed her to little Jerry's room. "Please, Vaneta," I said, "tell me."

She turned on me. "Have you really been converted, like you say?" she demanded.

The question was like a slap across the face.

"How much time have you spent with me or Jerry since you say you became a Christian? You were a better husband and father before."

215

"Vaneta!"

"Oh, don't try to play on my emotions! I tried not to see it Aunt Lydia's way. But it's true."

What's true?"

She tried to speak, her lips beginning to form words, but made no utterance. Abruptly, she placed little Jerry into his crib and stalked away.

I did not immediately follow. I looked down at my son. I looked at my hands. I turned to a mirror on the nearby wall and looked into it. The pang of failure came to my heart. I had basked in the Sunlight of God, oblivious of the potential of clouds in the heavenly skies. Glaring at myself in the mirror, I very nearly said aloud, *Jerry Pew, ol' boy, you're still a human being!*

"Vaneta," I called out, moving in the direction of her departure, finding her in the kitchen. "I'm sorry, sweetheart," I said.

She turned to me. Hurt was in her eyes.

"I've done a terrible thing," I continued.

Her eyes widened. Her lips parted slightly. Anticipation rose across her countenance.

"It's been such a tremendous experience, finding the faith I've wanted for so long. I've taken you and Jerry for granted, let myself get all wrapped up in witness to the community, and . . ."

There came such a strange turn of expression to her face, I broke off speaking and could only look at my wife, puzzled.

In a scarcely audible monotone, she said, "I thought you were going to say something else."

"Like what?" I asked.

"O Jerry!"

"What's wrong?"

I stepped toward her. She stepped away.

"How can anyone become a Christian without repenting? You haven't said a word about your adultery with Hillary. And what are you and Pastor Mallory up to anyway?"

I was stunned.

"I don't know what you're talking about," I managed to say.

"You're lying, Jerry. How can you claim to be a Christian and stand there and lie to me?" She burst into convulsive sobbing, and for the remainder of that week we became as strangers to each other.

In the days immediately following, I grew listless, in a half-stupor, clinging to my faith and yet unsure of its validity. My ef-

216

fectiveness at work came to such straits Mr. Vamp took me to task, cautioning me that if my attitude were an example of how religious experience was to affect my productivity, I had better do some careful thinking.

I didn't consult with Pastor Mallory. I, in fact, avoided him. I also avoided Uncle Rufus. I was confused, overcome with self-pity. Hostility supplanted the glow of love that had pervaded my thought mechanisms.

On the following Sunday, Vaneta and I went silently to church, then to Aunt Lydia's house. Other members of the clan also came. Moments before we partook of the carry-in dinner, Pastor Mallory and his wife arrived. It was not customary for Aunt Lydia to invite them to family functions, so I couldn't quite decide what might be in the offing, especially when Aunt Lydia transgressed protocol by commissioning Uncle Eliad, instead of Pastor Mallory, to offer the blessing.

The meal was eaten mostly in silence. Several of the Pews tried to make conversation. No one succeeded, except for brief moments. Had it not been for Pastor Mallory, conversation might have fallen off completely. Warmly, tactfully, he spoke with all in the room, an intermittent exchange but sufficient to ward off periods of extended silence.

Once, when I returned to the table for additional helpings, Pastor Mallory joined me. We were alone.

"I'm sure you realize this is not a social occasion," he said.

"I know."

"Then perhaps you also know it is both of us who are suspect in your Aunt's eyes."

Someone else came to the table, thus ending our brief exchange.

When all had eaten, the women began stacking soiled dishes and taking them to the kitchen.

"We'll wash the dishes later," Aunt Lydia said. "Everybody come to the parlor."

Everybody came.

Thereafter ensued moments of silence the like of which I had not previously endured. The eyes of those in the room drifted to Aunt Lydia, to Pastor Mallory, to me. My mind reverted to childhood again, when I wanted to run outside and be gone. It seemed endless, how long in actuality I do not know, but at last Aunt Lydia spoke.

"I may not be on this earth much longer," she began plaintively, "and once old Lydia is six feet below the sod, I don't suppose there'll be much of anybody left in this family to care about what happens. The coming of the Lord surely draweth nigh."

I had not expected this kind of introduction. It gave temporary relief to the tension I felt. I thought she perhaps might be announcing some terminal malady the doctor had discovered. Transforming though my spiritual experience had been, I could not feel apprehensive about the prospect of my aunt's departure from the earthly scene.

I promptly learned she had no such pronouncement to offer.

"Many's the night I lay awake," she began, whimpering. "I cry, I go into my sanctuary to pray. The burdens get so heavy sometimes I ask the Lord to take me home, away from this world with all its wickedness. Once it was only wickedness in the world. Now it's wickedness in the church. That's what hurts those few of us who really care about the Lord's work."

She stepped beside Vaneta, who sat directly opposite from me across the room. I am not sure if it was to be closer to Vaneta or to have a better vantage of me.

"I can't suppose it hurts the others of you as it hurts me, but we all know the sorrow and embarrassment that has come to our family by the young man who bear the name most precious to all of us, Jeremiah."

My ears began to burn.

"I don't just blame him. His own parents are at fault. For those of us that God never allowed to have children—and I can't expect you who haven't borne that cross to know how it feels—it hurts to see parents in our precious circle who have failed in their responsibility, who don't even speak up when their own first blood goes astray."

I glanced at my father. He sat staring at the floor. My mother twisted her handkerchief.

"You all know how Jeremiah resisted the gospel, year after year. You know how he went to college and would have fallen completely by the wayside, if the Lord hadn't answered prayers and sent this precious girl across his path. You know the shame Jeremiah has brought to her heart, even deeper than to ours."

At first I was disgusted. Then I became angry. I wanted to defy Aunt Lydia to her face, as I had done before, but I glanced at Pastor Mallory. He smiled assuringly. I held my peace.

"Knowing these are the last days," Aunt Lydia continued, "when

218

the Bible tells us wickedness is going to spread like a flood across the earth, I s'pose we would have kept quiet, myself included, if it had been just a matter of Jeremiah's sinful conduct. But the Bible also tells us in the last days not only shall evil men and seducers wax worse and worse but there shall be men who have a form of godliness but deny the power thereof."

She looked squarely at me now. Her eyes flashed. Her lips trembled.

"Jeremiah," she said, pointing, "I accuse you of blasphemy. Not just the blasphemy of taking the Lord's name in vain. That's small compared to those who profess to become His children in order to cover over the rotteness inside them."

"I declare," Uncle Eliad spoke up. "I don't see what's eatin' on you, sister."

"O Eliad!" Aunt Lydia gasped. She broke into weeping.

"She seems a mite soft in the head," Uncle Eliad whispered to Uncle Rufus. "You noticed anything special lately?"

Uncle Rufus offered no comment.

Aunt Lydia collected herself and resumed speaking. "There's just no discernment anymore," she said. "If that isn't a sign of the last days, I don't know my Bible."

She again turned her attention to me.

"Jeremiah, precious boy," she said, "Aunt Lydia loves you and weeps over your hypocrisy."

Pastor Mallory now stood.

"My dear lady," he began, "I commend you for whatever desire you may have to uphold true righteousness. But I simply cannot understand on what basis you question the conversion of this young man."

Aunt Lydia quickly regained her full composure.

"Now isn't this interesting?" She glared at Pastor Mallory. "Here's a man—and my heart is heavy for you, dear brother. I've laid awake many a night weeping because of you, praying for you, asking the Lord . . ."

"I thank you for your prayers," Pastor Mallory broke in.

"You hold still!" Aunt Lydia stormed. "This is my house, and I'll do the talkin'! Of course, you stand up for Jeremiah. It's precious few converts we ever see anymore and so naturally you take sides when someone has the courage and discernment to see what's happening."

"Now my dear woman . . ." Pastor Mallory began.

"I told you to be quiet. Sit down."

Pastor Mallory sat. It disappointed me to see him do it.

"It may interest you to know, Pastor Mallory, that I'm not the only one in our church who believes your ministry with us should end, because it never ever really began!"

Deathly silence fell across the room under the sweep of the woman's brash boldness.

"If that statement wasn't true," she continued, "then it wouldn't be up to me to take matters in hand, as I'm doing this afternoon."

"Tell me what you're driving at, Aunt Lydia," I spoke up.

"You be quiet, too."

"I certainly have a right to speak up in my own defense."

"You know very well what the matter is."

"Believe me," I said, "I don't."

"You lie! Can't you understand, Jeremiah, that guilt before God becomes doubly worse when the guilty one tries to cover his wrong?"

"Believe me," I insisted. "I don't know what you're talking about." I looked at my wife. "Do you know what she's talking about, Vaneta?"

Vaneta stood and hurried out of the room. Aunt Lydia watched her go, then slowly turned back to me. "Now do you undersand what the problem is?" she asked.

"Aunt Lydia," I said, "I am not aware . . ."

"Oh, you insolent young fool!" she broke in. "I suppose you sit there, thinking we can believe you've been converted as you claim, that your life has been changed, your heart made clean."

"That's exactly what's happened to me," I said.

Aunt Lydia now only looked at me, shaking her head.

"Why should you think otherwise?" I asked.

"Why do you suppose your dear wife went crying out of this room?"

"You know, dear," Uncle Rufus put in, "it could be that you're wrong."

"I'll thank you not to meddle, Rufus."

She returned her attention to me. "Jeremiah," she said, almost a touch of tenderness in her voice, "when people get converted, really converted, two important things happen. They confess their sins, all their sins, and they forsake those sins. Maybe you've grieved the Holy Spirit beyond a chance of redemption. I don't know. But in case this isn't true, be honest. Confess your adultery with Hillary

220

Vamp. Don't try to cover it over anymore. Confess that you're running around with the worldly crowd in town, shaming the Lord you've claimed to profess, gaining prominence with the worldly young businessmen that are practically taking over our community. Confess, Jeremiah!" Her voice rose until she was virtually screaming. "Confess, my boy! God have mercy on you! Confess! Do it for dear Vaneta's sake, if no other reason." She sank to her chair, sobbing. No one offered her comfort. We only sat there, stunned. After a moment, she got up and left, weeping convulsively.

I didn't know what to say. My tongue lay dry in my mouth. Myriad thoughts bombarded my mind. I looked at Pastor Mallory. His head was bowed in prayer. I, too, whispered a prayer. A measure of peace came to my heart.

"Naturally," I began, "this is all very upsetting to me. I didn't realize these kind of thoughts existed relative to my discovery of the Christian life. If I were guilty of the sins Aunt Lydia spoke about, I would confess them. But believe me, as God surely knows, I am innocent."

It was all I could say.

Pastor Mallory stood. He came over, gripped my arm a moment, then whispered to his wife that they would be leaving. As they walked toward the door, I turned to Uncle Rufus and said, "Will you drive Vaneta and little Jerry home? I better leave now."

He nodded.

I walked to the door.

"Jerry!" Uncle Rufus called.

I turned.

He smiled, a smile full and warm. I looked about the room. The others only sat there, staring at me. I didn't know what they were thinking. But I could tell Uncle Rufus believed me. I would rather have him believe me and all the others doubt, than to have him doubt and all the others believe.

I returned his smile and left.

Chapter Twenty-three

Vaneta remained with Aunt Lydia until late that evening. I imagined a myriad of things, pitied myself for the sorry web with which fate had entangled me, indicting myself for those past circumstances which, had I avoided them, might have left Aunt Lydia with nothing to surmise.

I paced the floor, coming to Vaneta's Bible left atop some magazines. I picked it up, it's damaged binding a cruel reminder of that day when Aunt Lydia first accused me of consortment with Hillary.

I prayed. Prayer brought peace, like the hush of shelter in the howl of a storm. There was vindication in that peace, hope and assurance.

At ten o'clock, Vaneta came.

"Hello, sweetheart," I greeted.

"Hello," she managed.

I took little Jerry from her arms. He was asleep. I removed his clothes, dressed him in his pajamas, and put him to bed.

Vaneta went to our room and closed the door. We had not shared the room for several nights.

I called to her.

She didn't answer. So I went to the room and, without knocking, opened the door. She turned, startled.

"May I talk to you?" I asked.

She didn't reply.

"Please," I added.

"Yes," she said quietly.

She went to the vanity dresser and began brushing her hair. I walked slowly across the room and glanced at the mirror. Our eyes met in its reflection.

"I love you, Vaneta," I said.

"Do you?" she asked. There was an edge to her voice.

I put my hands on her shoulders. She winced lightly so I took my hands away and put them on my hips.

"If my actions, my attitudes," I began, "if somewhere I've failed to show you I'm sorry and . . ."

"You know what the problem is," she broke in.

"Yes," I said, "I know."

"Then why don't you do something about it?"

"The problem," I said, avoiding her question, "is my failure, my inability, to prove my innocence."

"Jerry!" She tossed the brush aside and leaned forward, thrusting her fingers into her hair. "Why won't you confess your wrong, like Aunt Lydia said?"

I turned away, striking the palm of my left hand with my right fist. "How can I confess a wrong I didn't do?" I asked. "I'm a man. When an attractive woman throws herself at me, I have a rough time. I admit it. But I've never defiled myself with Hillary Vamp or any other woman. I never will."

Vaneta turned to me, raising her eyebrows. "So now you at least confess she throws herself at you? You must be quite the Lothario." She was being catty. It was utterly unlike her. "Such masculine charms that a stunning woman like Hillary Vamp throws herself at you!"

"You don't understand me, sweetheart! I . . ."

"Precisely how does she throw herself at you? Perhaps I could learn the technique."

"You're impossible," I snapped. Anger rose in me like a suppressed torrent. "You don't want to know the truth." I wheeled away out of the room.

"Oh yes, I do," she called, trotting after me. "I want to know the truth, Jerry! I want to know the truth. The morbid, rotten, filthy, horrible truth." She began to be hysterical, weeping, screaming. "Tell me the truth! Tell me all about it! I want to know everything you did. I want to know the truth, Jerry; I want to know the truth."

I took her by the arms and shook her.

"Vaneta," I cried, "act like you've got some sense!"

She struck me hard against the arm, hard enough to have broken her hand. I released her. "Tell me the truth, Jerry!" she screamed. "Tell me how she threw herself at you. Tell me about the nights you spent together. Tell me. Tell me!"

She threw herself onto the couch and sobbed convulsively. I stood a moment, helpless.

I prayed. You've got to help me, God, I breathed, Please help me.

I went to the couch and sat beside Vaneta. She didn't try to push me away. I put my hand on her shoulder, massaging it gently. She quieted. We sat that way a long time, how long I haven't the slightest notion, and then slowly she turned.

"I love you," I said.

There was a first glimmer of belief in her eyes.

"May I please tell you what happened in Chicago?"

"Tell me," she said. The words were like an unvoiced sound.

"In Chicago," I said quietly, "I made a mistake. It was thoughtless and stupid. Halford Vamp engineered it all, though I take my share of the blame. He didn't need me at the convention. He just had the idea of getting me together with his daughter. He kept steering us together, Hillary and me, all the time. We ate together. She wanted to go to Marshall Fields, but didn't want to go alone, so her father told me to go with her. She wanted to walk along the lake front, and he sent me with her there. It turned out I was her escort wherever she went."

"Day and night," Vaneta asked?

"One night," I said hesitantly, "after we had been to see a play . . ."

"Yes?" She raised herself to an elbow.

"She invited me to her room."

Vaneta's eyes were like glass, staring at me.

"I . . ."

"Go on."

"I told her I wouldn't go."

"Did you really?"

"God knows it's the truth."

"What happened?"

"I refused."

I saw the hunger for belief in my wife's eyes.

"She got angry," I continued. "She said my marriage was like a prison sentence to me and that I was spineless not to break it."

"You agreed?"

"Of course not. I told her that I loved you. I told her I intended to be faithful to you always. And I do, Vaneta." I leaned down and kissed her forehead. She didn't resist me. The thrill of young romance coursed for a moment through my body. I silently thanked God.

"What happened?" Vaneta asked.

"Hillary was furious. Look, sweetheart, it wasn't that I was such an attraction to her. But I was a conquest. And the very fact that I resisted her wiles made her . . . well . . . that's why she would throw herself at me."

"She threw herself at you then?"

"She went to her room."

"And you?"

"I went out onto the streets and walked—walked and walked and walked, Sweetheart, like I said, I'm human. For awhile, I was disgusted at myself for not taking Hillary's proposal. But more, much more, I was thankful I hadn't."

She looked away.

"Can't you understand, sweetheart? I love you. If I had defiled myself with Hillary, and if I confessed it to you and asked your forgiveness, I believe you would forgive me. You're that kind of a wonderful person, Vaneta. But I'm innocent. God help you to see it. How can I confess guilt when I'm innocent?"

I began to cry. It came suddenly, like a summer squall when one has not been watching the sky. I caught control of myself as quickly as I could. I didn't want her to think I was being theatrical.

She reached up and touched my head, drew it down to her shoulders.

"I wish I could believe you, Jerry," she said. "I guess I'm stubborn. But I want to believe. I'm trying, only . . ."

I drew back so I could look at her.

". . . only I can't."

"Why?" I asked desperately.

"I don't know. I just can't."

We were quiet for several moments, looking at each other. I caressed her. She didn't resist. I saw love come back to her eyes. I felt it in the warmth of her hand.

"I don't mean to make a scapegoat out of Aunt Lydia," I said at last, "but, for some reason, she's never cared for me. Maybe it's because, as a very young boy, I couldn't equate her ideas of the Christian life with . . . . Look, I don't want to put her down. I'm sure it's partly my fault, the rift between us, but that's another matter. I love you. Our marriage disappoints me . . . in some ways . . . because we so seldom seem to be very close to each other. But I'll accept whatever blame is mine. I pray . . . how I pray, sweetheart . . . that some way . . . somehow . . . I don't know . . . that things can be right between us."

I waited for her to speak.

She said nothing.

I again saw her Bible. This time I reached for it and took it, opened it, browsing. I came to the book of Proverbs where she had underscored.

I read aloud, just above a whisper. "Lying lips are an abomination to the Lord, But they that deal truly are His delight . . . Hope deferred makes the heart sick; but when the desire comes, it is a tree of life."

I looked at her. She got up, holding my hand.

"You may sleep in our room," she said.

I stood.

"Where will you be?" I asked.

"With you," she said, resting her head against my shoulder.

We walked toward the bedroom.

"Let's see if little Jerry's asleep," I said.

We went into his room.

He was asleep, a deep, beautiful, peaceful sleep known only to childhood. As we stood at his bedside, I put my arm around Vaneta. In the dim light falling into the room from the hallway, I could see her looking intently at the bed.

Suddenly, she began to cry.

"It isn't right," she exclaimed. "It isn't right that things have to be this way!"

"What's wrong?" I asked.

"All men are the same," she snapped.

She walked briskly to our bedroom, closing the door against me. I went to the door.

"Vaneta."

There was no answer.

"Vaneta," I repeated.

"Leave me alone," came a muffled cry from inside.

I turned away.

In the weeks that followed, the state of our marriage came to its lowest fortunes. Even yet, it pains me to speak of it. The afternoon in Aunt Lydia's parlor not only brought to light suspected skeletons in my closet, but also revealed the disinclination of several older stalwarts in our church toward Pastor Mallory, with the result that, a few weeks later, he tendered his resignation.

It was a stunning blow.

"I've come to value your friendship," he said, as we played golf immediately prior to his leaving. "I'm grateful for any help I've been able to be to you. But keep in mind that, important though it is for spiritual inter-relationship through fellowship such as we've had, in the final analysis, Jerry, the test of our Christian life lies in the flow of our personal communion with Jesus Christ."

This communion, this personal sense of relationship with the Son of God, became my vital source of spiritual sustenance in the month ahead. A new minister came to the church, one much more to Aunt Lydia's liking, and though he was, I am sure, a good man, we had little rapport—a circumstance very possibly more my fault than his. Uncle Rufus remained a strength in my life, as much by his attitude as by anything he said.

For the most part, though, I stood alone. It was good. It impelled me to renewed searching of the Scriptures. It strengthened my faith. I missed Pastor Mallory, as one misses a brother. We exchanged letters for a time, but as the press of responsibilities at the office intensified, I grew lax in my replies and the line of communication severed.

Laxity came also to my spiritual life. I continued my study of the Bible. I was sure of my faith and gave witness to others. But there seemed to come a status quo, an end to climbing and growing. It came so slowly, so unobtrusively, that it did not frighten me. Why it happened, I do not know. Possibly it was because of the one great emptiness of my heart, the leanness which had come to my marriage. It was not an all together blissless union, however. Vaneta was a basically good person, conscientious, considerate of others.

As I have indicated, the several weeks following Aunt Lydia's disruption of our relationship were characterized by frightening shadows of incompatibility. But Vaneta could no more sustain the rift than could I. Gradually, with the sheer force of time upon our temperaments, we renewed our affinities. We had moments of deeply enriched devotion, moments in each other's arms more meaningful and sustaining than the awe of our first wedded hours.

"I love you, Jerry," Vaneta whispered on one of those occasions. "Let's try to live for the future. I'll try. I'll try real hard."

There came times when the shadow of my suspected guilt seemed completely removed from the glow of our marriage. Slowly, but unmistakably, Vaneta accepted the fact of my conversion. I made it a point to read the Bible and offer prayer at the conclusion of each meal. She liked this. It was the only spiritual communion we had with each other apart from public worship, but it became increasingly meaningful.

It was little Jerry who forged the strongest bond between us. He grew like a weed, as people say. Vaneta mothered him wisely. I made a continuing effort to help her.

One evening, just before our son was old enough to enroll in kindergarten, he resisted the main dish at the evening meal. We both insisted he must always eat at least something of every kind of food on the table.

"Eat some of it," Vaneta encouraged, "so we can hear daddy read the Bible. See, he's finished his food. He's the nicest daddy in all the world."

It was a small thing.

It was a very big thing.

Autumn came, and little Jerry started school—a profound experience for the both of us, watching the little life we had generated take his first full step into the world beyond our shelter.

Autumn passed, and winter and spring came again, spring and the months of summer beyond which our son would enter the first grade, a full-fledged student.

But then calamity struck our community. Those were the years prior to the advent of polio vaccine, and summer after summer brought epidemics to many areas—this summer to ours.

Vaneta grew apprehensive, watching every move little Jerry made, leaving no suggested precaution unheeded.

"Don't worry," I said one evening, as we sat at the conclusion of dinner.

"I can't keep from worrying," she told me.

"But he's in God's hands," I said.

"Children in other families have the disease," she said. "What about them?"

To this I could not answer, though I nurtured confidence in my

228

heart. Daily, and often many times during the day, I prayed that the disease might not touch our son. But it did.

Returning from work one mid-July afternoon, I found Vaneta in great distress.

"Little Jerry has a fever," she said. "His neck is stiff. I'm afraid it's polio." She broke into hysterical sobbing.

I went into the child's room. She followed me.

"He was out in the yard," she sobbed, "just sitting there. I'm all upset. Call the doctor."

Momentary panic gripped my heart. It was a breach of doubt, for I had believed our son would be spared, and he was not. My faith had experienced dimensions of renewal, but now it plummeted.

Why, God? I questioned silently.

A breath of peace came to my heart. I turned Vaneta to me, lifted her chin so her eyes met mine.

"Hurry," she cried out. "Call the doctor!"

"This is no time to be upset."

"Call the doctor," she pleaded. "We musn't waste a minute. Please!"

I stooped and put my hand to little Jerry's forehead. It was hot.

"There is no time to loose. You've got to call the doctor."

"Don't worry, Vaneta." Then, looking at our son, I whispered, "How are you Jerry, boy."

"Call the doctor," Vaneta urged.

"God is going to make you well," I whispered to my son. "We're going to pray, and God will make you well."

Like a hastened sunrise, assurance dawned in my heart.

I turned to my wife.

"Bring some oil," I said.

"Oil?" she asked. "Why?"

"Any kind. Olive oil, some of that left over baby oil you had for little Jerry. Go get it, the baby oil."

"Why?"

"God is going to heal our son," I said. "We'll annoint him with oil and God will heal him."

"Call the doctor."

"Bring the oil," I urged. I again put my arm around Vaneta.

"Jerry!" She screamed.

"Maybe we don't even need oil. Maybe we can just pray for little Jerry, and God will heal him. I think that's what Mr. Sommerford would have done. He wouldn't have used oil."

"Mr. Sommerford?" she questioned.

I took Vaneta's hand and guided it toward little Jerry. "Let's put our hands on him, and God will heal him. I know he will."

"Call the doctor!" Vaneta protested.

"God is greater than any doctor," I insisted. "Let's pray together."

She wrenched free. "You go ahead and pray," she exclaimed, the tearfulness giving way to indignation in her voice, "but I'm calling the doctor." She hurried to the telephone. I was sorry for her impetuousness, her lack of faith.

Alone in the room, I hesitated a moment, looking at our son. There was joy and peace in my heart, for at last I stood on the brink of the great experience I had so longed for as a child. Faith loomed in my heart, as still another thought came to me. If I prayed for little Jerry and God instantly touched his body, healing him, then Vaneta would know for sure the Master's blessing was upon us. She would no longer have reason to doubt unconfessed transgressions in my past.

I paced the floor, thinking. But suppose I asked for healing and nothing happened? What if little Jerry should die?

From another part of the house, I could hear Vaneta talking to the doctor. I listened, experiencing a momentary concern that the doctor be brought as quickly as possible.

But then I returned to my son's bedside.

"It hurts, daddy," he whimpered.

I knelt by his bed.

"I'm going to pray for you," I told him. "There are naughty germs in your body. We're going to ask God to take them away. He can take them away and heal you the way Jesus healed people in the Bible. Do you want that?"

The little fellow nodded. I saw faith in his eyes, and thanked God. I put one hand on his feverish forehead, took his little hand in the other, and bowed to begin my prayer.

Then Vaneta burst into the room.

"I'm sorry," she cried out, "but we mustn't even take time to pray. The doctor says we don't dare lose another moment getting him to the hospital!"

I looked up.

"Hurry," she tugged at my shirt, trying to lift me.

I stood.

"We've got to go right away."

"But . . ."

"Please, Jerry! Please! Please!"

I picked up our son and followed Vaneta to the garage. In the silence of my heart, I felt again the remorse of disobedience I had so often experienced in childhood. It was as though I had one more time seen God's countenance in the sun, only to allow that sun to set before calling out to Him.

Chapter Twenty-four

Medical procedure in those days was for polio patients to spend a minimum of two weeks in total isolation. During that agonizing interval, Vaneta and I had only the reports of the doctor to sustain the link between us and our son.

"Your boy has partial paralysis," the doctor told us. "At this point, no one can predict the outcome."

We were numb. For two days, Vaneta prepared no food. It didn't matter. Hunger was a forgotten emotion.

Aunt Lydia fluttered in upon us like a mother hen. To her credit, I will say she did us well. She lifted household responsibilities from Vaneta's shoulders. She tried to bring a spirit of confidence and cheer to our lives—incredibly so, by revealing a strata of herself I had never before witnessed.

"Aunt Lydia's praying for you dear kiddies," she told us. "She's trusting the Lord with you for His very best on dear little Jerry's body."

She came to me, and we put our arms around each other. She was the same Aunt Lydia, quaint and crotchety, but there was good in her marrow, and it came out like the sun breaking through clouds of leaden winter gray. But it was inevitable for inclement moments to taint the goodness Aunt Lydia brought to our distressed circumstances.

One evening, when at her insistence we had each agreed to a small bowl of broth, she came with her Bible and asked if she might read a portion. Taking this to be another dimension of her turn to kindness, I readily agreed.

She read from the fourth chapter of Hosea:

Hear the word of the Lord, ye children of Israel: For the Lord hath a controversy with the inhabitants of the land, because there is not truth nor mercy, nor knowledge of God in the land. By swearing, and lying, and killing, and stealing, and committing adultry, they break out, and blood toucheth blood. Therefore shall the land mourn . . ."

Aunt Lydia stopped reading.

She turned to me, and there was nothing of the old unkindness in her countenance. There was pathos, as tears sought out the furrows on her skin.

"O Jeremiah!" she gasped.

I looked at Vaneta. Vaneta dropped her eyes. I knew what was coming.

"I spent until long after midnight last night in my prayer chamber," she bemoaned. "I cried to God for you, Jeremiah. Hasn't He answered my prayer? Don't you see this terrible sickness, which has touched your darling baby, can be God's voice to you, pleading for you to turn from your disobedience?"

Anger rose with the crimson that touched my cheeks.

"There has been disobedience," I said.

"Praise the Lord!" Aunt Lydia exuded. "Be out with it, Jeremiha. Be out with it, once and for all."

"We should never have taken Jerry to the hospital," I snapped.

"Whatever are you saying?" Aunt Lydia asked.

"God could have healed him, right in his bed," I continued.

Glancing at Vaneta, I said no more. I had hurt her. I was sorry and the anger left me. I got up and left the table.

"Whatever is he talking about, Vaneta?" Aunt Lydia asked.

Without replying, Vaneta also walked away. She came to me in our room. She came to me like a child pleading forgiveness for the security of a parent's love. She put her arms tightly around me, as though afraid I would try to push her away.

"I'm sorry," she whispered. "I didn't mean to do anything wrong. I thought little Jerry needed to get to the hospital as quickly as we could take him. Maybe we should have done as you said. I'm sorry."

I turned Vaneta's face to mine and kissed her longingly and

deeply—our tears mingled at our lips like the salt of unrequited thirst.

On the fourth day, the doctor came to our house.

"I've just been to the hospital," he said. The gravity of his bearing foretold the content of his tidings.

"Little Jerry is . . .?" Vaneta began, fear stifling her voice.

The doctor shook his head and sighed.

"What is his condition?" I asked.

"There is no improvement. The paralysis is critical."

"His arms? His legs?"

"His left arm and his left leg."

"Paralyzed?" Vaneta asked.

The doctor nodded.

"He'll never walk normally?" she asked.

"We can't say that now."

"But he might not?"

"That's correct. The only assurance I can give you is we are doing everything humanly possible." The words were mockery to me . . . humanly possible . . . but I bit my lip and did not speak.

When the doctor left, I paced the floor, tension building up in me like boiler pressure. Vaneta came and touched my arm. I didn't look at her. It was not that I was avoiding her, it was the pressure bursting inside me.

"I know what you're thinking," she said.

I didn't answer.

"But you know every moment is important in a time like this," she continued. "We had to get him to the hospital. Can't God touch him there as much as if we had kept him home?"

I stopped now, looked at her.

"Can't God heal him now," she asked, "in the hospital?"

"I don't know." It must have been the way I said it, or something about the way I looked at her. In any case, the plaintiveness departed from her eyes.

"Then you doubt God as much as you accuse me of doing," she snapped.

"We both doubted Him," I said quietly. "We stood in His way at a time when He could have spared little Jerry from what he's going through now."

It grew into an argument. I had no intention of being abrasive. I was upset, and had no thought of irritating her. But in moments we were hurling accusations and unkindness at each other.

234

"I suppose you hope little Jerry dies to prove your point!" she screamed.

"Don't say that!" I thundered.

"It's true, isn't it?"

"Of course, it isn't true."

She put her hands on her hips mockingly and scoffed, "You can tell people I was the one who prevented God from healing him. Then the score would be even between us—you and your infidelity with Hillary, I in the murder of our son."

I was dumbfounded. The fight went out of me. In one split second of weakness, I could have slumped to the floor.

"Isn't it true?" she asked.

O God, I prayed silently, what are we doing?

"You could answer me!" she bellowed.

I did not answer. I felt ashamed. I loved this woman. I could not understand her, but doubtless I was at times incongruous to her.

"I'm sorry, Vaneta."

"Heartbroken, I suppose," she countered.

I shook my head. "You're a very complex person."

"More and more disappointing to you?"

"I didn't say that. I didn't mean to offend you."

"You were trying to change the subject. Well, I'd like to stick to the subject. Isn't it true you would like to find a scapegoat for your past?"

"Redemption needs no scapegoat," I said.

She looked at me a moment. I stepped toward her. She stepped back.

"Go to the office," she said in a low voice. "Go visit Hillary. Do whatever you want. I want to be alone . . ."

I stood my ground.

"Please go," she said.

I stayed.

"Please, Jerry," she said. "I really want to be alone."

"Sure, sweetheart." I went to her, and this time she did not step back. She did not resist me, as I kissed her cheek and patted her arm.

"I love you," I said. "Some day you will know."

I went outside. It was incredible, the peace that came to my heart. It was buoyantly existential. Whether the affliction of little Jerry disciplined me back to full trust in God, or if it was simply the implanted Presence taking control of me apart from anything

I had done or encountered, I cannot say. I wanted Vaneta's love, her confidence, to be sure. But, more than these, I wanted her to share the reality that was dawning in my heart. I wanted an end to abrasions between us, and would do all I could to facilitate this goal.

How many times had I walked these streets, questioning the state of my circumstances? I was in turmoil now, but not as before. Once I had been as a man swept into the waves of a storm, now I was as one tossed in an angry squall, yet riding secure in a strong and weathered craft. In my aimless wandering, I passed Uncle Rufus' place. The light was on in Aunt Lydia's prayer room, and I did not scoff. It was out of character for me to so react.

After some time it came to me that I was heading toward the residence of Halford Vamp. I did an immediate turn and walked resolutely toward the church. In small communities such as ours churches are rarely locked. I slipped inside and stood for several moments at the back of the sanctuary, then slowly approached the altar. There I knelt.

"Please, God," I prayed aloud, "I can't make Vaneta believe me. I'm human, I'm not free of sin. I was tempted by Hillary. I looked at her with lust. But you know, I never defiled myself. I have been true to Vaneta. Help her to believe that.

"And forgive me for accusing her about Little Jerry. You can heal him right now, right there in the hospital. I only want your will to be done. I . . ."

My own words became sustenance to my troubled spirit. *I only want your will to be done!*

That was it. I arose from the place of prayer, walked slowly up the aisle, a thrust of moon glow giving definition to each pew.

Here was where Aunt Lydia always sat. Here Adelia had kept vigil over the congregation, watching for raised hands. She had pursued me along this pew, and at this side of the aisle I had fled to the outdoors. The sonorous thunder of a thousand sermons seemed to echo from the walls, the memory of endless hours spent in this place, hours of fear for the impending judgments of God, hours of hungering to know His forgiveness.

This had been the place of turmoil for me.

Now it was the place of peace.

Why should I demand exploits of my God, when in quietness He could mold my needs? Did I not want flamboyant answers to prayer, so I could thus vindicate myself, so I could startle the complacent ones with the furor of my faith?

236

It must be so no longer. I would wait for God's time, for His way. I returned home.

"It was a short visit," Vaneta greeted curtly. "Wasn't Hillary home?"

"I've been to the church."

She looked at me disbelievingly.

"It is true," I told her.

"You met someone there?"

I nodded.

"Who?" she demanded.

"I met God," I said quietly. "There was no one else."

She studied me—Vaneta in all her dimensions—distrusting, fretful, but loving me and wanting to believe. I had never felt more strongly her desire to believe.

"Did you pray?" she asked.

"Yes."

"What did you pray?"

"The prayer I pray over and over, sweetheart—that you will one day believe the truth I have told you."

She lowered her eyes. I went to her and touched her arm. She looked up and her eyes glistened with the mellowing sheen of tears.

I silently thanked God.

"We need each other," I said.

"I'm sorry," she whispered. "I get so upset sometimes I could scream. Please don't talk any more about what happened in little Jerry's bedroom that day. Promise me?"

"I promise."

I kept my promise.

A new kind of rapture came to our lives, not the excitement of young love, not the adjusted emotion of an enduring marriage, but the needing of each other, each other's confidence, each other's strength, the openness of a father and mother whose child was in dire need. Perhaps, I reasoned, I had been too sentimental in expecting of wedlock that which was not it's norm.

It may be I would have settled for a renovation of concept except that Vaneta's mother and her sister, Winona, came to see us. We had not gone to their community, since the letter accusing me of consortment with Hillary, and so it was awkward to have them come, awkward for all of us. Yet I did not begrudge the visit. A daughter and sister, a grandson and nephew, had need. It would have been more awkward for them not to have come.

"We have been very concerned," Mrs. Logan said to me. There was propriety in her manner, but there was also warmth. "We just had to come."

"It means a lot to Vaneta having you here," I said. "It means a lot to me."

Winona looked at me with a disbelief akin to Vaneta's, yet I sensed an awe in her eye, as though she were unable to overtly discount my sincerity.

Winona and I did not speak to each other directly during the entire visit. It could have been a bad situation, but the mother was a woman of admirable poise and astuteness and introduced moments of protocol which greatly lessened the possibility of tension.

"Your mother is a wonderful person," I told Vaneta. "It's great to have a mother-in-law who doesn't fit the traditional pattern." I meant those words. Yet, for all my good intentions and in spite of the elderly woman's finesse, shadows of the past came inevitably to my thoughts. I knew she and Winona thought of me as a tragic encumberance to Vaneta's life. They accepted me because they were stalwart in the morés characteristic of the past, but they wished for Vaneta a better lot in life.

It came to me like a floodtide, how good it would be if, during their visit, Vaneta might be brought to see the truth in my innocence. I prayed that this might occur. But it didn't.

I struggled to avoid a recurrence of earlier disillusionments when I asked favors of God, with, seemingly, no response to my implorations.

Then I received a letter from Pastor Mallory. He had learned of little Jerry's illness. "Put the child completely in God's hands," he wrote. "Ask only for His will, not yours. Whatever happens, remember that God's power is not necessarily for our convenience but always for the vindication of His name in every circumstance of life. It is as important for you to discover His peace in time of disappointment as it is for the miracle of healing to instantly occur in your son's body."

My spirits rose.

Slowly.

Surely.

I showed the letter to Vaneta.

"What do you think?" I asked, as she finished reading.

She looked at me with moist eyes. "This helps me very much."

Vaneta sat at the table and reread the letter. I paced the floor.

238

"Why are there so few people in the world like Pastor Mallory?" I heard her say.

I turned to her. She could be so surprising. Like this, saying things I'd never expected to hear from her lips.

"He meant a lot in your life, too?" I asked.

She nodded.

The name Mallory was a catalyst between us. It drew out the gold in our relationship. It rendered the dross.

"Write to him, Jerry. Thank him for the letter."

"I will. First, though, I need to go someplace where I can walk and think, like down to the river. Will you go with me?"

"I need to be alone, too," she said. A smile came warmly to her lips. "You go. I'll stay here."

I held out my hands to her, and she came to me. We embraced possessively and gave our lips to each other in searching endearment.

"This hasn't happened for a long time," I whispered.

She nestled her head on my shoulder. "I'm sorry." she whispered in return. "It's been my fault."

I stroked her hair.

"Little Jerry is in God's hands," she said. "That's better than the best doctors or the best hospital in the world."

"Much better," I said.

"Maybe . . ." she began.

"Maybe, what?"

"When . . . when you wanted to pray . . . not call the doctor . . . maybe it's better this way. I don't mean to justify my rebelliousness, but we're both leaving little Jerry in God's hand. We're united in trusting the Lord."

"That's good."

She pushed herself lightly from my embrace and looked into my eyes. "I'm such a selfish person," she said. "I'm learning. You have been very patient with me."

"I've got lots to learn, too."

"Not as much as I have," she countered gently.

She slipped her arm around my waist. I put mine across her shoulders. By her impetus, we walked to Jerry's room. There we stood, looking down at the empty bed.

"Many times," she said, "I've known you wanted more children. But the way things have been . . . my attitude . . . I don't want to talk about it now, except that even in this I have been very selfish." She looked up at me. "Whatever God's will is for little Jerry, and I feel it strong in my heart that he is going to be all right, let's have another baby real soon. Let's have as big a family as you would like to have."

I began to weep, unashamedly.

"Please believe in me, Vaneta," I whispered, "believe in me for the future, if you can't believe the past."

It was late afternoon, when I at last drove down to the river road, parked, and set myself to strolling along the meandering water line.

Thank you, God. I prayed silently. You've shown me miracles. You sent Vaneta into my life. You've kept me only for her. You spared me in the war. You've redeemed my soul in Christ. You're making of Vaneta the woman I want and need for a wife. You know what is best for me, God. I will accept whatever You send. Thank you, God! Thank you!

I came to a bend in the river, into full view of the day's final spectacle, and beheld, with newness in my heart, the embered beauty of the setting sun. There was no emptiness now, no seeking—only the assurance that the God of greatness and beauty was making of me a man who could honor His name.

It was a time of beginning.

Chapter Twenty-five

Our son had a lingering convalesence. The paralysis subsided, leaving him with a weakened left hand. By careful exercise, the doctor assured, he had an excellent chance for full recovery. Like seasoned physiotherapists, Vaneta and I took turns looking after him. There were games he could play, feats of skill to master—all adeptly programmed to correct his remnant weakness.

It came to me that I could thank God for this, the skills of modern medicine, the new frontier for a man and his wife to conquer. It was good. Not only did God give us back our son, but the whisper of Genesis came once again to the cradle of my wife's heart. To what measure the Puritanical ways of my forebears may have stinted the development of my personality, I cannot say, and many a modern would doubtless pity my celibate years of youth, yet there is a harvest of goodness in knowing that the love I shared with Vaneta and the love she shared with me had never been shared with others.

Like the rising of a great oak, our love grew strong, so sheltering at times I all but put away from my mind the skeleton in our connubial closet. We never discussed Hillary. If Vaneta thought of her, she neither mentioned the name nor implied the woman's existence. She seemed to trust my present and my future, and for this I thanked God, thanked Him and prayed for the one miracle sure to forever satisfy my desire for celestial exploits—the miracle that would restore Vaneta's confidence in my past.

241

I seldom saw Hillary. Her's was the gay life—New York one month, Los Angeles the next—and tales of her private involvements became legend among the glib tongues of our town. Whatever those involvements, be they fact or fabrication, I knew Hillary Vamp was a woman of emptiness, a vessel off course, a blighted flower, laughter without merriment in a life without meaning, and I pitied her.

But I left her alone.

She came infrequently to her father's office, at which time we exchanged brief pleasantries. I supposed she had gone permanently out of my life. I was glad.

Then one morning Mr. Vamp called me into his office.

"Well, Jerry," he bantered, "it's good to hear that boy of yours is doing so well. Got to keep new blood developing for this community. It's really booming around here and, I hardly need to say it, the Wilding Corporation is mostly responsible. About your boy, a lot of us were mighty concerned. Here at the plant we tripled our contribution to the polio fund this year."

"That's good," I said.

"The polio fund helped you on hospital bills?"

"It really took the sting out."

"Good. From what I read, they're really down to business researching this polio disease. They'll come up with a solution one of these days, a serum or something. Of course, there's a lot doctors can do now. I guess you found that out. They used some of Sister Kenny's methods on your boy, I suppose?"

"We're grateful for what the doctors did," I said. "But to be real honest, we depended more on God than on medicine."

Walter Vamp was a man of profane eloquence and nothing made his speech more maledictive than to introduce religion as a subject of conversation. He launched now into a barrage of invectives about the church, the people around town who prayed for a man's soul out of one side of their mouths while they preyed upon his reputation out of the other side. He insisted that money motivates all men, ploughman or prelate, and that every human being is first concerned for his own welfare, and that people who do good outside the church are markedly more righteous in God's sight than the many hypocrites who frequent the sanctuary.

"No, Jerry," he said, slapping me on the shoulder, "it wasn't God who made your boy well, except I suppose we should give Him credit for creating the ingredients in the medicine the doctors used. If you want to thank God, that's fine with me, but thank Him that we live in the twentieth century when a man can go to the medicine cabinet and get a couple of aspirins instead of lumbering off to Lourdes to cure his headache."

I kept quiet.

"No," he continued, "I don't believe in prayer answers. I don't believe in miracles. Neither do you, if you'd be honest about it. I believe in using my head. I believe in working harder than the next guy, thinking faster than he does, jumping after an opportunity while the other guy is still thinking about it. I believe in money. So does everybody else in the world, preachers and the whole lot. Why, there's not a preacher in America who wouldn't resign his church next Sunday if he got an offer of enough raise in pay to make it worth his while moving someplace else, especially if it was in Florida or Arizona."

His eyes were ablaze, his face taut. An impish smile played upon his lips.

"I don't agree with you," I broke in. The tone of my voice was argumentative, and I felt it putting me on the defensive.

"No, I don't suppose you do. I guess I'd have a different viewpoint myself, if I'd been raised in your kind of surroundings, which, thank the Good Lord, I wasn't." He pointed a finger at me. "Yeah, if I ever get around to thanking God for anything, that's the one thing I'll thank Him for.

"Oh, I don't say there couldn't be miracles. I suppose maybe there could be. But before I put up any odds over the likelihood of somebody being raised from the dead around here, I'll tell you one miracle I'd like to see. I'd like to see somebody in this town, just one, living the way the Bible teaches, really doing the things Jesus said a Christian ought to do. That would be a miracle."

"Are you sure . . .?" I began.

"Oh come on, Jerry," he intercepted, "don't be so serious. Sure, I know there are good church folk in this town. I'm sure there are people who live closer to God than I do. Maybe they're better off for it. I don't know. But you call the money and I'll double the odds there's nobody in this town—nobody, Jerry—who can play the Christian bit straight under any kind of circumstance. Whoever the most religious person in this town is, and I suppose it's a woman, she'll crinkle under when things get in rough shape just like the rest of us.

"God, whoever that is, didn't put us into the world to sit around with our hands folded singin' hymns. There isn't anything phonier, Jerry, than these Bible carryin', hymn singin', sick-faced Christians who amen and hallelujah all the time and worry themselves sick trying to convince the rest of us heathen how pious they are. I don't know if there's a heaven or a hell. If there is, I'll play the odds and take whatever turns up on the dice for me. But I wouldn't think much of a God who equated piety with any brand of religion that ties a man all up in knots, gives him a holier-than-you-are attitude toward everybody else, keeps him from raising a finger to do anything for the good of the community unless it has something to do with religion, and generally speaking is so heavenly minded, like I heard a preacher on the radio say once, he's no earthly good.

"Nope, Jerry, whoever God is, He's the one who made the rose bushes I grow in my back yard. He gave me a brain to think with. He gave a man his sex drive. He made a lot of women beautiful. He made us so we get hungry and taste what we eat. He filled the world with raw materials that a man can make no end of products of.

"And if there is a difference between Christians and guys like me—I'm not sure but, I say, if there is—then it's my opinion a Christian is somebody in tune with the world, somebody who makes sense when he talks "God talk" instead of always wantin' us sinners to go against our normal desires, live opposite to what makes sense to us, and get so dog-fired hypocritical we can't stand to live with ourselves, much less qualified to dictate to others how they should live.

"Now you come up with one person in this town that can stand up under that kind of demands and you've got yourself a convert. Until then, don't come to me about praying being better than medicine. Just don't talk to me about religion, Jerry. I've heard lot's of talk. My problem is that I've got the kind of brain that pays twice as much attention to my eyes as it does to my ears."

With that, he changed the subject to the item of business which prompted my being called into his office. He opened the top drawer of his desk and drew out a set of blueprints. At first, I thought it was some new product for which he had purchased rights. But a second glance told me he had building expansion in mind.

I moved for a closer look.

"I'm taking you into my confidence," he said. "What I'm showing you will set this town on it's ear the minute it becomes news."

"Building expansion?"

244

"We're going to double our facilities," he exclaimed.

It was obvious he wanted me to be as excited as he was, but though our business was good, I couldn't imagine what might prompt this kind of expansion.

"Jerry," he said, "I'm about to take the biggest gamble of my whole life. I'm a gambler at heart. I love it. But I've been matching pennies compared to the stakes we're calling now."

"I'm all ears," I said.

"We're just inches away from a big Harvest Craft contract. They are coming out with this new combination unit that handles small grain, corn, beans, anything a farmer grows that goes into a bin, and we're biding on the rollers, the knives, and a couple of other parts they job out."

"We'll have to build if we get the contract?" I asked.

He stood erect, threw back his shoulders, looked me full in the eye and said, "We're going to have to build to get the contract."

"I don't read you," I said.

"It's pretty simple, Jerry. Harvest Craft likes the prices I quoted. They think we could give them a good product. But they question whether we're big enough to produce in quantity. They've got a good point.

"Now here is what's going to happen. I've already got sets of prints out for bids. I would have told you about this before, but I had to keep it under wraps. It's not that I don't trust you, Jerry, but there is too much at stake. Okay, bids are to be in by the end of next week. We're in good enough shape so a bank in Chicago will cover us with a mortgage for the building. I think I can lease or get long term payment arrangements on the extra machinery we need. I feel we can have our new unit up in four months. Six at the very latest."

"And you're going to do this before you sign the contract with Harvest Craft?"

"It better be while we sign the contract," he said, his eyes flashing. "That's where you come in. As you probably know, Harvest Craft has a new purchasing agent. I want you to go see him."

"Glad to," I said. "He's in Chicago, I suppose."

"Yep, his name's Pierce Roberts."

My jaw sank.

Mr. Vamp saw it. He took a long draught of the cigar he had just lighted and billowed the smoke in my direction. He walked up close to me, grasped me by the lapel, and laughed. "I'm as nosey as the next guy, Jerry. Besides, a man with ears couldn't live in this town and not know you're on the odds with your wife's relatives." He relinquished his grip, paced back to his desk and grew serious. "I understand Roberts stool pigeoned about you showing my daughter a few innocent courtesies in Chicago just after you came with us. I gave him the raspberries about it, and I'm pretty sure he not only believes you're clean, but would give an awful lot to make it up to you for the way he's inconvenienced you. The way he could make it up to you, Jerry, would be to be sure we swing these Harvest Craft assignments."

"I, uh . . ."

"Now, look, it's a straight business deal with me at Harvest Craft. I can swing it myself. That's part of my gamble. It would make it a little easier for me if you carried some of the weight. Forget about the family involvement. That's up to you. But we could have us quite a success story to spread around town about you, Jerry, if word got out that you brought in the job that necessitated this big expansion. Some of your church people might even call it a miracle."

He looked at me penetratingly, and he began to laugh, the full-from-the-belly laugh of a man who deems himself in full control of his destiny.

"Get a move on!" he shouted at me, waving me to leave. "Give the boy in Chicago a call. Let's move, Jerry. Let's make work out of the stuff the good Lord's given us to work with."

Chapter Twenty-six

I wanted to make that telephone call but couldn't bring myself to do it. "Did you know Pierce and Winona had moved to Chicago?" I asked Vaneta, as we sat at dinner later in the day.

She nodded. "Mother wrote. I guess he has a very good job."

"Mr. Vamp told me," I said, giving no further details. Vaneta asked for none. We rarely discussed her relatives, never her brother-in-law.

During those next days, I castigated myself for not calling Vaneta's brother-in-law. I would put my hand to the telephone on my desk, again and again, and then withdraw it. When I heard Mr. Vamp's voice, his unmistakable footsteps, I cringed at the anticipation of his ire, but he didn't ask about my calling. He was like a child keeping secret some promised gift or excursion. He was at times effervescent, at times brash and didactic, but always intent upon his new plan.

Our town's weekly paper, which was published on Thursdays, rarely ran headlines. But the following week, no newspaper in America ran an edition that more effectively caught the eyes of its constituents. HALFORD VAMP ANNOUNCES EXPANSION.

"I think the man's crazy," I told Vaneta. "He only has an expression of interest from Harvest Craft. Not any contract as the newspaper puts it."

"Are you sure?"

"Absolutely."

"Then why does he move ahead?"

"He's a gambler. He believes this show of strength will dissipate any qualms Harvest Craft may have over our being able to handle the assignment. He was smart enough never to mention Harvest Craft in the release to the newspaper. People around town just think we're growing that much."

"Does Pierce know anything about this?"

I turned away.

"Is he involved?" Vaneta asked anxiously.

I turned back to her. "Mr. Vamp wants him to be. He wants me to go see him."

"Will you?" she asked, seeming anxious for me to do it.

"I'm not sure."

After the meal, I went out to try a few golf swings on the lawn. While I was out, Vaneta called her mother.

"Pierce and Winona expect to be home this weekend," she told me. "Let's drive home, the three of us."

"The doctor said you shouldn't make any trips."

"It's not all that far. Besides, I feel wonderful. Please, Jerry. Let's go. Let's go this weekend and surprise them."

I couldn't resist her exuberance, her wanting to see me involved with the success of the company, her desire to reactivate good relationships with her relatives.

The following Saturday morning, we drove to her home. Her mother wept at the joy of seeing us. Her father greeted me as though I were his own son, as though there had been no abrasion to our relationship.

Meeting Pierce and Winona, I realized, might be another story.

"We were so lonesome," Vaneta said, as we sat in the house and the grandparents got over their first bit of doting our son. "Then, too, Jerry's boss wants him to talk to Pierce."

"Oh," Vaneta's mother said, a touch of sadness in her voice. "He called just before you got here."

"Called?"

"His new job is very demanding, it seems, and he couldn't get away. I told him you were coming." Mrs. Logan looked directly at me. "He sent special greetings."

I was disappointed, but also relieved.

Early Sunday afternoon, we set out for home.

"I'm so glad we came," Vaneta said. "You were wonderful to my folks."

"Thanks, sweetheart."

"Maybe it was better Pierce and Winona didn't get back."

"Why?"

"I don't know. Just maybe it was better. I hope you don't get so involved in business you have to go, go, go all the time."

Traffic was light. I eased the footfeed and put my arm around Vaneta. She rested her head on my shoulder and for several miles we drove like young lovers on a Sunday afternoon.

After a bit, she lifted her head.

"How are you?" I asked, taking my arm away so she could be more comfortable.

"Sleepy," she said.

"You're sure this weekend won't be too much for you?"

"I'm fine. I was a little tense, thinking about going, but everything turned out so well."

We arrived home about church time, but Vaneta did not mention going. After a light snack, she retired. I took a book to read but couldn't concentrate. I kept thinking about the expansion at the plant, about my failure to contact Pierce Roberts.

I went early to my office the next morning. I wanted to be ahead of Mr. Vamp, but he was already at work, waiting for me.

"Come in, Jerry," he called briskly.

"Good morning," I said, entering his office.

"How did you do with your brother-in-law?" He asked. It was a militant question.

"I struck out," I said.

Mr. Vamp stood startled to his feet. "What do you mean, you struck out?"

"Oh," I said, feeling myself tremble, " I didn't mean there was any problem about the contract."

"He wants to negotiate it?"

"I told you we were driving down to my wife's folks."

"Yes?" he prodded.

"Pierce was to be there and . . ."

"What did he have to say?"

"He wasn't there."

"You mean he avoided seeing you?"

"N-no. I think he got tied up with . . ."

"He knew you were coming, didn't he?"

"Well, uh, we . . ."

"You idiot." Mr. Vamp looked at me in disbelief. "You went

down to call on a possible client and didn't even check for sure if he was coming?"

"Our idea was to make it a social call," I said.

"But you still could have told him you were coming."

"I'm sorry, Mr. Vamp. I . . ."

"The contractor'll be coming in here by the end of this week, Jerry. This is no time for games and surprises."

I suspected a note of panic in his voice, couldn't quite understand why, and then it occurred to me. For all his talk of being able to sew up the Harvest Craft contract himself, he must have been depending more heavily upon me than he wanted to admit.

"When will you see him?" he asked.

"I'm not sure," I said.

He evoked an obscenity, "If I were you, young fellow, I'd get some hustle into the sloppy way you've handled a few things lately."

The town was ablaze with excitement, as the contractor moved in to begin work.

"I can't imagine a builder of any size being able to free a crew this soon," Uncle Rufus commented. "Halford must have had this up his sleeve for a long time."

"When he wants action," I said, "he's got a way of making people move."

"It'll do wonders for our community," Uncle Rufus said. "My land, I was down there and watched as they staked out the foundation. That addition is as big as the whole plant is now. I understand it's going to be as modern as anything in the state."

"It'll be quite a place," I said.

It was difficult to believe my own eyesight—the rapidity with which the contractor moved into the project. Mr. Vamp was with him constantly, making observations, demands, until I found it less difficult to understand how a crew could be brought in so quickly. The contractor might be competent—I know too little about such things to say—but he seemed completely subdued by Mr. Vamp's overpowering image about the place.

More days went by. I didn't call Pierce Roberts. I despised my cowardice, but this man had hurt me deeply, more deeply even than Aunt Lydia's accumulated tirades, and I simply could not bring myself to call him.

I expected Mr. Vamp to be on my back about it, but he was so consumed by the building project, I rarely saw him. Then one afternoon, late, he came to my door.

"Say," he said, "there's so much happening around here I haven't had much chance to talk to you." He was unusually pleasant. But then, with characteristic possessiveness, he added, "I want you to come to my house tonight. Go ahead and eat with your family, but let's try to get together for a couple of hours starting say about eight."

At eight o'clock, I rang the doorbell to the Vamp residence. I had told Vaneta my boss needed me to help him with some work that evening. I didn't say whether it was at the office or at his house.

Hillary answered the door.

"Hello," she greeted awkwardly.

"Hello," I returned.

For a moment, she only looked at me. I didn't like the idea of standing in the full glow of the porchlight, on display for the beholding of any commuinty wag who might be peering from a nearby window.

"Come in," she said at last.

I stepped inside.

"How have you been?" she asked, closing the door.

"Fine. And you?"

"Comme ce, comme ca," she said.

"Isn't that all of us?" I commented.

She looked at me. Her eyes were troubled, evasive.

"Come in and sit down," she said.

I complied, and she took a chair nearby.

Except for the ticking of a big clock in the corridor, the house was utterly silent. The silence compounded by the way the two of us sat there, aware of each other but neither of us speaking.

"Your father . . ." I finally introduced.

He isn't here," she told me.

I looked at my watch. It was ten minutes past eight.

"He and mother went out to dinner," Hillary explained. "Then they are going to a movie."

"Now wait a minute!" I stood abruptly, anger quickening my pulsebeat. "I don't appreciate being maneuvered like this."

"Please don't be offended," she said, slowly standing, an uncharacteristic mellowness to her voice.

I turned to go. She hurried and stood in my way.

"Now that you're here," she said, "can't you stay just a moment? It's terribly important that I talk to you."

For one blazing moment I was angry enough to strike her. Yet she was different somehow, not the siren I had known, not the seductress, but a frightened thing.

"Okay," I said. "But let's make it short."

Against my better judgment, I returned to the chair I had occupied.

"Thanks, Jerry," Hillary said quietly. She also came and sat down.

For a moment, she picked pieces of small lint off the arm of the chair.

"It is a little off-color," she said, not looking at me, "our getting you over this way. I guess that's our trademark, manipulating people for our own designs."

She looked up at me now, searching my eyes for reaction.

"Let me be honest with you, Jerry," she said. "I know it's hard for you to believe anyone in this family can be honest, but I'm trying.

"Dad asked me to talk to you tonight. At first he planned to be here, but then he got the sudden impulse that it would be better if I saw you alone. I told him you wouldn't appreciate it. God knows it's the truth, Jerry, but you know my dad. He decided I should see you alone.

"I thought of calling you and telling you not to come, but I knew what a *faux pas* it would be if Vaneta answered the telephone. So I didn't call. But give me credit for at least realizing it's what I should have done.

"Jerry, I'm scared about this expansion dad is going into at the plant. He finally confided in mom and me that it's really a big gamble. Except for the possibility of lining up something with Harvest Craft there was no reason for expansion. And if the Harvest Craft contract shouldn't come through, dad admits to mom and me it could be disastrous.

"He needs you to swing the Harvest Craft contract, Jerry. Can you do it?"

"I don't know," I said.

"But won't you try?"

"Well, sure," I stammered, "I mean . . ."

"Dad wanted me to be more casual about it, but I've got to be honest, Jerry, I think he's a little desperate. He's depending on you to bring in the deal. Do try right away. You've just got to."

"I'll do all I can," I said. I began to stand. "Was that all?"

"Please don't go yet," she interrupted. "There's one more thing."

I sat down.

"I hardly know where to begin," she said, her eyes downcast, her fingers picking again at lint on the arm of the chair. She began rambling about herself, about there being so many inequities in life, about the importance of right decisions. At first, because her speech was so abstract, I failed to catch the one strain of impression underlying everything she said. She talked about frustration in a childhood surrounded by affluence. She had almost wanted poverty, she said, in order that their family might experience something of the need for each other and for sustenance beyond themselves.

"I don't suppose I'm making any sense. I guess it's because I don't know how to say what I feel. Nobody really knows me, Jerry. I don't even know myself.

She held up her hand as though I had attempted to say something. I hadn't.

"Please let me talk," she said. "Then you may go."

"This all relates to that first afternoon, when we were kids and my dad hired you to do some odd jobs for him. I mentioned it to you once. I wanted to tell you then, but I couldn't.

"Whenever anyone new came to town, and please understand I'm not trying to hurt you, one of the first things they heard about was the Pew family. I remember the first time we heard. It was from one of our neighbors. My dad laughed and laughed. He wanted to hear every little thing about your family, about your grandfather, particularly, and your Aunt Lydia. He thought it was so funny.

"Long before he ever met any of your people he talked about you. He would come home from work and tell some new funny he had learned about the Pews. Really, Jerry, you were quite the topic of conversation—your people, I mean.

"I got awfully, awfully curious. Naturally, I didn't have the discernment then that I hope I have now. My folks had bred into me the importance of pride for our family. The day we arrived in town, my father made it clear to me that there was a new first family. So I looked down on people like you because I looked down on everything.

"But I was curious, Jerry. From some of the things my father said, even as young as I was at that time, I kind of envied you. I guess I envied anybody who wasn't supposed to be self-sufficient the way we were. That can give you a lot of insecurity, having it drilled into you that you're not supposed to depend on anything outside yourself.

253

"Well, anyway, my dad had this little job he wanted done, things in the barn straightened. You remember. He was wondering who he could ask. I had seen you around, and so I suggested you. I suggested you, Jerry. I really did. He thought it was a great idea. He wanted to be around to egg you a bit, but mother wanted to do some shopping or something, and so he just showed you what it was he wanted done and let it go at that.

"I think I said some hurtful things to you that day. It's awfully late to be doing it, but I apologize. You see, when I came out to the barn, I intended to make fun of you. I watched you for a long time. You were working hard, doing a good job without anybody around to tell you you should. I liked you from the beginning. I liked you very much. I wanted you for a boyfriend the way young girls do. But I got scared when mom and dad came home. If I'd have shown any interest in you at that time, dad would have whipped me for sure.

"So I ignored you after that. That is, I tried to." She laughed, a dry, non-humorous laugh. "But I didn't forget you. I would fall asleep pretending you weren't a Pew. I'd pretend you were the coach's son or your father was Mr. Wilding or some other prominent man in town.

"As I grew older, I became less fearful of punishment from my father. I wanted to show more interest in you, but you always seemed so inhibited when I was around. I was full up to my ears by that time of the tinsel our family is made of, so I'm sure my displays of ego didn't encourage any interest on your part. I know you had your frustrations as a child, Jerry, but you had values. Thank God that you had values."

I was amazed at what I was hearing from the lips of this woman!

"As we got older, I realized how different you really were, a genuine person. Kids who went to your church said you didn't go along with the fanaticism. They said you weren't like the rest of your family. This encouraged me, and by the time we were in high school, though I know a person has a lot of unstable emotions at that time, I'm pretty sure I was in love with you. But, proud the way I was, realizing what would happen if I expressed interest in someone my dad made fun of all the time, I didn't give you much encouragement."

Tears came to her eyes.

"Remember when the scholarships came up for the valedictorian and salutatorian honors in our class?"

254

I nodded.

"I was so proud of you for winning one of them and hated myself for reacting the way I did. I'm sure you must remember. My pride was hurt, because, of course, my parents expected me at least to be the salutatorian. I hated myself for not telling you how proud I was. I know this sounds kind of funny, but though I wanted to win one of these scholarships to stay in the best graces with my family, I was secretly glad my father's scheme had been upended.

"Actually, it was to my best advantage that you came out ahead of me. Until that time my father hadn't really understood what I was driving at when I said you were different, that you would rise above your family, become known for something other than religious fanaticism. In the way he thinks, no religious fanatic could win a scholarship. Your brand of Christianity was synonymous with low mentality in his estimation. So it impressed him that you did better than I scholastically.

"I wanted to go to the university to be near you. But I played my hands too quickly. I admitted to my parents how I felt about you. The old evaluations were somewhat dimmed in my father's mind, but he still couldn't bring himself to accept the thought of my ever marrying you. So they sent me off to a different school, and I made a mess of things.

"I can't fill you in on all the details, but your Aunt Lydia must have done something that reminded my father of how hyper-religious your family was because that first summer after your freshman year he made it very plain he didn't want me to stay in town. That was the summer I went to Europe on a student tour and met this character I eventually married just after the war started.

"Oh, there's a lot I could tell you in between, but I'm taking too much of your time. I didn't want to get married. I guess it was mostly to put you out of my mind. But on the honeymoon, more than once, Jerry, I pretended I was married to you. I actually fell asleep in my husband's arms one night and dreamed I was in your arms."

She broke into sobbing. There had been too much evidence of honesty in the way she spoke for me to think she was merely currying my sympathy. I sat there numb. Slowly, she regained control of herself.

"All I've ever known of love," she continued, "how it is won, how it is expressed . . . well, you know what I mean . . . a girl, a woman, making herself available to the one she wants. Like in Chicago. I'm so sorry, Jerry. To you, I probably seemed like a very bad woman. I didn't mean to be."

She stood again, walked slowly back and forth.

"When I got my divorce, I told my father I had really wanted you. I came right out and told him. I caught him in one of his good moods, I guess, because he wrote to the university. I'm sure you didn't realize that. He found out how well you had done in business administration, so he got to seeing things my way. Together, we began to scheme how we might bring something about.

"Oh, we were schemers, Jerry. We thought all we had to do was push buttons and the world was ours. Whenever he wanted anything, he just pushed a button. I was so convinced about it myself, I felt it was simply a matter of time after you got back from the war until we would be married.

"Then you announced your engagement to Vaneta. I was hurt and angry. Hurt and angry and humiliated."

She paced the floor for several moments.

"This is a cruel community," she said. "To me, it seems all the more cruel because so many people in it are supposed to be religious. But people talk. There just isn't anything that people would rather do than tear other people apart. I'm not speaking about the talk that goes on about me, though I'm very much aware of it. I'm talking about you and Vaneta."

"There was gossip about us?" I asked.

"Isn't there gossip about everybody and everything in this town?"

"What was it about us?"

"People said your Aunt Lydia arranged your romance."

"Oh, my back!"

"I believed it. It seemed logical. And subsequent circumstances verified what I had heard people say."

"How?"

"Well, almost right away people began saying you had an endured marriage. They've said it even more lately. You must surely know, Jerry, how cruel people can be around this place."

"What are some of the things people say?" I asked.

"I'm sure you don't want to sit here and listen to me all night," she replied.

"Give me an example."

"An example? Well, people say your Aunt Lydia has done everything she can to keep Vaneta from being the wife she would like to be."

256

I stood.

"I'm only telling you what I've heard, Jerry," she said.

"Go on," I told her.

"People know your aunt is at your house practically every day. They know you and she are on bad terms. Pardon my frankness, but your Aunt Lydia has a voice like the siren on the water tower and when she gets worked up on a subject, and if a window happens to be opened at your house . . ."

The telephone rang. Hillary glanced at it but didn't go to answer. She waited for it to stop ringing.

"People distort facts," she continued. "I've learned that often enough by hard experience. But gossip is based on what people have actually heard, distorted though the reports may be."

She wrung her hands for a moment and looked at me intently, then asked, "Is your marriage satisfying, Jerry?"

"Of course," I said.

"Please don't lie to me," she interrupted.

"Well . . ." I couldn't bring myself to speak further.

"Trust me, Jerry, she pleaded. "I'm not trying to get some more fuel for the gossip fires. My reason for asking is that when I hear these things, your unhappiness, your dissatisfaction with the way your marriage has gone, it makes me all the more want to become the person that's really inside me, to steal you away for myself, to surround you with the kind of love a woman is supposed to give a man. I love you so much, Jerry!

"My dad knows all about this. We've grown closer these last few years. He's an enormous conundrum to me. In some ways, he's the most noble man I know—in other ways, the most despicable. He can read a person like a book. You know that. I can't hide a thing from him. Again and again, he's egged me on, telling me I was crazy not to openly go after you, to steal you away from your wife. This would be success in his way of thinking. If I want you, and especially if I believe you're not happy, then I should go after you. Please don't hate my dad for this. It's life the way he understands it. For all the religion in this community, and I don't mean just to knock religion, it doesn't seem to have done anything to make him think otherwise.

"You're Uncle Rufus played a part in all of this. I guess my dad admired him about as much as any man in this town. I don't know your uncle at all, but he must be a wonderful person."

"One of the greatest I've ever met," I said.

"When dad began to sense my feelings toward you, especially when my marriage was going on the rocks, he talked to your Uncle Rufus. Your uncle helped him to see what kind of a believable person you really are."

The telephone rang again. Hillary seemed not to hear it, except that she broke off speaking.

"The phone," I said, after it had rung several times.

She started toward it, then hesitated. "Dad gets lots of calls at night. They'll call back tomorrow."

She came toward me, so close I sat down again. I could see she wanted to sit on the arm of my chair, but I gave her no encouragement.

"Are you happy with your wife, Jerry?" she asked. "Please tell me. If you are, then I promise never to bother you again. I'm not Hillary Vamp, the seductress. That was just a facade. If you believe anything, Jerry, believe that, deep down inside me, I am a worthwhile person. At least I want to be."

She went to her chair and sat.

"I appreciate your telling me these things," I said. The words came with difficulty. "It's good to get to see a person as she really is."

"But what about your marriage?" she asked. "If it isn't working out, if Vaneta could be just as happy with alimony, letting her have the house—and dad would give you advance funds to more than take care of the cost—Jerry, I'm sure you must hate me for saying this, but is there any chance?"

I could only sit there for the moment, staring at her. It was plain enough that marriage to Hillary would be a good deal different than marriage to Vaneta and there was enough of mere humanity in me to be tempted by the potentialities. But there was more than humanity now. I experienced an inner strength, a surrounding restraint. Explain it as you wish, but I sensed an unmistakable Presence in the room.

"Our marriage has required adjustments," I said, "I'm sure most marriages do."

"But do you love your wife?" she asked with marked anxiety.

"I love her."

"Really?"

"Yes."

"Jerry," she gasped softly.

"But even if I didn't," I said, "even if our marriage were only tolerable to me, before God I pledged myself to Vaneta. I would never break that pledge. It would be the same if I were married to you."

"This view of marriage is based on your religious convictions?"

"My faith in God is the most vital aspect of my life."

"It helps to make your marriage tolerable?"

"I told you, I love my wife."

The telephone rang again. This time we continued speaking above it's ringing.

"The transformation Christ gives could fill the emptiness in your life, Hillary," I said.

"You admit there is emptiness in yours?" she asked eagerly.

"There was emptiness," I said. "There is emptiness in every life without Christ."

"But what about your marriage?"

"We had problems. I don't deny that."

"You've had terrific problems. Your wife believes you were immoral with me in Chicago." Hillary looked at me with eyes more penetrating than a probing shaft of sunlight.

"She doesn't want to believe it," I said.

"But she doesn't really trust you. Isn't that true?"

"We have a growing trust for each other," I countered. "I think every good marriage is that way. Vaneta is a wonderful woman, Hillary. I'm not just whistling in the dark. She's a complex person, just as many people are, and I'm sure I'm not the finest catch for a husband, but we're building a good marriage."

The telephone continued ringing. Hillary glanced toward it.

"Marriage, even to someone you feel you're very much in love with, can't give you the real answers for life," I continued. "You've got to see this, Hillary. You've got to see that Christ, before anything else, is what you need."

She grew restless, looking toward the phone.

"If you have a Bible handy," I started to say.

She bolted toward the phone, mumbling, "I'd better answer it. If it's important, dad'll never forgive me."

She picked up the phone.

"Vamp's residence," she said. She waited a moment, then repeated, "Vamp's residence. Hello."

She put the phone down and came toward me.

"Must've given up just as I answered it," she said.

"If you're really interested in the Christian faith. . . ."

"Maybe I will be someday," she said, "but right now, I'm passionately and completely and terribly interested in one thing—you, Jerry."

She reached out her hands towards me. I stood. She tried to come into my arms, but I restrained her.

I excused myself and left.

Outside, moments later, I paused to look up into the clear bejeweled sky. I had a new freedom in my heart. I felt clean from the top of my head to the bottom of my feet.

Yes, it was a temptation to think of a change of marriage status, but it was far better to know I lived my life by the kind of faith that was one day going to bring my marriage to Vaneta into a deeper enrichment than any other union for me could possibly have known.

"Thank you, God," I whispered.

I walked circuitously toward home. There was buoyancy in my heart. I sang: Give of your best to the master, Give of the strength of your youth.

I laughed. It had been a long time since I sang these words. I whistled the tune, and I was whistling it when I entered the house and came full into the presence of Aunt Lydia, trembling with anger, eyes ablaze.

"Where have you been?" she demanded.

"I . . ."

"No more of your lies!" she bellowed. "We called the office. The cleaning woman said you hadn't been there. We tried to call Mr. Vamp's house . . ."

"I was at Mr. Vamp's house," I broke in. I realized in an instant that I shouldn't have.

"Was Mr. Vamp there?"

I quickly gained control of myself. "Why don't you go see?" I snapped.

"If he was there and it wasn't just you and that horrible Hillary, then why didn't you answer the phone?"

"Why don't you go and ask him?" I said.

"You're covering over something, Jeremiah Pew, and you know it. Well, let me tell you something. While you were once again unfaithful to your dear wife, she took sick and had to call me."

"Vaneta?" Fear rose in my heart. "Where is she?"

"She's on her way to the hospital."

"You idiot," I flared. "You stand there lecturing when my wife needs me?"

"You should talk about her needing you!" Aunt Lydia snapped.

I pushed her aside and headed toward the door to drive to the hospital.

"The Lord may have to take her away from you, that's what," I heard Aunt Lydia cry out, as I left. "Vaneta is probably going to lose her baby, and its your fault. You mark my words."

Chapter Twenty-seven

I rushed to the hospital.

"Your wife is under medication," a nurse told me, "but you may go into her room."

Vaneta was tossing on the bed. She was frightfully pale. Her eyes were closed. I touched her hand and spoke to her. She opened her eyes briefly, smiled, but did not speak.

The doctor came. I was asked to leave the room. I paced up and down the hallway in a state of slight shock.

After several moments, the doctor came to me.

"How is she?" I asked anxiously.

"Your wife is in no danger," he said.

"The baby?"

"It'll be touch and go. I can't give you any assurance as to the fetus. We will do all we can."

"What causes something like this?"

"Pretty hard to say, Jerry. Could be a number of reasons. She hasn't done anything overly strenuous lately, has she?"

I remembered the trip to see her parents and told the doctor. He made no comment.

"May I go back into the room?" I asked.

"Better not. There's a waiting room at the end of the hall. Wait there. We'll keep you informed."

I tried to sit, tried to thumb through a magazine, but was restless. I stood and paced the floor.

Aunt Lydia and Uncle Rufus came. The first I knew of it was the pall of Aunt Lydia's voice coming down the corridor as she protested the doctor's forbidding her to enter Vaneta's room.

"Quiet, dear," Uncle Rufus admonished.

"That's doctors for you everytime," Aunt Lydia whined. "How could anybody be so sick their own flesh and blood can't be at their side to minister to them?"

Uncle Rufus and Aunt Lydia entered the waiting room.

"Hello, Jerry," Uncle Rufus spoke up softly.

"Well," Aunt Lydia exclaimed, "they keep you out of the room, too, do they?"

"It's getting a little late, Aunt Lydia," I said quietly. "A lot of people are trying to sleep."

She looked at me with indignation.

"I should have invited you to ride with me to the hospital," I said, "but I was upset."

"I can imagine you were," she retorted.

Ignoring her comment, I said, "Please sit down. The doctor told me he would keep us informed."

"It won't surprise me none if you lose the baby," Aunt Lydia said after a good deal more silence than she was accustomed to.

"Lydia!" Uncle Rufus scolded.

Glancing momentarily toward her husband but keeping her gaze fixed upon me, she continued, "You just don't play with God. But maybe it has to be this way to wake you up, Jeremiah."

I clenched my fists, breathed a prayer, relaxed my hands again. Aunt Lydia chattered on. I didn't listen, but I did saunter out into the corridor to get away from the sound of her voice.

Uncle Rufus came to me there.

"I don't know what's getting into Lydia," he said. "Old age, I 'spect. It's been weeks since I've seen her happy about anything. We should've stayed home, but I couldn't keep her."

"I appreciate your coming," I said. "Hospitals can get pretty lonely."

We talked for several moments. I told him about my conversation with the doctor.

"Medicine can do wonders these days," he encouraged. "I'd say you can be pretty sure doc will save the baby."

He went back to the waiting room. I returned for a moment, but there was always the threat of a new tirade from Aunt Lydia, so I did a good deal of pacing up and down the hall. Shortly before midnight, Uncle Rufus persuaded Aunt Lydia it was no use to remain any longer.

"Well, I can pray at home as well as I can pray here," she said. "But sometimes it's past the good of praying."

After they had gone, the doctor came to me. "Better go home and get some rest, Jerry."

"How's it going?" I asked anxiously.

"I'm encouraged," he said. "I think we're going to make it."

"She won't lose the baby?"

"I don't think so. No promises, understand. But it's beginning to look good."

Driving home through the night, I prayed aloud in the car. I thanked God. I renewed my commitments.

Vaneta's parents came to see her. They spent their time mostly at the hospital. I both hoped and feared that Pierce and Winona might come. But they were now fully settled in their Chicago surroundings.

Vaneta weathered the crisis. When she returned home, I inundated her with attention and concern. I spoke often of my love, my gratitude to her for mothering our offspring, and she responded with warmth and appreciation.

I warned her she would be hearing new accusations from Aunt Lydia and told her in detail exactly what had happened at Hillary's home.

"You believe me, don't you?" I pleaded.

"I want to," she said.

With the surge of development in the new project, I knew I had to call my brother-in-law and finally got around to placing a call late one morning. He had already gone to lunch the operator was told, and I was to replace the call that afternoon. I fully intended to but didn't.

The next morning, Mr. Vamp came prancing into my office. I cringed, sure he would ask about the Harvest Craft contact, but he didn't. He only stood at the front of my desk a moment, staring at me, and then, as though he had forgotten what he was going to say, wheeled about and left.

None-the-less, I promptly placed another call to Pierce Roberts.

"He's in conference at the moment," I heard his secretary say. "Could you replace the call a little later?"

That convinced me. He was avoiding me, just as I avoided him, and I would have to weather whatever the consequences might be so far as the contract was concerned. Besides, with Mr. Vamp acting so strangely, obsessed as he was by the insane building project, I wasn't sure how concerned I ought to be about my security with the organization.

I talked to Uncle Rufus about it.

"He's a hard man to figure," Uncle Rufus said. "The way that new addition is going up, I 'spect he's got a lot of big things taking shape."

"I hope so," I said.

Uncle Rufus was quiet for a moment. I could see he was thinking.

"Now Jerry," he began slowly, "it's none of my business what Vamp pays you. Whatever it is, I'm sure it's not what you're worth. I wish you would make me one promise."

"What's that?"

"You know that, with this new addition, it's going to throw an awful lot of responsibility on your shoulders. I don't suppose Vamp would want it known but I've heard some of the men around town say he attributes a lot of the growth to what you've done for the place. So I wish you'd promise me something. Before he throws any kind of responsibility to you make sure it involves better pay."

"I'm trying to conduct myself so that I can give this man some kind of an effective witness," I said.

"He won't understand Christianity if it's spineless, Jerry. He'll listen to you a lot faster if you stand up for your rights. I'm just a country storekeeper, but in this kind of business, you get to know an awful lot about people."

I got my chance sooner than I expected. For the very next day, Halford Vamp came bursting into my office like a sudden crack of thunder.

"What have you done on that Harvest Craft contract," he demanded.

"Not much," I said, trying to be casual.

"Look, Jerry," he stormed, "I told you this was a gamble. But even the best gambler in the world can't do much if he doesn't lay any cards on the table. I'm counting on you to get next to Pierce Roberts. He's a big man in the Chicago office now, you know."

"I know," I said.

He came at me like a threatening animal. I remembered Uncle Rufus' counsel and stood my ground. It threw Mr. Vamp off a little. I was encouraged.

"I know you're a lot smarter than I give you credit for sometimes," he said. "You realize we can't jump at HC as though we need the contract to justify our expansion. So I appreciate your playing it cool."

This turn of comment surprised me, for it was certainly something which had completely escaped my alleged wisdom.

"I've tried to call Pierce," I said.

"Tried?" Mr. Vamp's eyes widened.

"He's been gone or in conference, and . . ."

"You don't suppose he's trying to avoid us? You don't suppose he . . .?" He let his words trail off into nothingness.

"I plan to see him," I said, "but I've had a serious illness in the family."

"I know! I know!"

"Then, too," I continued, "there's something we haven't discussed."

"What?"

"Doubling the size of our operation is going to throw a lot of responsibility my way."

"So?"

"I think I deserve a substantial raise," I said bluntly.

He recoiled momentarily. It was something a man could be proud of, throwing Halford Vamp off-guard this way. I tried to swallow my pride. I really didn't care so much about the raise, but I wanted to prove myself to this man.

Yet I felt awkward, cheap. It was obvious he was upset about the Harvest Craft delay. Maybe he had begun to sense the potential folly of the building program. Anyway, I was sorry for having brought up a raise and would have tabled the subject if I could have.

"There is not much big money to be made in this town," Mr. Vamp said, becoming more casual.

"That's right," I said.

"You haven't been looking around in other directions?"

"I'd like to stay here," I said. I knew I had to stay with the dialogue or admit to my lack of wisdom in the timing of my approach.

"But it's gone through your mind, I take it, to look for something else? Maybe in a bigger town?"

I didn't say.

"You'd need recommendations," he said.

"It would help," I countered. I could see he thought he had me on the defensive, so I said, "Of course, photostats of memos and sales graphs would be helpful."

He reddened and I grew momentarily enthusiastic. Bringing him to this state was like pinning his shoulders to the floor.

"How much do you think you're worth?" he asked.

"Ten thousand dollars a year."

"Ten thousand dollars a year?" he gasped.

"Plus," I added calmly, "a schedule of increase pegged to rising sales."

His gaze went blank. It was a characteristic whenever he recessed his attentions for cogitation.

Suddenly, he said, "I'd be a mite careful, Jerry. This plant's been good to you. Even though you have no stock or family claim, it could be security for the future."

"That's why I want to see the line grow," I said. "I'm willing to work hard."

"What about Harvest Craft?"

"I'll try calling again" I said.

Without another word, Mr. Vamp turned and left my office.

I felt a little unsure about myself. I had a lot of confidence in Uncle Rufus and his counsel, but I knew I had made a poor move.

I talked about it to Vaneta.

She became quite upset. "You shouldn't have done it, Jerry," she said. "What if Mr. Vamp gets one of his sudden impulses, and you find yourself out of a job?"

"I suppose we'd have to move," I said. "At least I wouldn't have Aunt Lydia 's shadow over me all the time."

Vaneta grew irritable. It was the first marital abrasion we had had in a long time. At first, I tried to be reasonable. But she became upset, then critical. I finally stalked off to another part of the house. It was the last we spoke to each other the remainder of the evening.

I got up early the next morning, fixed myself a hurried breakfast, and went down to the office. I was being immature again, hurrying away from Vaneta this way, but I also wanted to plan a strategy for getting in touch with her brother-in-law.

I was about to place the call when Mr. Vamp came into my office. "You may want to start looking for that other job," he told me bluntly.

He caught me completely off-guard.

"I've told you and told you to cultivate this Pierce Roberts character so we could land the HC contract."

"I was just going to call him," I said weakly.

"Save your energy." He slammed his fist on my desk. "I went after Roberts myself. I was on the telephone with him an hour last night. I'm going in to Chicago tomorrow to cinch the deal."

I just stood there.

"I might keep you on," he continued, "if it hadn't been for the foolish play you made for more money. You see, I run this place. I decide how much people are paid. And I can keep running this place successfully without upstarts who have too much personal ambition."

"I'm fired?" I managed to ask.

"We won't rush things," he replied. "I'm a fair man. I don't want any stink in town, and neither do you. You go ahead and look around. Give yourself a month or so. I'll wait for you to resign."

I was stunned. I put my hands in my pockets, walked back and forth in the office. After a moment, I looked up. Mr. Vamp was watching me. Like a sadist, he watched as though pleased to behold the suffering he had invoked.

"I hope you realize one thing," he said, breaking the long silence. "I'm doing this for your own good. I could have made a great life for you, young man. I've got a daughter whose crazy about you. You know that. But since you won't face up to facts and recognize that your own marriage is a farce, it's a lot better for you to move someplace else. Besides, it'll spare my daughter some of her misery."

Chapter Twenty-eight

Was this to be the sum of life—crisis upon crisis, a gleam of hope, a sky of discontent?

How would I tell Vaneta? How would her sensitive spirit react to the uncertainty sure to surround my search for new employment? What might this turn of events do to her physical condition? I decided to seek the counsel of Uncle Rufus.

"It's no surprise to me," he said. "Vamp has talked to people around town. He's been restless about you. The problem is, you see, you're too valuable to him. He can't face up to having people around who are capable of doing their jobs without his supervision."

A customer came to the store, asking for my Uncle's specific attention on a matter. I sauntered away. It was like a walk into the past each time I came to the store. Uncle Rufus had made few changes, except to keep abreast with new products. Here, where it had always been, was his candy case. There was a coffee grinder, electric driven now, but in the same location. The radios, the phonographs were gone, commodities too specialized now in a day when sales involve maintainence, but it was nostalgic to browse through the area where my grandfather had once listened enthralled to the Farmer's Favorite Fiddlers.

His business of the moment dispatched, Uncle Rufus came to me.

"Don't let it upset you too much," he said. "I've wondered many's the time how long you could stand it working for the man. Better to have this happen now than ten or fifteen years from now after you're more settled. Vamp's the kind of scoundrel who would fire somebody a month before he's due for retirement."

"How do I tell Vaneta?" I asked bluntly.

Uncle Rufus pursed his lips thoughtfully.

"I've got to tell her.

"If you don't," he cautioned, "she'll soon hear it from somebody else. This is a small town."

"But with the scare we just had . . ."

"I know," he sympathized.

More customers came. I waited several minutes. There seemed no prospect of further discussion so I left.

I decided on the tactic of informing my wife by stages.

"Mr. Vamp's going into Chicago in the morning," I told her.

"Oh." Her response was casual.

"He's going to meet with Pierce about the Harvest Craft deal."

"He is? With Pierce?"

I nodded. Taking her hand, we walked to the living room. I gestured for her to sit.

"You may hear some rumblings around town," I said.

"About what?"

"I had a bit of a run in with Mr. Vamp."

I studied her face closely. Her eyes expressed alarm, but she was poised, in good control of herself.

"Is Pierce involved?" she asked.

"Indirectly," I said.

She frowned. "Are you trying to get something back at him for that Chicago situation?"

"No, sweetheart." I sat beside Vaneta now, drawing her to me. "I'm trying to put that all in the past. Mr. Vamp asked me to go see him. That's not easy to do, but I would have tried, except for your illness."

"Then it's my fault?" she asked, hurt.

"Please, sweetheart," I said, "it isn't anybody's fault. I just talked with Uncle Rufus."

"About what?"

"About all this. I told him I may resign."

"Jerry!"

"Like Uncle Rufus said, better to face up to things now than wait ten or fifteen years and have Mr. Vamp . . ."

"But what will we do?"

"Please, Vaneta," I begged. "Don't jump to conclusions. I'm

going to look around, see if I can't find something more interesting and secure for us."

"But will we have to leave our house?"

"I don't know. I hope not. There's always the chance I could get the kind of work that would let me stay right here. I haven't resigned yet. I just wanted you to know first from me in case you hear any talk around town."

"If you mean Aunt Lydia," she said, "she hasn't been here since I got home from the hospital. I called her this morning. She's not well. You could hear it in her voice on the telephone. I thought I'd go over and see her this afternoon."

"Why don't you?" I asked. "I'll stay here and look after little Jerry. I could quick drive you over."

"I'd like to walk," she said. "I need the fresh air and exercise."

I thought it might be helpful, being in the house alone. I needed to think, to formulate a plan, but I was too confused to think. I tried not to be morose about it, to face up squarely to this initial threat upon my responsibilities as a family man but, frankly, I was a little scared.

I tried to read the Bible. I tried to pray. But I was so out of contact with myself, I didn't seem to be able to make any contact with God.

I paced the floor from one end of the house to another, each step adding to the weight of my disconsolation. Finally, coming into our bedroom, I dropped to my knees.

"Please, God," I cried out, "You've got to help me. I've asked You and asked You, and so many times there doesn't seem to be an answer. I don't ask for miracles, God, I just ask You to clear my head somehow. Help me."

I got to my feet, a boy again for a moment, expecting the skies to rend, angelic visitations to answer my summons with some cataclysmic evidence of divine favor on my behalf.

It was only a moment. I would have to work out my own problems.

Pacing the floor for several moments, more confused with each step it seemed, trying to take an adult view of my circumstances and yet wondering why I couldn't see, just once, some more overt instance of God's presence in my time of need.

Then the telephone rang. A sudden mood of expectancy came over me.

I walked briskly to the telephone, reached to pick it up, then

271

hesitated. Suppose it was only some casual call, some friend of Vaneta's?

I picked up the phone.

"Hello," I said.

"A person-to-person call for Mr. Jerry Pew," the operator said.

"This is Mr. Pew."

"Go ahead, please," she said.

"Jerry," came a man's voice booming across the wire, a voice I could not at first identify.

"Yes," I said.

"I just talked to your uncle."

"My uncle?"

"Your Uncle Rufus. He called me, filled me in on the situation you're facing just now."

"Pastor Mallory," I exclaimed, recognizing the voice.

"How about a few holes of golf?"

"Sure!"

"I'm tied up over the weekend, naturally, but I found an excuse to drive down your way first of the week. I figure I could meet you at the golf club by two o'clock Tuesday. I'll grab some lunch along the way."

"You're not coming here just to see me?" I asked.

"Can you make it Tuesday afternoon?" He ignored my question.

"Yes, but . . ."

"Good, I'll see you at the golf course at 2 o'clock. How's Vaneta?"

"My uncle told you about . . ."

"Yes, he did. How's she doing?"

"Seems okay."

"Maybe I could drop in and see her after the golf game?"

"I'm sure she would want you to have dinner with us," I said."

"If it works out, fine."

He terminated the call. I told Vaneta the moment she returned.

"That's wonderful, she exclaimed. "Maybe he could go see Aunt Lydia."

"Don't bring Aunt Lydia into this," I snapped.

"But she's not well, Jerry. Really she's not."

I could see I had hurt Vaneta.

"Sorry, sweetheart." I apologized. "But you know she wouldn't be helped by a visit from Pastor Mallory, or from me either, for that matter."

272

Vaneta went to the kitchen.

"Can he stay for dinner and spend the night with us?" she called.

"That'd be great," I replied. "We'll see."

Mr. Vamp would be in Chicago for at least ten days so I spent some time in my office. I wanted to make several exploratory calls relative to future employment but the prospect of seeing Pastor Mallory so overpowered my thinking I could scarcely bend my mind to anything else. I awaited the coming of Tuesday like a little boy anticipating one of the gala events of childhood.

Pastor Mallory and I spent a half-hour in animated chit-chat before moving out to the first tee.

"It was great of Uncle Rufus to call you," I said, hoping to introduce the discussion for which he had obviously come.

"He loves you like a son," Pastor Mallory said. "You know that."

"I sure do."

"He couldn't go into detail on the limited phone conversation. Why don't you do that?"

I brought him up-to-date on all that had happened.

We began to play.

"How's your spiritual life, Jerry?" Pastor Mallory asked, as we walked down the fairway. It was good being asked a question like this, so casual and yet so meaningful, as a friend would pleasantly and sincerely inquire about the health of another.

"Up and down," I said.

"For instance?"

"Well, I want the Bible to have real meaning in my life," I explained, "but I've seen so many people read it without getting any value out of it that I guess I'm afraid the same thing's going to happen to me."

"Looks like we're kindred spirits, Jerry."

"How do you mean?"

"Just because a man's a preacher doesn't assure him of a vital relationship with the Scriptures. One of my problems was reading the Bible to find sermon texts instead of reading it to seek God's guidance for my life. I sometimes wonder if a lot of people wouldn't be better off not to read the Bible at all."

I was startled by such a statement.

"Really, Jerry, the thought often comes to me. Some people starve themselves spiritually by little or no reading of the Bible but others have what you might call Bible gout."

"From reading the Bible too much?" I asked.

"As I say, the thought has crossed my mind," he replied.
"How could that be?"

"Reading with the wrong objective in mind—you know, to confirm a pet doctrine, or reading as a kind of spiritual rigmarole. It can be like a fetish to some people."

It was a new thought to me. We separated for several strokes. I watched Pastor Mallory closely. He was tensely serious, more than simply having his mind on his golf game, and the measure of his intent bolstered my anticipations.

When we met again on the green, there being benches in a shady area nearby, he suggested we sit out a foursome just behind us. Other than to his own wife or to a fellow pastor, I question if he ever opened his heart to anyone more fully than he did to me that afternoon. He had told me previously of his childhood frustrations, some of them similar to my own, but now he spoke of the frustrations of a minister. Sincere though he may have been in his desire to exhalt Christ, he had again and again found himself slipping into the rut of spiritual professionalism, pleasing his parishioners rather than standing alone for what he knew to be right.

"It gets a little wearying sometimes, being a minister," he said. "You come to call on someone and everybody suddenly snaps to attention as though God Himself just walked through the door. I guess we talked about this before, how people get the idea that only the pastor has a direct line through to Heaven.

"But preachers are men, Jerry. At least this one is. And men need God, whether they admit it or not—a God who reveals Himself and is more than a figment of the imagination. I'm sure God could reveal Himself through angels, through any number of ways, but I've discovered He wants to reveal Himself to me by becoming part of every detail of my life."

"Tell me more."

"Maybe I should go back to the beginning—yours and my beginning, that is. A lot has happened in my life since those days. I cooked up quite a martyr spirit when I left the church here. I sort of looked upon myself as one of God's special heroes. To be truthful, it was just as much my fault as the fault of anyone at the church here. I could have stayed and had a rewarding ministry. I'm sure of it. But I guess I needed experience to bring me to some of the discoveries I've made."

"Discoveries?" I asked eagerly.

He smiled. "I was reading my Bible one afternoon, (He reached down, plucked a stem of grass, studied it for a moment) looking for sermon material. I happened to come to the book of Joshua. My heart was empty, Jerry, and that bothered me because a man can't preach from an empty heart, and I sensed desperately the need for some answers in my life personally.

"I don't know how familiar you are with the book of Joshua. Moses had died and the Israelites were pretty upset, but God raised up Joshua, a man with lots of courage. Because of this, God gave Joshua some very meaningful promises.

"There in the first chapter, the eighth verse, God said,

> This book of the law shall not depart out of thy mouth; but thou shalt meditate therein day and night, that thou mayest observe to do according to all that is written therein: for then thou shalt make thy way prosperous, and then thou shalt have good success.

"It took a moment before it hit me, Jerry. But it hit me hard. Three words in that verse. I'd read it many times, memorized the verse shortly after my conversion, thought it meant that if anyone reads the Bible regularly, God will reward him by blessing his life."

"You're saying that isn't true?" I asked.

"Not simply reading the Bible, Jerry. A man can read the Bible and have it mean no more to him than reading the newspaper. But there are three words in that verse. They gave me a key that's unlocked a lot of doors. God told Joshua to not only make His word a part of his thought processes day and night, but he said *observe to do*. There's the key, man."

"Observe to do," I reflected.

"Remember the verse I shared with you here on the golf course when we talked about faith?"

"I sure do," I replied. "Romans 10:13. Faith comes by hearing and hearing by the word of God."

"That's part of what I'm talking about, Jerry—the Bible is a living book that only relates to us by application. I've got to come to the place where everything I do . . . everything Jerry . . . my thoughts, my motivations, my decisions . . . where the total me is related to obedience to God.

"Unless I come to the Bible asking God to speak to me, unless I ask for guidance from what I read, unless I'm willing to let God show me the rough edges that need to be squared off in my life—in short, unless I'm willing to *observe to do* what the Bible says, I probably would be better off not reading it at all."

275

"How about that?" I mused. The concept was beginning to get through to me.

"I said those three words gave me the key to unlock a lot of doors. One of those doors involves an understanding of the verbs of the Bible. Get your hands on a concordance. Look up verbs like *trust, believe, study, rest, obey.* The Bible says, As you have therefore received Christ Jesus the Lord, so walk ye in Him. If I am going to *observe to do* what that verse says, then it means I must *walk* in harmony with God. A lot of life's problems can become pretty insignificant when everything is predicated by the knowledge that we are walking in harmony with God.

"The Bible has come alive in my life, Jerry," Pastor Mallory exuded. There was a glow in his eyes I'd never seen in a man before. "Oh, I get in the middle of a lot of theological controversies. I don't know if you're aware of it or not but there is quite a hassle going on now in our seminary as to just what is meant by the inspiration of the Scriptures. I'm sure that's an important question. But somehow I can't help believing that if, as a church, we would bring people to a discovery of what our relationship to God can be, if we will simply *observe to do* what the Bible says, well, if this could happen, a lot of the theological controversy would be pretty meaningless.

"What I'm saying is that a lot of people would go to their graves defending the word for word inspiration of the Scriptures, and yet their own lives are fallow because they have never let the Book come alive in the day by day, moment by moment guts and grind of life as it really is."

"If I dig out the verbs of the Bible . . ." I began.

"Let me take you through one more door, Jerry. What all this has added up to for us, by the grace of God, is that I'm beginning to form the habit of being a Christian."

"The habit?" I asked.

"Reading the Bible, making a study of the verbs as I indicated, this is all important. It's vital. But I must make this so much a part of me that, as a kind of spiritual or reflex action you might say, it becomes normal for me to apply the valid, living concepts of the Bible in every detail of my life."

"Habitual Christianity," I mused.

"That's it," Pastor Mallory reacted with enthusiasm. "Great, Jerry! I've been trying to put a handle on it. Habitual Christianity!"

276

I must have looked a bit dubious, for he sobered quickly. "I'm taking too much for granted," he said. "Let me detail this a bit more. For years, I've been trying to nail down the real meaning of dedication. Like you, I was reared in an evangelical setting. I saw people again and again make promises to God. I, too, made such promises. But always it was the same story. Sincere though I may have been in that moment of dedication, deeply concerned because, somehow, my previous dedications hadn't proved really vital, I always slipped back into the same rut.

"Then, while sharing with a friend in the ministry shortly after I left the church here, the two of us came upon a definition of dedication which has played a tremendous part in my own spiritual metamorphosis. I know we've got to be careful with definitions and philosophic formulae, but this one makes sense, Jerry. Let me share it with you. *Dedication is a lifetime process, in which a Christian forms the habit of consciously involving Jesus Christ in every event of every day of his life!*"

I took from my pocket the card on which I had been keeping our score.

"Repeat that," I said. "I want to write it down."

He repeated it.

"Habitual Christianity," I mused again. "Yeah."

"Jerry, I believe every trait of the human mechanism was designed by God to equip us for glorifying Him. One of the strongest forces in our own lives is the capacity for forming habits. Kind of strange, isn't it, that we so often think of habits as being bad? This just could be one of the devil's choicest tricks.

"I believe that, in it's finest use, the capacity for habit forming can be our most vital response as human beings to the Bible concepts we were talking about."

"Is there any special way you go about this process?" I asked.

"Yes, there is," he said, nodding, "If your wife asks you to go to the store, is there any particular thing you do to serve as a reminder?"

"From force of habit, I turn my wrist watch so that the face is below my wrist instead of above it. It really bugs me until I remember what I was asked to do, so I can turn the watch back again."

"Like tying a string on your finger, right?"

"Right," Then I caught the full impact of what he was saying. "The thing I need to do," I said, "is to develop some kind of reminder. Is that it?"

277

"That's it. It's surprising how little time it takes but once you've done it, Jerry, once you've literally formed the habit of being conscious of Christ in everything you do, until that consciousness becomes a vital part of your subconscious motivation, once you've done this, you've at last plumbed the secret of letting God's perpetual presence into your life.

"With me, there was a ring my wife had given me. I just wore it on special occasions. But I started wearing it all the time. Naturally, it felt awkward at first, but every time I felt the ring, I reminded myself that that moment consciously belonged to God. Whatever was happening, however trivial or meaningful it might be, I related it to the fact that I wanted God to be absolutely central to everything in my life.

"Remember those verses in Proverbs, in the third chapter, Jerry? "Trust in the Lord with all your heart, and lean not unto your own understanding. In all your ways acknowledge Him, and He shall direct your paths." That's what you call making it a habit. "In all your ways!" That's your part. "He shall direct your paths"; that's God's part."

It was strange, strange and downright tremendous. We didn't talk about my employment circumstance, though I'm sure Uncle Rufus had appraised Pastor Mallory of this. We did not speak of the sword that continually hung above my head concerning Hillary. We talked about the reality of God, about the full life found only in His Son, the penetrating dynamic of the Holy Spirit.

It was a day of awakening for me, a day of new beginning!

Chapter Twenty-nine

Observe to do.

In all your ways acknowledge Him, and He shall direct your paths.

Simple concepts, within the grasp of any mortal who recognizes that terrestrial dimensions cannot, of themselves, bring a man into the kind of purposeful living for which the Creator designed him. It was not a cataclysmic discovery, not an orbiting emotional experience, but rather the sounding out of bedrock upon which I could build the super structure of the life I dared to believe was within my province to envision.

Quietly, but relentlessly, I put these new concepts into practice. I did not even speak of them to Vaneta. They must first be tested in the laboratory of my own experience, put to the fire of my obsession for discovering the totality of faith in the human equation.

As would be expected, I related my spiritual research to two areas—my terminating relationship with Mr. Vamp and the perpetual outreach for some way whereby I could convince Vaneta of my moral integrity.

In all your ways acknowledge him, and He shall direct your paths, served the first purpose. I simply told God of my need for employment, my family responsibilities, leaving my lot in His hands. I didn't understand the present circumstance, and the future was like an ominous haze, but I would leave it all in His care, trusting Him to guide my thinking as I sought to make the right moves.

The Hillary nemesis was something else.

I wrestled with it in new determination, recognizing more fully than I had ever known how deeply this frustration lay embedded in the mainstream of my thought processes. I grew restless about it, fitful because no promise leaped from the Bible's pages to assure me of a sudden solution. Then, recognizing the wrong of my questioning, I simply began to search the Bible's pages with the prayer that God would show me His way.

He did!

"Commit your way unto the Lord; trust also in Him, and He shall bring it to pass . . . the trial of your faith brings patience . . . He knows the way that I take. When He has tried me, I shall come forth as gold." That last quotation, from the experiences of Job, became the most vividly relevant of my quest.

Then one day, reading the Apostle Paul's first letter to the Corinthian church, I came upon this admonition. "Whether, therefore, you eat, or drink, or whatever you do, do all to the glory of God." Even in this early stage of my new spiritual development, I immediately caught the import of this statement.

God, I prayed silently, I've been wanting to straighten out this Hillary mess to absolve myself, but, Lord, if it will bring more glory to you for me to carry this suspicion of guilt the rest of my life, I'm willing.

It was like lifting a bag of rocks from my shoulders. Let me never be accused of presuming God intends a Christian's life to be an aesthetic superimposure of some sort in which the participant so lives above the give and take of life as to be immune to innate human attitudes. It is nothing of the sort, for the here and now becomes the grist, the catalyst, through which the Divine experience flows and by which it is verified. In fact, the deeper my exploration into this new way, the more I became aware of my humanity, the more I saw the utter folly of supposing anyone, however gifted, could structure within himself even so much as the semblance of that which only the Spirit of God can breathe into a man.

No, it must become habitual—a liberating habit like the learning to walk, to speak, to drive a car or fly a plane—this Christian life devoid of parenthesis. With God's help, I would make it so.

Pastor Mallory suggested a physical reminder so I wore a rubber band around my wrist. No one noticed it, but I felt the pleasantly incessant nudging to relate every event of the day in a continuous acknowledgment of my need for God. By far the greatest attain-

280

ment was the sense of peace I found regarding Hillary. Once, when an attitude of Vaneta's indicated she might be alluding to the situation, I reacted with resentment as I normally would, but then the new learning process intervened, and so it was only a moment's rift to the peace in my heart, to the poise in my life.

I was learning, for this is the scheme of life brought to its foremost scholastic, the search for God. And each rising above myself, each putting down of carnality, touched my mind and my emotions with the elated senses given by the Creator to those who walk always toward the sun. But wherever the finite form intercepts the infinite light, shadows must fall.

They fell upon my way.

I had confidence, such as I had not known before, but I also felt the press of circumstances, the loom of uncertainty. On the morning of Mr. Vamp's return from Chicago, for example, I was at peace and yet fretful with the continuing radiance deep inside but wisps of duress at times unnerving me. Whether my problem stemmed from a lurking hostility toward's Vaneta's brother-in-law or disdain for Mr. Vamp, I cannot say.

In any case, I was most surely unprepared for the turn my situation took.

"Say, Jerry," Mr. Vamp exuded, coming into my office as though there had been no inclement turn to our relationship, "I hope you haven't looked too seriously for another job."

"As a matter of fact, I haven't," I said, his cordiality having so surprised me that I blurted my state frankly.

"Good," he exclaimed. "I'd like you to stay with us for another sixty days anyway. I'll tell you what. Go and look for the work but don't announce any resignation for sixty days. Can you arrange that?"

"I suppose," I said.

"Fine!" He slapped my arm.

By this time, a bit more acclimated to the change in his attitude, I grew suspicious.

"Any special reason?" I asked. He looked at me, puzzled, so I added, "For my staying on?"

"I'm not the kind to turn anybody out into the cold, Jerry m'boy," he effused. "Say, this Pierce Roberts is one whale of a fellow, isn't he?"

I offered no comment. This seemed to upend my employer somewhat.

"He thinks the world of you," Mr. Vamp said, clearing his throat, "sends greetings as a matter of fact. Say, isn't he a little on the order of your religious opinions?" Not waiting for any reply, he added, "We talked business, Jerry!" He clapped his hands joyfully. "We sure did. Yes, sir, we talked business!

"The new addition's coming along great, eh? Makes this little burg look like a metropolis. Yeah, things are looking great. Real, real great.

"Well, like I say, you plan to stick with us for at least sixty days before you announce any changes, okay?"

I felt sure he was up to something but couldn't ferret out the faintest inclination of what it might be.

"Tell you what, Jerry," he put in, growing noticeably uneasy for a moment. "Tell you what let's do. You don't announce any change here for sixty days. Then go ahead and resign and I'll pay you cash in advance for three more months but you'll have no responsibility at all here at the plant. Okay?"

"You'll put that into writing?" I had the presence of mind to ask.

"Over my signature," he promised.

His signed memo was on my desk within the hour. He was an incomprehensible man and, of course, I was puzzled by his action. But I thanked God. In sixty days, Vaneta would be far enough along in her pregnancy to be able to withstand any distressing announcement. Until then, I could assume a normal stance in my activities.

That very night she asked me about what was happening at the plant, and I could tell her truthfully that Mr. Vamp had told me to stay on. Before the week was out, life resumed a placid course for us. I continued my quiet search for future employment. Several new potentials increased my confidence that all would be well.

Then one morning, as we sat at breakfast, the telephone rang. I answered.

"Jerry?" It was Uncle Rufus. "Can you come over and lend me a hand?" He had a knack for facing distressing circumstances with a poised attitude, but his voice plainly told me this was no ordinary circumstance.

"What's wrong?" I asked.

"Lydia," he said. "I think she's had a stroke. I can't lift her off the floor. I've called the doctor."

"I'll be right over," I told him.

"What is it?" Vanetta asked anxiously.

282

I told her.

"I was afraid this was coming. Should I go with you?"

"If you like," I said. "But I'm sure they'll just move her to the hospital. You could see her there."

"I'll stay here," she said.

I drove quickly to Uncle Rufus' house and entered without knocking. It was pathetic the sight that greeted my eyes, Aunt Lydia prone upon the floor, Uncle Rufus looking down upon her helplessly, his unshaven face white with drying lather.

We did not speak, but got quickly to the task of lifting her to the couch. Her eyes were closed. She was like a woman dead except for the faint rising and falling of her bosom.

"What happened?" I asked.

"We got up like usual," Uncle Rufus said. "She went to the kitchen to fix breakfast. I was in the bathroom getting ready to shave. All of a sudden I heard this thud. I came down right away. I knew it was trouble. I found her like you saw her. Guess she must have felt sick in the kitchen and tried to get in here to the sofa."

"Too bad," I said. It surprised me—the love and the pity in my own voice.

"The doctor told me he'd be right here," Uncle Rufus said.

"How are you?" I asked.

"I'm all right."

"Can you go back to the bathroom and finish shaving?"

Uncle Rufus put his hand to his face, felt the shaving cream, and smiled momentarily. "I can do it," he said and left.

I stood alone in the room. There had been the day when I would have disdained that prostrate form, delighting in my aunt's misfortune. It was in my heart to do this now. But I remembered reading in the book of Romans earlier in the week, "Recompense to no man evil for evil . . . as much as lieth in you, live peaceably with all men," and I stepped to my aunt, dropped to one knee, and placed a hand on her arm. It was old and withered like a branch one prunes from a tree.

"Oh God," I whispered, "give me love for this woman. Take the hate out of my heart."

When the doctor arrived, he diagnosed her condition as critical and asked for the telephone to summon an ambulance. Then I called Vaneta and told her to arrange for someone to look after little Jerry and so, shortly after the ambulance left for the hospital, we followed with Uncle Rufus.

283

Sentiment in some degree always surrounds the demise of any close relative, and I shall not enlarge upon the brief events which preceded Aunt Lydia's passing, except to say that I was able to show love to this one who had been so detestible to me, to bring a glint of wonderment and gladness to eyes that had so frequently looked upon me with scrutiny and scorn.

Aunt Lydia could neither speak nor move. Her eyes were as the eyes of a child, frightened at the thought of death, responsive to the touch of kindness, to the voice of sympathy.

"What are my wife's chances?" Uncle Rufus asked the doctor.

"It's difficult to say," the doctor replied.

"This thing's hit her pretty hard?"

"Yes."

When I told Mr. Vamp what had happened, he put his arm across my shoulder like a father.

"Your uncle needs you," he said. "You just take whatever time you want. Come in and check the mail if you can, but don't feel pushed. Don't feel pushed a bit. No, sir.

"Say, not to talk business at a time like this, but your brother-in-law called this morning. He's going to be out in Los Angeles for a week or so but plans to stop here on his way back to Chicago." Gleefully, he added, "Won't he be surprised when he sees the addition?

"But let's talk business later. You see what you can do for Uncle Rufus. Tell him I sure hope his wife snaps out of this."

Though Mr. Vamp's attitude continued to baffle me, I was sincerely grateful for the freedom to be of whatever assistance I could to my uncle. I helped him with odd jobs about the store, drove him back and forth to the hospital, tried to anticipate his needs and concerns.

"I'm being an awful bother," he said one day.

It was my chance to tell him, more forthrightly than I had ever been able to do before, how much he had meant to me in the past, how I had respected him, depended on him. Tears came to his eyes. I do not remember ever having seen such a response before in this strong and serene person.

I went to the church that afternoon, pleased to find it silent and empty. I walked among the pews. God, I prayed, I'm grateful. The hate is gone for Aunt Lydia. It's gone, God. Thanks so much.

We visited Aunt Lydia twice daily. Sometimes Vaneta was tired and remained home, but I never missed a visit. I brought Aunt

Lydia a plant one afternoon, and when I kissed her, she gasped for breath, as though trying to sob but unable to do so.

"I don't see how you can be so good to her," Vaneta said, as we left the hospital. "The nurse says she seems to wait for your coming more than any of the rest of us."

It was good to hear, to see in my own life the fruit of *observe to do*. I had not yet discussed this with Vaneta, but she was beginning to see.

Aunt Lydia died.

In his sermon, our minister spoke rather eloquently of how she had been a pillar in the church. I only heard snatches of it, for I kept looking back to the form in the casket, cold and silent like a gaunt and solemn tree that had given neither fruit nor shade to passers by. Was it fully her blame, or had the church, those who spoke for it, failed in not showing her, as I had been shown, the way that is higher and surer, closer to the sun? Perhaps she had done the best she knew. Though a stranger to the intended radiance of the life in Christ, she had championed righteousness and assaulted evil.

People from the church and townsmen who respected Uncle Rufus surrounded the casket with flowers of every hue and fragrance. Those flowers spoke to me that afternoon. Beautiful now, they would soon wither to a travesty of their present glory. Might it have been that Aunt Lydia in the moment of her first walk with Christ knew the fragrance and the beauty of the upward way? Was there a time when she stood within reach of the fulfillment I now experienced?

After the sermon, the mourners waited while members of the community filed past the remains. Then the family gathered around the casket. Some wept. Uncle Caleb sobbed uncontrollably for several moments. Vaneta stood arm and arm with my mother, each of them weeping quietly. Tears came to my own eyes.

I looked for Uncle Rufus wishing to give him comfort. He was not among those looking into the casket but was standing off to the side, alone.

I went to him. "It's not an easy time," I managed to say.

He did not look up, though I could tell from the expression on his face he had heard me. He broke a flower from a nearby stem and crushed it into his fingers. "I once loved her," he said.

He looked at me a moment a bewildered man.

The mortician came to us with that arctic professionalism so painfully characteristic of their trade and asked, "Shall I close the casket?"

Uncle Rufus nodded. He moved forward and stood looking down at his wife's body, as the others crept away. The casket was closed and sealed.

I stepped alongside my uncle and put my hand on his shoulder. He was trembling.

I had many times felt weak in his presence. Now I felt strong, a strength I was now sharing with this one who had so often been a fortress against the beleaguering elements in my life.

Chapter Thirty

There was death and there was life—the passing of Aunt Lydia
and the child Vaneta would soon bear. There was also the passing
of the old ways, the unrewarded seeking, the questioning.

Aunt Lydia's demise was like the last words of a prolonged end
of Pewdom. My parents, Uncle Caleb, Uncle Eliad, and the others,
whatever their adherence to the past, could scarcely be counted upon
to defend the cause, much less champion future conquests. But the
putting down of the old ways, rather than undermining my spiritual
foundations, forged new girdings to the strengthening tenacity of my
faith. *Observe to do* became even more meaningful in my searching of the Scriptures, and in my application of the divine precepts,
I saw, as one sees with the lifting of a dense fog, how much the life
in Christ is not ecclesiastical performance but the truly existential
encounter. "Christ in you, the hope of glory," the Apostle Paul put
it.

It gave new personality to our marriage, enrichment to all my
human relationships, poise and compassion and an outgoingness
compatible to the norm of my traits and characteristics and yet
simultaneously transcendent to them. It is both unbelievable and
utterly credible, simple and profound, the texture of life when a
man relates his faith to everything he is and does.

The passing of Aunt Lydia was a stone of many facets. It brought
a newness to our clan as, with the spending out of legalism, a kind
of liberation came to our people. Aunt Britta stimulated a renewed

social consciousness among us. My own mother, who had become very nearly a nonentity in my life, gave expression to latent graces I did not know she possessed. I developed the first real rapport I had ever had with my father.

Yet I did not applaud my aunt's departure. This gave me much encouragement—the absence of delight in my heart. I think I almost wished her alive again. I wanted more opportunities to express to her the genuineness of Christ's abundance in giving us love to the unlovely—not simply the turning of the cheek but the walking of the second mile in giving and forgiving, as we *observe to do* the Bible's transforming precepts for human relations.

Uncle Rufus received the largest share of attention beyond my immediate domestic circle. Though the passing of his spouse liberated him from a long and patiently endured encumbrance, he needed me. I stopped often at his store. We had him at our home frequently for meals. He and little Jerry became very fond of each other, and Vaneta and I loved him more than we loved our own fathers.

On one of my visits to the store he asked about my plans for future employment. I told him I had sent out several new queries, resulting in one particularly interesting offer from an insurance firm, but was not prepared to make any decision.

"I've been wondering," he said. "It may be you and I could work into some kind of partnership."

"Here in the store?" I asked. It didn't particularly interest me, and I'm afraid the fact showed in my attitude and in the tone of my voice. I saw Uncle Rufus' countenance fall.

"I was just wondering," he said. "It's probably not worth discussing."

"I'd be glad to discuss anything with you," I said.

"You would?" His eyes brightened.

"Of course."

A customer entered.

"For now," I said, "I'd probably better be getting back to the office."

"We'll talk about it sometime," he said.

"I'll look forward to that," I told him and left.

The following afternoon, Mr. Vamp came into my office. "You've been a little quiet lately," he said.

I didn't understand his question, so offered no reply.

"Have you found another job?" he asked.

I was about to give him a rundown on the status of my inquiries but decided against it. "I'll be giving you my formal resignation the first of next week," I said. "I can give it to you now, if you want it."

"Oh, no." He cleared his throat, subduing the obvious fact of concern of some sort. "No hurry, Jerry. I was just curious."

"Things are looking great on the building program," I said. "That new unit has gone up like a mushroom. How soon will you be installing new machinery?"

"I expect the first load in a couple of weeks."

He walked over to my window and stood a moment looking out. Without turning back, he said, "Got a note from your brother in-law. He'll be stopping here Tuesday on his way back from Los Angeles. Had to be out there longer than he first figured, I guess."

He turned, looked at me studiously and asked, "Have you said anything to him about leaving?"

"No."

"Good!" Mr. Vamp was obviously relieved. "When he gets here, I'd appreciate it if you'd meet him the way you would any client. Okay?"

"Of course."

I tried to fathom the man—more out of curiosity than for personal security, as I fully intended to terminate my employment—but his actions and attitudes defied rationalization.

"Plan to be at work as you've done in the past," he said. "On time, eh? You've been real good about that. Punctuality on the part of executives means a lot to a plant. Good for morale. Right?"

I smiled, wanly.

"I suppose you'd like Pierce to stay at your house?" he continued. "Hope you won't mind that I've already asked him to stay with us. Of course, now, if you really want him and if I can count on you not discussing the change in arrangements you and I have . . ."

"Whatever you decide," I said.

"Now I realize, Jerry," he said, "it's a little awkward, a relative of yours coming to town and me putting him up instead of having him stay with you. If we had a decent hotel . . ."

"How about Pike's Motel?"

"Say, now!" He cut off abruptly, his mouth remaining open as he studied my eyes with the thoroughness of a child fearing punishment. "Somehow, though," he continued, "it don't seem appropriate, putting a man in a motel unless he comes driving his own car. Then I could see it, Jerry. Sure, then it'd be the thing to do.

"Tell you what, Jerry. Let's keep him at my house. Okay? I'd just as soon we do it that way—have him stay with us."

"Like I say," I told him, "you're the boss."

"Good!" Mr. Vamp exuded. "Then you're agreed. That's good."

I told Vaneta. "He must be afraid we'd say the wrong thing to Pierce," she said. "I'm sure it'll work out all right. Maybe we could have him for a meal."

The morning Pierce Roberts arrived, Mr. Vamp tripped about the office like an obsequious vice-president. His eyes sparkled. He had music in his voice. He told my secretary she should speak with me about a new electric typewriter. He ordered a round of cokes for the girls in billing. He picked a string off the bent shoulders of our bookkeeper, a man who had been with the company for twenty-seven years but hadn't had a raise in the past five. In point of fact, from the manner with which he spoke to me in Pierce's presence, one might have thought I was the plant president and he chairman of the board.

When time came to get down to the negotiations, however, he took Pierce into his office and closed the door, without so much as a suggestion as to my involvement. In the light of his prior insistence that I give no indication of my impending resignation, this confused me somewhat. I lingered in my office for perhaps an hour, then decided to leave.

"Don't forget to order that typewriter," I said to my secretary, chuckling.

"That'll be the day," she returned.

I stopped at Security Mercantile Store for a chat with Uncle Rufus, telling him of Pierce Robert's arrival and of my disinvolvement with proceedings.

"Like I said once before, Jerry," Uncle Rufus comforted, "better have this happen now than a few years later. It's just the way Halford Vamp does, using people to his advantage, moving them out of the organization if they threaten his job in any way."

"How could I threaten his job?" I asked. "I don't know how much corporation stock he holds. I have heard it is just about all of it."

Uncle Rufus chuckled. "There's more than one way to skin a cat," he said. "Vamp could control 100% of the stock and the place be making an enormous profit, but if somebody came along

290

who looked more important to the company than he did, that would be the end of it." He paused for a moment, then added, "Even if it might mean hurting the company financially I venture to say. No. Jerry, he's used you well, probably adding the finishing touch with this Harvest Craft situation."

"But it doesn't seem he's used me at all in the HC deal."

Uncle Rufus lifted his eyebrows and peered momentarily over the top of his glasses. "Oh," he said. That was all he said.

"I told you how Mr. Vamp claimed Vaneta's brother-in-law was concerned about the Hillary affair and supposedly told Mr. Vamp he wanted to make things right with me."

"A likely story," said Uncle Rufus dubiously.

"He must've told him something."

"Why so? Vamp's heard all the gossip around town. He knew your brother-in-law was involved. He could make up any story he's of a mind to."

"I suppose."

"Bury the past, Jerry."

"It's not easy. Vaneta's forgiven me to a certain extent, but it still stands between us and . . ."

"Don't be imagining things now."

"I'm not trying to, Uncle Rufus."

"I've lived a long time, a good long time, and I've observed a few things about the shape of this old world. For one, if a man's guilty, all the saying he isn't won't prevent his being shown for what he is sooner or later. And it's vice versa if he's innocent."

"Say," he said, changing the subject, "we're not very busy today, as you can see. Let's take a drive, maybe have lunch down at the county seat."

The thought didn't especially appeal to me, but it engendered such enthusiasm on my uncle's part, I couldn't decline.

We drove leisurely, following country roads. Uncle Rufus pointed out farms where people he knew had homesteaded. He talked about the radical changes in farming, the future forebodings. He noted crops where rainfall had been especially heavy and where a light but damaging hail had fallen. I only half-listened to his chatter. I kept thinking about Pierce Roberts. Had he told Mr. Vamp about the Chicago affair? Did he want to help me set the record straight with Vaneta? He had been unusually pleasant when we met at the plant. I thought I had detected a compassionate glint in his eye. Might I only have imagined it?

Then after some distance of travel, I made two discoveries. I was driving dangerously as one does when a consuming thought so preoccupies the mind that driving occurs mechanically. Secondly, Uncle Rufus was calling my name.

"Yes?" I said, turning to him.

"You just drove past the last turn to the county seat."

I put my foot to the brake. The car lurched.

"Land sakes, boy," Uncle Rufus cried out.

"Sorry," I said. I took a quick look to get my bearings. "We can cut back next corner."

After I had turned, correcting our route, my uncle said, "It bothers you quite a bit, having this Pierce Roberts fellow come to town."

"I guess so," I admitted.

It then occurred to me why Uncle Rufus had suggested the drive, why he had been chattering so. He had wanted to divert my thought, making the day easier for me, and I appreciated it.

We went to a small restaurant for lunch.

"Still no definite decision on a job?" he said, after we had placed our order.

"No," I replied. "I plan to nail something down in two or three days."

He took a drink of water. Picking up a spoon he idled with it for a moment, glanced out the window toward main street, and then turned back at me.

"Never having had any children," he began, "I've about been limited to my wife for sharing confidential business matters. There were a few things I didn't even share with her."

He paused again, this time scratching on the placemat with the opposite end of the spoon. I waited for him to continue. When he did, he lowered his voice so I had to lean across the table to hear him distinctly. "I'm not a wealthy man," he said, "but I bought a little land out in Oklahoma a good many years ago. It's a section of farmland. I never told Lydia a thing about it. Most of the money the store made I needed to keep up inventory. I've got some savings, some securities, and, of course, I've got the business, whatever it's worth.

"But this here land down in Oklahoma has started to look like it might be pretty valuable. It's farmland, pasture land mainly, I should say, hilly and lots of rocks." His eyes began to sparkle. One

292

did not often see this kind of zest in his manner. "The way it's turning out, what's above the ground isn't so much. It's what's down underneath."

"Oil??" I asked.

"Oil," he replied.

The waitress came with the first of our order.

"Real valuable, Jerry."

"Has their been any drilling?"

"Not right in my area. But apparently the survey shows my land is sitting on one of the biggest basins down there. I may be a rich man, Jerry. I don't know."

"For you, I hope there's no question about it."

"Suppose I'm a millionaire," he said. "I doubt that, but just suppose. I'm also an old man. What have I got, six or ten years left, a dozen maybe? No family. Just myself."

He stopped eating, looked about cautiously.

"Jerry," he said, his voice softer than before, "I've watched you for a long time. Ever since you were a boy I saw you had the makings of something. Especially now that you have this Christian view of things, I see it all the more. I had a simple will made out when Lydia was alive, but with her gone now, I'm having the will changed. I'd like to make you my beneficiary, you and Vaneta."

I was startled and humbled by his announcement.

"I've been going over things with the lawyer," he continued. "As I understand it, there's ways we could work this so taxes wouldn't eat up everything when I'm gone. One way would be to form a partnership, you and me. I'd want you to talk to the lawyer yourself, but from what he's explained to me, that's what I'd like, a partnership.

"I don't know how much of your time it would take, Jerry, but it would sure set my mind at ease if you'd help manage things. Oh, I'd keep puttering away at the store, it's something for me to do, but I'd sure appreciate it if you'd look into the land. I've had a real good offer to sell the mineral rights, but, sakes, Jerry, it might be a good sight better for us to drill a well ourselves. Would you be interested?"

"Of course," I said. I wanted to say more, to express my appreciation for his love and confidence, but it was difficult.

Wisely, he spoke as though he had delved my deepest thoughts, for he said, "Oh, I know you pretty well, Jerry. You don't want to take advantage of me. You want to make it on your own, and I appreciate that. I'm not one to express much emotion and sentiments, but I know how you've felt toward me all these years. It's meant a lot to me, son, the feeling between us."

My uncle's acknowledgement of our camaraderie loosened my tongue and we talked for over an hour. It was all summed up in our final remarks. Uncle Rufus said, "If this Oklahoma proposition should prove to be valuable, I'd like to see you use the capital to develop commercial ventures in our community. My roots are deep there, you know."

"So are mine," I said.

Leaving the restaurant, we drove leisurely homeward. Uncle Rufus began to reminisce once more. But I had seen that there was also vision left in the man.

"We're losing too much store business to the county seat," he said. "If you check the assessor's records, though, you'll see farm population centers more in our area than it does down there. I figure if we could build up a shopping center right out along the highway, we just might stimulate things."

Arriving back at our little town, we parked along the area he had in mind.

"I looked into a few things," Uncle Rufus said, "and found the land out here has been plotted for selling as house lots. It's been that way for two or three years and nobody has built."

"There would need to be streets put in first, wouldn't there?" I asked.

Uncle Rufus smiled knowingly. "That's just it," he said. "The party that owns this land hasn't been able to get it ready so it will attract people who want to build their own places. I figure we might just be able to buy this whole area at a pretty decent price. Why, Jerry, if we had a shopping center—you know, start with something small at first—it would attract farm business from all around here, business from a lot of the smaller towns, too. What do you think?"

"I think it has possibilities."

We got out and walked like pilgrims in a new land, like the old homesteaders Uncle Rufus had spoken of earlier.

"You've got to remember," I said. "Real estate is all new to me. I'd want to move cautiously.

"That's what I like about you, Jerry. I know you'd be careful. We're in no special hurry. I don't know what Mr. Vamp pays you, I'm sure it's not enough, but I'll do my best to come close to what you're making while we develop our partnership."

"I wouldn't . . ."

"Don't worry about money," he interrupted, smiling pleasantly. "I'm not the richest man in town," he winked, "not yet anyway, but I've got a comfortable account put aside and I don't owe a soul." He drove his fist into the palm of his hand. "Oh, I think we could have something real interesting here. Yes, sir, I do."

We talked more, dreaming, planning. He wanted me to find the earliest possible date to slip out to Oklahoma. He would get his complete financial information together and go over it with me. We would move cautiously but we would move steadily.

It was nearly three o'clock by the time I let him out of my car back at the store.

"Going to the office?" he asked.

"I think I'll slip on home," I said. "I told Vaneta I might be out to lunch with Mr. Vamp and Pierce, but I've been getting home about this time afternoons."

As I drove toward our street, I felt a new liberation and exuberance.

"Jerry," Vaneta exclaimed, as I entered the house. "Where have you been?"

For one brief moment, the old animosity returned, but I squelched it.

"I was with Uncle Rufus," I said. "We went for a drive and had lunch down at the county seat."

"You shouldn't have," she protested.

"Why?"

"Mr. Vamp has been calling. He seems all upset."

"Let him be."

Vaneta's eyes widened.

I shrugged my shoulders, went to the kitchen, and drew a glass of water. Vaneta came to the doorway. I glanced at her before beginning to drink.

"Have you had trouble with Mr. Vamp?" she asked.

I drank the water slowly. I drank it all.

"Shouldn't you call him?" Vaneta asked. "Really, Jerry, he was terribly upset."

The telephone rang.

"Please," Vaneta said, "you answer it."

I went to the telephone and picked it up slowly. "Hello," I said with a casual air.

"Jerry?"

"Yes."

"You rascal you. We've been calling all over town for you. Stay there at the house. I'm driving out to see you."

I put down the phone and said to Vaneta, "It was your brother-in-law."

"What did he want?"

"He'll be here in a couple of minutes."

"Oh!" she gasped.

Then, in the manner typical of a housewife, she began to scurry around, tidying the place. I slowly paced the floor.

It was awkward at first, when Pierce arrived. He kissed Vaneta and asked about little Jerry. He offered chit chat about my wife's relative. Then he grew restless.

"You want to talk to Jerry alone?" Vaneta asked.

"No," he said, "that's not necessary."

"Would you sit down?" I asked.

He sat. So did Vaneta and I.

Then he said, "I couldn't quite figure what was coming off down at the plant."

"What do you mean?" I asked.

"Well, Vamp came to see me in Chicago."

"I know."

"Things have gone well for me, Jerry. I've got a responsible job at Harvest Craft, and the nature of the job is such that I'm the one for Vamp to work through if he's to do business with HC.

"Well, when he came to see me in Chicago, I didn't like the look in his eye, when I told him I was mainly interested in swinging a contract because of you."

"Because of me?" I gasped.

"How nice," I heard Vaneta say.

"Blood is thicker than water," Pierce said. "Actually, I've given Halford a lot of encouragement, and I guess that's why he leaped into this expansion program. Frankly, I think he's a little nuts going as whole hog as he has, and I'm afraid if I gave a full evaluation to my boss back at HC, he'd say to forget about subletting anything out here."

"That'd be disastrous!" I exclaimed.

"I suppose it would," Pierce replied.

"He's gone into this expansion on a gamble."

"Obviously. Without an HC contract, he just could break his back."

296

"You're not going to sign a contract with Harvest Craft?" Vaneta asked.

"Not unless Jerry's involved," Pierce said.

I was dumbfounded. Suddenly, Mr. Vamp's ambivalent attitudes began to have meaning.

"What's your status with the company?" Pierce asked. "Halford slobbered all over his chin when I tried to pin him down."

"I'm planning to leave," I said.

"Jerry," Vaneta gasped.

I took her hand and stroked it gently.

"Just today, I had a very attractive offer," I said.

"He's been crowding you out?" Pierce asked.

When I didn't reply, Vaneta said, "Mr. Vamp has been very difficult."

"Well," Pierce said, "I'd like to work with him, but not unless you handle the account, Jerry. I'd want to work directly with you. But if you're leaving . . ."

"Couldn't you stay?" Vaneta asked.

For a moment, I lost touch with reality. It was a dream, surely. I would awaken soon.

"Frankly, I've been finangling the last couple of years to swing something big between HC and this Vamp character," Pierce said, "because I figure I owed it to you and Vaneta. But, like I said, when we were talking in Chicago, I didn't like the way Halford's eyes kept switching away from me whenever I talked about you. We could have signed a contract right there, but he started giving me such a song and dance, I suspected a rotten apple in the barrel. Well, I came here and he acted like everything was fine. When I asked why you weren't with us in our first discussion, he said you had some things to look after, but would probably be in later. Well, when he saw how serious I was that you be involved, he checked your office. He was routine about it at first, but then when he heard you were gone and when he couldn't give me any satisfactory explanation why, knowing that I had sense enough to understand you wouldn't be floating about if you were involved in a big deal for the company—well, that sort of started bringing things to light.

"He got so rattled, I was able to talk a good deal of information out of him, until he realized what he was saying. He started at first trying to tell me you were restless in the company and one of the reasons he was going into the big expansion was to give you more challenge. But he said a couple of things that contradicted that. Well, I told him in no uncertain words that there were several places we could place contracts and that I was at liberty, in fact it's my responsibility, to pick the best supplier, and so far as management of HC was concerned, there was no obligation whatsoever for me to sign a contract with him. Sure, I was interested because of you, being married to my sister-in-law here, but also because I had a lot of confidence in you personally."

I glanced at Vaneta. Tears moistened her cheeks.

"I'd hate to think I was the cause of Mr. Vamp . . ." I began.

"Any chance of your staying with the firm?" Pierce broke in.

"Well . . ."

"He wants you to stay. There's no doubt about that. He'll agree to any reasonable arrangement you propose."

"I sure don't want to crowd the poor guy into a corner."

I felt Pierce's eyes studying me closely.

"Say," he said, "you are a decent sort of person, aren't you? If it was me, I'd shove the guy down the sewer."

"Jerry's wonderful," Vaneta exclaimed. Her voice was like a chord from the spheres.

Pierce sat alone on the couch. He motioned for Vaneta and me to come sit beside him. We complied. He took me by the arm. He put his other arm around Vaneta.

"I feel real bad about the trouble I've caused you two," he said.

I looked at Vaneta. Our eyes met for one brief moment. Then she lowered her gaze.

Pierce coughed nervously. I felt a light tremor in his grip upon my arm.

"I hope you'll forgive me," he said.

Vaneta looked up at her brother-in-law.

"It's pretty serious," he said, speaking with difficulty. "You know, it's pretty serious to hurt any innocent person."

Now it was I who coughed nervously.

"Honest, Jerry," Pierce continued, "it was a long time before I realized the casual statement I made to my wife stirred up all the trouble I now understand has been going on. I saw you with Vamp's daughter in Chicago, sitting in the hotel restaurant. That's all I saw, and I just happened to mention it to Winona when I got home. Actually, I was just joking, when I told her."

I heard Vaneta gasp softly.

"I did get a little bit suspicious at the time," he continued. "That girl looked to me to be as sticky as a strip of fly paper. So I asked around there at the convention. Her dad had been doing a lot of talking. He didn't make it any secret that he was perfectly content for you to have any kind of relationship you wanted with his daughter. But he had also said to one of the men I knew that his daughter was pretty upset about the fact you'd kept putting her off. I couldn't find anybody who had any kind of a case against you. I didn't try real hard. I wasn't trying to stir up anything, but being Vaneta's brother-in-law, you know . . ."

Vaneta bolted to her feet. She stood a moment, looking down at her brother-in-law.

"It's the truth, as God knows it," he said, "every word of it."

Tears came to her eyes, then a sudden outburst of sobbing, as she turned and fled toward our bedroom.

I stood to accompany her, but Pierce restrained me.

"I suspect Vaneta's a good deal like Winona," he said. "At times like this, they like to be alone. She's a real good girl, Vaneta is. Let her have a cry and do some thinking."

I put out my hand. "Thanks," I exclaimed. There were tears in my own eyes.

"I should have done it long ago," Pierce said. "I guess I hoped it'd blow over. I think of myself as being pretty fearless as a salesman, but I sure was chicken about this situation. I apologize, Jerry.

We gripped each other's hands warmly.

"Let's go down to the shop and see Halford," Pierce said. "That is, if there's any chance of your sticking with the poor guy."

I led the way toward the door.

Chapter Thirty-one

It could have been the *l'heure de triomphe* of my business career, our moment of entry into Halford Vamp's office. There was enough of the Pew fabric in me to make it so. Mr. Vamp was obsequious to the point of the ridiculous for, at Pierce's insistence, I was to co-sign the contract as account executive, with my personal responsibility for all Harvest Craft relationships written into the text.

But a spiritual concept came to mind, one I had chosen in search of *observe to do* motivations, a verse from Proverbs which says "By humility and the fear of the Lord are riches, and honor, and life." I was a man, and as a man I wanted those terrestrial merits which come to one who rises above another, in particular above one from whose hand mistreatment has come. But I was also a child of God, intent upon obedience, and thus a stronger desire came to my heart, the compulsion to do good in return for evil. It may seem strange to some, such a compulsion, but I am coming to learn that the practice of those actions, which result from spiritual obedience, is such a sound procedure that God's child must take care lest he practice them for personal gain.

"I, uh . . ." Mr. Vamp stammered, looking first to Pierce and then at me. "I look for Jerry to have a long relationship in the company, long and profitable. How about that, Jerry? Here, you sign first. Okay, Jerry?"

It was a strange phenomenon, having been one day so thoroughly stripped of any future in the company, and the next day inundated with the promise of security. It gratified me to look back upon the past weeks in which I had almost nonchalantly gone about the chore of seeking another source of livelihood. It was the fruition of faith, the intervention of God on my behalf, those manifestations of His hand I had so fervently desired to witness as a child.

I felt as though the adventure of life was but just begun!

There is much I could relate concerning this adventure during the time that has ensued since that momentous hour in Mr. Vamp's office.

I could, for example, relate the continuity of events which, during those subsequent months, brought out with unmistakable clarity the fact that my employer had far over-extended himself in the enlargement of our plant facilities, so much so that, by the mere threat of an unrenewed contract, Pierce Roberts and I could have brought him to his knees, thereby projecting me into control of the organization, even as he had once maneuvered himself. But I refused to be a part of it. Pierce at first resented my decision, presuming my intentions were to utilize my heroic stance as spiritual pressure against Halford Vamp's benighted heart, but I was able to assure my brother-in-law I harbored no such intention. Consequently, so far as I am now able to ascertain, we facilitated negotiations in such a way as to leave Mr. Vamp with no suspicion of a possible coup.

I made a trip to Oklahoma, carefully looking into the circumstances relating to Uncle Rufus' land, and discovered the reports he had received to be somewhat exaggerated. We may one day find oil on the land, but any action we take will need to be carefully calculated, since there have been several abortive drillings in adjacent areas.

We are going into the shopping center project, however, working cooperatively with two men of means from our church, men to whom God has helped me relate some of the dynamics which are becoming increasingly normal to my life.

I must, of course, tell you of Behrend, our second son, named after a favorite uncle of Vaneta's. We named him Behrend Robert.

Our marriage grows increasingly rewarding to both of us. It is a disappointment to me, but we have never discussed her brother-in-law's momentous visit. It troubled me greatly at first. I almost introduced the topic but felt any initiative should come from her.

I believe I understand the reason.

It is difficult to know anyone, even a lifemate. I suppose Vaneta and I will never fully know each other. But I have learned that, whereas I experienced frustrations of one texture, she, too, is beset by lingering influences of childhood.

Vaneta is a lovely person, a woman of poise and radiance rarely found so profusely in members of her sex. But beneath her poise, her frequent display of outgoingness, lurks a dominant pride.

Pride!

The most formidable of all foes in the progress of the pilgrim.

Do not mistake my thoughts at this point, for I stand in judgment of no one, but I have suspected that Vaneta needed this specter of my alleged affair with Hillary to nurture that pride.

So it seems to me, and it has concerned me.

But in my pursuit of the great adventure, which is mine to experience in the life Christ gives, I see, with increasing clarity, what the Apostle meant when he cautioned the people of God about the two powers continually at war in a man's spirit. So that it is not our weaknesses by which are judged, but, rather, the measure in which we submit our weaknesses to that affirmation which promises, "I can do all things through Christ, who strengthens me."

No doubt there are couples better matched than Vaneta and I, for whom domestic tranquility comes easier. I envy them not. For I see in Vaneta and myself the making of a relationship more rewarding and enduring, by virtue of our need for the touch of God to lift us beyond ourselves into that greater reality known only in submission and obedience, to the fact of God and His willingness to touch and transform mortality.

Hillary has remarried—a wretch of a man, I fear. I pleaded with Vaneta to have her visit our home, for I feel sure Hillary would have listened intently to the witness of those who could honestly display the kind of love and concern that transcends and forgives and forgets. Vaneta refused.

It is my prayer that I may yet touch Hillary's life, and the life of her father, one day bringing them to that knowledge of God which has become so vital and genuine to me. But perhaps it shall never be so.

I have no delusions of grandeur. I cannot transform the world. No man can. But, God helping me, I shall be a valid demonstration of what can happen to a man who submits to the eternal. I must bring my beloved Vaneta into the reality of this experience. It must be lived before my sons and those other children yet to be conceived by our union.

I have come far on the upward journey. Beneath me lies the great valley of my past, with it's penetrating shadows, it's threatening pinnacles, it's treacherous ways.

The path ahead winds upward. I would not foolishly presume it to be devoid of footfalls and impending perils, but it is an upward path and I shall claim it. I may never reach the summit, for I am a man, mortal, and I think perhaps the summit towers beyond the reach of mortality, and that one is always climbing.

I am beginning to discover the length and the breadth and the depth of it all—the meaning of the definition Pastor Mallory shared with me.

Dedication is a lifelong process.

It is the good way!